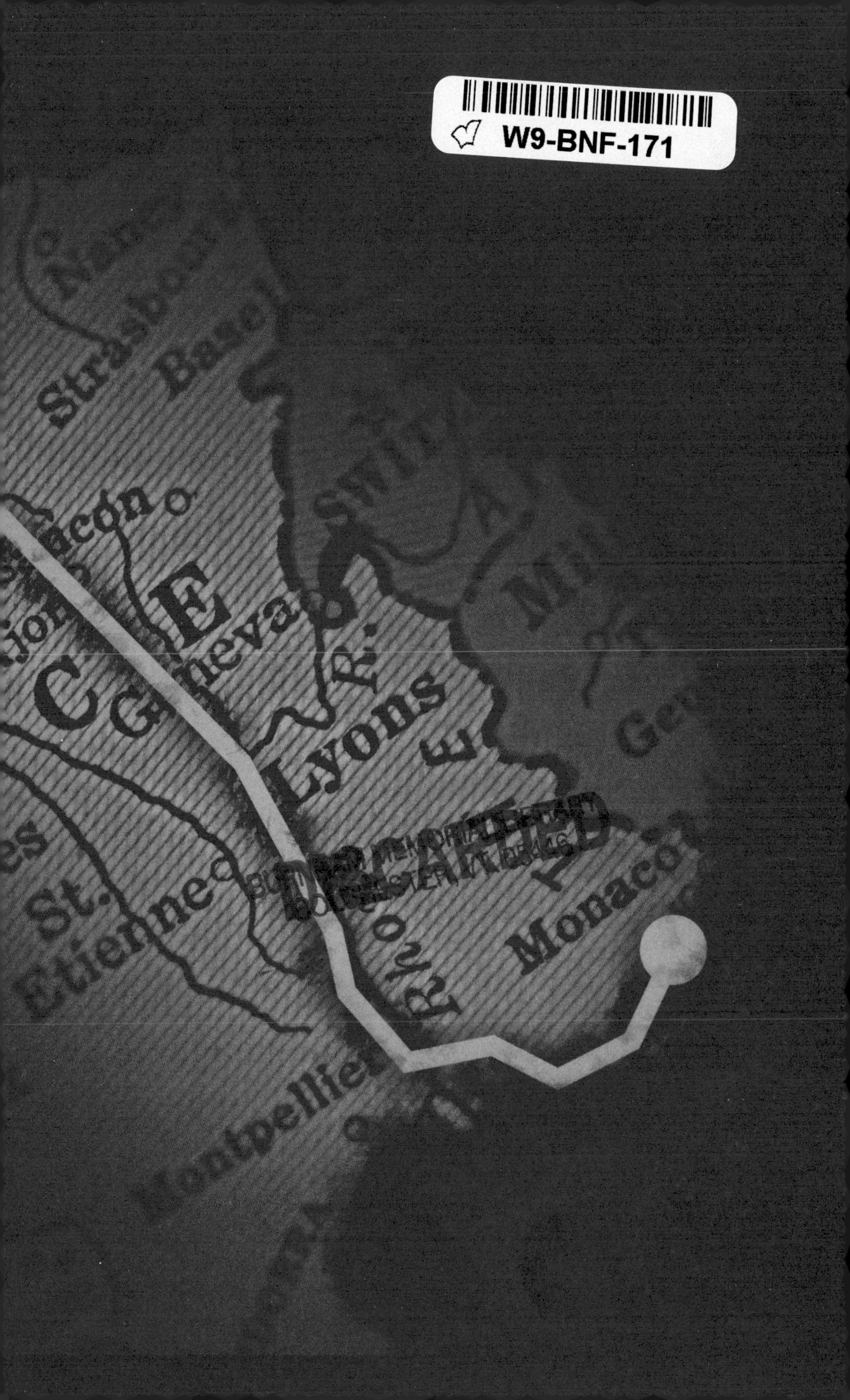
St.
Etienne
Lyons
Monaco
E
C
R.

Praise for

THE DOPPLE GANGER CHRONICLES

What Readers Are Saying

"I was so absorbed in this book that it only took me two days to read it. (I couldn't put it down!) I loved the way it was part graphic novel and part book. That really made me understand what the characters looked like. And my favorite parts made me laugh out loud!"

"I absolutely love The Dopple Ganger Chronicles—the story line is good and exciting and gripping. I especially like Sadie and Saskia because I have a twin, so I like stories about other twins growing up."

What Teachers Are Saying

"I was a reluctant reader when I was a child, and comics were about the only thing I would read cover to cover without interruption. . . . The Dopple Ganger Chronicles will be a permanent part of my classroom for sure. I only hope it is the dawn of a new format of book so others can jump on the bandwagon."

"The children at our school have been so excited by THE FIRST ESCAPE. We have set aside twenty-five minutes every day to read it, and that is not enough, as we have children begging to take it home. We even have a waiting list of children who want to read the book. It's not often that reading can cause such a buzz."

"From the first paragraph we knew this book would be the key we needed to unlock the minds of reluctant readers. For those who already enjoy reading, this is one of the most atmospheric and enjoyable books I've ever seen. I can't wait to unleash it on my reading groups! The illustra-novella is here to stay."

What Parents Are Saying

"My son is almost thirteen, has ADHD, and has a hard time staying focused, so reading is a chore for him. But he is totally into The Dopple Ganger Chronicles! When he's not doing his schoolwork, he has his nose in that book! We're so happy to see him enjoying a book on his own!"

"My eleven-year-old daughter had a reading age of seven and would 'switch off' whenever she encountered a book, as her dyslexia and special needs made reading tedious. But G. P. Taylor's visit to her school inspired her to try THE FIRST ESCAPE. It was the first time she'd ever grasped a book, and she read it all from cover to cover and even wrote a final chapter of her own. The teachers were astonished. . . . It was the mixture of words and illustrations that made her want to read it. It's almost a miracle."

"My eight-year-old son, who has been reluctant to read chapter books despite his abilities, devoured the first Dopple Ganger book, and then his eleven-year-old brother did as well. They are very eager for the next book!"

"I want to thank you for writing The Dopple Ganger Chronicles. My son does not often enjoy reading, but he loved your book—in fact, he couldn't put it down. He keeps asking when there will be another addition to the series. I can't thank you enough; we'll be anxiously awaiting the next installment."

G. P. Taylor

DOPPLE GANGER
CHRONICLES

BOOK III: THE GREAT MOGUL DIAMOND

SALTRIVER®

AN IMPRINT OF
TYNDALE HOUSE PUBLISHERS, INC.
CAROL STREAM, ILLINOIS

Visit Tyndale's exciting Web site at www.tyndale.com.

Visit Markosia's Web site at www.markosia.com.

Visit the Dopple Ganger Chronicles Web site at www.doppleganger chronicles.com.

THE GREAT MOGUL DIAMOND

Designed by Erik M. Peterson | Art directed by Stephen Vosloo | Edited by Elizabeth R. Kletzing

G. P. Taylor is represented by the Caroline Sheldon Literary Agency.

For manufacturing information regarding this product, please call 1-800-323-9400

Library of Congress Cataloging-in-Publication Data

Taylor, G. P.

The great mogul diamond / G. P. Taylor.

p. cm. — (The Dopple Ganger chronicles ; #3)

Summary: When an anonymous note threatens someone they love, twins Sadie and Saskia Dopple are thrust into a series of crimes that look suspiciously like something from the pages of a mystery novel.

ISBN 978-1-4143-1949-0 (hc)

[1. Orphans—Fiction. 2. Twins—Fiction. 3. Sisters—Fiction. 4. Robbers and outlaws—Fiction. 5. Supernatural—Fiction. 6. Mystery and detective stories.] I. Title.

PZ7.T2134Gr 2010
[Fic]—dc22 2010004260

Printed in China

17 16 15 14 13 12 11
7 6 5 4 3 2 1

TO SANJA BESAROVIC

AND ALL THE WONDERFUL STAFF

AT HULL ROYAL INFIRMARY.

YOUR CARE GOES BEYOND WORDS.

Contents

Chapter One

The Unsigned Letter

IN THE VAULTED LIBRARY of Spaniards House, all was not well. Three figures stood motionless in the doorway, shadows looming over them like menacing giants.

"Sadie . . . Saskia . . . did you hear that?" whispered the dark-haired boy to the identical twin girls on either side of him.

"she's being
threatened."

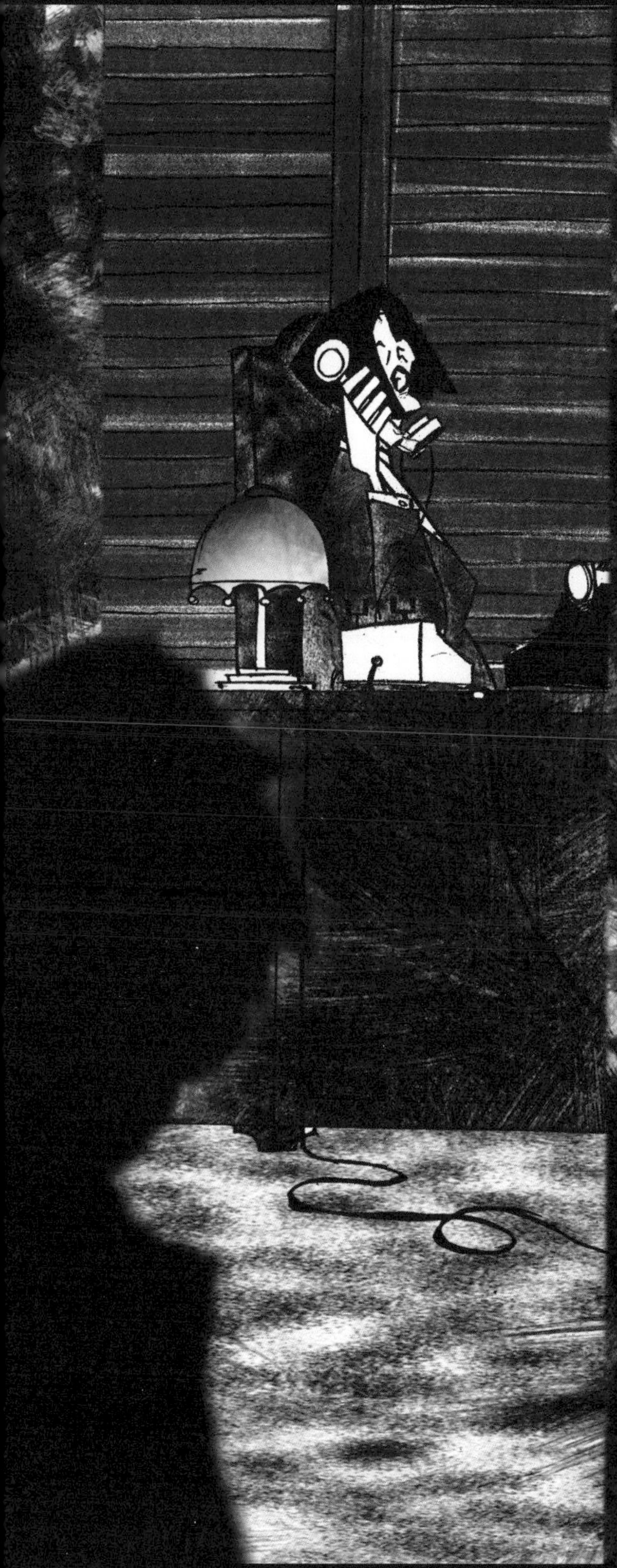

The eyes of every portrait in the great hall behind them seemed locked in their direction.

Through the open doors, they could see Muzz Elliott sitting at her mahogany desk, the telephone clutched in her stony hand. Her face was as white as the crisp paper that was sticking crookedly out of the typewriter in front of her. She stared straight ahead, unaware of the three pairs of eyes now fixed on her.

"Are you sure you heard right, Erik?" Saskia replied.

As if in answer, Muzz Elliott spoke into the telephone, her voice growing louder with every word. "I got your note, and I cannot agree with what you have to say. A letter like that can be seen as nothing but a threat—and a threat to commit murder—if I don't comply."

"Who is she talking to?" Sadie murmured quietly.

Suddenly the one-sided conversation from inside the library went strangely silent.

"She heard us!" squeaked Saskia. "Quick!" She dragged her companions away from the door.

"Very well . . . if you insist . . . the Hotel Carlton . . . Cannes . . . in three days," Muzz Elliott said. The shadowy figures tiptoed to the other end of the hallway.

There was a soft click as Muzz Elliott hung up the phone.

Without speaking, Saskia opened the large front door and then slammed it shut.

"We're back," she called, striding across the hall and dragging the others behind her.

"In here," Muzz Elliott said tiredly.

Saskia put her head around the door of the library and peered in. Muzz Elliott was still sitting at her oversize desk. To one side was a glass lamp connected to the floor by a thick black cable that looked like the coiled tail of a lizard. The windows of the room were shuttered, and several were double darkened by thick green curtains hanging from large white poles that resembled the tusks of elephants. The main light in the room came from what looked like a veiled golden orb. It shone from a vast disk suspended by a wire from the ceiling and dangled like an iridescent halo just above the writer's head.

Muzz Elliott was rearranging the papers on her desk, and Saskia saw her quickly slip an envelope inside that day's copy of the TIMES.

"Erik has to be going soon," Saskia announced. "Dorcas Potts is coming to take him home to Lord Gervez's house."

"Dorcas Potts?" asked Muzz Elliott. "Soon?"

"Eight o'clock—I think that's what she said," Erik replied.

"And you're happy at Lord Gervez's house?" Muzz Elliott asked, as if she wanted to fill the air with fresh conversation.

"Very," Erik replied.

Sadie laughed. "He's training to be a detective with Dorcas Potts. She's opened up her own agency."

After Sadie, Saskia, and Erik had helped Dorcas Potts, the American journalist and detective, discover the secret of Indigo Moon and capture the criminals responsible for the burglary of her uncle, Lord Gervez, Erik had left Isambard Dunstan's School for Wayward Children and gone to live with Gervez. He was now spending a lot of time assisting Dorcas Potts in her work.

"Good . . . good," replied Muzz Elliott, sounding like she wasn't really listening. "He's a nosy boy, and that always helps." She paused and then stood up. "I would like to see Potts as soon as she gets here and perhaps take a walk with her—will you convey that when she arrives?"

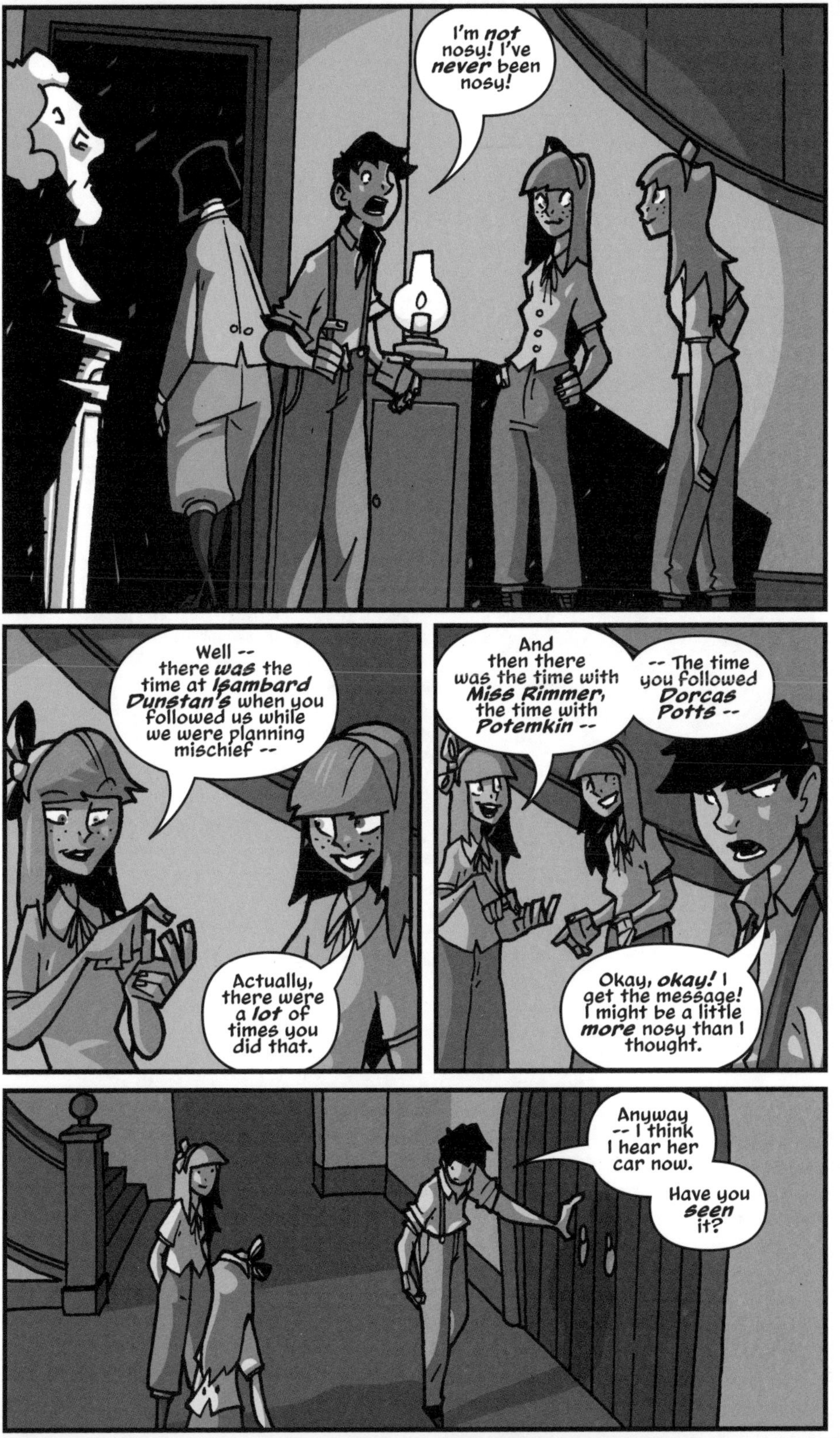
I'm not nosy! I've never been nosy!
Well -- there was the time at Isambard Dunstan's when you followed us while we were planning mischief --
Actually, there were a lot of times you did that.
And then there was the time with Miss Rimmer, the time with Potemkin --
-- The time you followed Dorcas Potts --
Okay, okay! I get the message! I might be a little more nosy than I thought.
Anyway -- I think I hear her car now.
Have you seen it?

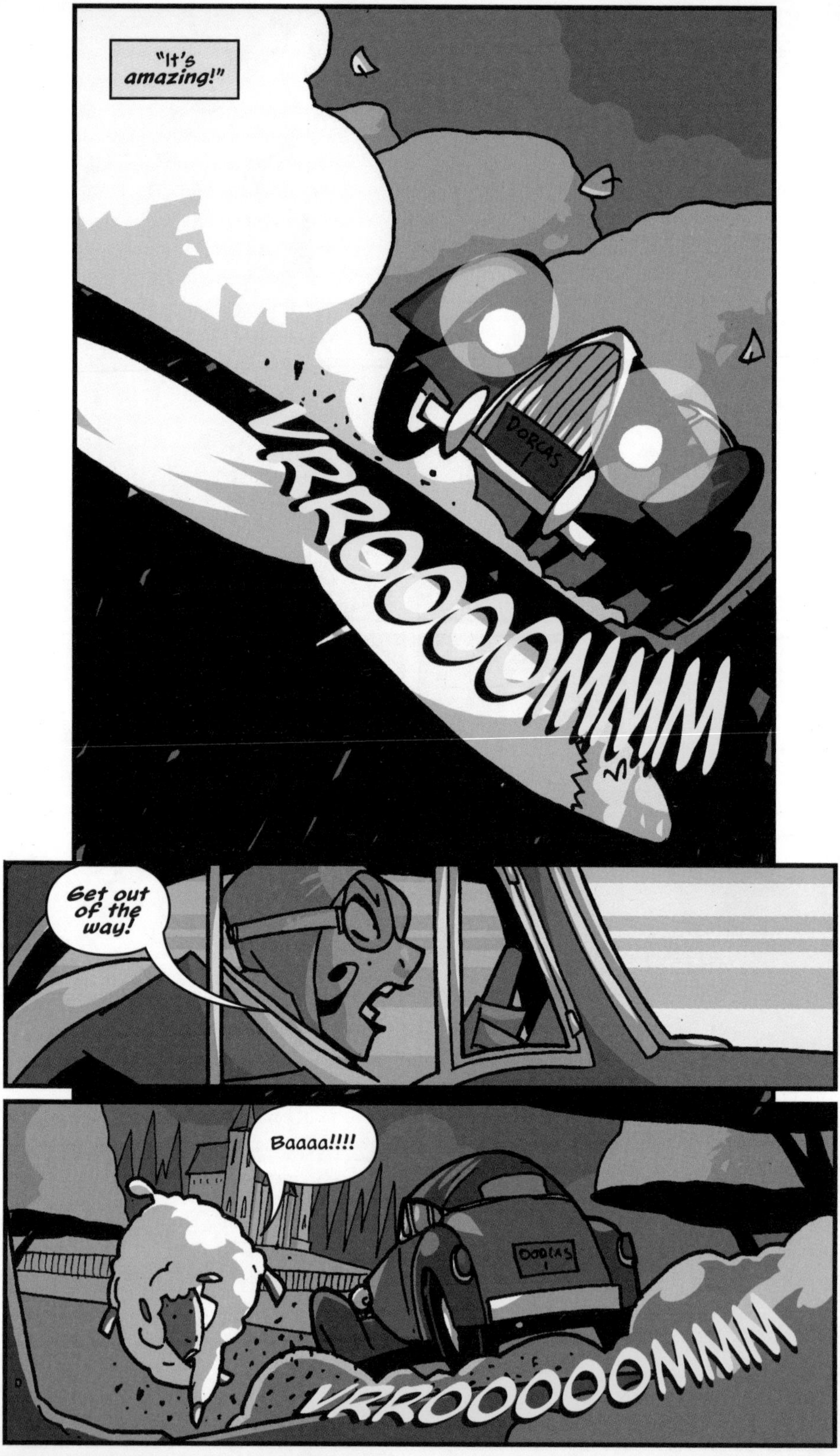
"It's amazing!"
VRROOOOMMMM
DORCAS 1
Get out of the way!
Baaaa!!!!
DORCAS 1
VRROOOOOMMMM

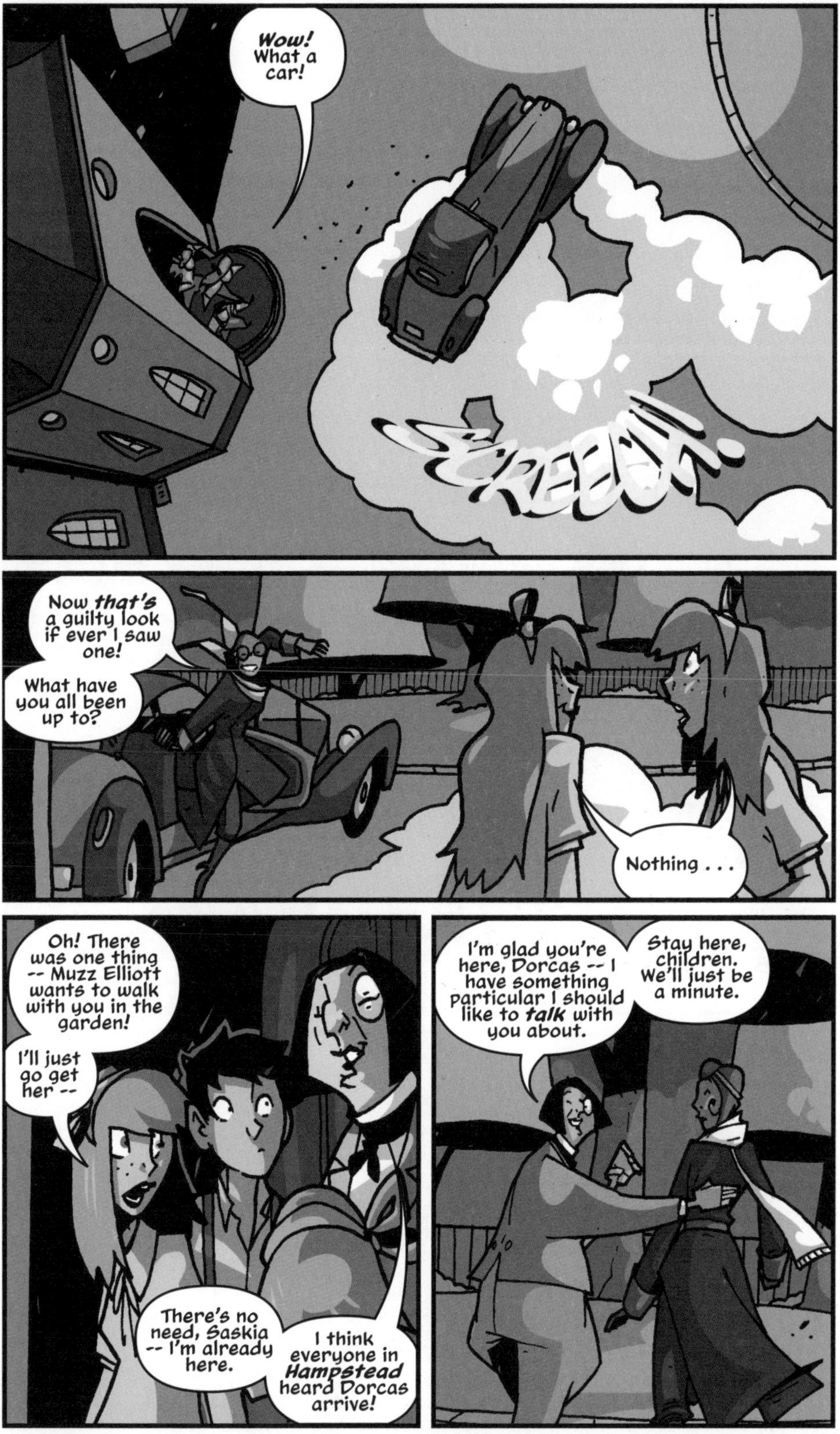

Wow! What a car!
SCREECH!!
Now ***that's*** a guilty look if ever I saw one!
What have you all been up to?
Nothing . . .
Oh! There was one thing -- Muzz Elliott wants to walk with you in the garden!
I'll just go get her --
There's no need, Saskia -- I'm already here.
I think everyone in ***Hampstead*** heard Dorcas arrive!
I'm glad you're here, Dorcas -- I have something particular I should like to ***talk*** with you about.
Stay here, children. We'll just be a minute.

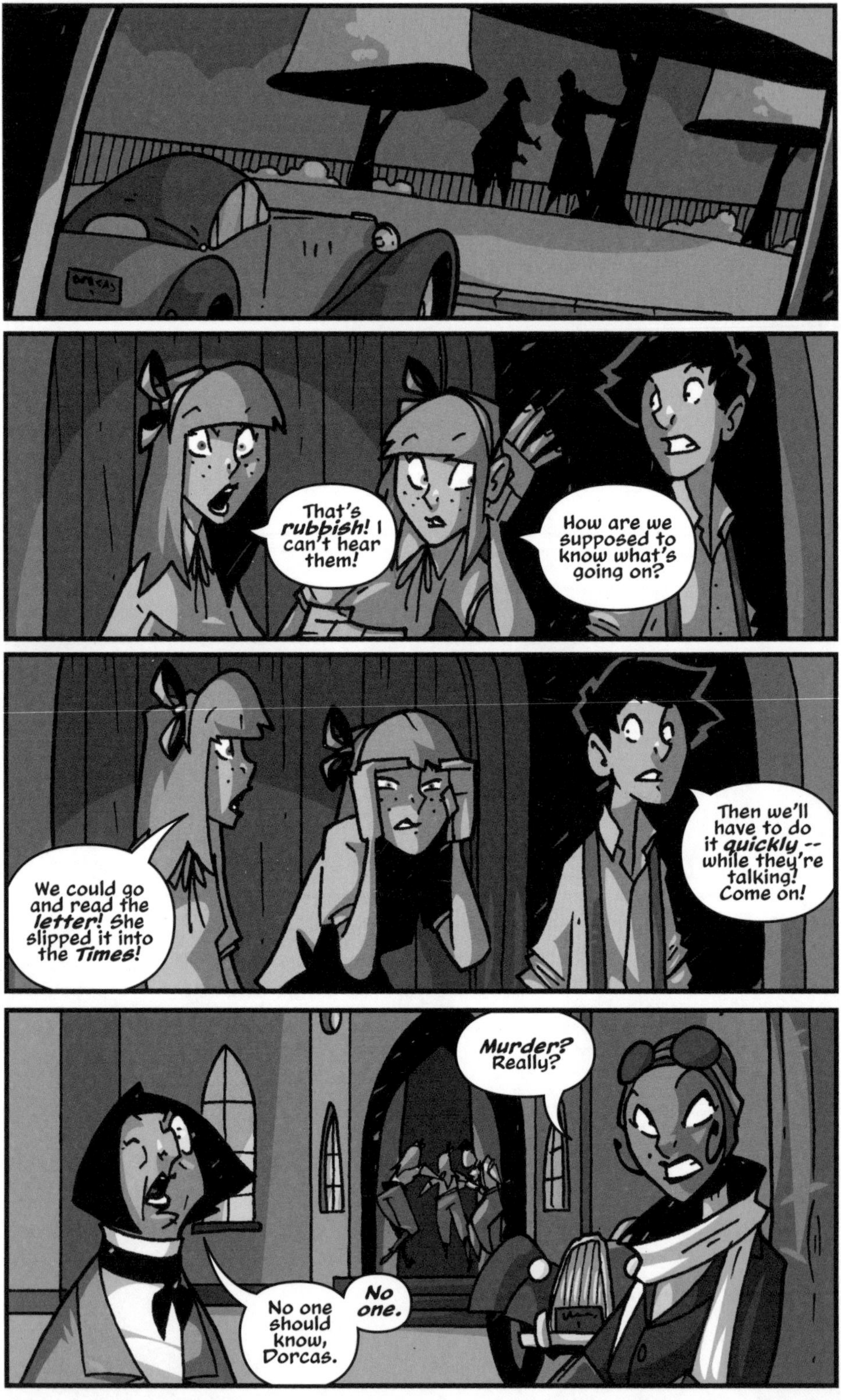
That's *rubbish!* I can't hear them!
How are we supposed to know what's going on?
We could go and read the *letter!* She slipped it into the *Times!*
Then we'll have to do it *quickly* -- while they're talking! Come on!
Murder? Really?
No one should know, Dorcas.
No one.

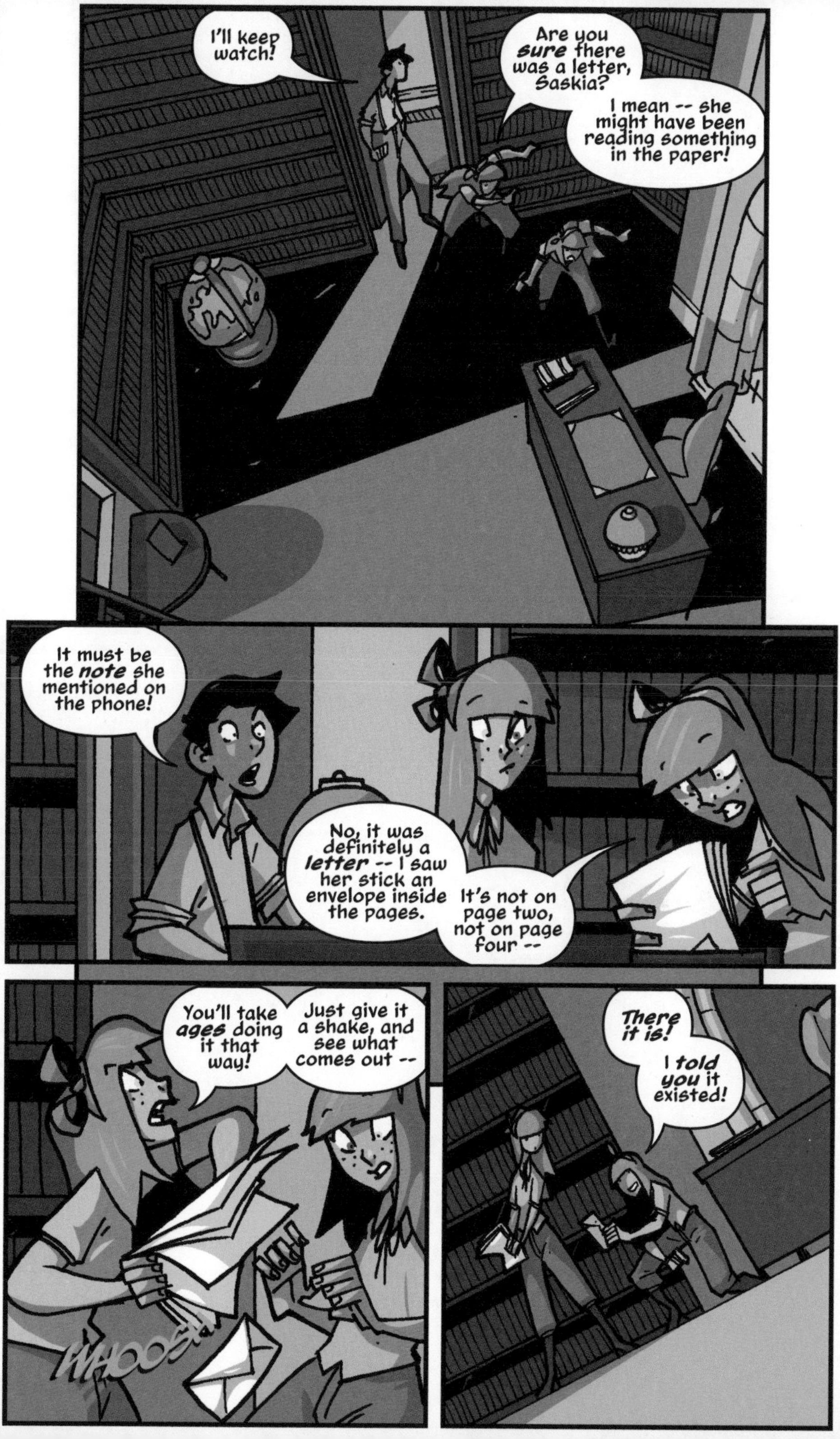
I'll keep watch!
Are you *sure* there was a letter, Saskia?
I mean -- she might have been reading something in the paper!
It must be the *note* she mentioned on the phone!
No, it was definitely a *letter* -- I saw her stick an envelope inside the pages.
It's not on page two, not on page four --
You'll take *ages* doing it that way!
Just give it a shake, and see what comes out --
WHOOSH
There it is!
I *told you* it existed!

Erik crept from the open door toward the desk, where Saskia stood holding the letter in her trembling fingers. The envelope was crisp and had been sealed with candle wax, but the seal had been broken. The postmark spelled out "Paris, France" in smudged letters. Saskia pulled a folded sheet from the envelope, and her eyes flicked across the page.

"Blackmail." She handed the note to Sadie. "That must be what the phone call was all about."

Erik snatched the letter from Sadie's hand and held it up to the light. It was written with a quill pen on thick vellum. It was not signed.

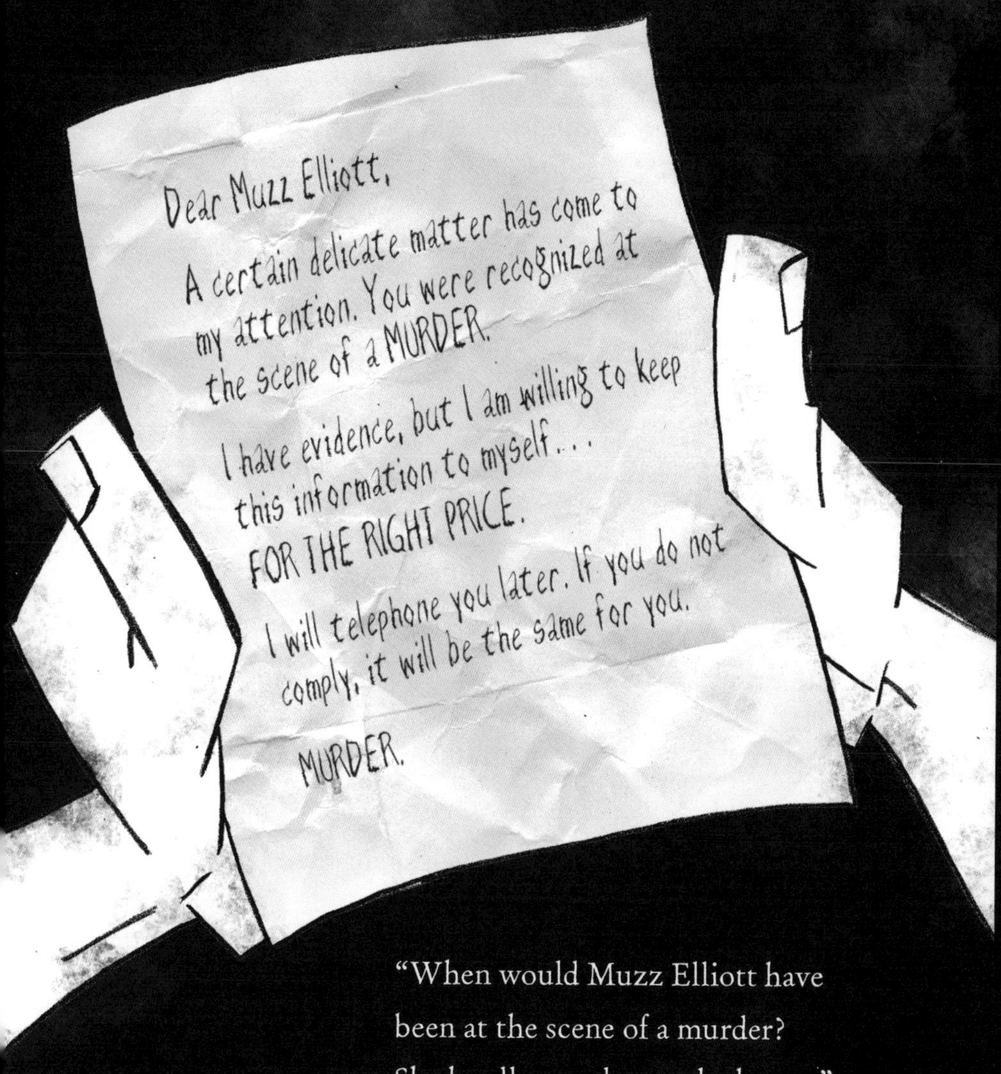
Dear Muzz Elliott,
A certain delicate matter has come to my attention. You were recognized at the scene of a MURDER.
I have evidence, but I am willing to keep this information to myself. . .
FOR THE RIGHT PRICE.
I will telephone you later. If you do not comply, it will be the same for you.
MURDER.

"When would Muzz Elliott have been at the scene of a murder? She hardly ever leaves the house," Saskia said vehemently as she screwed up her face in disgust.

"Whoever wrote this thinks she has." Erik put the letter back in the newspaper and returned it to the desk.

A thick black book lay on the desk next to Muzz Elliott's typewriter. Erik picked it up. "THE WOLVES OF TANKERVILLE," he read aloud. "Dorcas Potts is always going on about this book. I wonder why she likes it so much. . . ." He opened the book and started leafing through the pages.

"It's one of the most famous books Muzz Elliott has written," said Saskia. "Actually, I thought it was pretty exciting myself."

Erik looked up in surprise. "You've read it?"

"She got tired of exploring the house," explained Sadie in a bored voice. "And Grimdyke isn't around to pour porridge on."

Soon after the twins had left Isambard Dunstan's School— and their old enemy Charlotte Grimdyke—and come to live with Muzz Elliott, they had spent their days wandering the vast halls of Spaniards House. Sadie had hoped that Madame Raphael would reappear to her, but Saskia assured her that angels tend to come when they are needed most—or when they're least expected. When the twins were exploring the library one day, secretly hoping to find more hidden treasure, Saskia had come across

Muzz Elliott's famous work. Remembering how much Dorcas Potts had talked about it, she had decided to give the book a try. Since then, she had spent much of her time in the attic reading.

"Which reminds me," said Saskia, walking across to one of the many tall shelves lining the walls of the library, "I need a new book."

So far Muzz Elliott had written thirteen volumes of detective novels, two love stories, and one thriller. Several copies of each stood proudly on the shelf opposite the desk. Saskia pulled a fat book off the shelf. "Hmm . . . MURDER TRAIN . . ."

The latch jangled on the large front door. "Quick— they're back!"

Erik, Sadie, and Saskia ran out into the hall just as the front door was opening.

With narrowed eyes, Muzz Elliott looked from them to the open door of the library.

Saskia held up the heavy volume. "Just getting another book to read," she explained innocently.

Muzz Elliott smiled and relaxed. "It's nice to know I'm not the only one in this house who appreciates good literature," she said.

Sadie snorted and changed the subject. "Do you think Dorcas Potts will take us for a spin in her Bugatti?" she asked as the reporter appeared in the doorway behind Muzz Elliott.

"I would love to, but not tonight. I have to get Erik back to Lord Gervez's house," replied Dorcas Potts, fastening the chin strap on her flying helmet and turning up the collar of her long coat.

"I heard it was the fastest car in London," Sadie said.

"Faster than Muzz Elliott's Jaguar," boasted Erik.

"It all depends who's driving," interrupted Muzz Elliott with a benign growl. "I still think I could race her to the aerodrome and win."

“I’ll have to take you up on that, Muzz Elliott,” replied Dorcas Potts. “Come on, Erik. We can practice on the way home.” Dorcas Potts raised a wary eyebrow across her forehead and smirked with a slight twitch of her painted red lips. She turned to Muzz Elliott. “It was good of you to have him for the afternoon. I know how he misses the girls.”

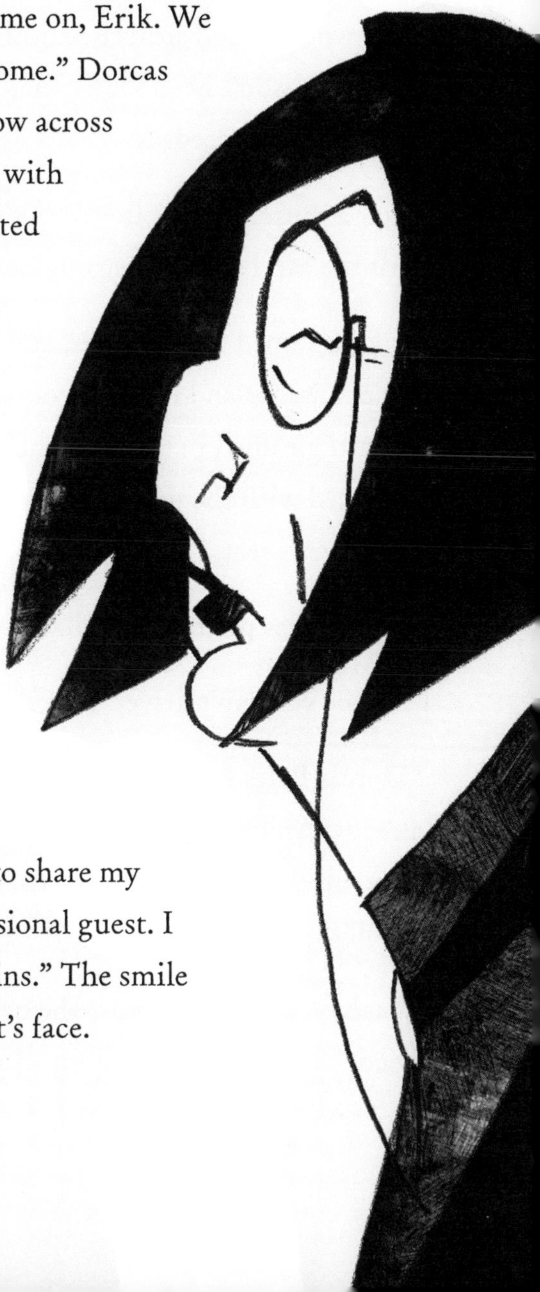

“I enjoy the company—as long as they don’t interrupt my writing schedule. Who would have thought—two girls to share my home and Erik as an occasional guest. I do have a fondness for twins.” The smile slipped from Muzz Elliott’s face.

Saskia and Sadie shared a look. In that strange way of theirs, the girls seemed to read each other's thoughts. Was Muzz Elliott thinking about her own twin sister, Cicely Windylove? Had she forgiven her sister for trying to do away with her and steal the family fortune almost a year ago? If it hadn't been for Saskia, Sadie, and Erik, she might have succeeded.

After a pause, Muzz Elliott went on. "Erik, go and show the girls the car. I have something more to say to Miss Potts."

Erik beckoned to the twins, and they followed him out the open door and into the cool of the evening. The Bugatti gleamed in the twilight. Its silver-spoke wheels glistened with the dew. In one movement Erik slid into the driver's seat.

"Sixty miles per hour," Erik boasted.

"Shame you can't drive," Saskia teased.

"Dorcas Potts will teach me everything I don't know already. Anyway, I can drive—ask Sadie. Don't you remember when we escaped from Dunstan's, and I drove the police van to rescue you?"

"Yeah, you drove it across the heath and crashed into the pond," Sadie said as she jumped in next to him.

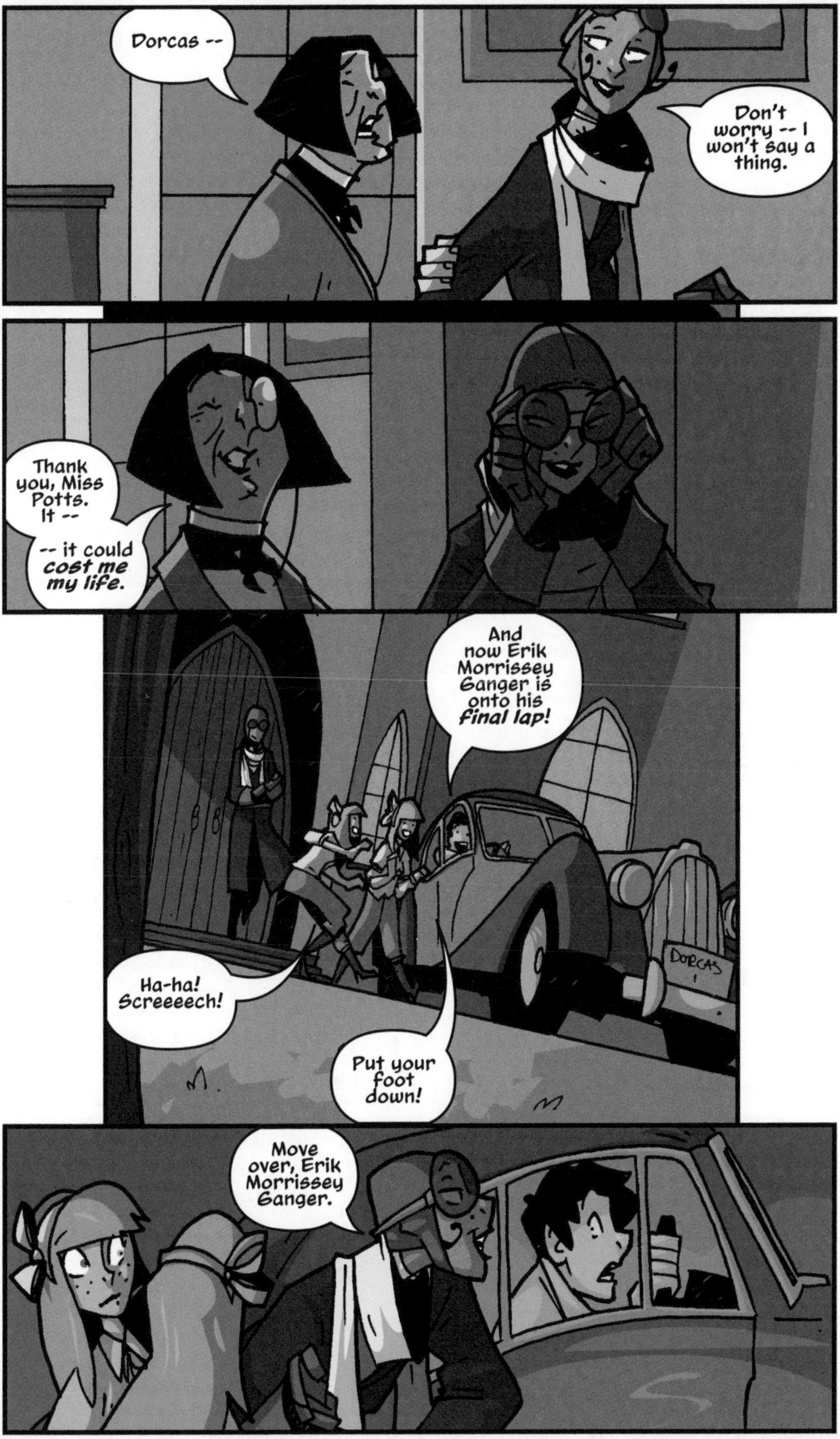
Dorcas --
Don't worry -- I won't say a thing.
Thank you, Miss Potts. It --
-- it could *cost me my life.*
And now Erik Morrissey Ganger is onto his *final lap!*
DORCAS
Ha-ha! Screeeech!
Put your foot down!
Move over, Erik Morrissey Ganger.

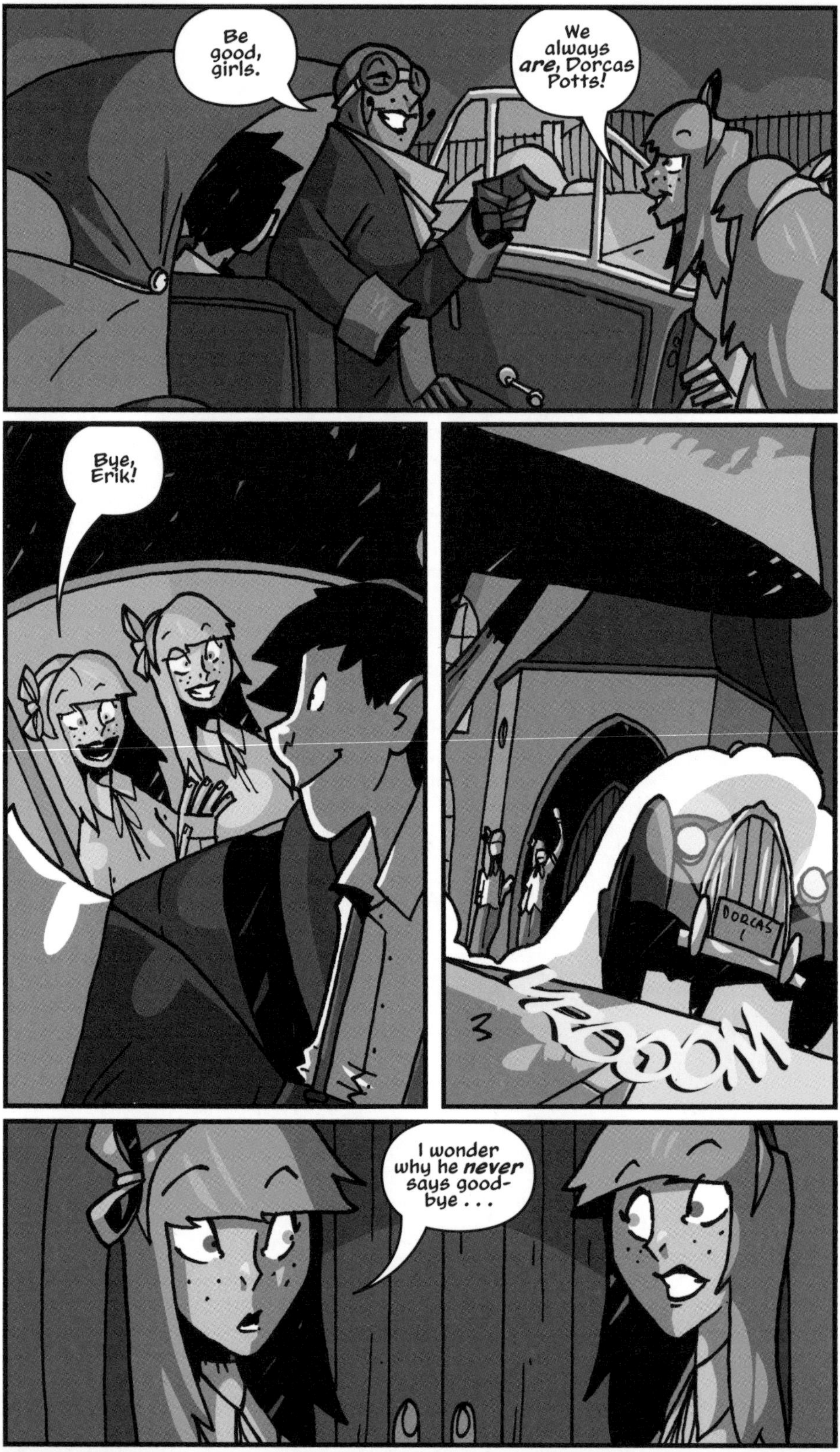
Be good, girls.
We always are, Dorcas Potts!
Bye, Erik!
DORCAS
VROOOM
I wonder why he never says good-bye . . .

As they walked back into Spaniards House, Muzz Elliott stopped them both by the door. Her forehead was creased with worry, but she tried to hide her concerns with a smile.

"I think it is time for a vacation," she said suddenly. "I know of a nice hotel in the south of France. The Hotel Carlton in Cannes. I think you will both enjoy it very much."

"France?" muttered Sadie.

"We'll take a night train and a boat to Paris and then a Pullman to Cannes. We leave tonight. It will all be arranged," Muzz Elliott said as she walked into the library. Just as she was about to close the door, she turned. "It will be good for us all— possibly the greatest adventure of our lives.

Go and pack, and be ready to leave in two hours. We shall soon be on the midnight train to France."

The door of the library closed, and the twins heard the squeak of a leather chair and the click of a light switch. They knew Muzz Elliott was at her desk. She would not want to be disturbed.

"We are going to FRANCE," Saskia whispered. They started up the long staircase to their tower room on the top floor of the vast house. "Don't you realize? It's the hotel that she talked about on the phone. The Hotel Carlton."

"And," grunted Sadie as they turned onto the landing, "we're going with an alleged murderer."

We are Going to fRANce

Chapter Two
Midnight Train

WITHIN THE HOUR,
the Jaguar was waiting
at the wide front doors
of Spaniards House.
Like the day before and
the day before that,
it was raining.
Saskia stood waiting.
She held a large suede
umbrella with one
hand, and with the
other, the book she'd
taken from the library
that evening.

“We have to be

Muzz Elliott shouted from inside the cavernous house. “The train departs Victoria Station at midnight.”

Muzz Elliott appeared at the door. She was dressed in riding boots and a long coat. On her head was a broad-brimmed hat with a band that was tied tightly under her chin. She carried her small case, and as she came out of the darkness within, she looked at Saskia.

“We won’t be late, Muzz Elliott. The car is ready, and our cases are in the trunk.” Saskia’s smile did not mask

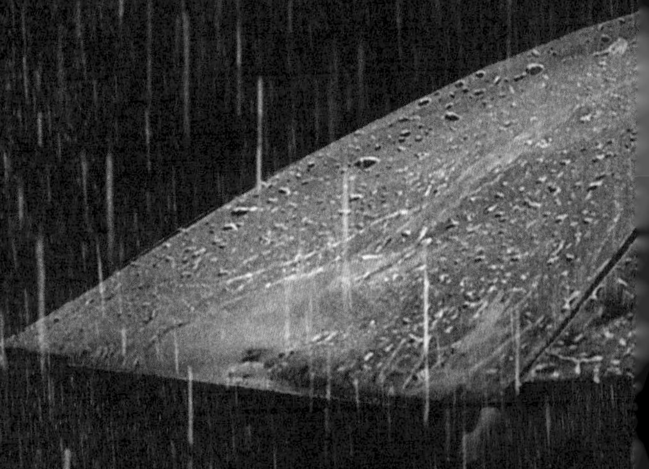

Quick, Sadie,

her anxious glance back into the house. Just then Sadie
emerged from the doorway.

"Come along," said Muzz Elliott, closing the front
door and locking it with a large brass key. "We mustn't
be late."

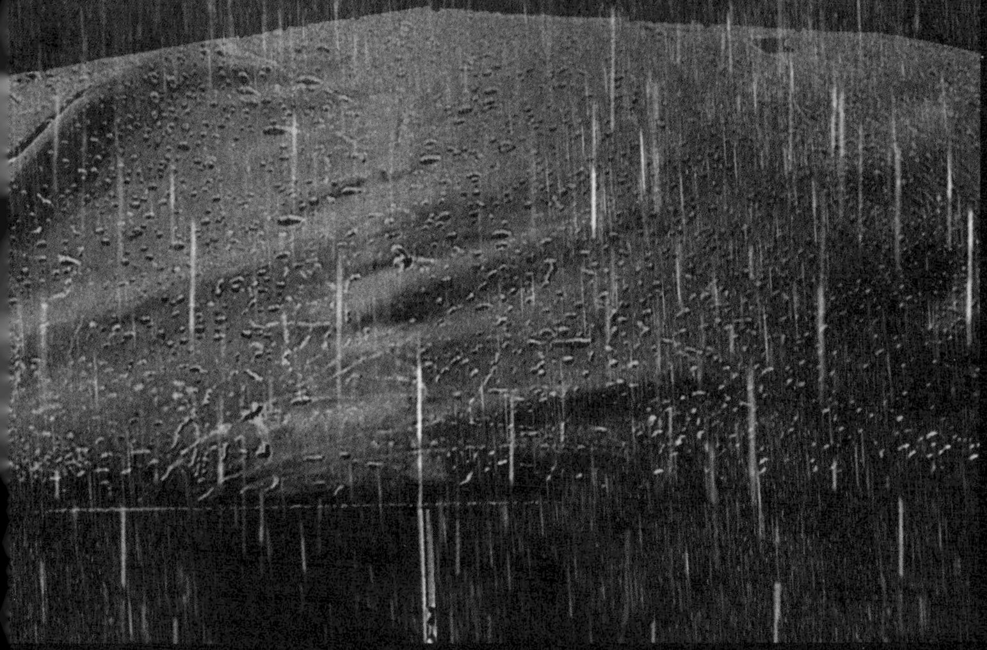

As soon as Muzz Elliott's back was turned, Saskia turned to her sister and whispered urgently, "Did you call him?"

Sadie shrugged her shoulders helplessly. "I tried three times, but no one answered. I stalled for as long as I could, but Muzz Elliott was getting impatient."

"We'll have to try again at the station," said Saskia. "Look for an excuse to get away for a few minutes."

The girls followed Muzz Elliott down the steps.

Muzz Elliott addressed the man waiting politely beside the car. "Mr. Crowley, how good of you to come. I still haven't found a chauffeur as good as Brummagem. Shame he tried to rob me."

Mr. Crowley had been present on the night when Muzz Elliott's twin sister, niece, and former chauffeur had tried to steal the family fortune, and he had helped to thwart the villains. He remained a great friend of Muzz Elliott's—not least of all because he shared her love of fast cars.

“Victoria Station,
Mr. Crowley,”
Muzz Elliott
informed the
white-haired man.
“We can’t be late,
and London traffic
is getting worse. . . .”

Mr. Crowley nodded
as he got into the
driver’s seat.

“You’ll be taking the SILVER ARROW?” he asked Muzz Elliott. He started the car and sped off down the drive.

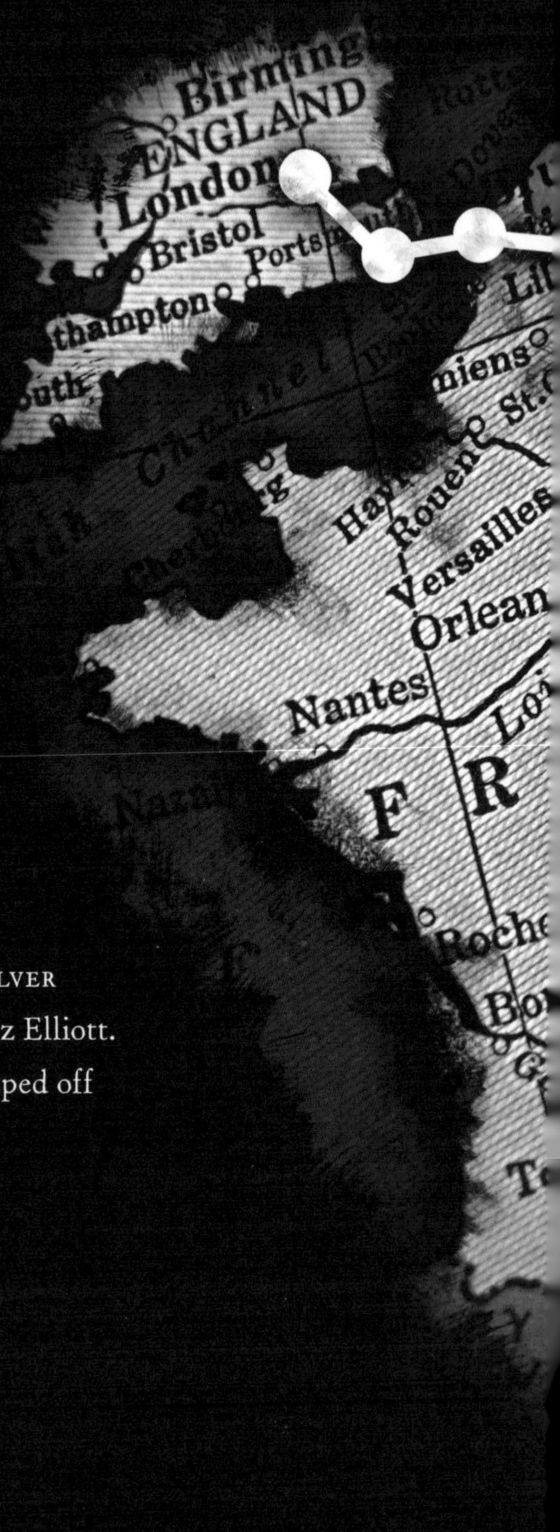
ENGLAND
London
Bristol
Rouen
Versailles
Nantes

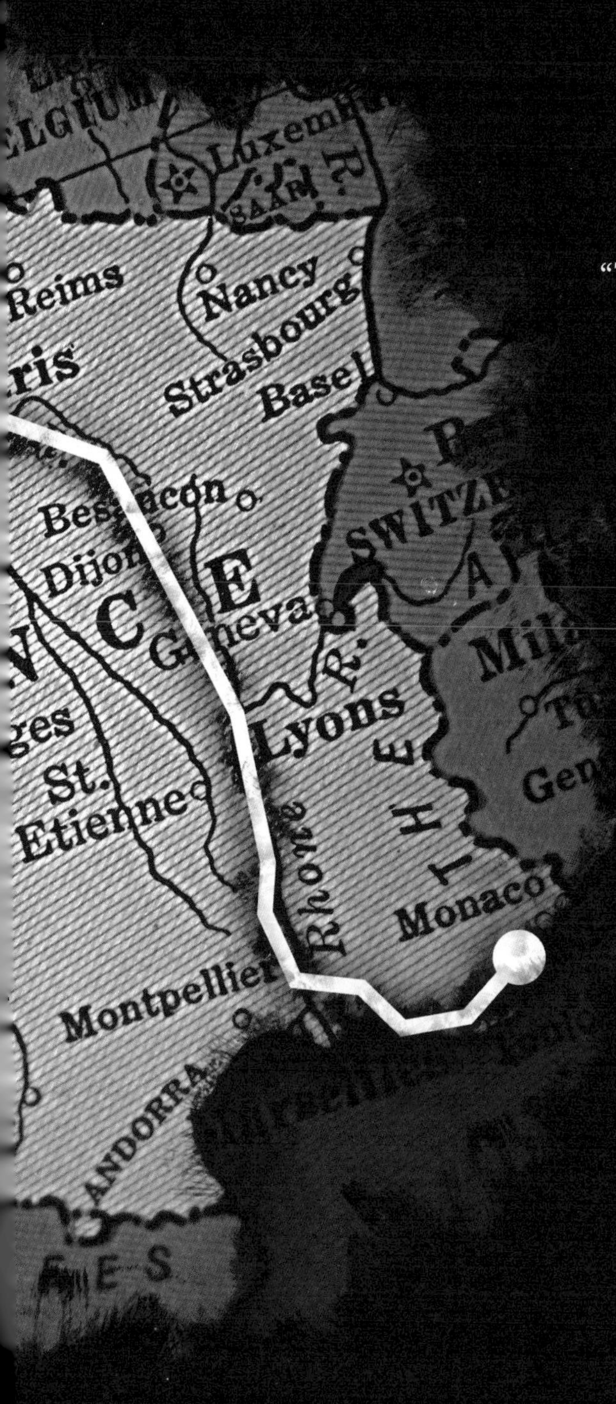
Reims
Nancy
Strasbourg
Basel
SAAR
Lyons
Rhone
St. Etienne
Montpellier
Monaco
ANDORRA

"The SILVER ARROW?" echoed Saskia.

"Yes. The train to Dover—we take the SILVER ARROW from London, change to the SS JUBILANT, and then take the ROTHSCHILD EXPRESS to Cannes. It will take us two nights."

"Is Mr. Crowley coming with us?" Sadie asked.

"He is looking after the house. I think it best if we go alone," Muzz Elliott replied as sweetly as she could.

"Is Cannes a busy place?" asked Sadie.

"Quite," answered Muzz Elliott. "But very English— similar to Ramsgate, but it smells less fishy."

"Does it have a theater?" Sadie went on cautiously.

Saskia knew what her sister was going to say. In the same way and at the same time, she had been thinking exactly the same thing.

"She won't be there," Saskia whispered so that Muzz Elliott wouldn't hear. "Mother isn't coming back." It had been years now, but both twins still found it painful to remember the woman who had abandoned them at Isambard Dunstan's to pursue her career as a vaudeville star.

"What?" asked Muzz Elliott as the car screeched through the London streets.

"Nothing. We're looking forward to the boat," Saskia answered.

Saskia had once mentioned her mother to Muzz Elliott. The woman had merely raised an eyebrow and asked if she

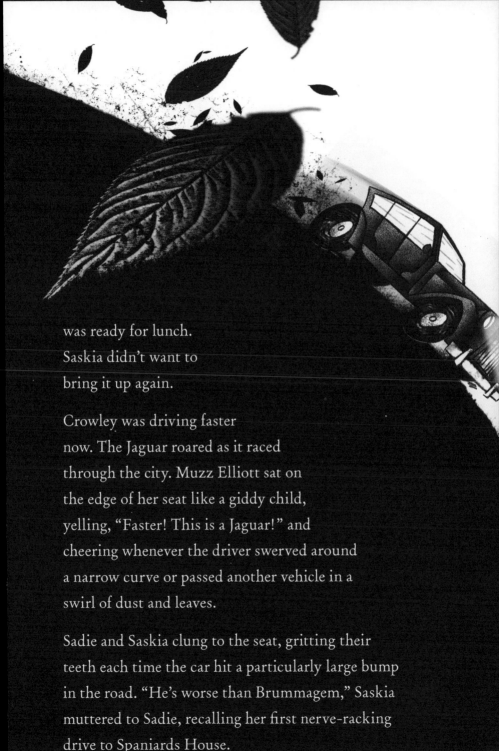

was ready for lunch.
Saskia didn't want to
bring it up again.

Crowley was driving faster
now. The Jaguar roared as it raced
through the city. Muzz Elliott sat on
the edge of her seat like a giddy child,
yelling, "Faster! This is a Jaguar!" and
cheering whenever the driver swerved around
a narrow curve or passed another vehicle in a
swirl of dust and leaves.

Sadie and Saskia clung to the seat, gritting their
teeth each time the car hit a particularly large bump
in the road. "He's worse than Brummagem," Saskia
muttered to Sadie, recalling her first nerve-racking
drive to Spaniards House.

It was only when they got to Regent's Park that the car slowed down.

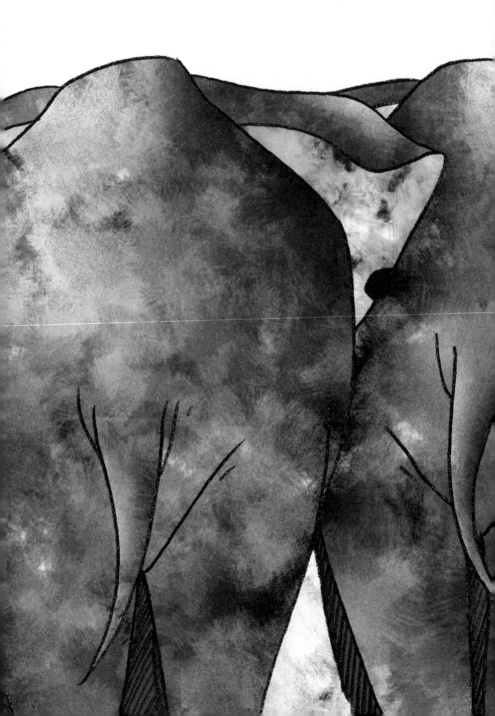

A procession of elephants blocked the road toward the zoo.

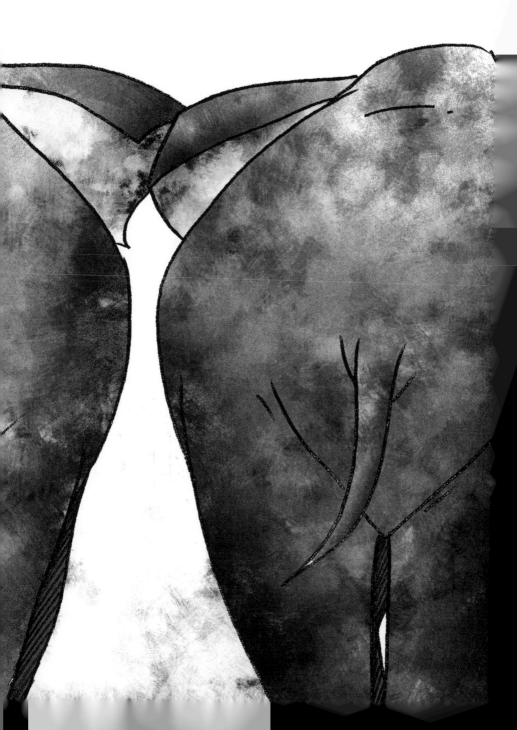

Crowley stopped, put the car into reverse, and drove the wrong way down the entire street. Muzz Elliott did not respond. She now had a faraway look in her eyes and seemed to be hearing something over and over in her mind.

"The note," Sadie whispered to Saskia as the car drew closer to the railroad station.

"I tried to find it, but the newspaper was gone," she replied through pursed lips.

"Muzz Elliott must have it with her," Sadie said.

"We have to tell Erik where we are going," Saskia said with a hand covering her mouth so that Crowley couldn't read her lips in the rearview mirror. "You have to try calling again."

"Phone box . . . station . . . I'll say that I'm going to the bathroom," Sadie coughed as the Jaguar pulled up outside Victoria Station. The door was opened, and Muzz Elliott stepped out.

"Hurry up, now. Trains don't wait—not even for first-class travelers." She snorted briskly, gripping the umbrella that Crowley had handed her from the trunk.

Soon they were all in the station. Muzz Elliott collected the tickets she had reserved by telephone, and their cases were packed on the waiting train. The SILVER ARROW steamed at the head of the long platform. Smoke spewed from the green and brass smokestack and filled the station with an acrid smell.

Saskia looked at Sadie, who nodded. Neither of them noticed the man in the gabardine suit standing by the red phone box near the gates to the platform.

"I think I just need to go to the . . . ," Sadie said, pointing to the drab sign for the public restroom opposite the train.

"Very well, Sadie, but you'll have to be quick. Go with her, Saskia—five minutes." Muzz Elliott snapped the orders and then turned to Crowley. "Thank you for driving us."

"I think I should come with you," he insisted. "It would be far safer. . . ."

"No, keep an eye on the house. This may be a trick to get me away," she replied genially. "Besides, I have this." She pulled a mysterious thin box from her large purse. "My grandfather was a genius in the art of perfecting secret weapons."

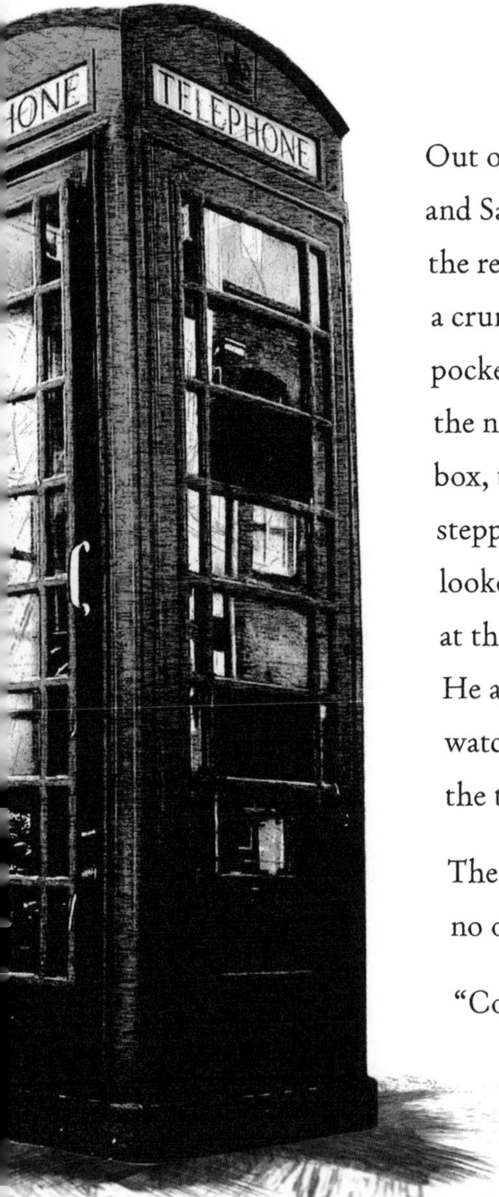
TELEPHONE

Out of sight of Muzz Elliott, Sadie and Saskia pressed themselves into the red telephone box. Sadie pulled a crumpled piece of paper from her pocket as Saskia furiously dialed the number. Outside the phone box, the man in the gabardine suit stepped closer. Instinctively, Sadie looked through the misted glass at the vague outline of the man. He appeared to smile, took a fob watch from his pocket, looked at the time, and then walked away.

The phone rang and rang—
no one answered.

"Come on, Erik!" Saskia pleaded.

"Come on!"

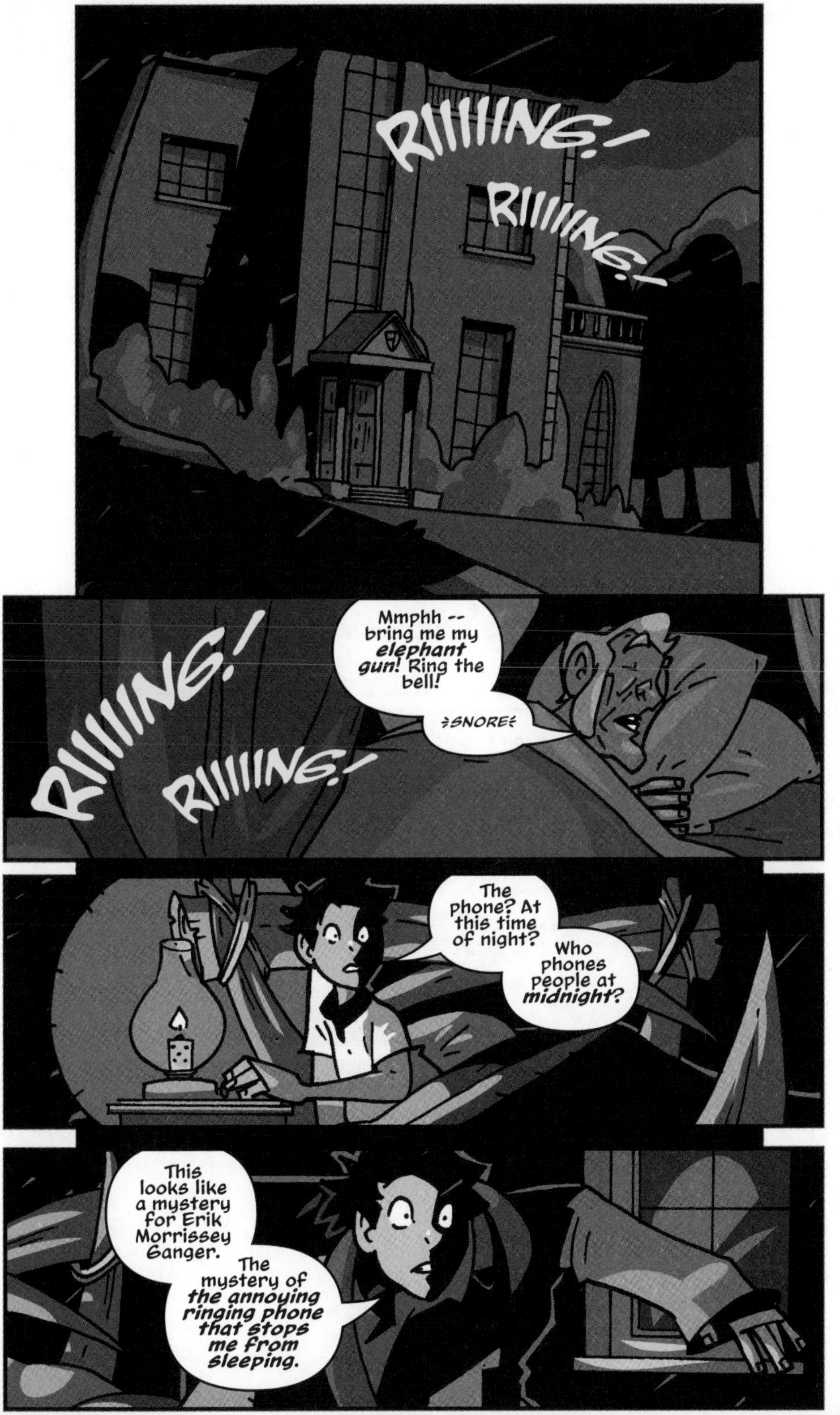
RIIIIING!
RIIIIING!
RIIIIING!
RIIIING!
Mmphh -- bring me my *elephant gun*! Ring the bell!
SNORE
The phone? At this time of night?
Who phones people at *midnight*?
This looks like a mystery for Erik Morrissey Ganger.
The mystery of *the annoying ringing phone that stops me from sleeping*.

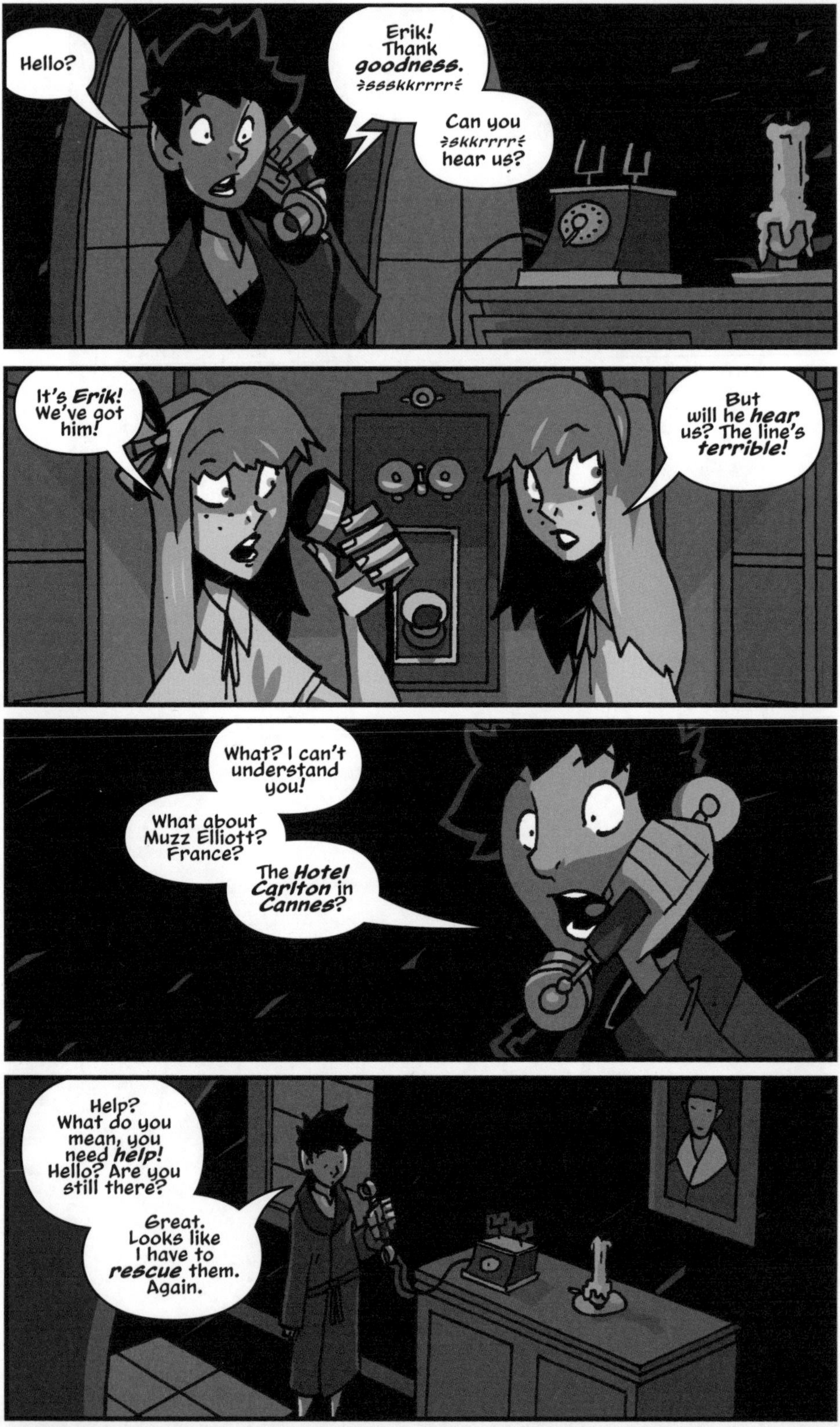
Hello?
Erik! Thank goodness. ≈ssskkrrrr≈
Can you ≈skkrrrr≈ hear us?
It's Erik! We've got him!
But will he hear us? The line's terrible!
What? I can't understand you!
What about Muzz Elliott? France?
The Hotel Carlton in Cannes?
Help? What do you mean, you need help! Hello? Are you still there?
Great. Looks like I have to rescue them. Again.

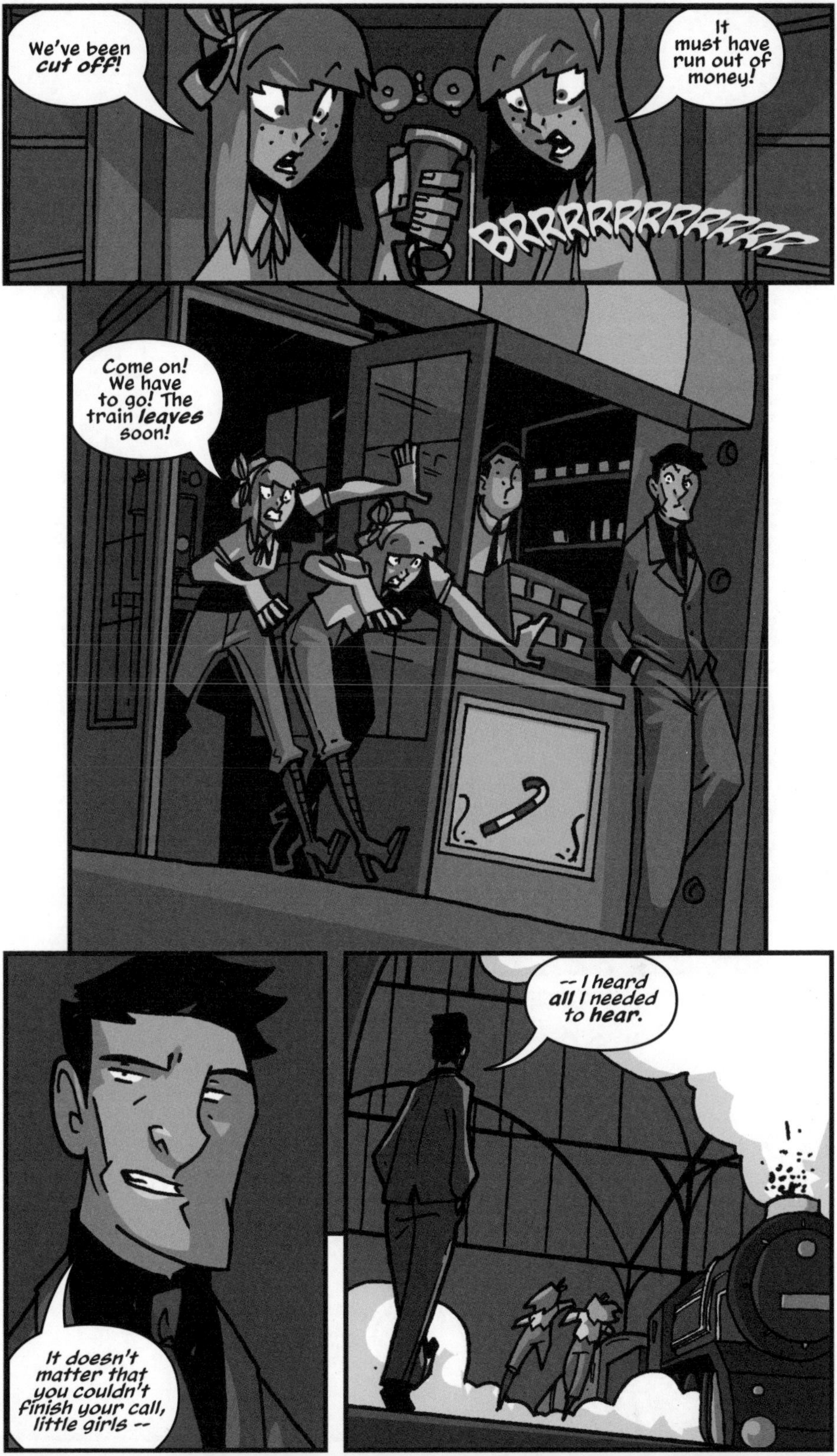
We've been cut off!
It must have run out of money!
BRRRRRRRRRRRR
Come on! We have to go! The train leaves soon!
It doesn't matter that you couldn't finish your call, little girls --
-- I heard all I needed to hear.

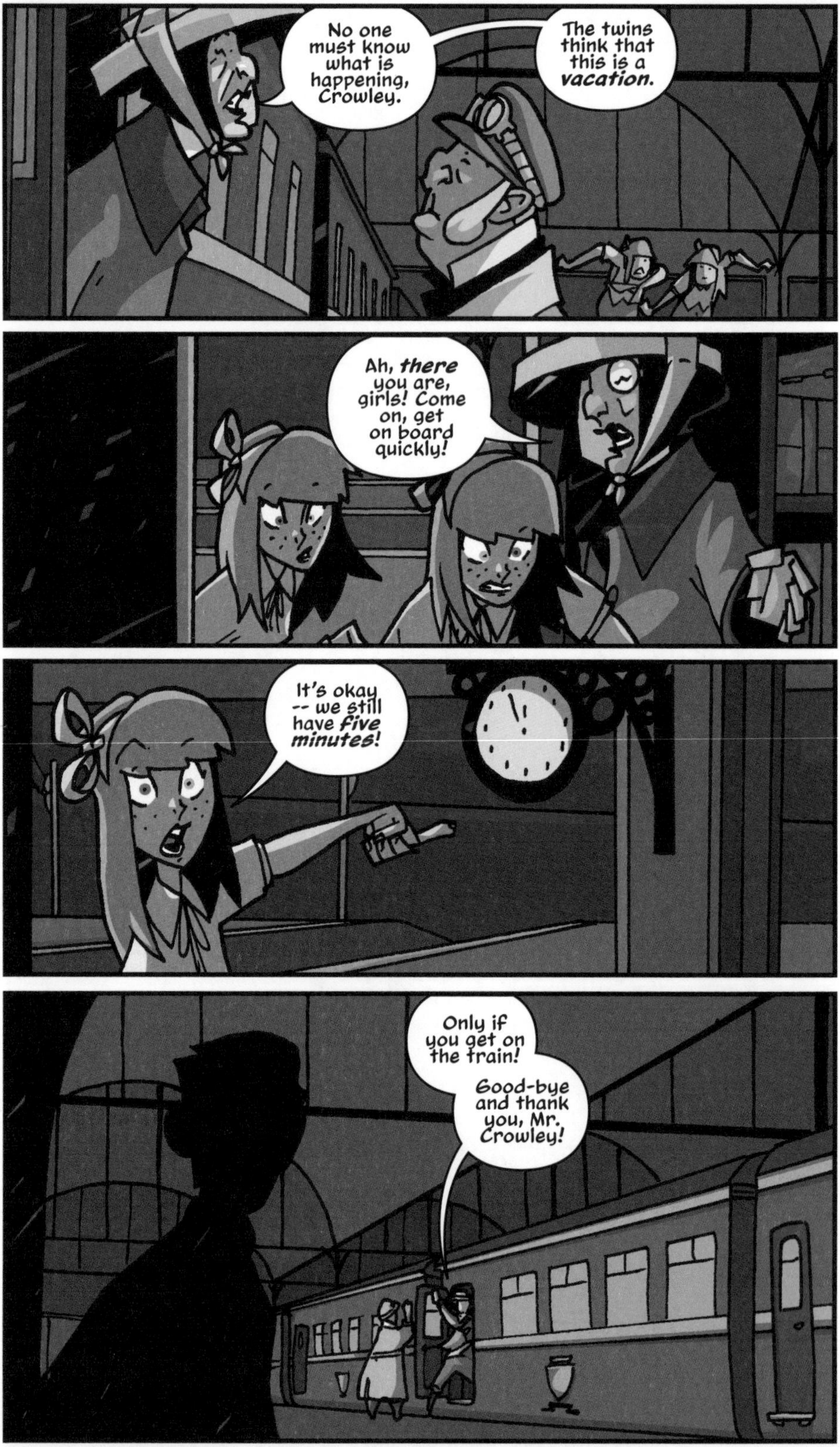
No one must know what is happening, Crowley.
The twins think that this is a *vacation.*
Ah, *there* you are, girls! Come on, get on board quickly!
It's okay -- we still have *five minutes*!
Only if you get on the train!
Good-bye and thank you, Mr. Crowley!

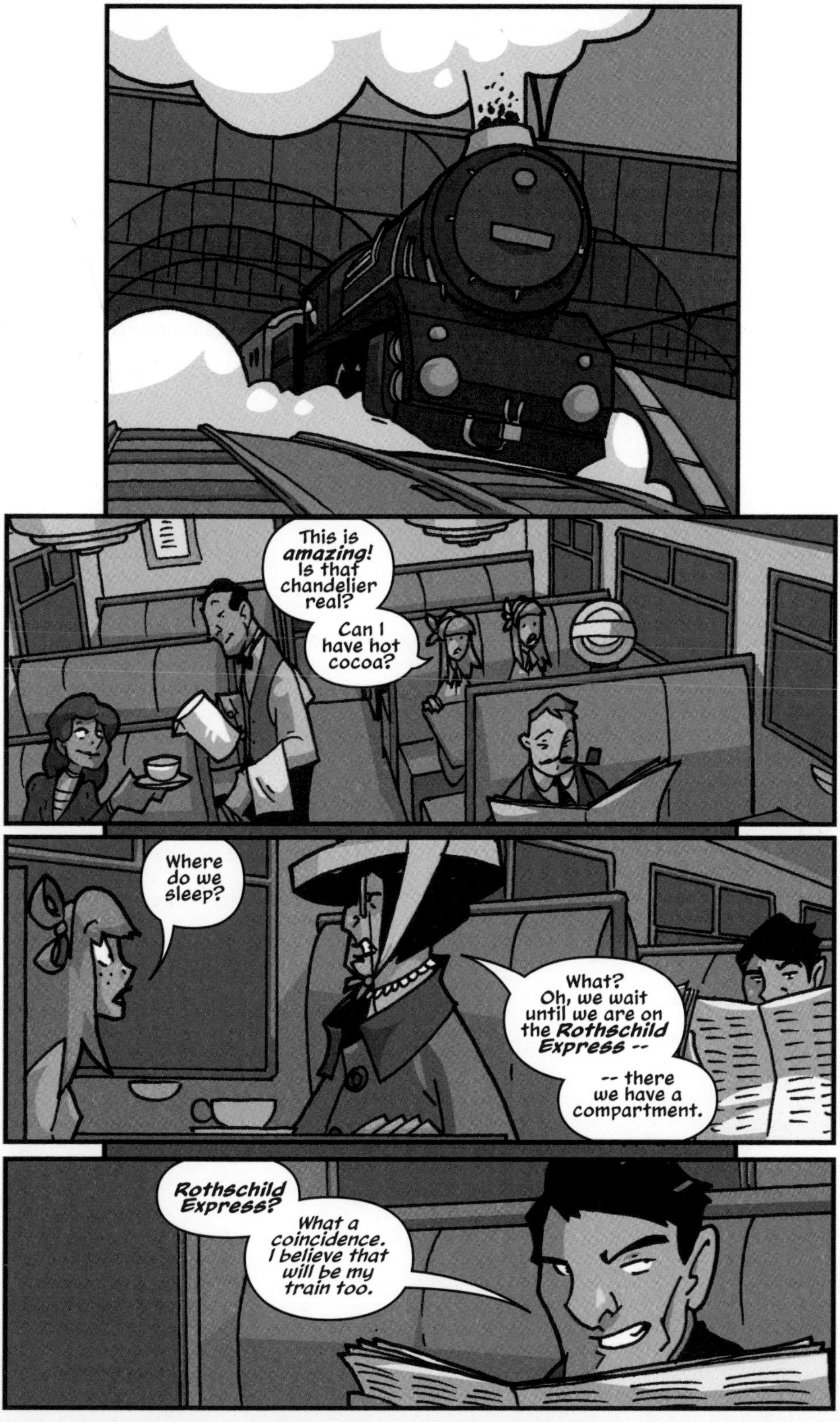

This is *amazing!* Is that chandelier real?
Can I have hot cocoa?
Where do we sleep?
What? Oh, we wait until we are on the *Rothschild Express* --
-- there we have a compartment.
Rothschild Express?
What a coincidence. I believe that will be my train too.

The chandelier swayed as the train pulled out of Victoria Station and gathered speed. Several waiters served the midnight buffet. They danced between the tables of the carriage like fleet-footed penguins as they pampered the first-class guests.

As the train sped into the night, Muzz Elliott stared in deep melancholy at her reflection in the window, eating nothing. The twins ate as much as they could. Plates of sandwiches and cakes were washed down with cups of hot cocoa. The SILVER ARROW rattled on through towns and villages, toward the coast. The steam engine hissed and blew like an abandoned teakettle.

By the time the train was nearing Dover, the plates had been cleared away, the tables wiped, and coffee served. Sadie and Saskia looked out the window as the train slowed. The outline of the ship awaiting them in the harbor was etched in white lanterns that hung from its funnel to its decks.

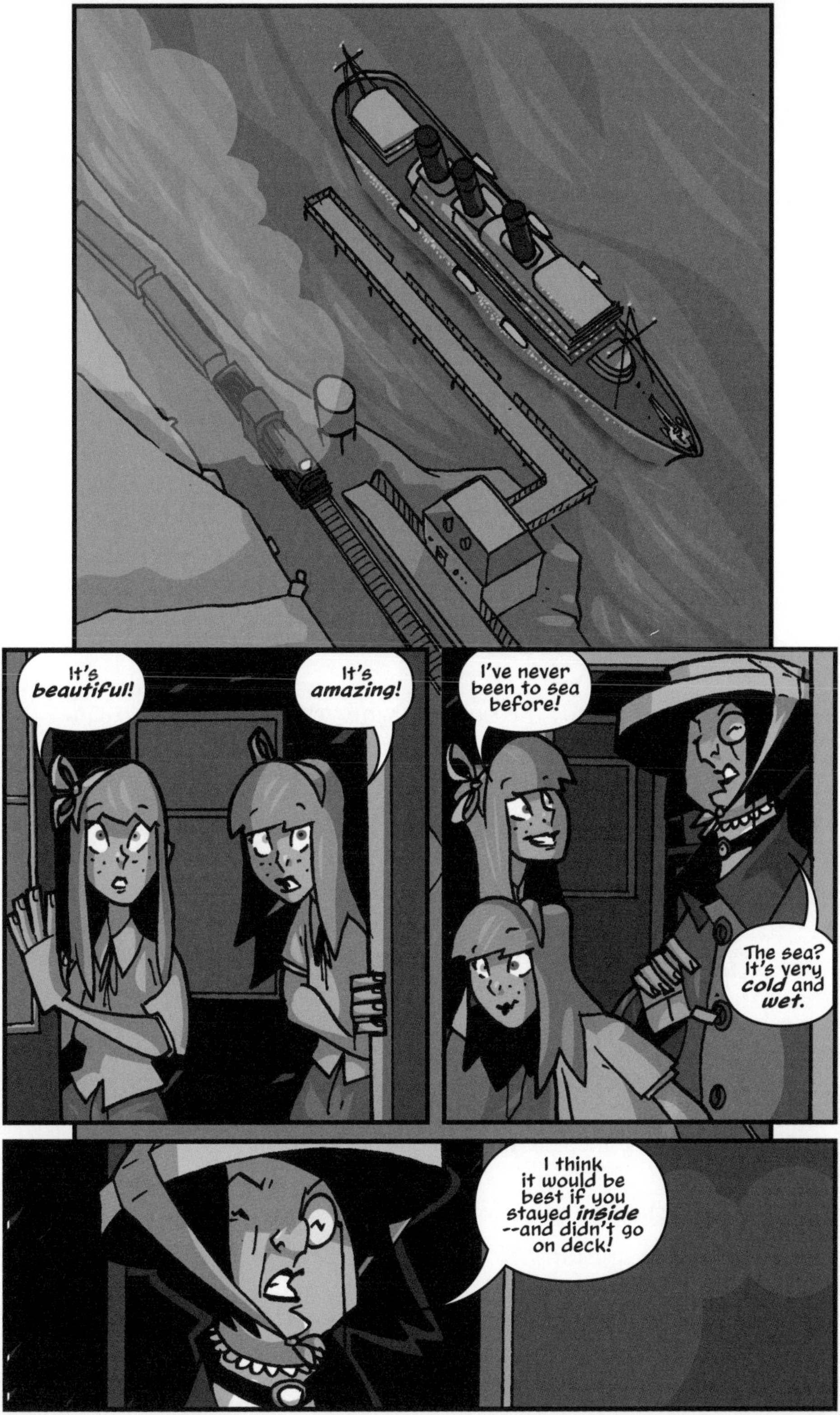

It's *beautiful!*
It's *amazing!*
I've never been to sea before!
The sea? It's very ***cold*** and ***wet.***
I think it would be best if you stayed ***inside*** --and didn't go on deck!

On the quayside, the passengers divided quite naturally into two groups by the make of their clothes: those who would travel on the SS JUBILANT and those destined for the tramp steamer moored at a nearby wharf. The SS JUBILANT was for first-class passengers only. It reminded the twins of a floating hotel. They felt out of place on the neatly painted, brushed, and polished gangplank.

Saskia noticed that most of the passengers never said thank you or even acknowledged that the stewards were there. "Do we have to ignore people too?" she asked as a jovial Irish steward with a red face led them to their cabin.

"So you noticed," he said in a whisper. "We are here to serve and not to be seen."

He stopped the cart and unloaded the bags in the room. "Will that be everything?" he asked Muzz Elliott in a louder voice.

"Thank you." Muzz Elliott smiled and looked him in the eye. "You're from Connemara. If I am not mistaken, by your accent, I would say . . . Scrahallia . . . Cashel Bay?"

The man looked surprised. "Why, yes—it's just as you say."

Muzz Elliott took a neatly folded five-pound note and handed it to him. "Not everyone on this boat is English. Some of us are Irish."

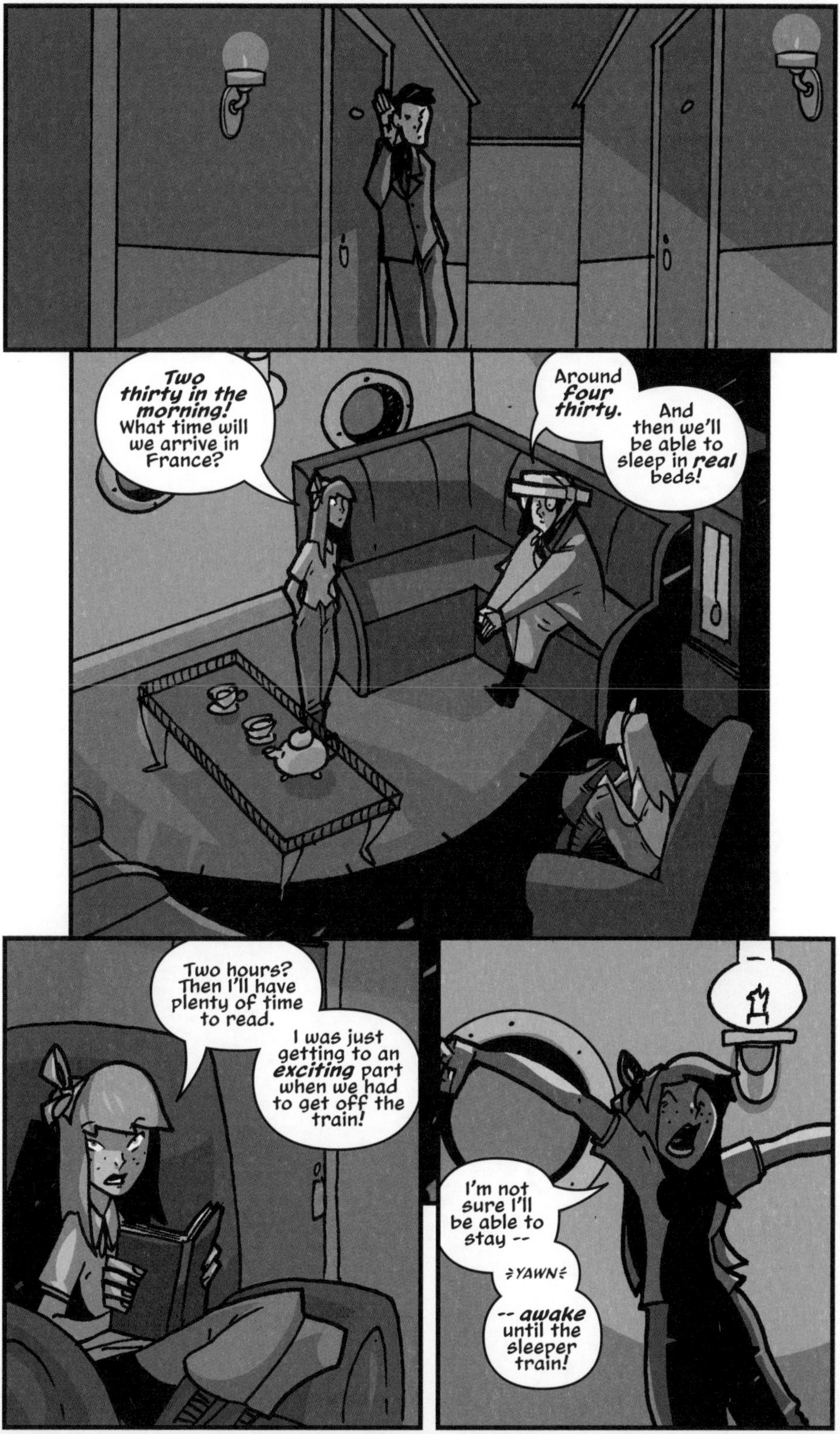
Two thirty in the morning! What time will we arrive in France?
Around four thirty.
And then we'll be able to sleep in real beds!
Two hours? Then I'll have plenty of time to read.
I was just getting to an exciting part when we had to get off the train!
I'm not sure I'll be able to stay --
YAWN
-- awake until the sleeper train!

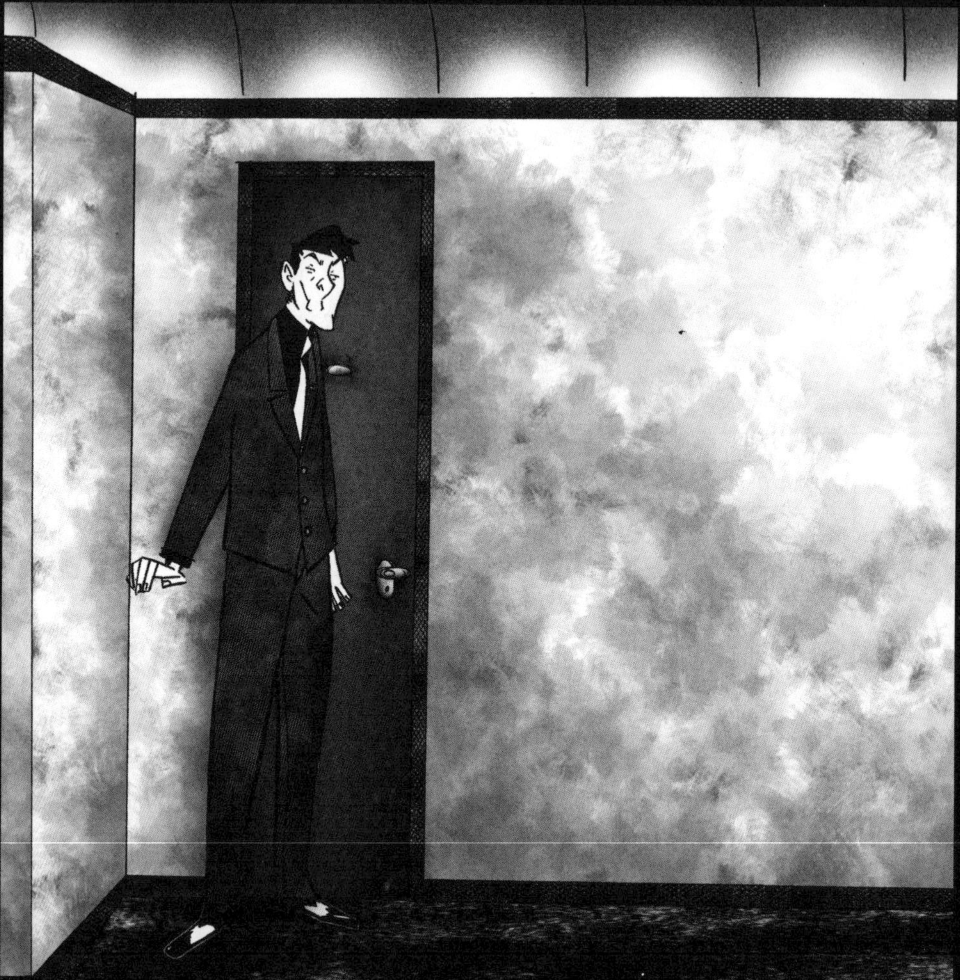

Outside the cabin, the man in the gabardine suit stood listening at the door. His face was grim as he muttered to himself,

"If you make it to the sleeper train. . ."

Chapter Three

Mystery on the ROTHSCHILD EXPRESS

THE CROWDS OF PEOPLE leaving the ship hemmed in Muzz Elliott and the twins. The kindly Irish steward made sure their cases were taken to the train for the last leg of the journey. As they left the ship, he smiled at them and waved. Saskia thought there was something about him that looked lost, almost forlorn.

Saskia stood on the quayside and sniffed the air. She didn't know what to expect. After all, this was France. It was a foreign country, and she and her sister had never been anywhere so adventurous—unless they counted Ongar, which, though it might sound exotic, was only about twenty miles from Isambard Dunstan's. It was the farthest they had traveled on the Underground when they had run away from school once.

Saskia looked around her and shivered. The night was cold. Muzz Elliott and Sadie walked ahead, unaware that she trailed so far behind.

"If you stand here long enough, you will miss the train, Saskia," a man's voice said warmly by her shoulder. "Your companions are far ahead of you."

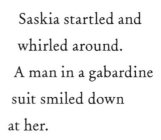

Saskia startled and
whirled around.
A man in a gabardine
suit smiled down
at her.

"Pardon?" she asked,
wondering how he
knew her name and
who her traveling
companions were.

"I saw you on the train
from London and then
on the JUBILANT," he
said charmingly. "Are you
going far?"

Saskia looked him up and down.
She was taken aback by his questions and his
brilliantly polished black shoes.

"Cannes," she said hesitantly. "On vacation."

"Such a coincidence. We must be traveling together," the
man said. "I am Max Taranis." He paused, waiting for
her reply, but all she gave was a worried half grin.

"And you are Saskia, not Sadie, right?"

"Right," she said nervously, moving to catch up to her sister and Muzz Elliott.

"Well, it is nice to meet you, Saskia," Max Taranis said, keeping stride with her. "I will doubtless see you at breakfast."

Saskia turned to reply, but the man was gone. She looked around the platform, bewildered.

It was as if he had just vanished from sight . . . or had never been there at all.

"Come on, Saskia," Sadie called. Saskia caught up as they turned a corner, following the tide of people who walked toward the train.

There before them was the ROTHSCHILD EXPRESS. It stood on the track panting like a living creature. Towering above the platform, it oozed steam and smoke while the fire from the steam engine glowed in the gloom. Flames leaped from

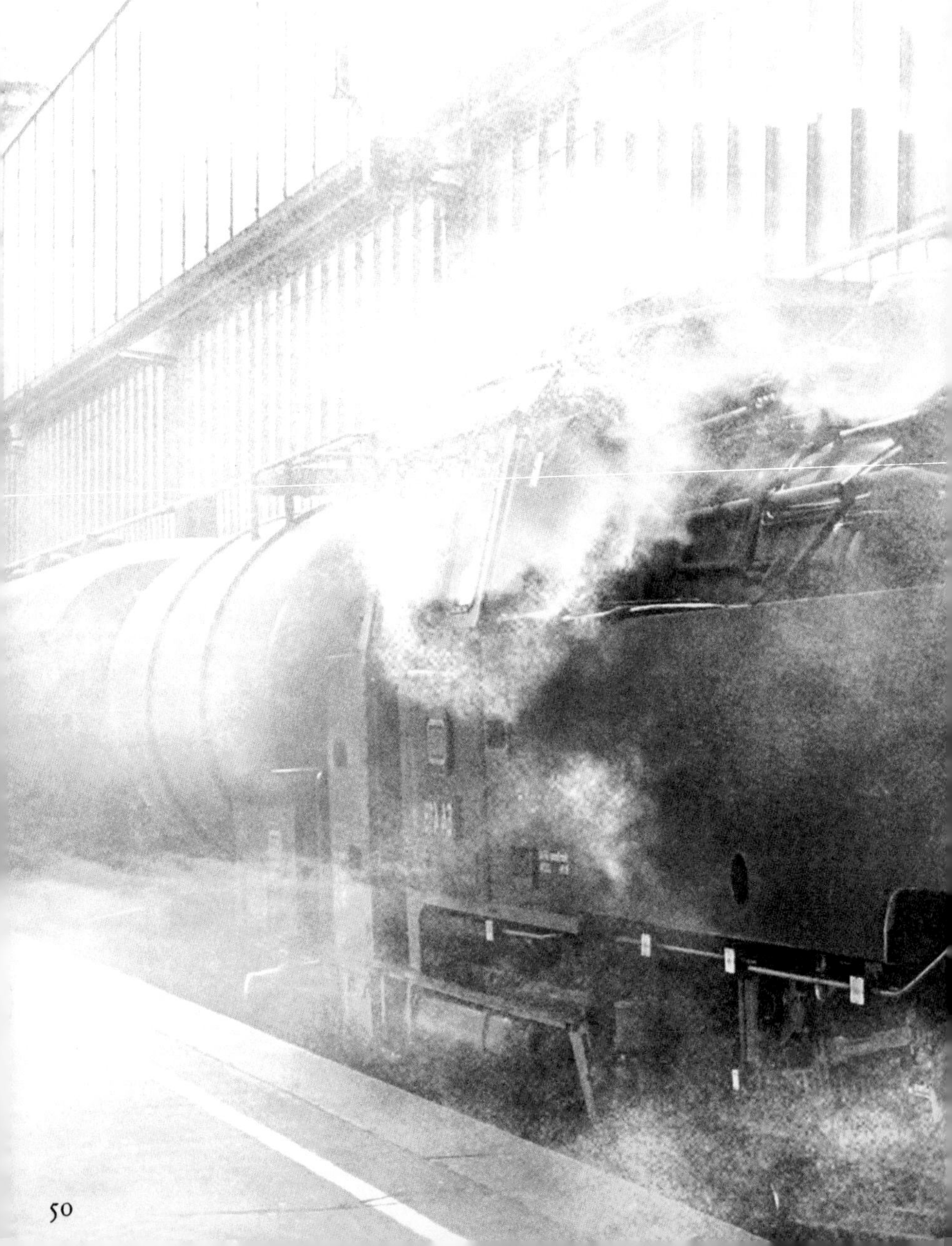

the smokestacks on top of the black engine. Disappearing into the distance were gold-painted Pullman carriages that stretched on as far as the eye could see.

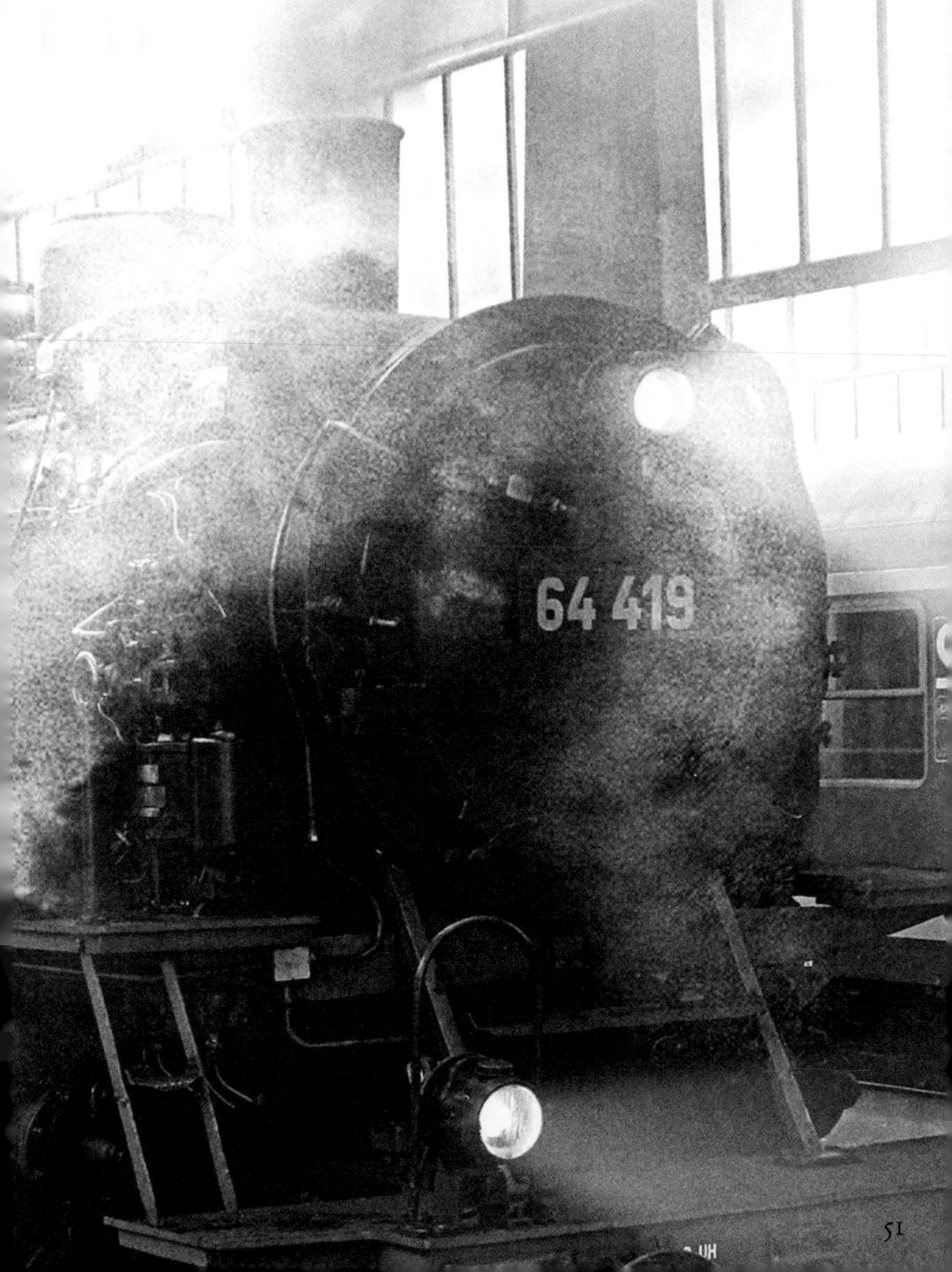
64 419

"Carriage number four," Muzz Elliott said, reading the tickets in her hand. "Our luggage should already be there."

She strode on confidently. Sadie and Saskia clutched each other's hands and walked eagerly behind her. They didn't say anything; each knew the other was excited by the iron monster that would carry them to Cannes.

"Do you think we should ask Muzz Elliott what is really going on?" Saskia whispered.

"I just hope Erik and Dorcas Potts will follow us—they have to do something. Muzz Elliott can't be on her own in this," Sadie said as they got closer to carriage number four.

"I was followed by a man on the platform," Saskia said. "He knew my name. He said he was Max Taranis and he was traveling to Cannes on THIS train."

Just as Sadie was about to speak, Muzz Elliott turned sharply in front of them and took off her hat and coat as she prepared to board the train.

"This is it: carriage number four," Muzz Elliott called to them.

At the door was a guard in a blue uniform with gold braid. He looked more like a sea captain than a train conductor.

"Madame," he said politely when Muzz Elliott showed him their tickets. He pointed into the carriage. "If you follow the corridor, your suite is at the end. Your luggage has already arrived."

Muzz Elliott nodded and, handing the guard her coat and hat, bid the girls to follow.

"I will not be needing these for the journey, if you would look after them for me," she said in a voice that he could not argue with. Sadie and Saskia climbed into the carriage after her.

The carriage was lit with electric light. It shone on the gold fittings that adorned the corridor. Each of the windows was made to look like an ornate baroque picture frame. There were several doors along the hallway that opened into rooms. Muzz Elliott looked at the tickets as she walked. She then stopped, opened a door, and stepped inside.

"Here we are," she said and disappeared into a room. Her voice echoed into the corridor. "Quite spacious for a train."

The twins stepped inside. Sadie gasped. The room was vast. There were three bunk beds attached to the wall with chains, a small dining table, and a long sofa in the middle of the room. Their luggage was neatly stacked on the rack by the door, and the sheets on the beds were turned down.

"Madame Elliott &

said a voice with an Italian accent from the corridor. "I am Luzio, your steward."

A man stepped into the compartment. He was short—smaller than Muzz Elliott—and very round. On the tips of his hands were stubby, fat fingers wrapped in white silk gloves.

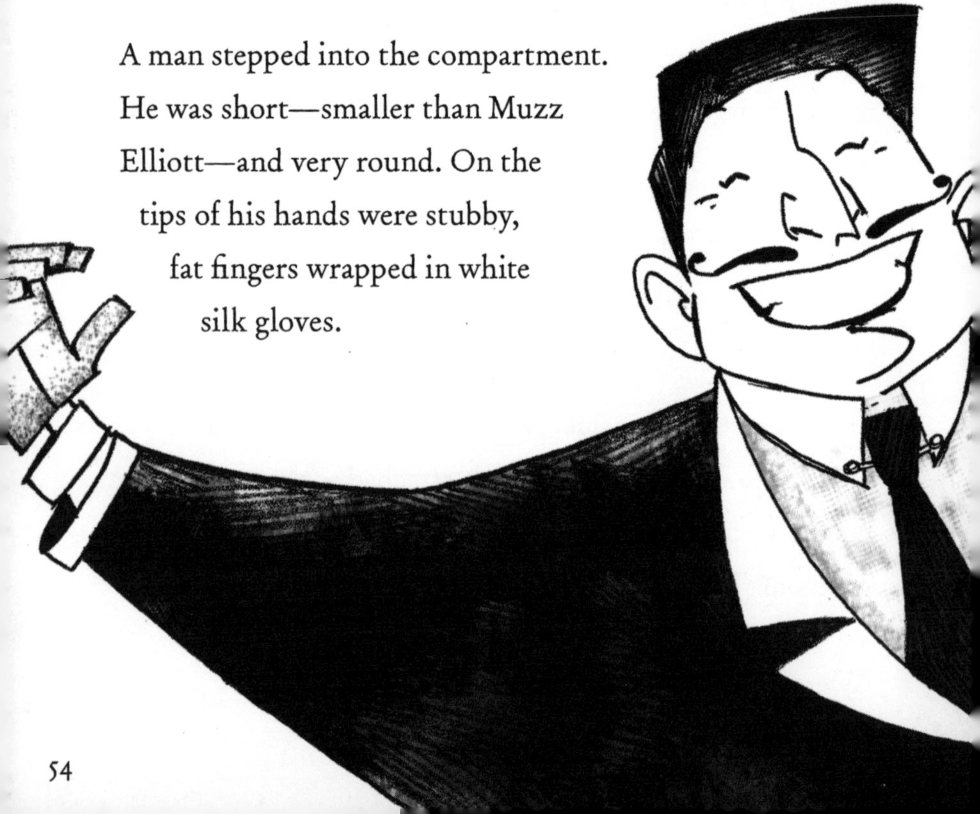

her children,”

He smiled widely and tried to fold his arms but only managed to rest them on his chest.

Muzz Elliott eyed him up and down.

“I am here if you need anything. I have put your coat in the locker outside. If you want anything—anything at all—please ask.”

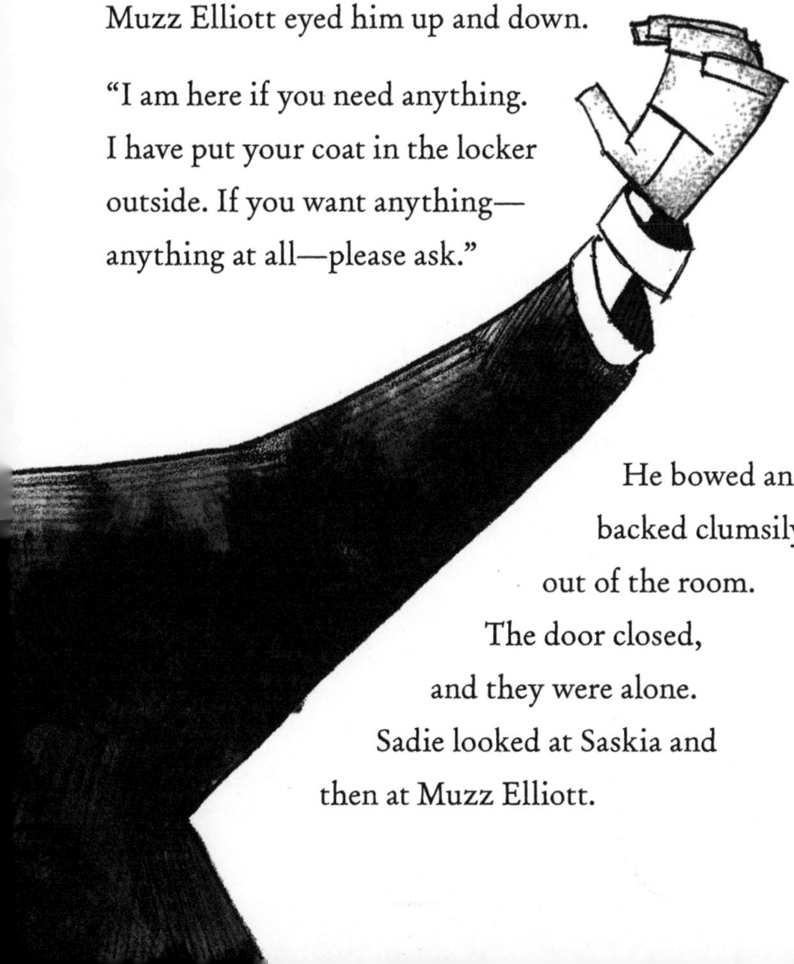

He bowed and backed clumsily out of the room. The door closed, and they were alone. Sadie looked at Saskia and then at Muzz Elliott.

"Is it safe to sleep?" she asked, pointing to the beds.

"Of course," Muzz Elliott replied. She sank into a large armchair by the window.

"But . . . ," faltered Sadie.

"Is it safe to sleep when the train is moving?" Saskia finished for her sister. "We've never slept on a steam train before. It goes very fast, and—"

"You will not be thrown from your beds, if that is what you fear. You will not even know that we are moving. I suggest you find out for yourselves." She pointed to the bunks. "I have some writing to do, and then I shall turn in."

Muzz Elliott opened her bag and took out her notepad and a neatly folded copy of the TIMES.

"Do you know a man named Max Taranis?" Saskia asked, climbing onto her bunk.

"Taranis?" repeated Muzz Elliott. "How do you know him?"

"He spoke to me when we left the ship. He seemed to know all about me."

"I . . . I . . . I don't think I do." Muzz Elliott stumbled over the words. "Perhaps he was mistaken."

"He was really creepy," Saskia added, while Muzz Elliott opened the newspaper.

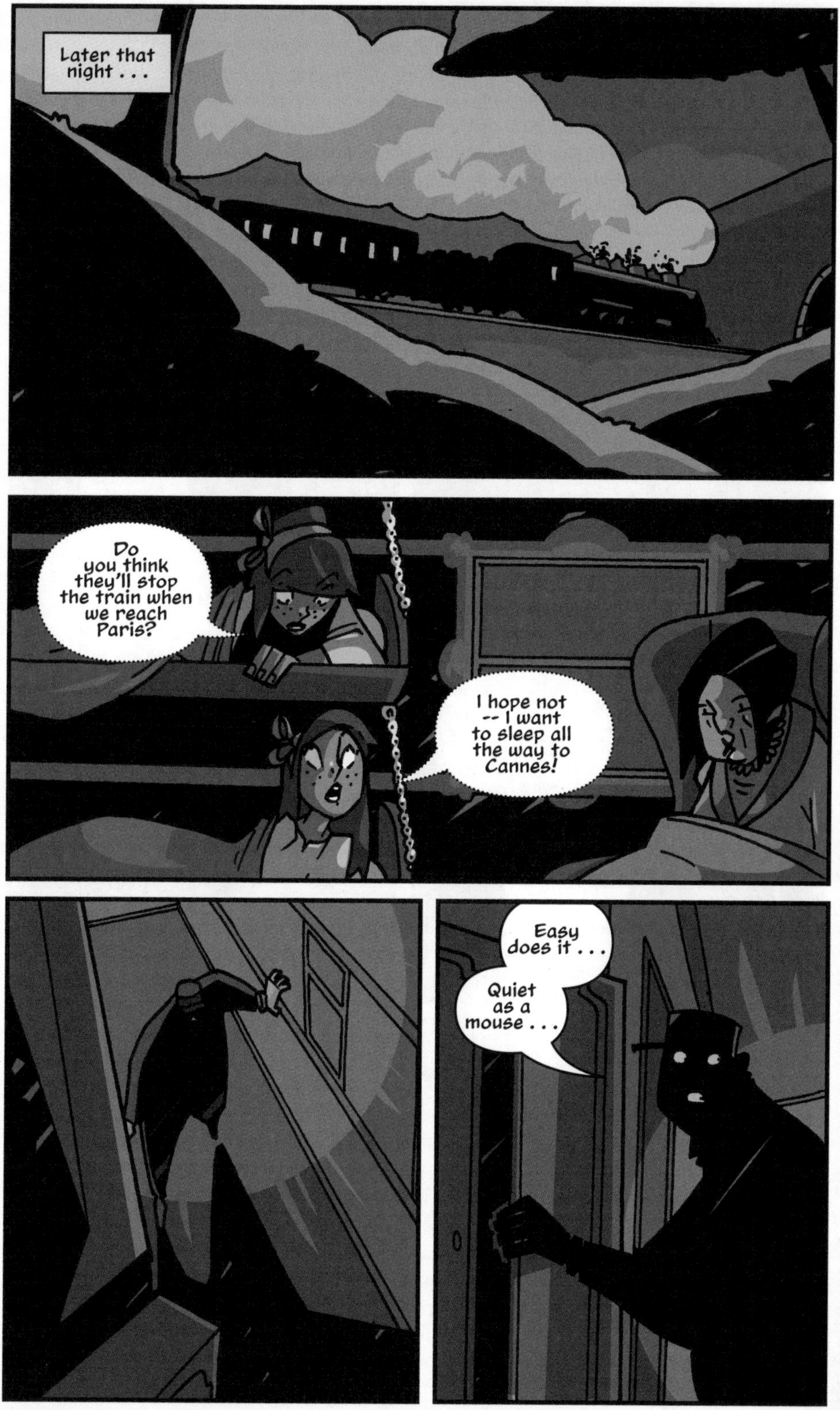
Later that night . . .
Do you think they'll stop the train when we reach Paris?
I hope not -- I want to sleep all the way to Cannes!
Easy does it . . .
Quiet as a mouse . . .

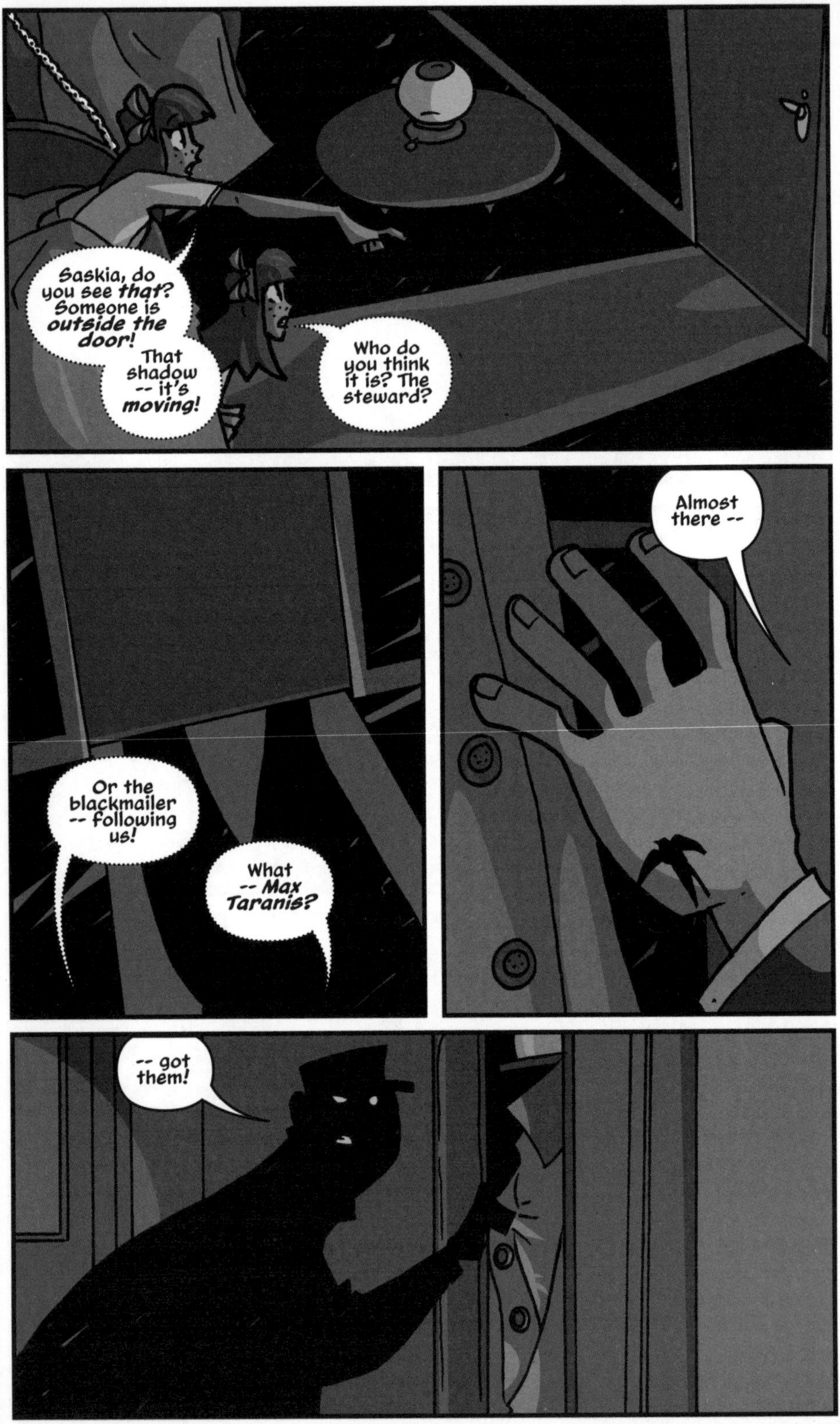
Saskia, do you see *that*? Someone is *outside the door*!
That shadow -- it's *moving*!
Who do you think it is? The steward?
Or the blackmailer -- following us!
What -- *Max Taranis*?
Almost there --
-- got them!

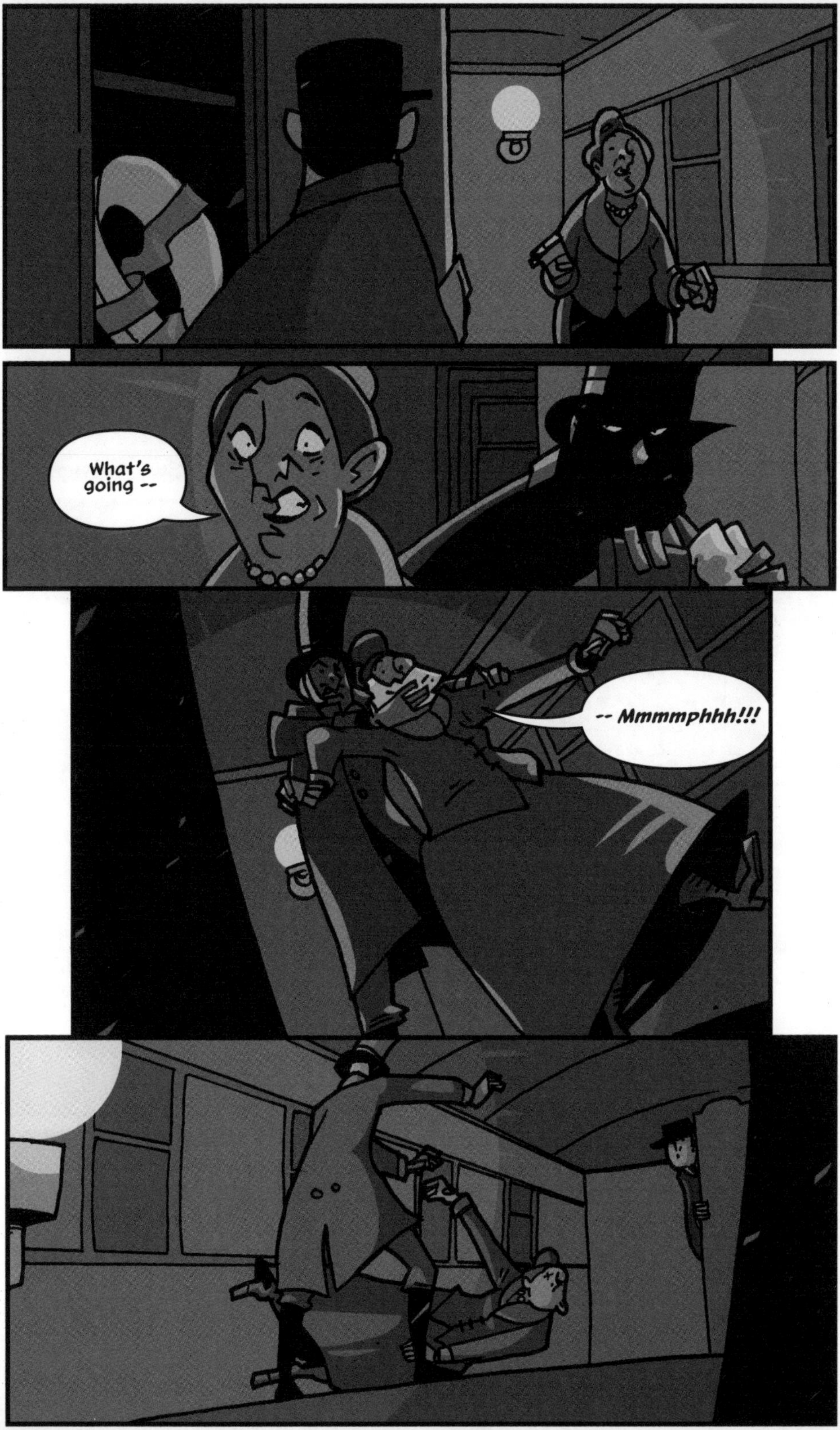
What's going --
-- Mmmmphhh!!!

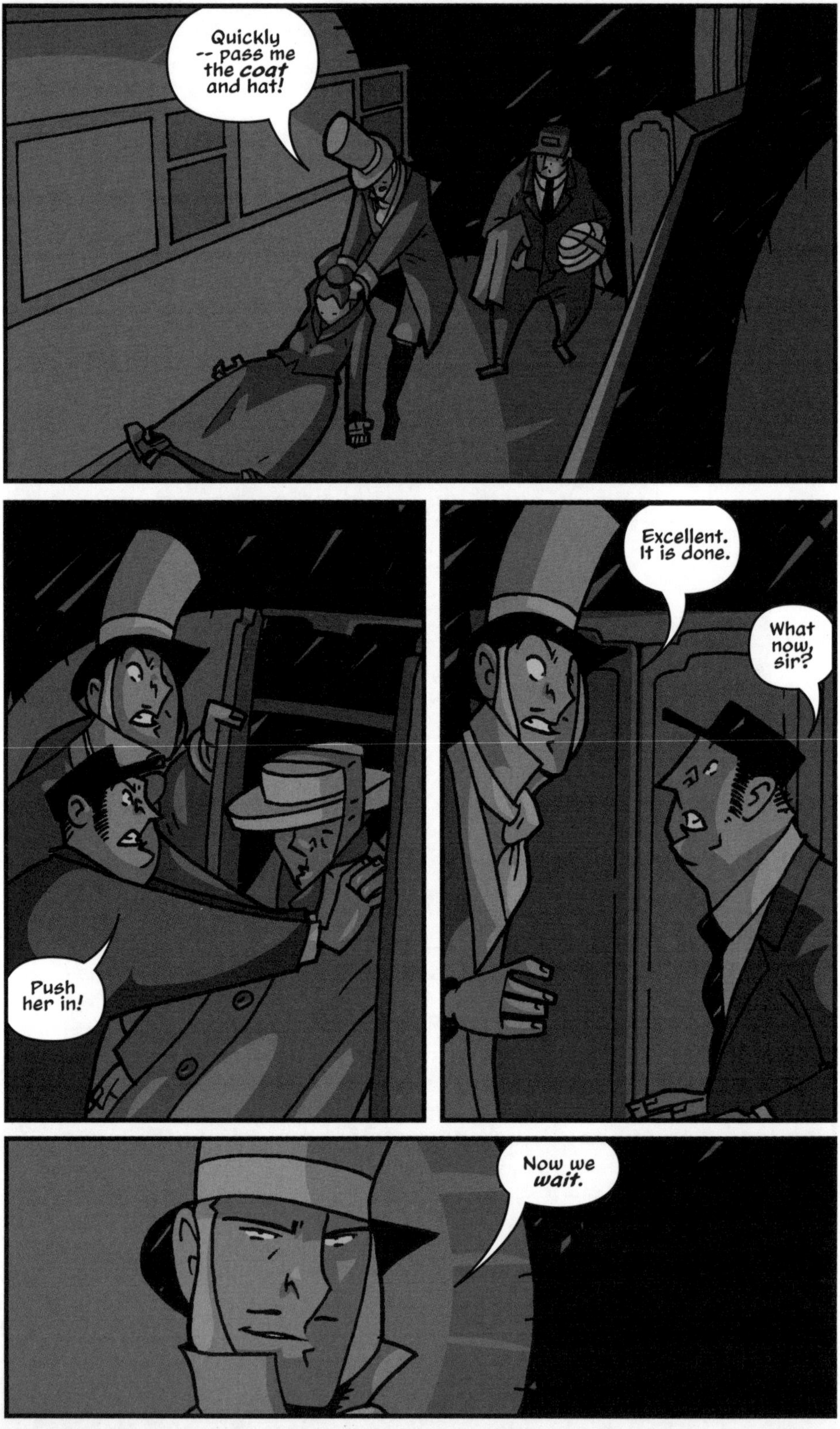
Quickly -- pass me the *coat* and hat!
Push her in!
Excellent. It is done.
What now, sir?
Now we *wait*.

Morning came quicker than the twins had expected. There was a tap on the door. A trolley laden with breakfast was wheeled into the room. Luzio greeted them with a loud and cheerful "Good morning," much to the annoyance of Muzz Elliott, who didn't usually speak to anyone until she had been awake for at least an hour.

"Breakfast," he said. "I thought you would want it in your room as the restaurant is now closed."

"Closed?" snapped Muzz Elliott.

"It is ten thirty—I let you sleep late," he replied sheepishly, knowing he had been chastised.

"But what about Paris?" Saskia asked. She had wanted to see the Eiffel Tower or at least the Isle de France—or a vaudeville stage.

"Paris comes and goes. It smells of cats," Luzio said, making a face like he'd just sniffed something quite vile. "It shall never be like Rome."

"So where do we stop?" Sadie asked.

"Lyon—to take on water for the engine. There are no other stations before then," Luzio replied. He pulled off the towel that covered the breakfast and silver jugs of coffee and hot chocolate. "That will be later this evening."

He smiled, turned, and left the room, closing the door behind him.

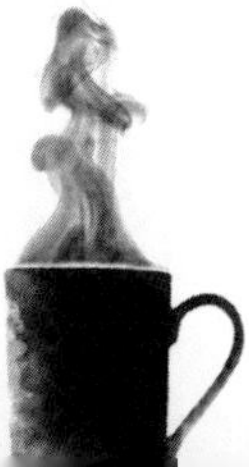

Sadie and Saskia ate their breakfast eagerly as Muzz Elliott watched. There were dark stains under her eyes, and she looked worried.

While the girls dressed, Muzz Elliott drank her coffee and put thick white face cream on her cheeks.

Sadie was pouring herself another cup of cocoa and Saskia was settling back on the sofa with her book when there was a horrendous scream from the corridor outside. Sadie jumped, dropping her cup and splashing cocoa across the breakfast tray. "What was that?" asked both twins at once.

Running feet pounded the floor outside. More shouts came from the other side of the door.

"Muzz Elliott—she is dead!" screamed Luzio in a high-pitched voice. "I take her breakfast and now she is DEAD."

"DEAD?" asked Sadie, looking at a perfectly healthy Muzz Elliott in the armchair.

"The man's mad." Muzz Elliott sniffed.

"How do you know it is her?" asked a voice they recognized as the guard's.

"This is her coat. You gave it to me, and look . . . her hat!" Luzio wailed in anguish.

Muzz Elliott sighed, crossed to the door, and flung it open. She stood in the doorway staring at them with a raised eyebrow.

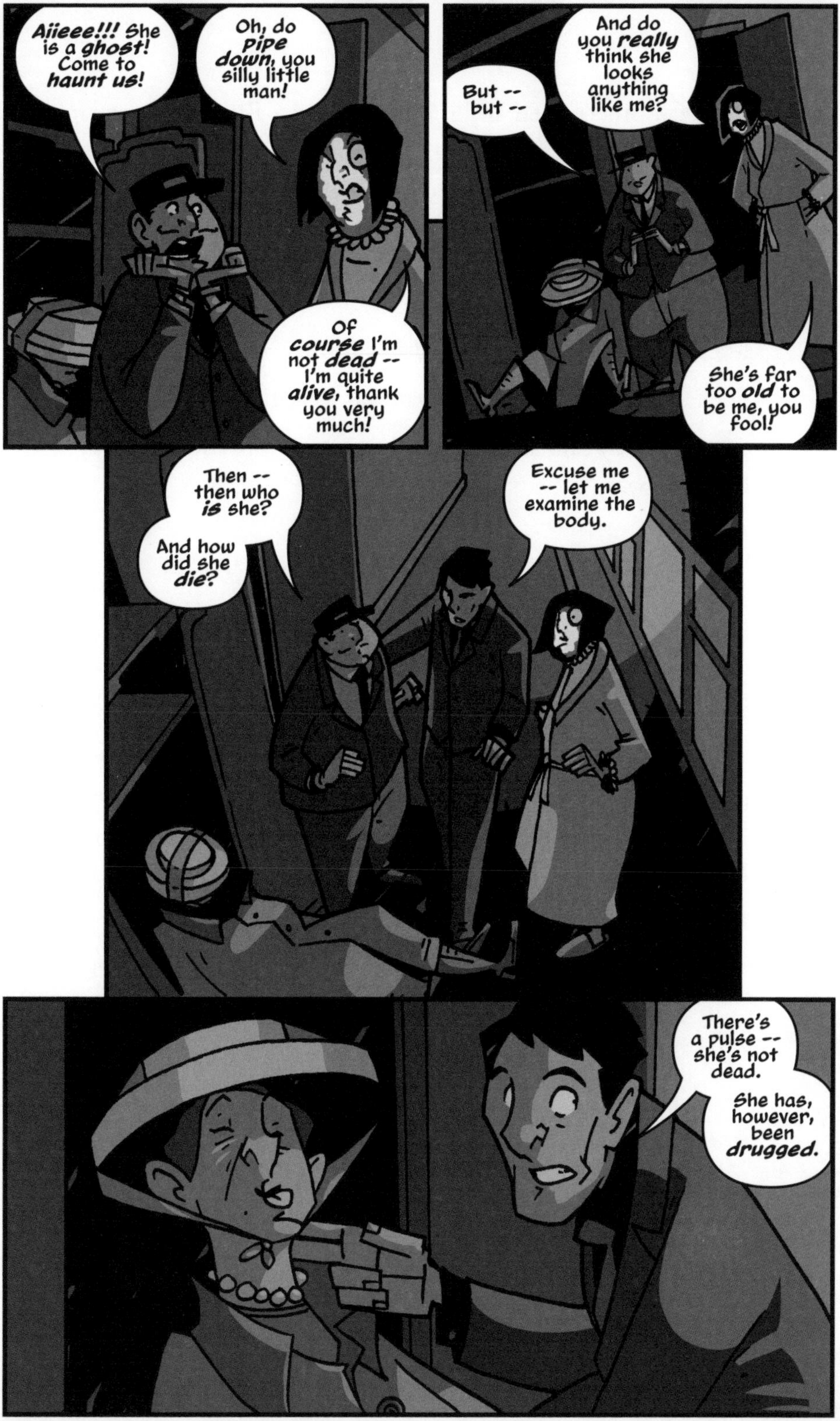

Aiieee!!! She is a ghost! Come to haunt us!
Oh, do pipe down, you silly little man!
Of course I'm not dead -- I'm quite alive, thank you very much!
But -- but --
And do you really think she looks anything like me?
She's far too old to be me, you fool!
Then -- then who is she?
And how did she die?
Excuse me -- let me examine the body.
There's a pulse -- she's not dead.
She has, however, been drugged.

Max Taranis turned and looked at Muzz Elliott. "I take it these are your clothes?" he asked in a sharp voice.

"My hat and my coat. I gave them to the guard," Muzz Elliott replied stoically.

Max Taranis leaned forward and rummaged in the inner pockets of the jacket the woman was wearing under the coat. "Ah," he said as he pulled a passport from the pocket. "Tamora Vallettzi."

"It can't be—she got off the train in Paris," Luzio protested.

"Did you see her get off?" Max Taranis asked sharply.

"She—she was not in her room. I thought she had gotten off the train. I left her trunk on the platform. . . ." Luzio trailed off, his mouth hanging open.

Max Taranis looked at the passport photo and back at the unconscious woman. "There can be no doubt. This is Tamora Vallettzi. But who would make her miss her stop, and why has she been drugged?"

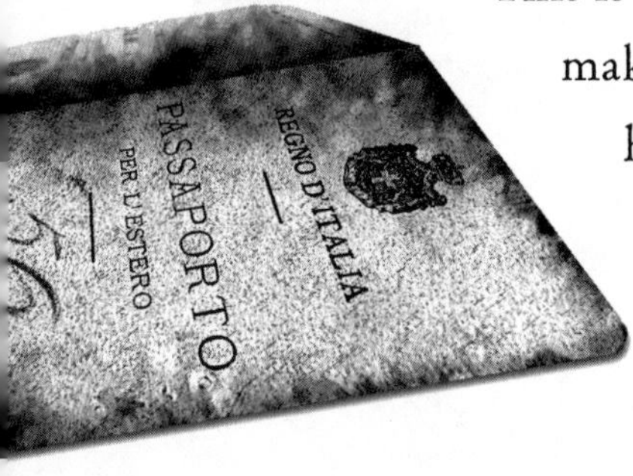

REGNO D'ITALIA
PASSAPORTO
PER L'ESTERO

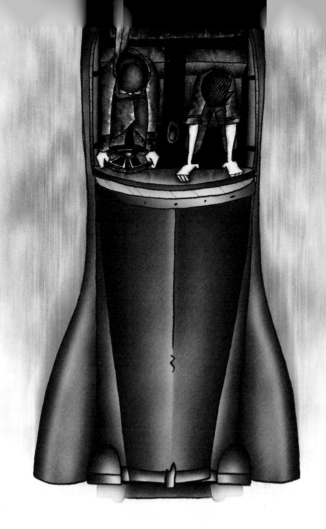

Chapter Four

The Mountain Pass

THE TIRES OF THE BUGATTI smoked as the car twisted and turned on the mountain road. Erik looked out at the vast drop that fell away to the lake below. The gravel path clung to the side of the Alp. Pockets of snow filled the ditches, and sharp scarps of rock stuck out like fingers high above the canyon.

Dorcas Potts looked straight ahead. She hadn't spoken for the last ten miles. They had driven through the night, leaving London soon after Erik had answered the telephone and told her what Sadie had said.

"To the car," Dorcas Potts had shouted as she pulled on her long coat and flying helmet. "An old warship has been converted to take cars across the Channel. If we go now, we can beat the train."

Erik now regretted agreeing to her plan. Dorcas Potts drove the Bugatti as though she were completely insane. The road from Hampstead to London had been a blur of dark trees, fast corners, and sudden stops.

The ship she'd referred to was an old iron barge with a giant crane that hoisted the cars and held them dangling throughout the voyage. The crossing had made him feel sick. Then the road to Reims had been a nightmare of donkey carts and irate Frenchmen they had forced out of the way. Now, twelve hours later, they were climbing into the mountains.

"It's a long way down," Erik said as they sped along the deserted road.

"It's like this most of the way to the sea. This is the Route Napoléon—I did it last year but not as quickly," Dorcas Potts shouted into the wind that blew over the windshield of the green, open-top vehicle.

"Do you really think we'll get there before they do? They are on an express train."

"As long as we don't crash." She laughed as she skidded sideways around a narrow corner.

Erik held his hand to his mouth. He had never been in a car that went so fast and for so long.

"Do you think they'll be safe on the train? Blackmail is dangerous business." His last words went unheard.

Suddenly two wheels of the car slipped over the edge of the ravine, and the Bugatti was momentarily suspended in midair.

Dorcas Potts spun the steering wheel and pressed hard on the accelerator.

She laughed as the car thudded back onto the road and sped toward another hairpin bend—this one on the ridge of a small mountain pass. "You'll love this, Erik. The view is amazing."

Erik wasn't looking. The view made his stomach drop to his knees. He stared into the footwell of the car and watched the grit and stones bounce around near his boots.

"Lovely," he muttered as the wind whistled over his head.

"You should look. It's not that bad," Dorcas Potts insisted. She slowed the car for the briefest moment.

"I'd rather—" Erik didn't finish what he was going to say.

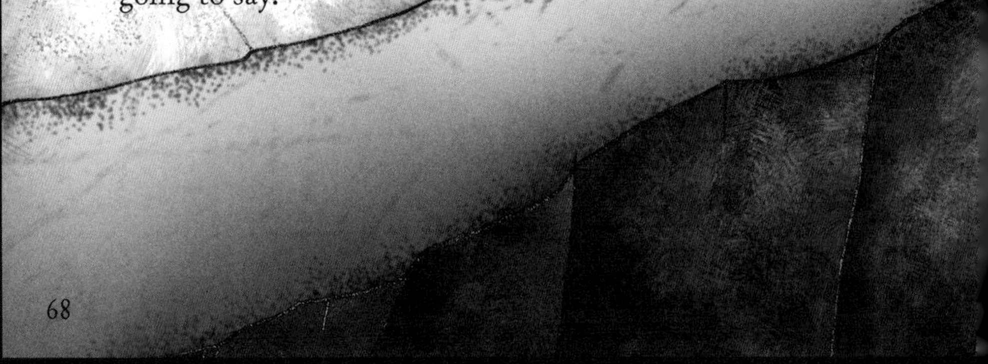

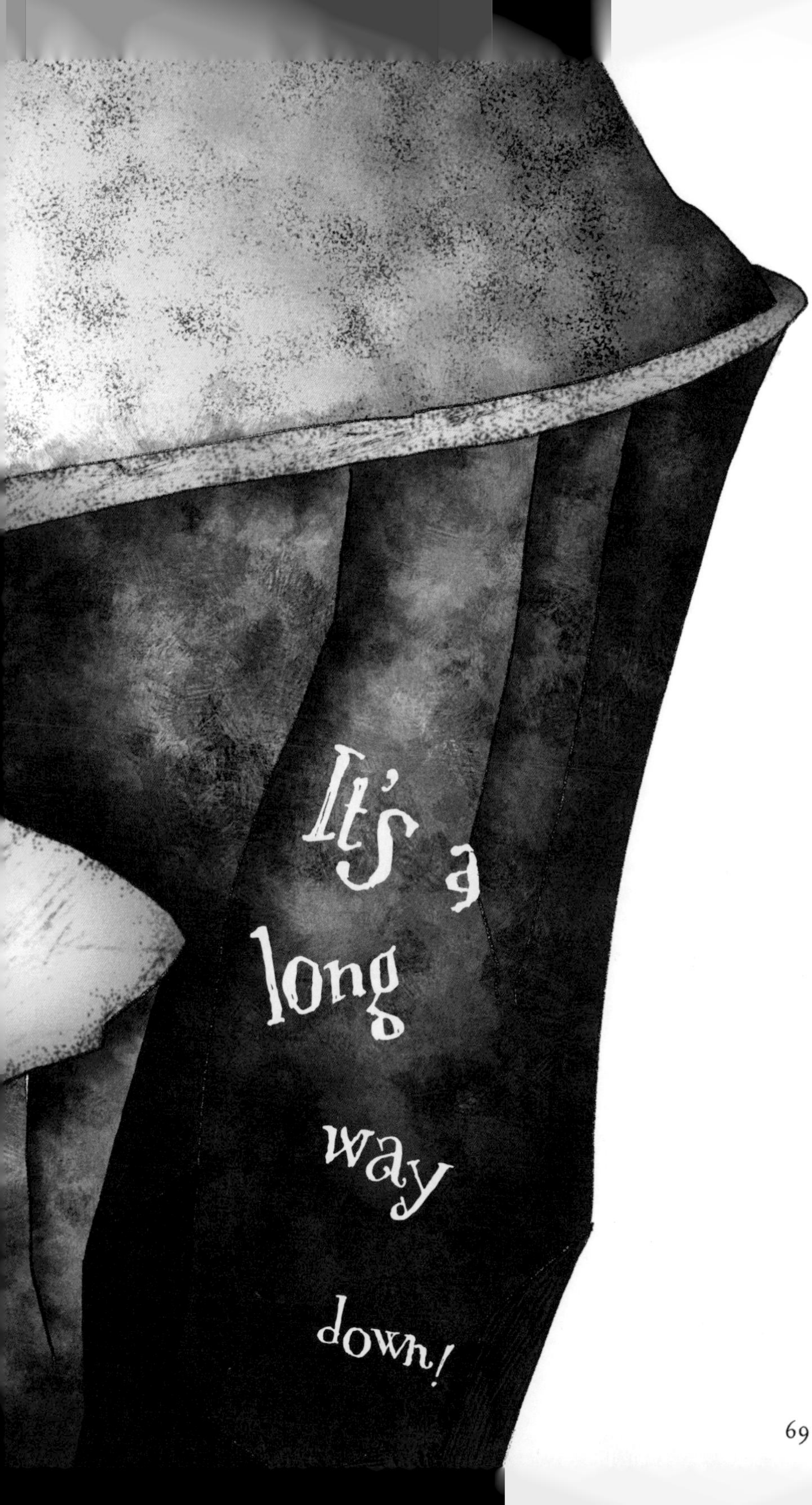
It's a long way down!

There, in the small gravel turnout on the next bend, was a long, black sedan. He hadn't seen anything like it before. The windows were darkened, so he could see only the faint outline of the driver. Headlights beamed from what looked like two gigantic eyes slung over the front fender. The car hugged the road like an enormous panther waiting to strike. Something inside Erik trembled. He suddenly knew the car was waiting for them.

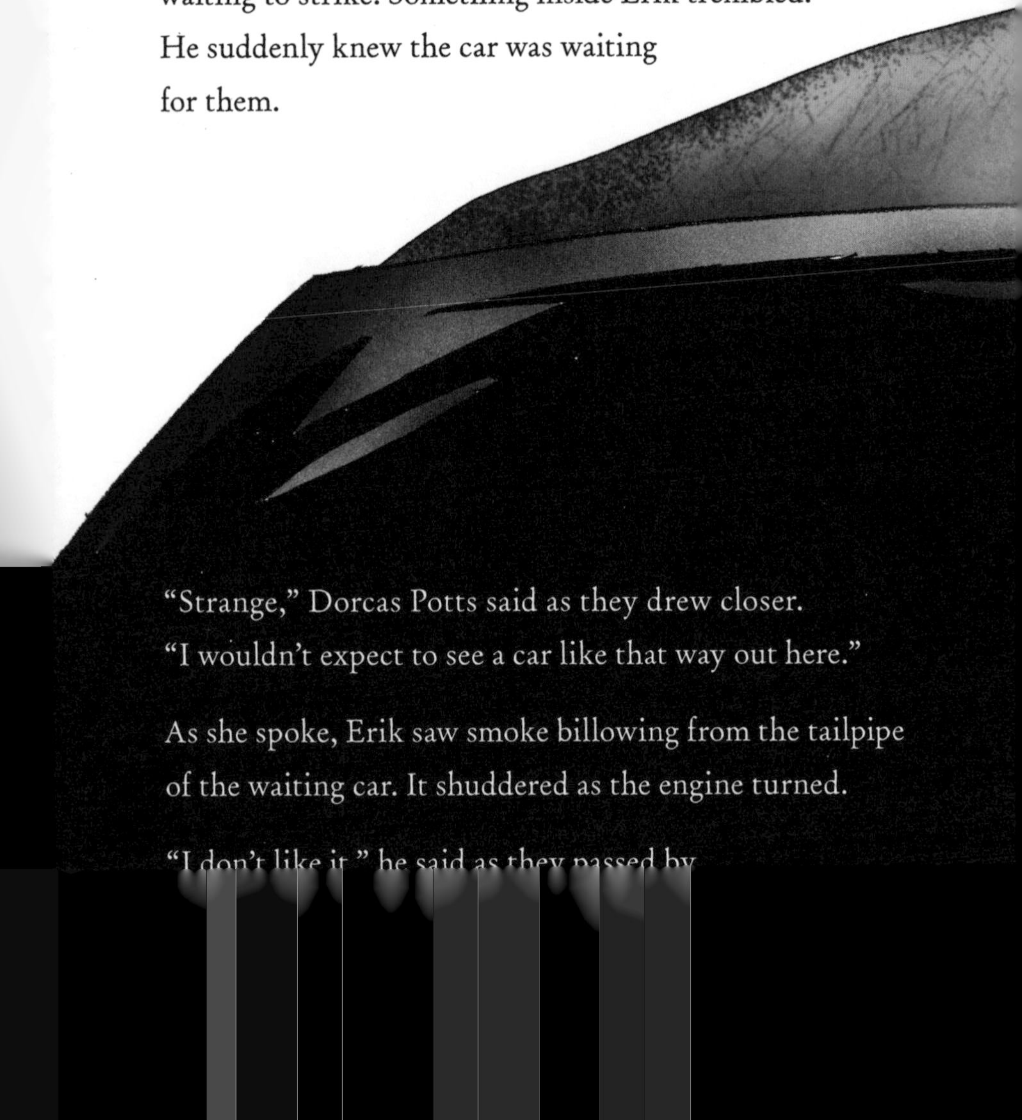

"Strange," Dorcas Potts said as they drew closer. "I wouldn't expect to see a car like that way out here."

As she spoke, Erik saw smoke billowing from the tailpipe of the waiting car. It shuddered as the engine turned.

"I don't like it," he said as they passed by.

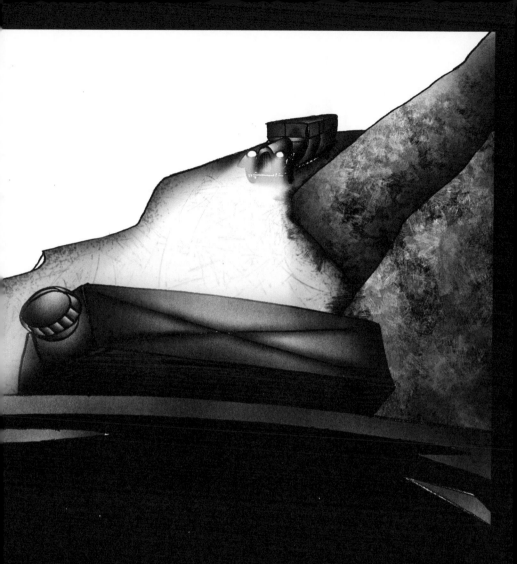

"Keep a lookout," Dorcas Potts shouted, flooring the gas pedal. "They're coming after us."

Erik turned in his seat. The black car had slipped onto the road and was keeping pace. It purred at a steady distance behind them—never getting closer, never falling back. There was no doubt: they were being followed.

"What do they want?"

Erik asked.

"They could be robbers. This road is notorious for bandits," Dorcas Potts said calmly. She took the curves even faster, heading toward the summit.

"What will they do if they catch us?" Erik asked, holding on to the side of the car.

"Probably steal what we have and then push us and the car off the cliff to make it look like an accident. Either that or steal the car and just throw us off the cliff."

Dorcas Potts had a habit of being able to say the most terrifying things in the most matter-of-fact way. Erik swallowed hard and looked back at the car that now appeared to be gaining ground on them.

"They're catching up with us!" he shouted above the whining of the engine.

"I know—and the engine is starting to overheat with this speed," Dorcas Potts replied.

Erik looked at the dial on the dashboard. The needle veered dangerously into the red zone. He knew that if they didn't slow down, the engine could soon explode.

"How long have we got?" he asked as he looked back again.

"Five minutes at this speed—ten, at the most," Dorcas Potts hollered. The car screamed faster up the side of the mountain toward a peak in the road. "If we can just get to that arch, the road drops down the other side, and I can take the turns quicker than they can."

Erik looked ahead. At the peak of the mountain road was an arch of solid rock. The road had been hacked through to form a small tunnel on the curve. On top of the arch, a man was crouching behind a boulder, pushing against it.

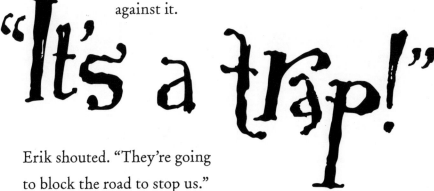

"It's a trap!"

Erik shouted. "They're going to block the road to stop us."

Dorcas Potts took her eyes from
the road. On the peak of the
stone arch, the large boulder
shuddered. The man
strained against it, and it
began to roll slowly
to the edge.

"Hang on," Dorcas
Potts screamed.
The car revved
even higher
and the wheels
spun faster.

Erik gripped the
seat. The wind
pushed against his
face. Around him was
a blur of flashing light.
He looked up. The rock was
falling toward them.

"NO!" he screamed.

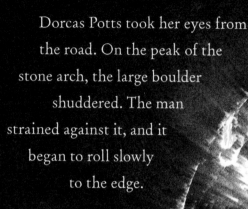

The boulder fell.

The car lurched to one side
as Dorcas Potts pulled the
hand brake. Erik was spun
sideways. He looked up
again and saw the falling
rock blotting out the
sky. Somewhere
nearby he could hear
the roaring engine of
the car behind them.
Dorcas Potts pushed
the Bugatti into
reverse and slammed
the accelerator to the
floor. The car shot
backward through
the stone archway. The
boulder hit the road and
shattered into a thousand
pieces of exploding rock.

"Get down!"

Dorcas Potts yelled, dodging shards of flying stone.

There was a loud groaning, and the arch above their heads began to crack. The mountain road trembled like an earthquake had struck.

"It's falling!" Erik cried as a fissure appeared in the rock above them.

Dorcas Potts didn't hesitate. She spun the steering wheel and turned the Bugatti just as the mountain pass began to crumble.

"Keep your head down. We should just be able to do it," she said and drove out of the tunnel and into the light.

Erik looked back. The tunnel had collapsed. Dust and debris billowed into the air. The road they had traveled on slipped down into the ravine. On a jagged outcrop of what was left of the stone arch, the man looked down at them. Slowly, carefully, he lifted a rifle and took aim.

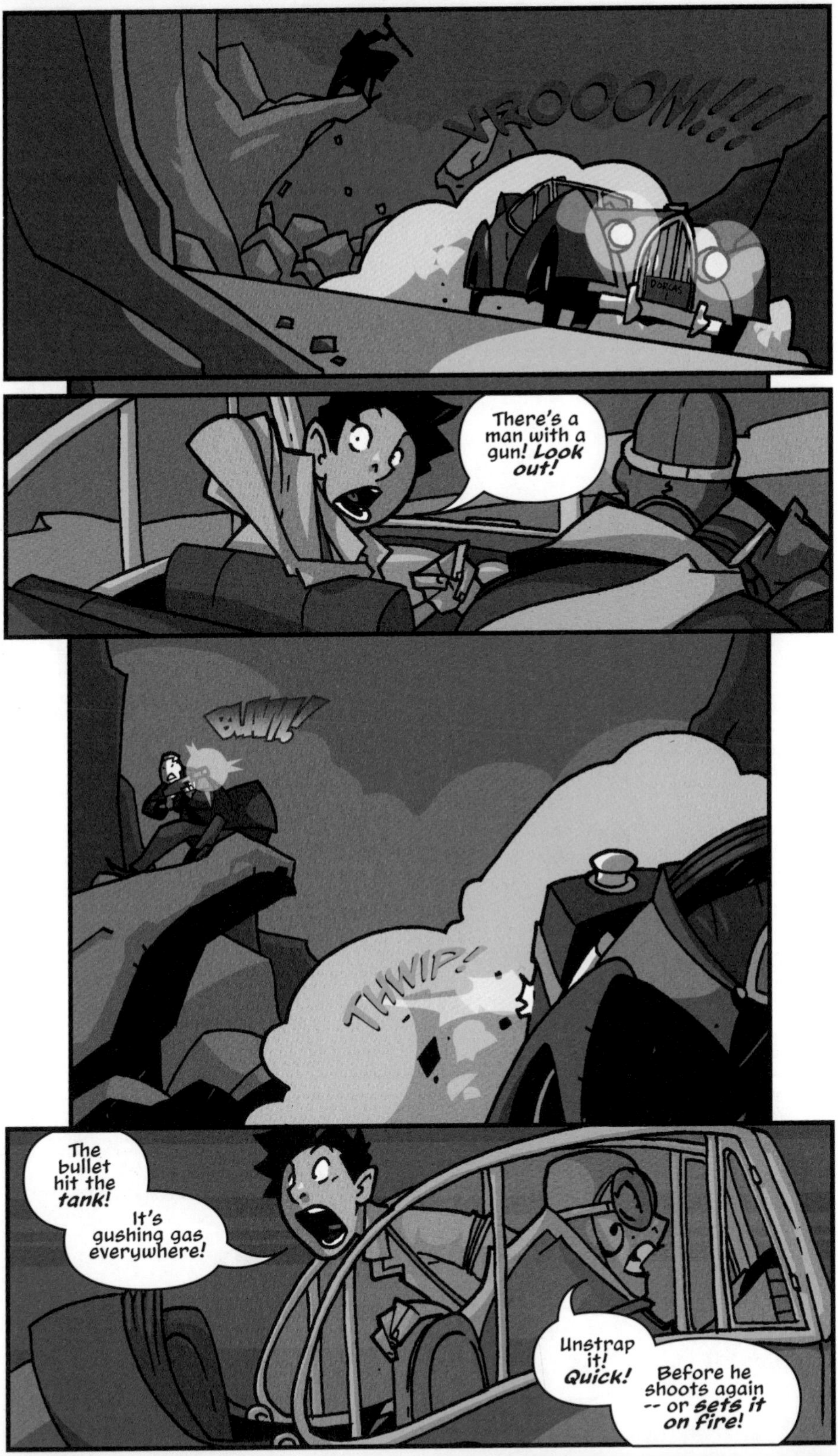
VROOOM!!!!
There's a man with a gun! Look out!
BLAM!
THWIP!
The bullet hit the tank!
It's gushing gas everywhere!
Unstrap it! Quick!
Before he shoots again -- or sets it on fire!

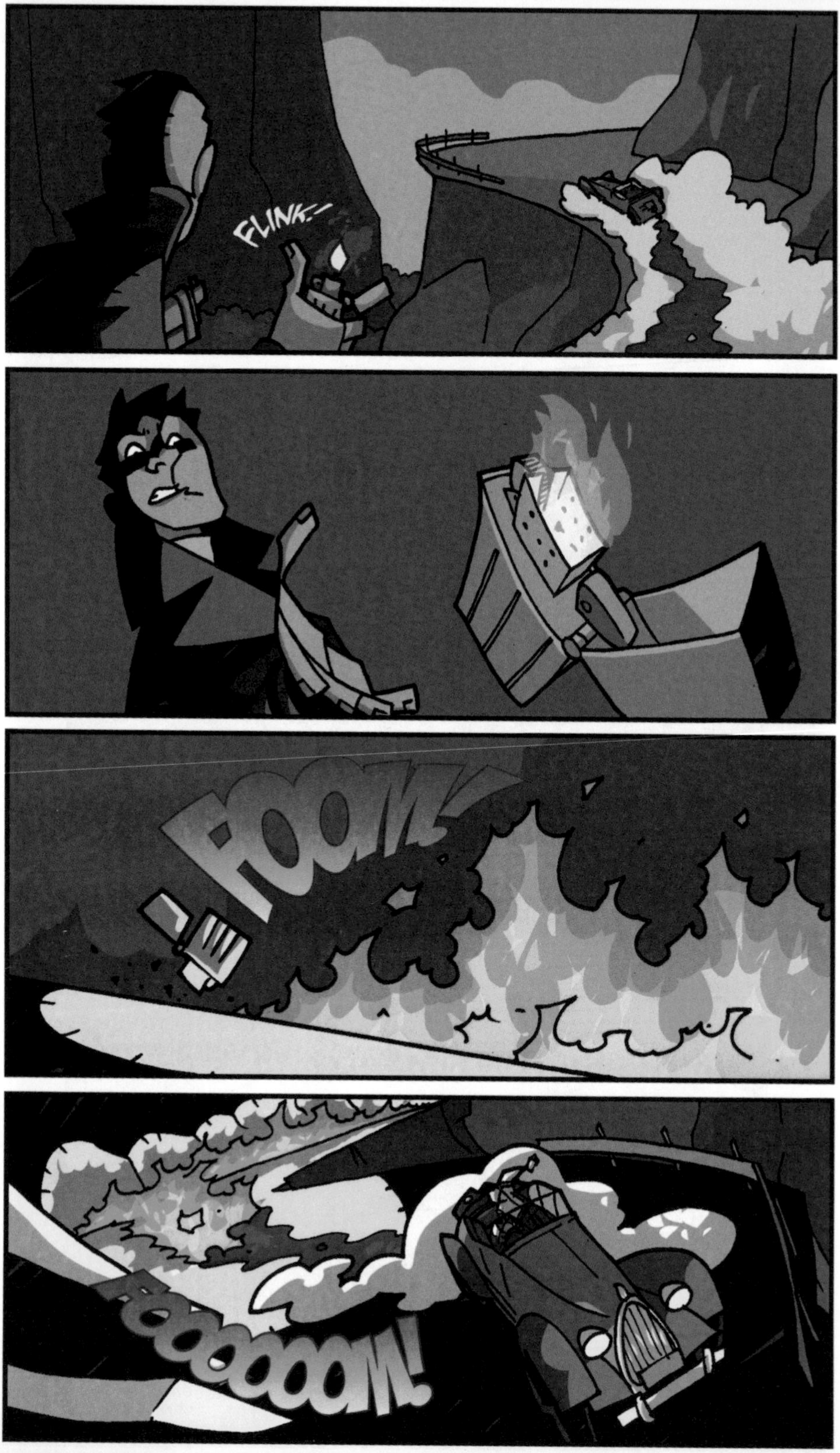
FLINK!
FOOM!
FOOOOOOM!

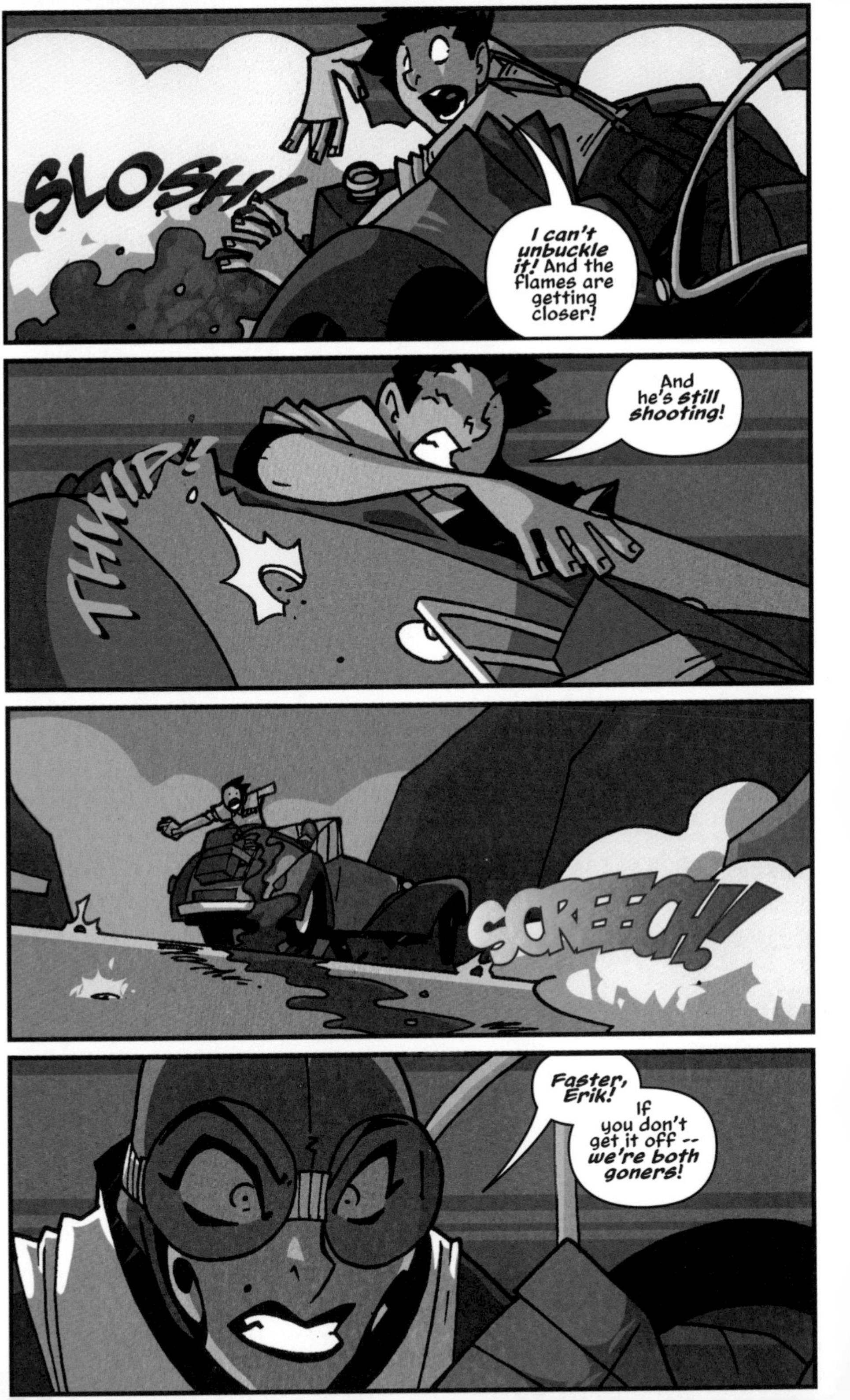
SLOSH!
I can't unbuckle it! And the flames are getting closer!
THWIP!
And he's still shooting!
SCREECH!
Faster, Erik!
If you don't get it off -- we're both goners!

The flames whipped closer and closer to his face, striking like an angry rattlesnake. He grappled with the strap, but it wouldn't budge. Erik knew time was running out, but by now his hands were slick with gasoline. Bracing himself against the seat of the car, he yanked hard on the strap. Finally it came loose, and he fell back with a thud. Erik pulled the canister from the rack and threw it from the car just as the flames leaped toward him.

There was a sudden, blinding flash as the gasoline exploded in a ball of acrid black smoke. It blew up in a dense, mushroom-shaped cloud that blocked the car from the gunman's view. Dorcas Potts turned suddenly, taking a narrow and far more treacherous road. It dropped down the side of the ravine toward the meandering river below.

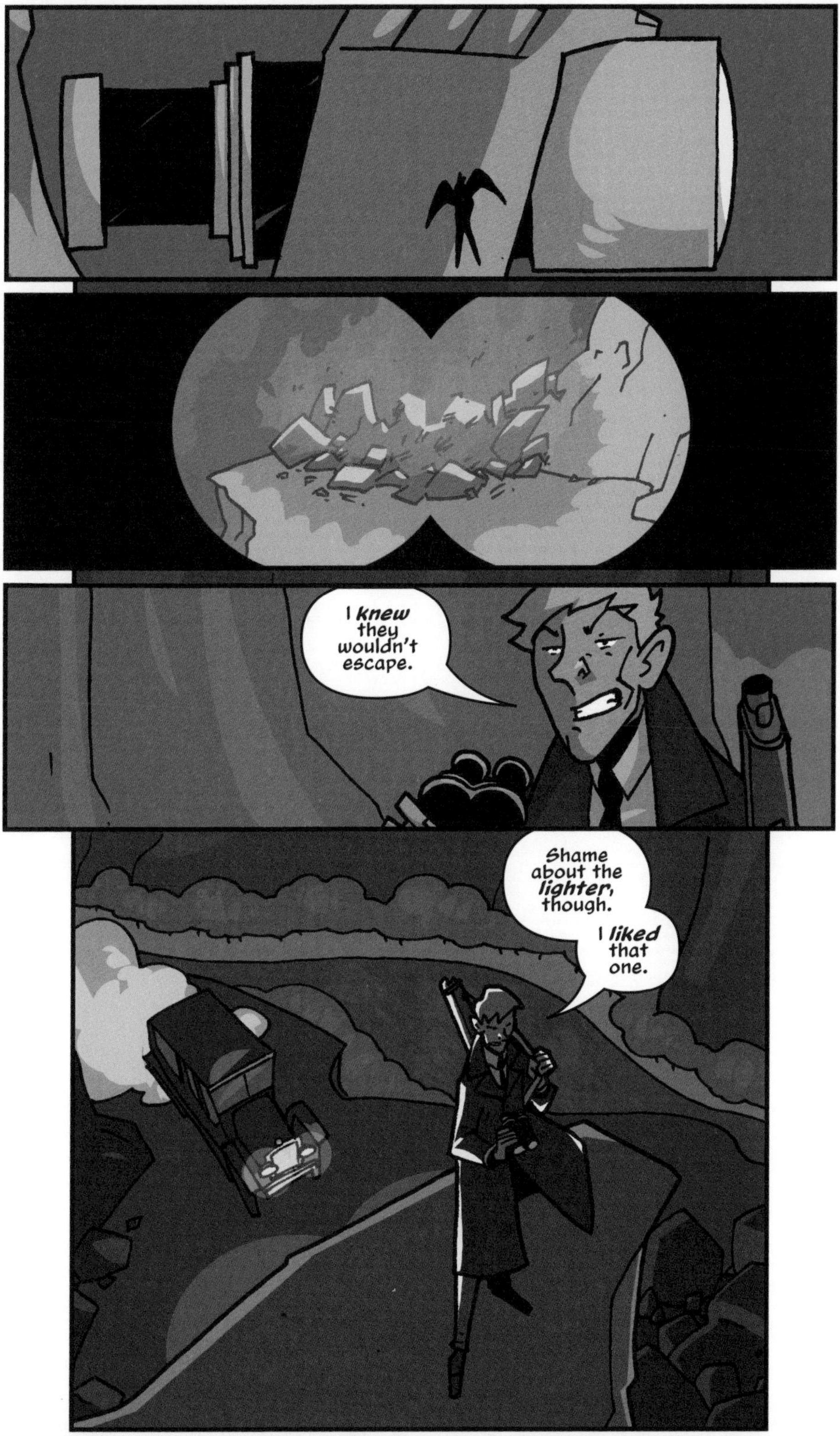
I knew they wouldn't escape.
Shame about the lighter, though.
I liked that one.

As the gunman peered into the smoke, he heard the sound of a car slowing to a halt on the road behind him. He turned. A man in a trilby hat and a long white coat got out of the sedan and looked up, shielding his eyes. "Did you get them?" he called.

"Of course. I never miss," answered the gunman smugly.

The man in the trilby hat smiled. "Good. Then they will not be able to get to their friends in time."

Chapter Five
The Twisted Plot

"IT APPEARS SOMEONE has been drugged and stuffed in the closet," Muzz Elliott said matter-of-factly as she closed the door and stepped back into the room.

"Who?" asked Saskia, although she had heard everything through the open door.

"Tamora Vallettzi—whoever she may be. Apparently she intended to disembark in Paris but has been unconscious in the cupboard this whole time, poor thing," Muzz Elliott said, staring around the room and looking perplexed. "She was wearing my hat and coat . . . quite strange."

"I saw someone last night. I saw a shadow under the door," Sadie said urgently. "It could have been her—"

"Or the people who drugged her!" cut in Saskia.

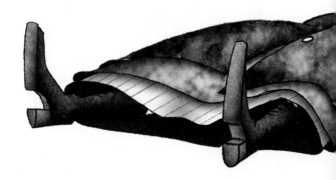

Muzz Elliott slumped onto the sofa, looked at the twins, and then stared at the floor. Finally she sighed and spoke.

"I haven't been completely honest," she said flatly. "This . . . 'vacation' isn't all it seems to be."

"We know," Saskia replied.

"I'm afraid I may have brought you into even more trouble," Muzz Elliott said, appearing not to have heard. She picked up a cloth and wiped a stripe of cream from her face.

"We know," Saskia insisted a second time.

"The trouble is—" Muzz Elliott stopped, the hand holding the cloth poised inches from her face. For several seconds she resembled a wax figure in a museum. Then suddenly she returned to life.

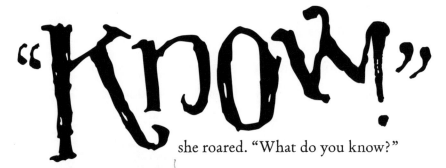

"KNOW!"

she roared. "What do you know?"

"You're being blackmailed," Sadie said in the same tone she would use to offer someone breakfast.

"But how . . . ?" Muzz Elliott glanced from one twin to the other, and both her eyebrows shot up.

Saskia looked at Sadie. Now they knew they had to be honest.

"We overheard your telephone conversation last night," Saskia said with a sigh.

"You were listening?"

"By accident," offered Sadie, as she picked up a biscuit from the breakfast tray.

"How much do you know?" asked Muzz Elliott, rising to her feet and pacing nervously.

"We read the letter—when you were talking with Dorcas Potts," Sadie told her. She poured herself another cup of hot chocolate. "Erik put it back in the newspaper."

Muzz Elliott glared.

"I guess that part wasn't an accident," Sadie admitted.

Muzz Elliott pursed her lips, drew in a breath, and opened her mouth to speak. But her anger seemed to soften at the last moment. "And you still came?" she asked.

"You can't go alone," added Sadie.

"We called Erik and told him to bring Dorcas Potts," said Saskia.

There was a frantic knocking at the door.

Mr. Taranis requires a Conversation with you.

"Madame Elliott! Madame Elliott!" shouted Luzio.

Before Muzz Elliott could get to the door, it opened. Luzio stood there, his face bleak, lips drawn tightly across his face.

"What is it?" Muzz Elliott asked. With a single glance, she bid the twins to be silent.

"Mr. Taranis requires a conversation with you," Luzio said, nervously bobbing up and down.

"Then tell Mr. Taranis he will have to wait until after breakfast." Muzz Elliott crossed to the door and pushed the short Italian man from the room.

As Luzio was pushed outside, the man in the gabardine suit stepped aside and leaned against the wall. He smiled.

"I didn't realize the brilliant Muzz Elliott was so forceful. I have read all of your books," Max Taranis said, bowing.

"Then you didn't read them well enough," she said and slammed the door in his face.

"That was the man from the platform—he knew my name and everything," Saskia said. Another knock sounded on the door.

"Then he knows too much," Muzz Elliott replied quickly. She flung open the door. "Don't you listen?" she bawled. "I said AFTER breakfast—"

The guard stood on the other side of the door looking stunned. The corridor was empty except for him.

"I came to say . . . I came to say that—" he began to whisper—"THEY have removed . . . HER." He pointed to the cupboard into which the body of Tamora Vallettzi had been stuffed.

"Good," replied Muzz Elliott as the twins peered nosily from behind her. "Tell THEM that I want my hat and coat. I can't go parading along the Boulevard de la Croisette half dressed."

"But she is still unconscious . . . ," faltered the guard.

"Then she is NOT in need of a hat or a coat," Muzz Elliott insisted.

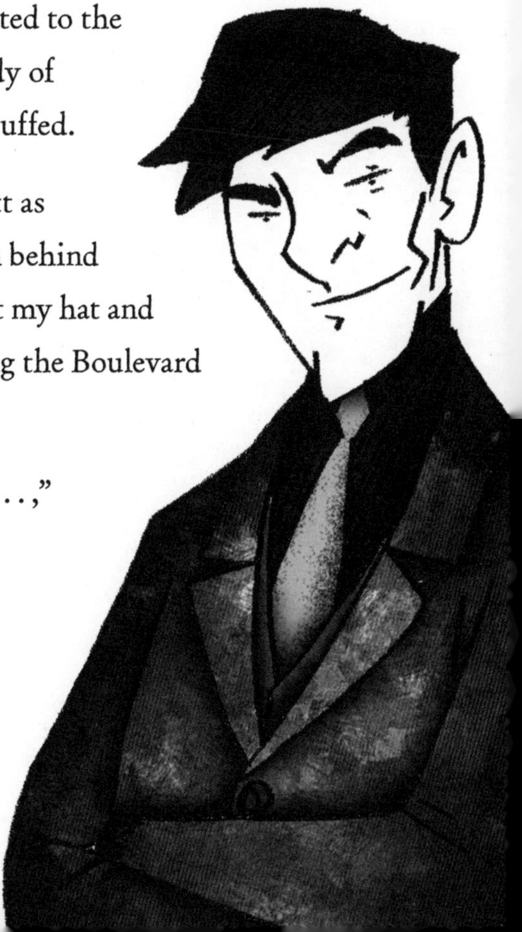

The guard looked sullen. He stared at the cupboard and lowered his head in false respect. "Very well, madame," he scowled. "I will have your things brought to you when THEY see to Madame Vallettzi."

The door at the end of the corridor swung open. Max Taranis pushed Luzio in front of him.

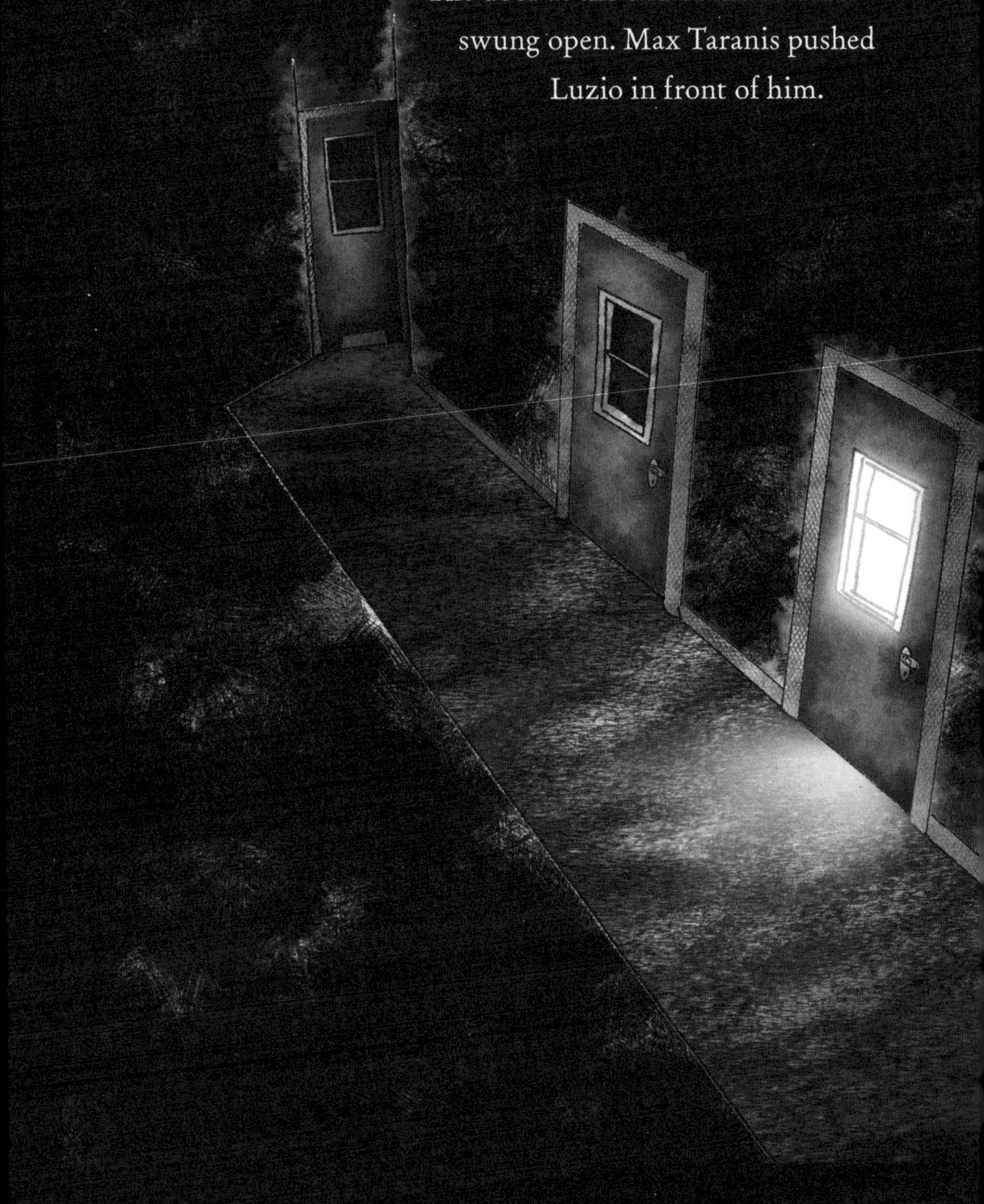

"Madame Elliott," Luzio squeaked, prompted by a sharp push in his back. "Mr. Taranis—he wants to—"

"Mind his manners," Muzz Elliott finished, marching back into her room and slamming the door. "When will people ever learn?"

"Do you know who he is?" Sadie asked.

"By the time we reach Cannes, I am sure we will know a lot about Max Taranis. In the meantime, we have to be very careful. I have a bad feeling about all of this," she said.

"Do you think he could be the blackmailer?" asked Saskia.

"His voice—from what I heard—is not the same. But you never know." Muzz Elliott tried to smile. "We will just have to stay together."

"He looks like a villain," Saskia put in. "His shoes are far too shiny for someone ordinary."

"Do you think the blackmailer is the same person who drugged Tamora Vallettzi?" asked Sadie suddenly.

"It's hard to say," began Muzz Elliott. "It could be merely a coincidence that she was found in the closet next to our compartment.

"But why was she wearing my hat and coat?" Muzz Elliott trailed off, lost in thought.

"What about the police—why don't they stop the train? Whoever drugged Tamora Vallettzi has to be on board," reasoned Sadie.

"There isn't a stop until we reach Lyon. The police will be informed then." Muzz Elliott looked out the window. "I know all the stops on this train. I researched it for a book I wrote called MURDER TRAIN."

"Isn't that the book you're reading, Saskia?" Sadie turned to her sister and immediately knew something was wrong. "Saskia? Are you all right?"

Saskia was staring at the open book in her lap like it was a poisonous toad. Her mouth hung open in horror, and her blue and yellow eyes were bulging.

"What is it?" Sadie asked as she saw the color drain from Saskia's face.

"It happened just like in the book! I can't believe I didn't catch it before," Saskia muttered.

"Catch what? Saskia, what are you talking about?"

"It was even on THIS train, the ROTHSCHILD EXPRESS," Saskia moaned.

Sadie groaned in frustration. She was not used to misunderstanding her sister's thoughts.

"The first murder in the book," explained Saskia, "takes place in the middle of the night. A woman is suffocated and hidden in the closet. The steward finds her the next day—she's even wearing a stranger's hat and coat! In the book, the woman stole the hat and coat just before she was murdered. It's just like what happened to that lady out there!"

"But she wasn't murdered," put in Sadie. "It could just be a coincidence that the woman in the book was wearing someone else's hat and coat."

"The details do seem eerily similar," mused Muzz Elliott.

"Well, what was the motive for the crime in the book?" asked Sadie.

"I don't know. I haven't gotten to that part yet," said Saskia. "And don't spoil it for me, Muzz Elliott."

Muzz Elliott drummed her fingers on her knee. "I think it's clear that whoever drugged Ms. Vallettzi has read my books," she said. "But why would they choose to mimic them?"

"Maybe it's the blackmailer trying to frighten you." Saskia gasped and jumped to her feet. "Max Taranis said he read all your books."

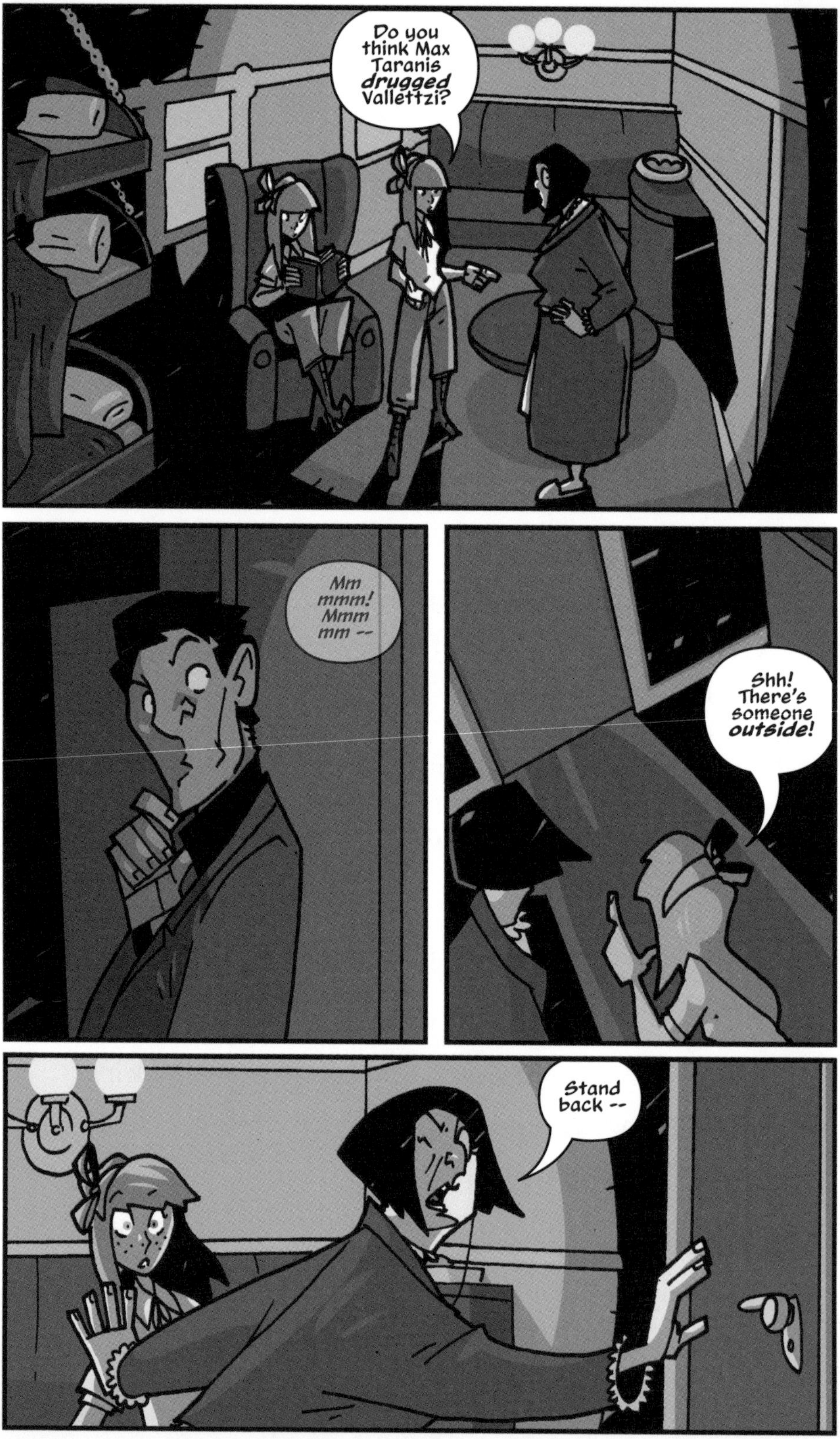
Do you think Max Taranis *drugged* Vallettzi?
Mm mmm! Mmm mm --
Shh! There's someone *outside*!
Stand back --

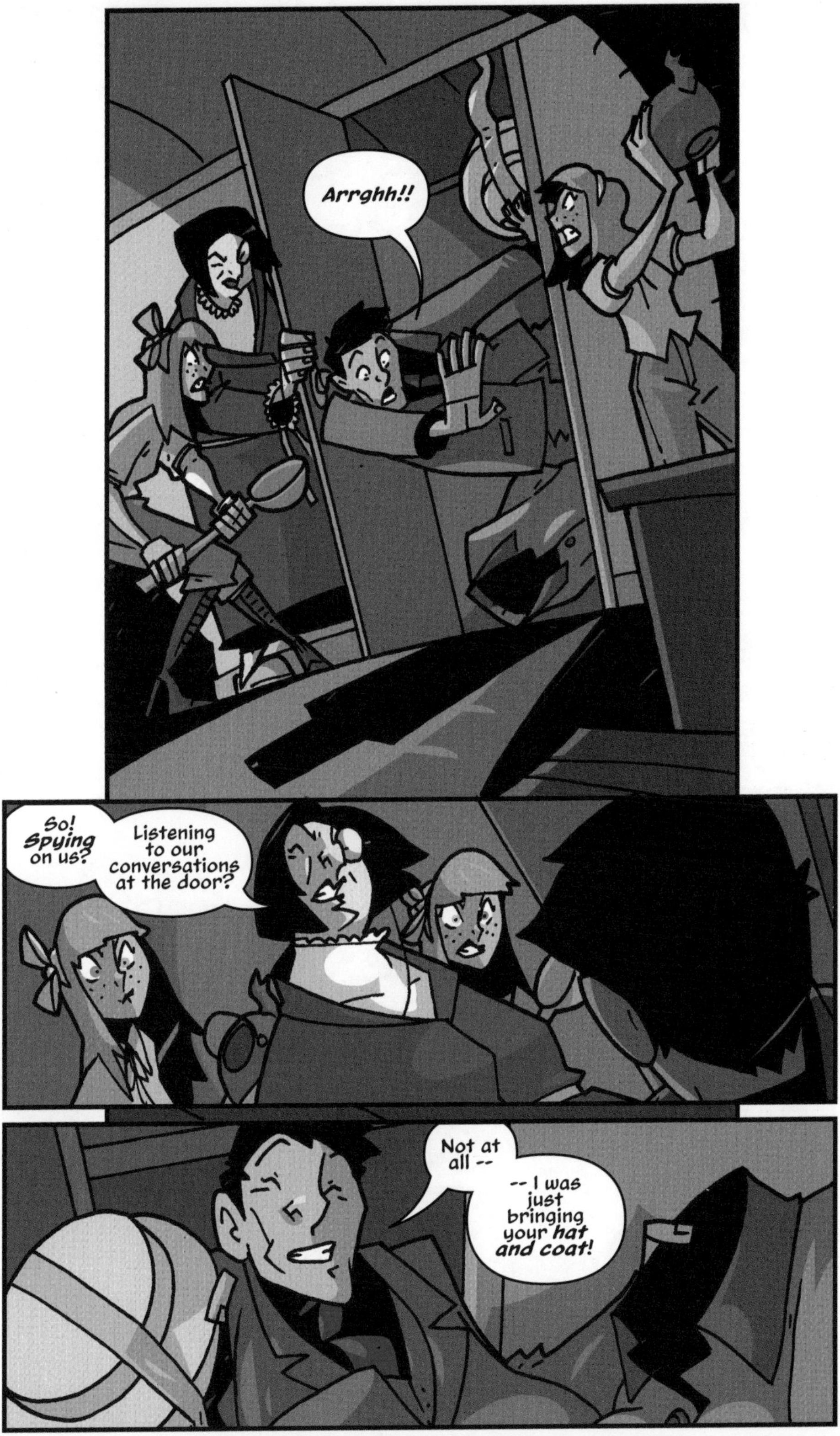
Arrghh!!
So! Spying on us?
Listening to our conversations at the door?
Not at all --
-- I was just bringing your hat and coat!

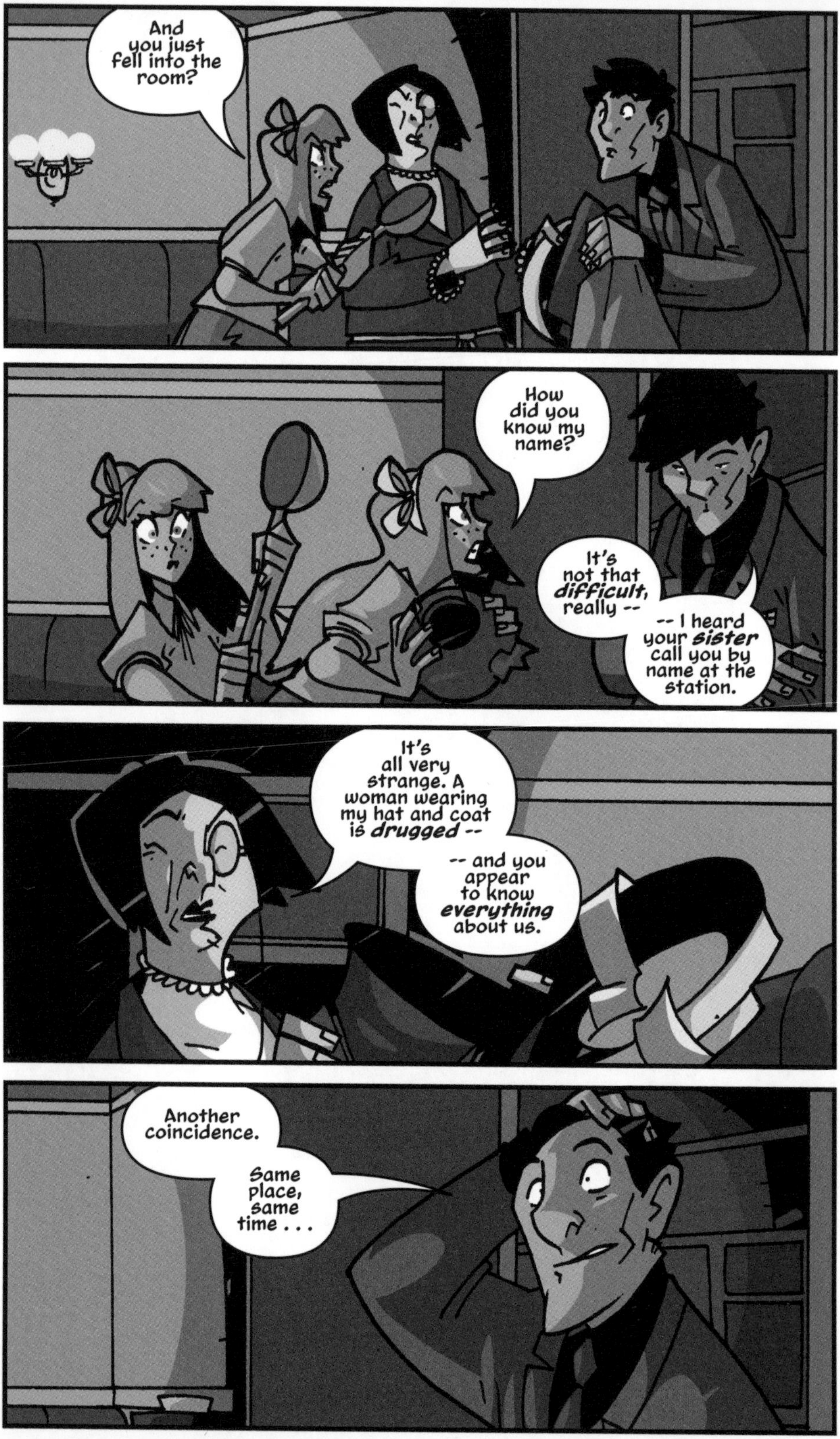
And you just fell into the room?
How did you know my name?
It's not that *difficult*, really --
-- I heard your *sister* call you by name at the station.
It's all very strange. A woman wearing my hat and coat is *drugged* --
-- and you appear to know *everything* about us.
Another coincidence.
Same place, same time . . .

"I hate coincidences," Muzz Elliott snapped as she threw the coat across the room and straightened the crumpled brim of the hat. "Luzio said you wanted to ask me something."

"It is all sorted out, Muzz Elliott. Luzio was able to answer what I desired." Max Taranis edged out of the room.

"Did you ever read MURDER TRAIN?" Saskia asked accusingly. "I heard you say you had read all of Muzz Elliott's books."

"Every one but that one," Max Taranis replied. He stroked his face with a long, thin finger.

"Why not that one?" Sadie asked, stepping forward and waving the spoon in his face.

"My, my," he said patronizingly, "you are both becoming proper detectives. I am sure you will want me to leave you in peace so you can solve this crime. I shall have to be careful—you obviously think I am a suspect." He coughed as he shuffled from the room. "If there is anything I can do for you, I am just two doors away—near the restaurant car."

"We'll be staying in our room," Muzz Elliott announced. "The girls are tired, and so am I." Max Taranis dived away from the door as it was slammed shut. Muzz Elliott stood there with a smug grin on her face. "We did well, girls."

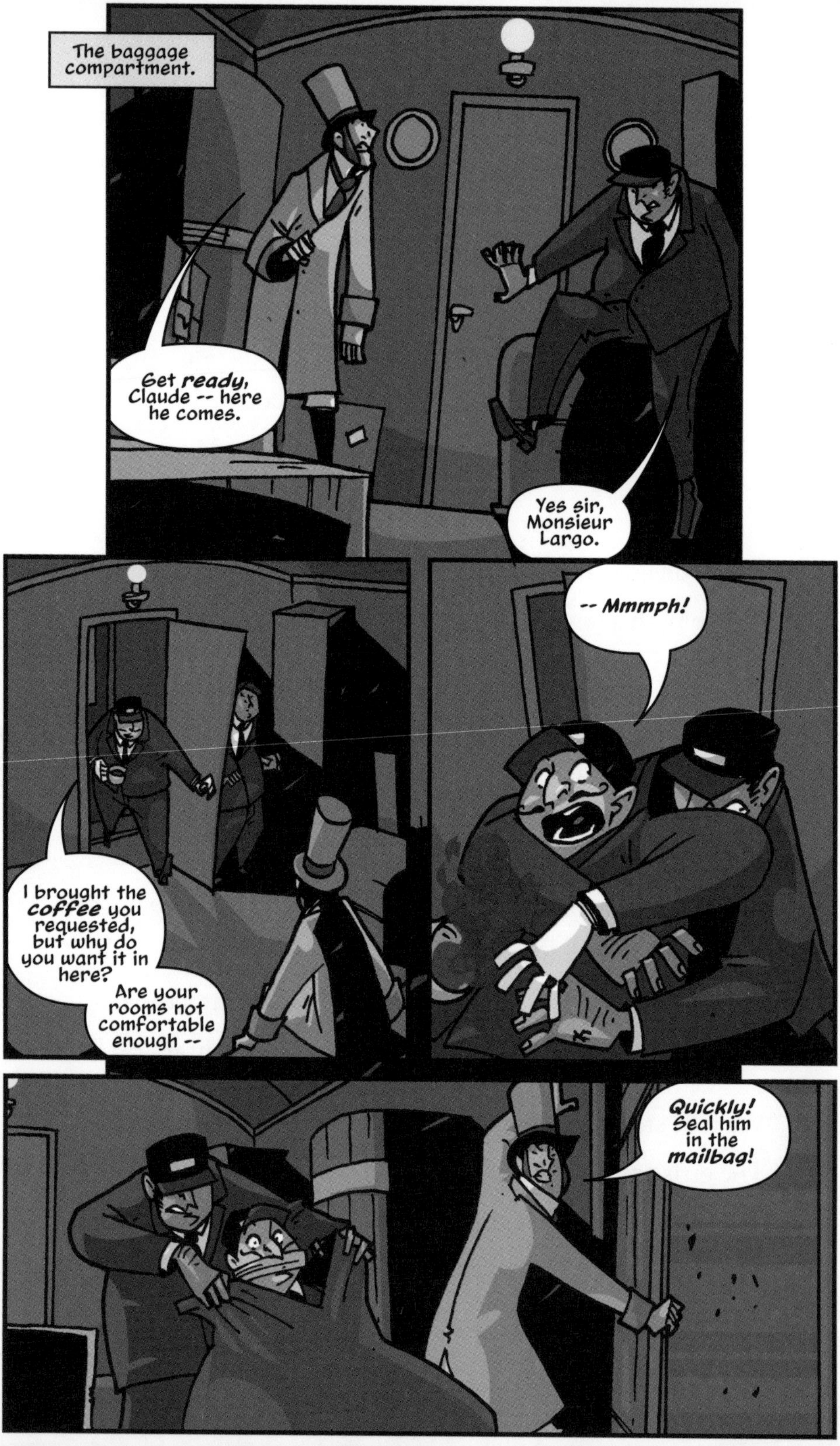
The baggage compartment.
Get *ready*, Claude -- here he comes.
Yes sir, Monsieur Largo.
I brought the *coffee* you requested, but why do you want it in here?
Are your rooms not comfortable enough --
-- *Mmmph!*
Quickly! Seal him in the *mailbag!*

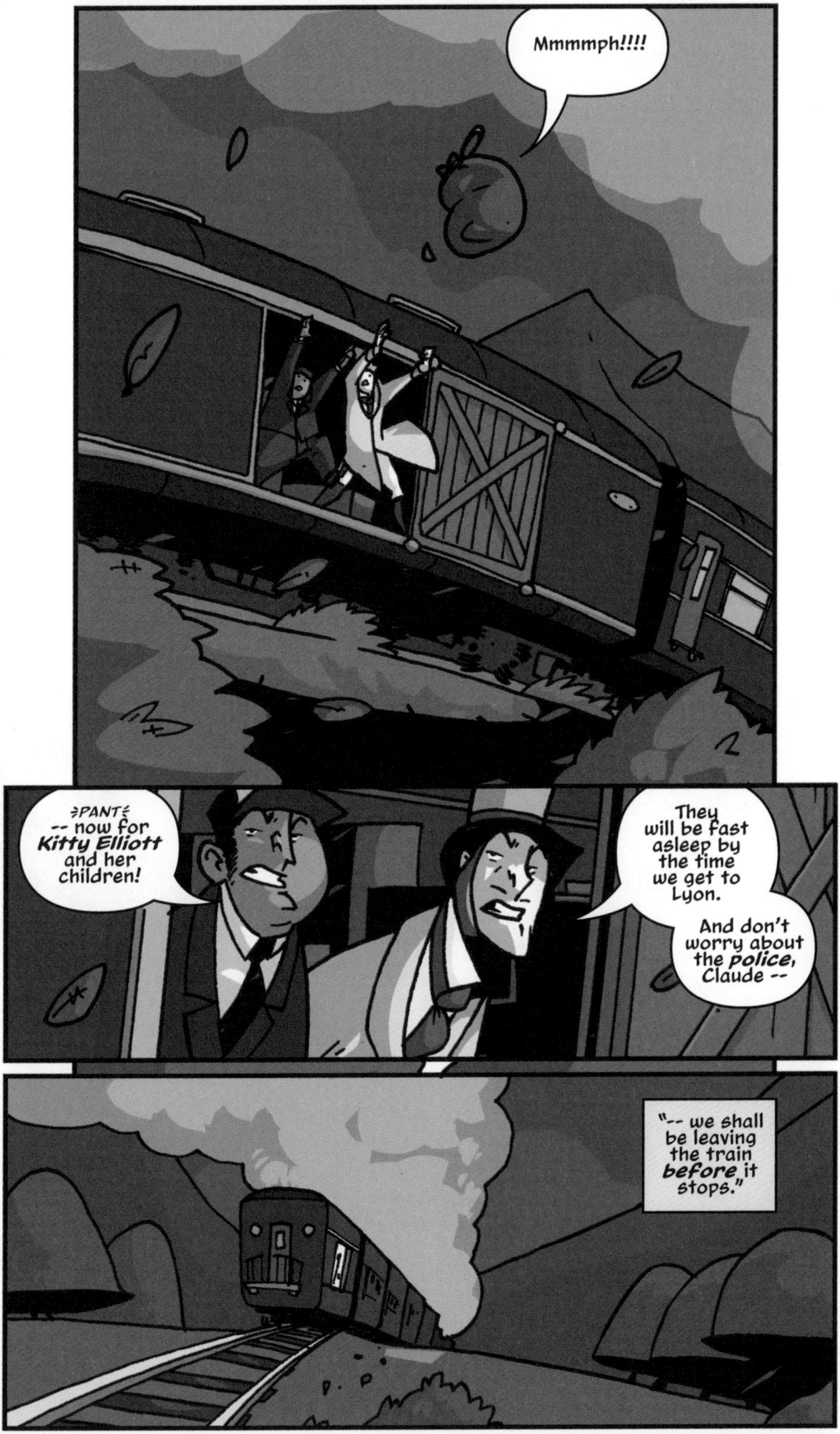
Mmmmph!!!!
≠PANT≠ -- now for *Kitty Elliott* and her children!
They will be fast asleep by the time we get to Lyon.
And don't worry about the *police*, Claude --
"-- we shall be leaving the train *before* it stops."

Muzz Elliott rummaged through her purse and pulled out the long, thin box that she had shown Mr. Crowley at the train station.

"What's that?" asked Sadie. She was sitting on the sofa next to her sister, who was once again engrossed in her book.

"Insurance," replied Muzz Elliott. She opened the box and lifted a shiny silver pen from inside. "My grandfather Lord Trevellyn learned of this sort of device on his travels, but he was the one who perfected it in pen form. The ink inside will cause someone to fall unconscious for several hours with one single prick of the tip."

"Lord Trevellyn? Wasn't he the one who hid his fortune in a stuffed donkey and forgot where he put it?" Sadie asked skeptically.

"Sadly, his memory did fail him in his later years, but you cannot deny that he was a master at hiding things."

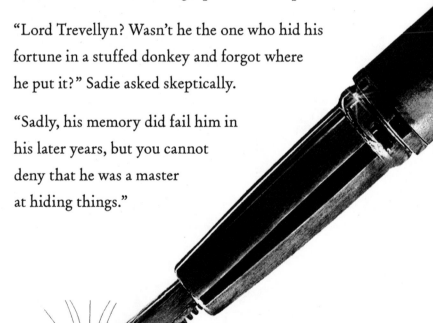

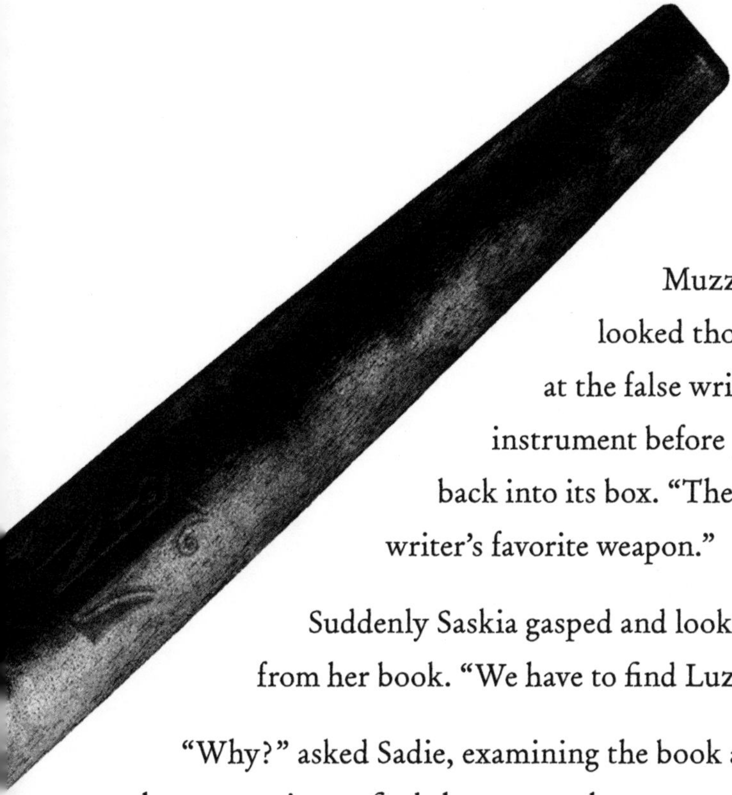

Muzz Elliott looked thoughtfully at the false writing instrument before placing it back into its box. "The pen is a writer's favorite weapon."

Suddenly Saskia gasped and looked up from her book. "We have to find Luzio!"

"Why?" asked Sadie, examining the book as though she were trying to find the answer there.

"In the book, the train steward is the next to die. The murderer gets him next because he was the one who found the body in the closet—just like Luzio did!"

"Nonsense, Saskia," Muzz Elliott interjected. "I admit the incident with Tamora Vallettzi was strangely similar to MURDER TRAIN, but why would anyone re-create the entire plot of my book?"

"Well, there's one way to find out if they are," said Sadie. She looked at her sister, and as one they stood and walked to the far wall. Sadie reached out and pressed the button labeled "Steward." Then they turned to look at the door and waited.

No one came.

Sadie rang the bell again and again. Luzio did not appear. Finally Saskia opened the door and shouted into the hallway.

"Luzio! Luzio!"

The words echoed down the empty corridor.

Muzz Elliott appeared at her side. "You may be right. I fear the worst. We have to find Luzio."

"Where should he be?" Sadie asked.

"There is a small room at the end of the corridor. He should be there. We can go together." Muzz Elliott put the box containing the pen back inside her purse and clutched it in her hand as she led the way down the hall.

"I wish Erik and Dorcas Potts were here," Sadie said.

Chapter Six

The Boy and the Bugatti

THE BUGATTI SLOWLY COOLED as the engine idled its way down the side of the Alp. Erik kept looking out the back. He was convinced the black car would be following, waiting to strike again. Dorcas Potts was silent. She stared at the road ahead. Erik knew what she was thinking.

"Those people who were following us—they weren't robbers, were they?" he asked.

"No," she replied in a voice slightly louder than the engine's hum. "They were not robbers."

"Do you think—?"

"They want to stop us from helping Muzz Elliott?" Dorcas Potts finished the question. "Yes, I think so."

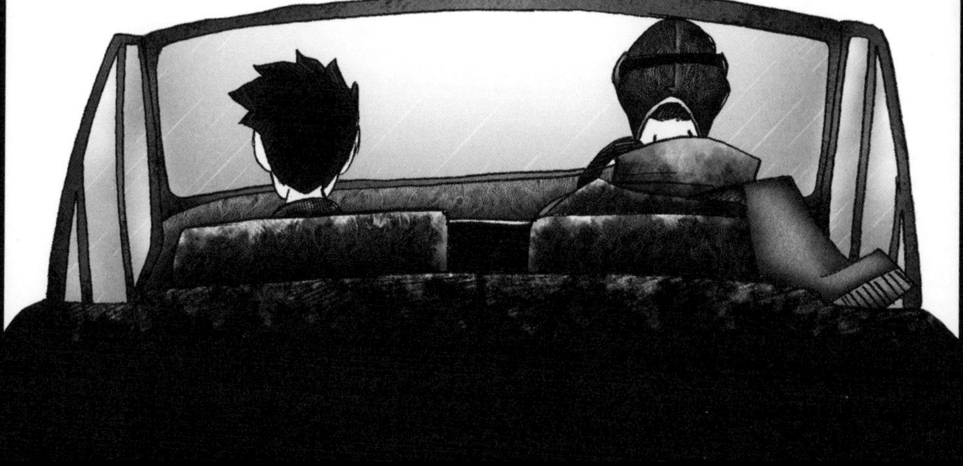

"But . . . how did they know we were here?" Erik asked.

"Fast car—on the way to the south of France. Not difficult to spot, Erik." Dorcas Potts sighed. "I am . . . well known among the villains of Europe."

"Should we go back?" Erik asked.

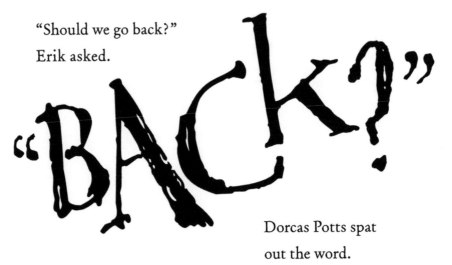

Dorcas Potts spat out the word.

"We don't go back, AND I'm certainly not put off by a halfhearted attempt like that."

"But they nearly killed us!" Erik protested.

"'Nearly' is not good enough. The guy couldn't aim, and you did a good job of saving us from exploding. I think we make a great team." She laughed. "We'll still be in Cannes by morning—just as the train arrives."

Erik sat back in his seat and folded his arms tightly across his chest. He had been through many close calls, but never like this, and the experience had taken its toll.

He could feel himself shaking from the inside out. His mind meandered to Saskia and Sadie. They were somewhere near on the ROTHSCHILD EXPRESS by now. A dark thought invaded his mind. Until now this had all been just a game, an adventure—fast cars, detectives, and ships in the night. Now there was a revelation of real danger, which, despite her coolheadedness, Dorcas Potts had etched on her face.

Neither of them saw the sleek Citroën parked in a clump of trees just off the road to the river. Its driver pulled his flat cap down over his eyes and slumped in his seat. As soon as the Bugatti had passed, he pulled onto the dirt road.

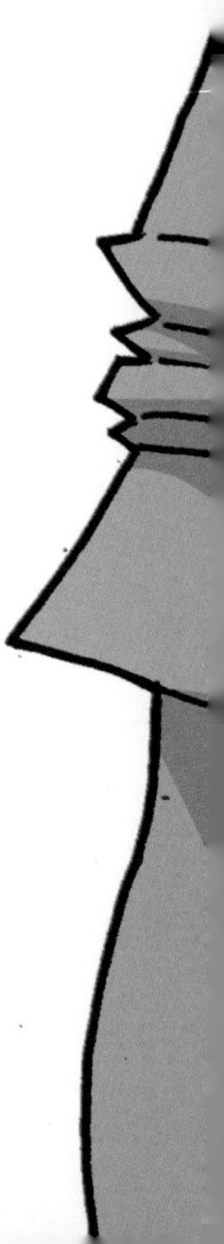

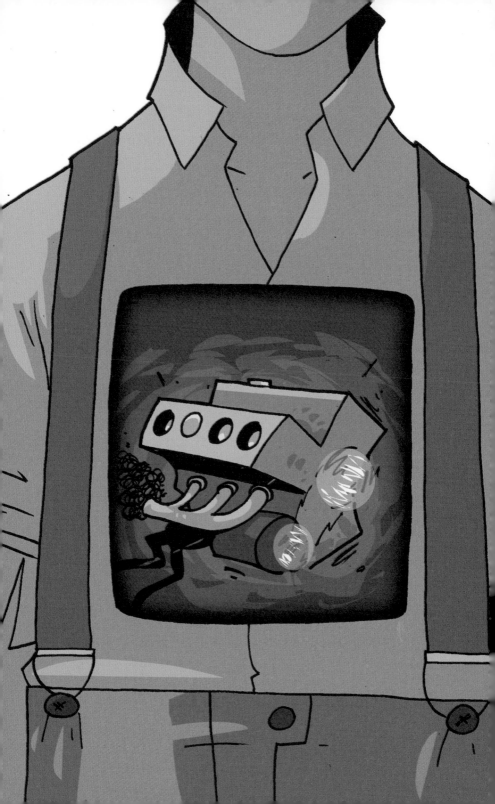

Dorcas Potts took the corner slowly. The road before them was empty. It followed the contours of the river that broke over boulders as it cut its way to the sea.

"Beautiful." She sighed, her eyes following the outline of the mountains through the trees.

"When do we get to Cannes?" Erik complained. "We haven't eaten since breakfast." On cue, Erik's stomach rumbled.

"Oh, you mean the croissant that you said looked more like a skinned rat baked in pig fat?" She looked at him out of the corner of her eye and smirked. "By the way, you still have some chocolate on your face."

The car swerved across the road as Dorcas Potts leaned to one side and reached into her bag. She tossed a small glittering object into Erik's lap. He picked up the tiny hand mirror and raised it to his face. A faint chocolate mustache lingered on his upper lip. Quickly, he wiped his mouth with the back of his hand and looked away, embarrassed. As he did, he caught sight of something by the side of the road.

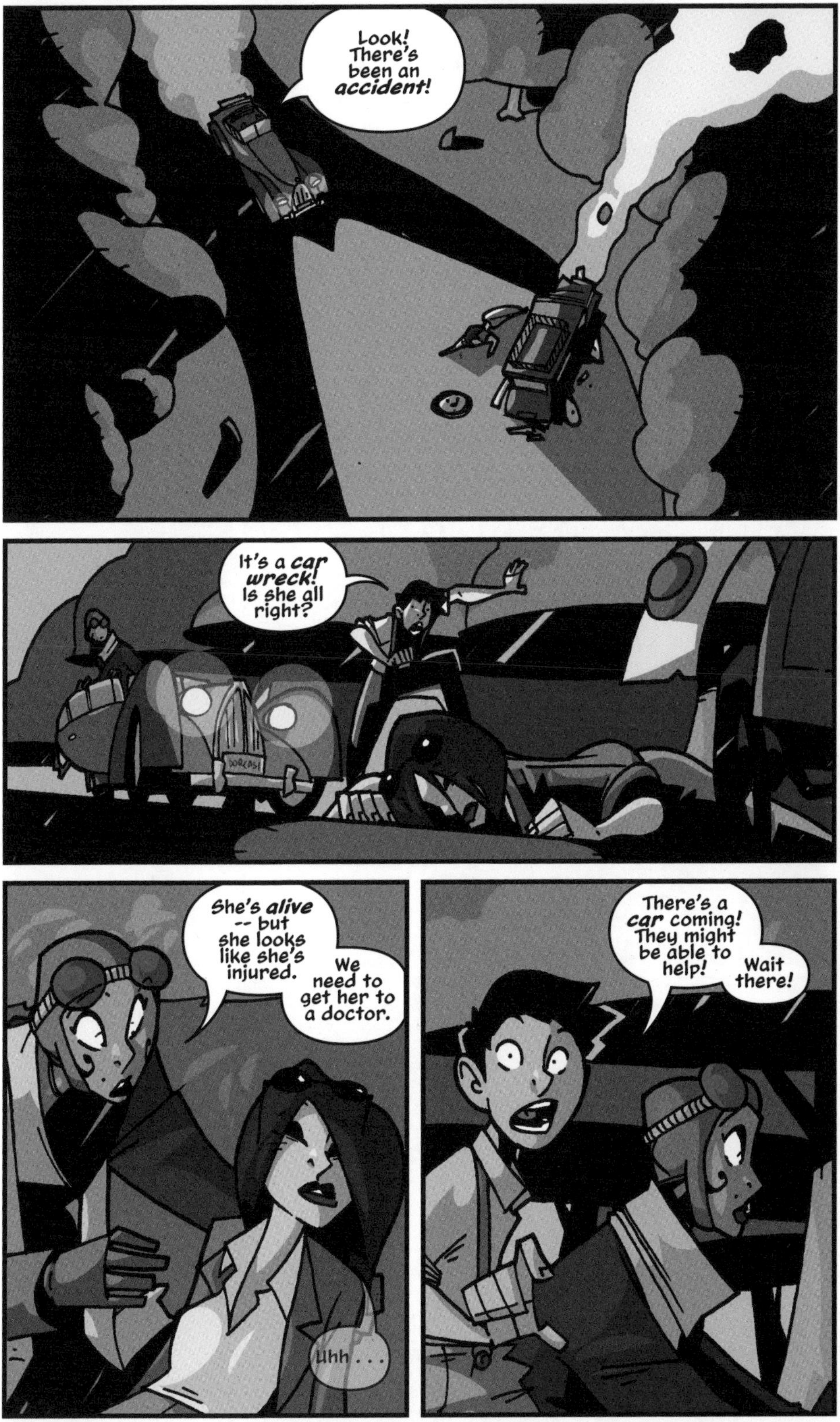
Look! There's been an *accident*!
It's a *car wreck*! Is she all right?
She's *alive* -- but she looks like she's injured.
We need to get her to a doctor.
Uhh . . .
There's a *car* coming! They might be able to help!
Wait there!

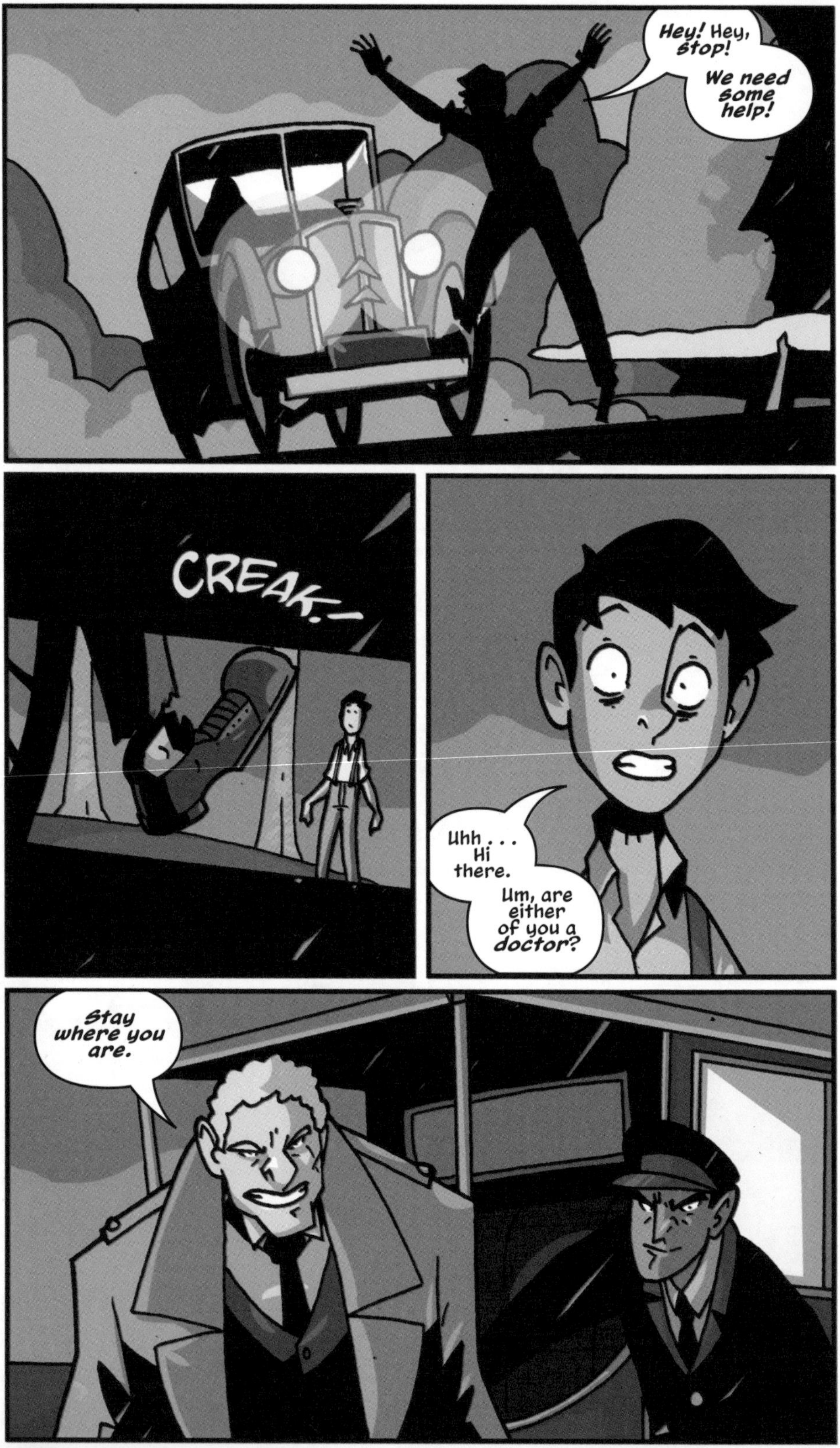
Hey! Hey, stop!
We need some help!
CREAK!
Uhh . . . Hi there.
Um, are either of you a *doctor*?
Stay where you are.

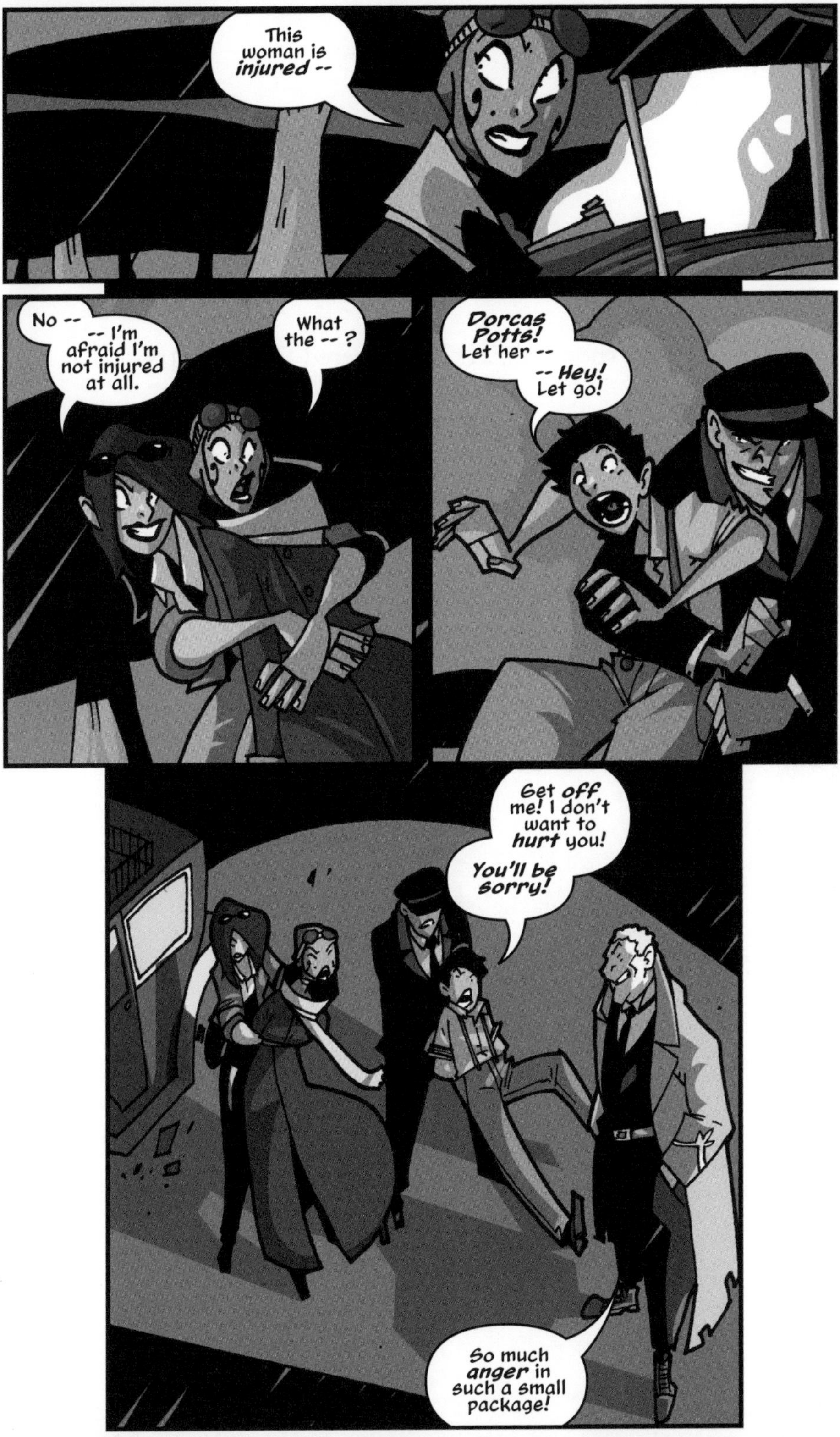
This woman is *injured* --
No --
-- I'm afraid I'm not injured at all.
What the -- ?
Dorcas Potts! Let her --
-- *Hey!* Let go!
Get *off* me! I don't want to *hurt* you!
You'll be sorry!
So much *anger* in such a small package!

Erik struggled to get free, but the man held him fast. "It was a trap," Erik moaned.

"Just do as they say, Erik," whispered Dorcas Potts.

"We'd better be quick," the woman said to the large man. "There could be another automobile along here at any time."

"What shall we do with them?" asked the man.

"Take them to the château. We can decide their fate there," the woman replied. "I will go with her and François. You take the boy and the Bugatti."

"But—"

"He's a boy, Foojack," she argued. "He won't do you any harm."

Foojack looked Erik up and down. "Very well. I'll take him to the château and see you there."

"Damage my Bugatti, and it'll be the last thing you do!" Dorcas Potts shouted as the man dragged Erik to the car.

Chapter Seven
The Missing Luzio

THE ROTHSCHILD EXPRESS rattled on. The countryside appeared to speed by faster than before as the landscape changed from verdant meadows to craggy valleys and high mountains.

Muzz Elliott stood in the corridor of the carriage and beckoned for Sadie and Saskia to follow. She kept her hand in her purse, clutching the silver pen with poisoned tip.

"We have to find Luzio," she demanded. "I fear that all is not well."

Muzz Elliott went ahead of the girls. They cautiously approached the small kitchenette, Luzio's home away from home. Here he would prepare the drinks and cook the toast to serve to the seven cabins under his care. Pushing open the door, Muzz Elliott looked inside. Not a thing was out of place. A small stove burned brightly in the corner. On top of that, a black kettle boiled its heart out.

Three china cups were upturned on the drainer. A poster adorned the far wall.

"He was a lover of musicals," Max Taranis commented from behind them.

"What?" gasped Muzz Elliott in surprise as she awkwardly pushed the purse toward him.

"From THE MIKADO—one of my favorites."
Max Taranis pointed to the poster that advertised the opening performance at the Savoy Theatre.

"You said WAS," Saskia commented, eyeing Max Taranis suspiciously.

"Was, is—what does it matter?" he snapped, pushing Saskia out of the way so he could look inside the room.

"Luzio has gone missing," Sadie explained.

"So that's why he never brought my coffee."

"This is serious, Mr. Taranis," said Muzz Elliott. "He has gone missing, and you could have been the last person to see him."

"So that makes me a suspect?" he replied with a smile.

"If he's been kidnapped," Saskia butted in.

"But you need a ransom note for a kidnapping—didn't they teach you that at crime school? Or are you just relying on the famous author?" Max Taranis leaned against the wall, blocking the doorway of the kitchenette so they couldn't pass by. He straightened his tie and eyed each one of them in turn. "He could be in a different part of the train."

"You might want to be careful of what you say," Muzz Elliott warned and pointed her purse at Max Taranis.

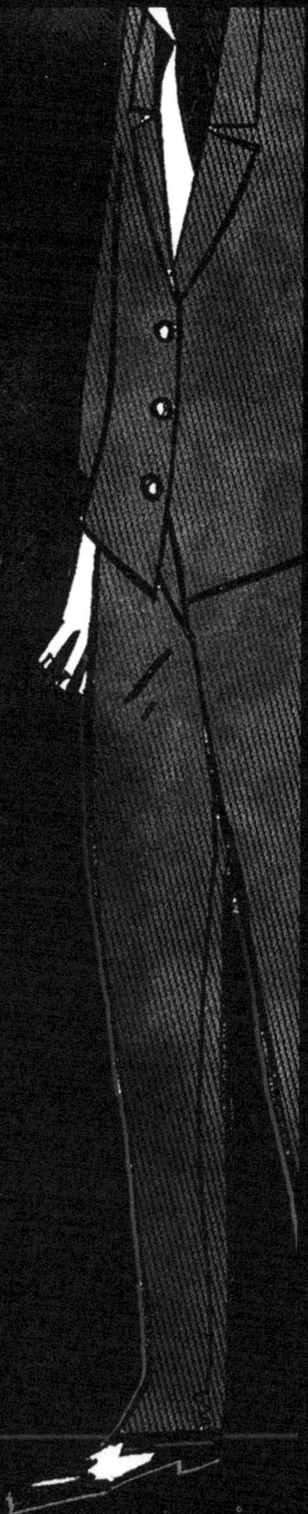

"Are you threatening me with your purse?" Max Taranis asked in mock horror.

"You don't even know what's in it," Saskia answered for Muzz Elliott. "We're going to find the guard and tell him what you have done to Luzio."

"I ordered coffee. I didn't kidnap him."

"Strange how there has been one unconscious body in a closet and one mysterious disappearance, and you turn up at both of them," Muzz Elliott said.

"If you look at the facts, the unfortunate Ms. Vallettzi was dressed in your coat and hat," he replied. "Perhaps whoever knocked her out was trying to get you?" He looked from Muzz Elliott to the twins and then to his shoes. "Unfortunately, she has no idea who drugged her and only a vague recollection of being grabbed from behind. One minute she was walking down the hall, and the next she was lying on the ground with the guard staring into her face."

"How do you know all that?" asked Saskia in an accusing tone.

"I happened to be nearby when she awoke, and I overheard her explanation," Max Taranis replied curtly. Sadie opened her mouth to ask if this was a mere coincidence, but he rushed on. "I did have a reason for wanting to speak with Luzio. I'll look for him with you and prove I have nothing to do with any kidnapping."

Muzz Elliott waved the purse in front of his face. "Lead on, Mr. Taranis. If you try to do anything suspicious, I will have no hesitation to use it."

"Your purse?" His lip curled up in a mocking grin. "I've never heard of anyone being wounded by a purse before."

"There is always a first time," Muzz Elliott replied. "The guard is further down the train—he should know where Luzio is . . .

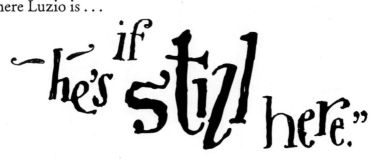
—he's if still here."

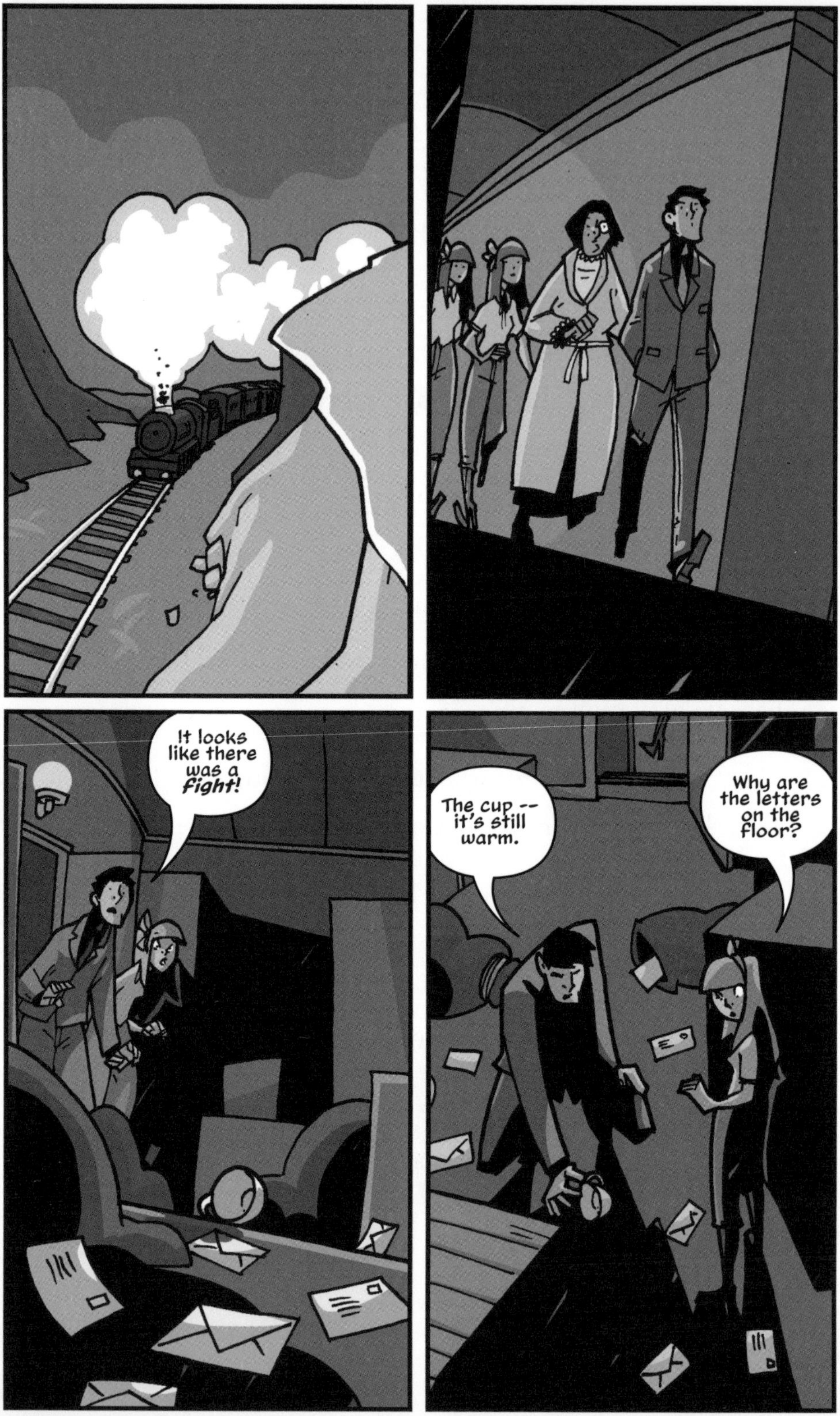
It looks like there was a *fight*!
The cup -- it's still warm.
Why are the letters on the floor?

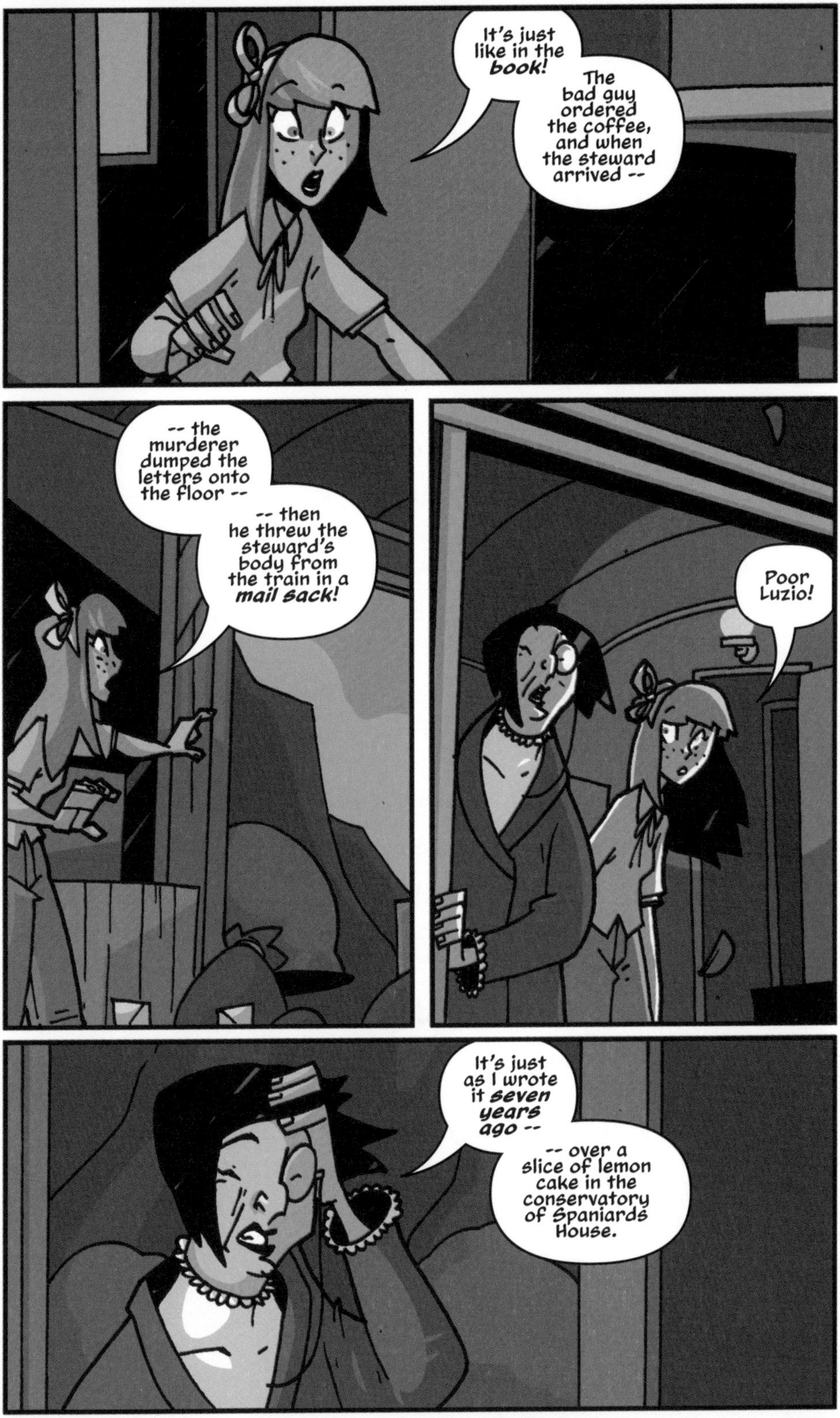
It's just like in the *book!*
The bad guy ordered the coffee, and when the steward arrived --
-- the murderer dumped the letters onto the floor --
-- then he threw the steward's body from the train in a *mail sack!*
Poor Luzio!
It's just as I wrote it *seven years ago* --
-- over a slice of lemon cake in the conservatory of Spaniards House.

Muzz Elliott's eyes flicked about the room. It was as if the place had been snatched from the pages of the book and re-created just for her. What she now saw was like a living dream. Slowly she slumped back against the cases in the beginning stages of a faint. Sadie and Saskia grabbed her arms.

"Muzz Elliott—are you okay?" Sadie asked.

"It's too real," mumbled Muzz Elliott as she dropped her purse to the floor. "Whoever is doing this knows me too well."

Max Taranis snatched the purse from the floor. He clutched it to himself, then bid their silence with a finger to his lips.

Sadie and Saskia turned and stared at him.

The door to the compartment opened. An elderly man in a London morning suit walked in and nodded politely. Max Taranis gave him a smile.

"My aunt is out of breath," he said as the man walked by and exited through the door at the other end of the compartment.

As soon as the man had gone, Max Taranis turned to Sadie. "Better take this." He handed her the bag. "I don't need a weapon."

"You just throw people from trains and poison them," Saskia muttered, helping Muzz Elliott to her feet.

"You would be surprised at what I do, Saskia Dopple," Max Taranis said.

"What ARE you doing here?" asked Sadie.

"I'm on vacation—by mistake."

"As are we," said Muzz Elliott under her breath.

"I would keep that to yourself, Muzz Elliott," Max Taranis replied. "There are some things better left unsaid."

"A criminal would say that," Sadie muttered, playing with a loose thread at the bottom of her shirt.

"It doesn't take a criminal to see that you, Muzz Elliott, are being blackmailed," he said.

"By you?" said Saskia and Sadie at the same time.

Max Taranis casually leaned back and pulled a small leather wallet from his pocket. He placed it on the pile of cases.

Sadie snatched it and looked inside. Saskia read over her shoulder. Without speaking, she handed it to Muzz Elliott.

"I think we owe you an apology, Inspector," Muzz Elliott said respectfully, shooting a sideways glance at the twins.

"He never said . . . ," Saskia protested.

"You never asked," Detective Inspector Max Taranis of Scotland Yard replied with a shrug.

"I liked you better when I thought you were a murderer," Sadie whispered, edging away from him.

"Enough, Sadie," Muzz Elliott snapped. "I think that Inspector Taranis owes us all an explanation."

Max Taranis nodded.

"It started five weeks ago, late one foggy night. . . ."

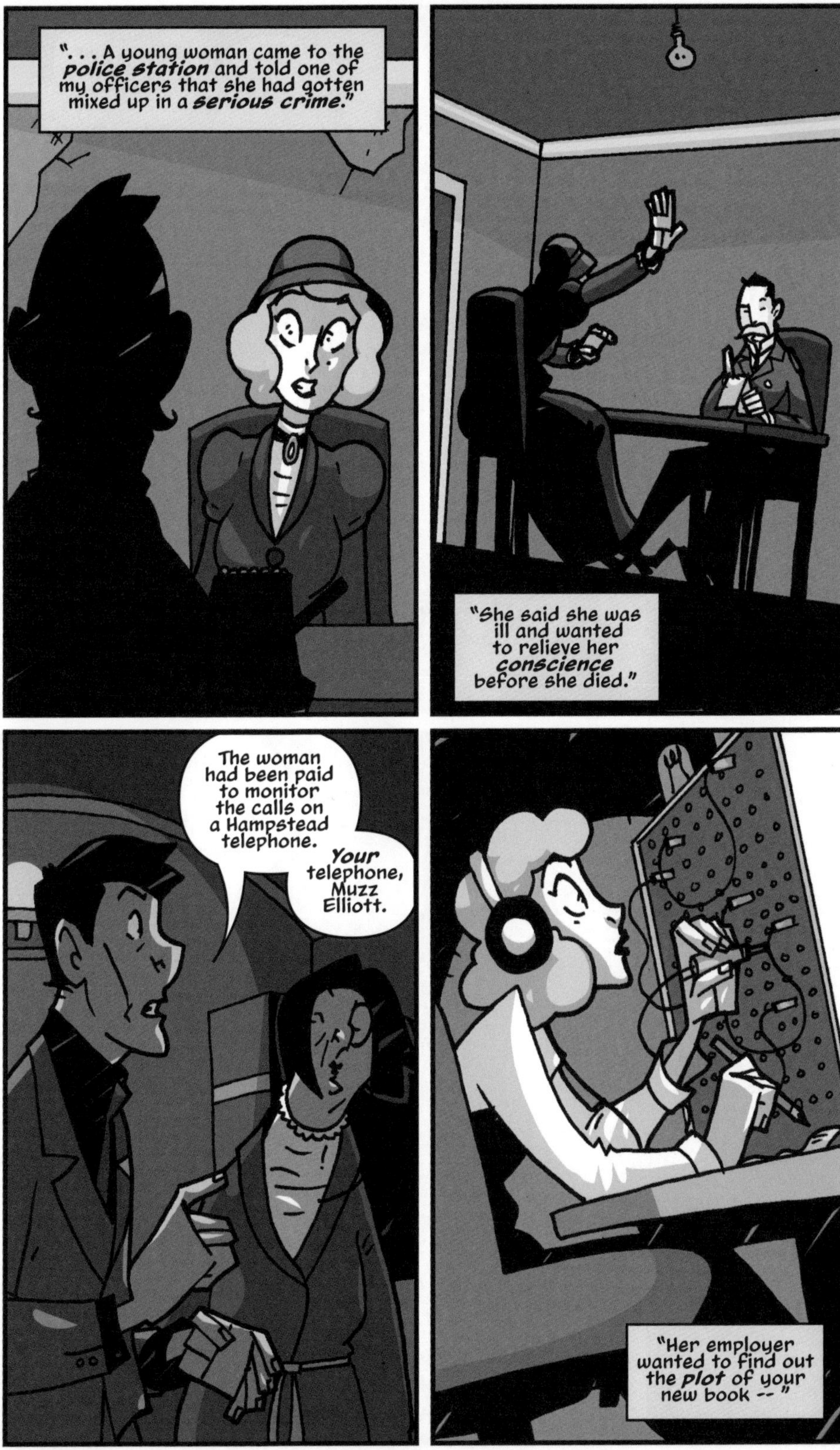
". . . A young woman came to the police station and told one of my officers that she had gotten mixed up in a serious crime."
"She said she was ill and wanted to relieve her conscience before she died."
The woman had been paid to monitor the calls on a Hampstead telephone.
Your telephone, Muzz Elliott.
"Her employer wanted to find out the plot of your new book --"

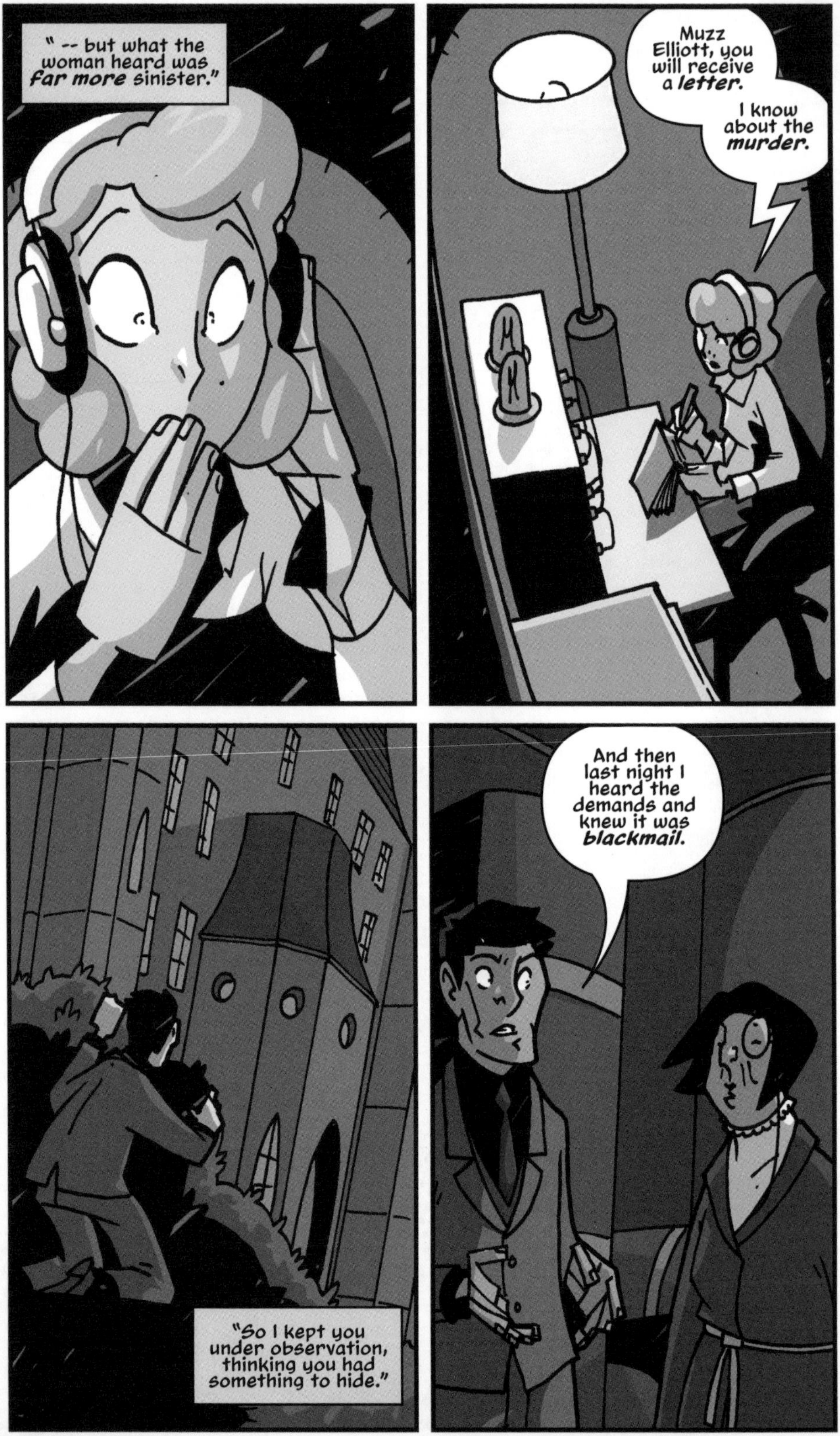
" -- but what the woman heard was far more sinister."
Muzz Elliott, you will receive a letter.
I know about the murder.
"So I kept you under observation, thinking you had something to hide."
And then last night I heard the demands and knew it was blackmail.

Muzz Elliott looked even more pale than usual. She touched her thin, quivering lips, but no words came out.

"You thought she was a murderer?" Saskia asked with wide eyes.

"Yes," he said. "Then we realized Muzz Elliott was the victim of two outrageous plots. One to steal her novel and the other to blackmail her."

"That's how you knew so much about us," Sadie said, thinking aloud.

"Precisely."

"And you had more than one call?" Saskia asked Muzz Elliott, who was still staring at a spot on the wall.

"Several," she said softly. At last she looked at Max Taranis. "I suppose you know of them all?"

"We took the liberty of recording everything that was said," Inspector Taranis replied. "If it is not inconvenient, Muzz Elliott, could you tell me who you were seen to murder?"

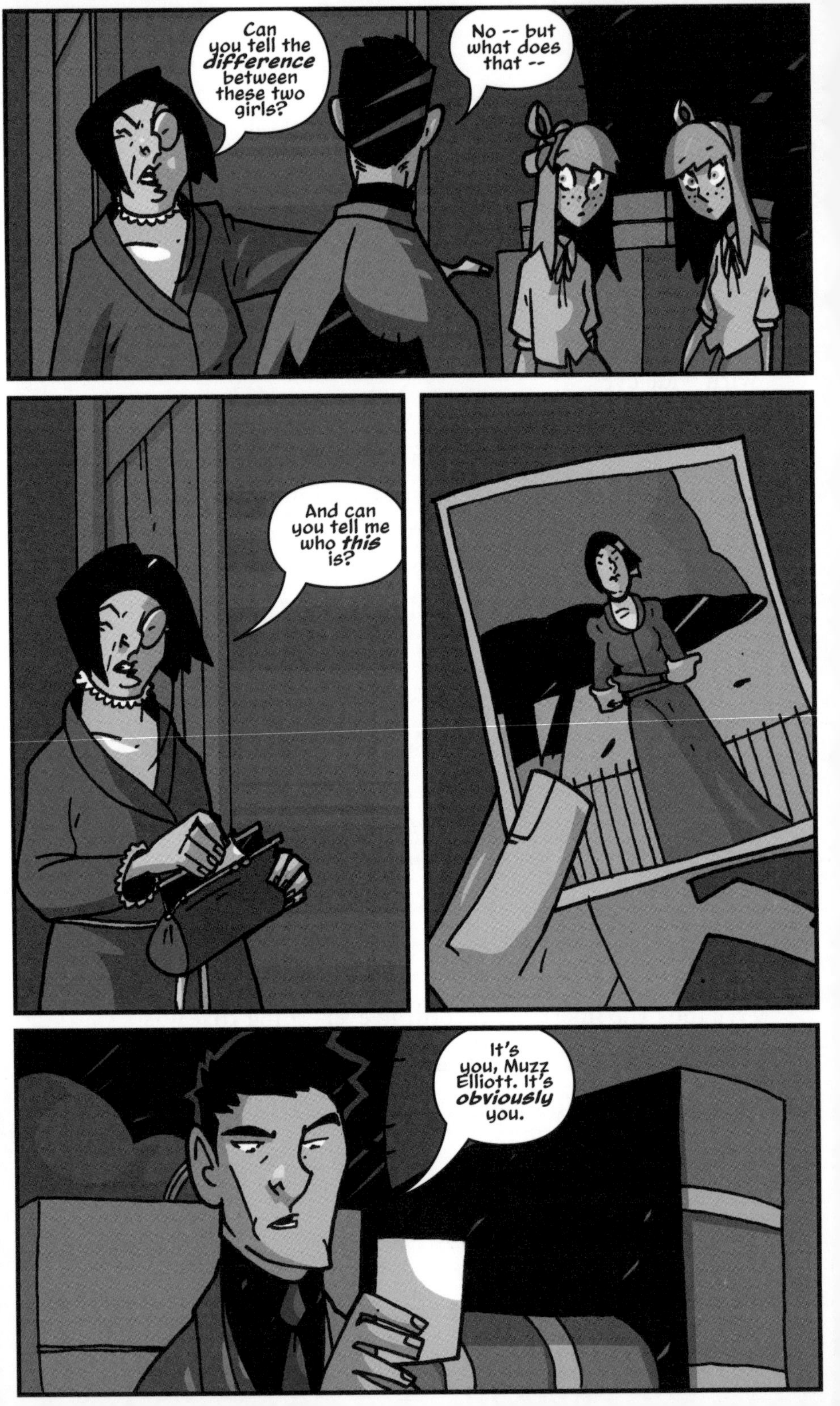
Can you tell the *difference* between these two girls?
No -- but what does that --
And can you tell me who *this* is?
It's you, Muzz Elliott. It's *obviously* you.

Then look *again*. Look at the back of the hand, and you will *see* the difference.

It is you . . . But if is *not* you --

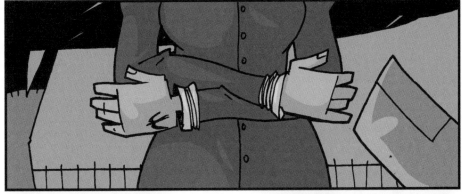

This woman has a small tattoo of a swallow -- old and faded. You do not!

"You have been negligent in your investigations, Inspector," said Muzz Elliott. "It should have been easy to ascertain that I, like Sadie and Saskia, am a twin—an identical twin." A tear came to her eye. "Sadly, my sister took a different path in life. She may be known to you as Cicely Windylove."

"The burglar?" Max Taranis replied.

"Among other crimes she has committed. She had even planned to murder me and move into my house. If it had not been for these girls and their good friend, she would have succeeded."

"And?" he asked.

"I think it was my sister who was seen and mistaken for me. That is why I have taken the bait. No matter what she has done, she is still my sister. Blood is thicker than water, Inspector.

"Come along, girls. It is time for lunch."

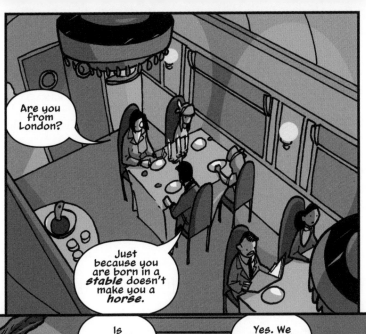

Are you from London?

Just because you are born in a *stable* doesn't make you a *horse*.

Is everything prepared?

Yes. We shall do it tonight.

I am sorry to say that we will *not* be stopping in Lyon.

There has been a *rockfall* -- we have been diverted straight to *Cannes*.

So we *won't* be able to talk to the police?

We have to get off this train! *Now!*

Though the girls had been desperate to know what would happen next in MURDER TRAIN, Muzz Elliott was so unnerved by the scene in the luggage compartment that she refused to talk about it. So the twins had been racing through the pages to find out if there were any more murders to come. Now they both stared at Max Taranis. "We have to stop the train—before the rest of the book comes true!" insisted Saskia.

"In the book, the driver is killed and the train crashes, so all the evidence will be lost," Sadie explained to Inspector Taranis.

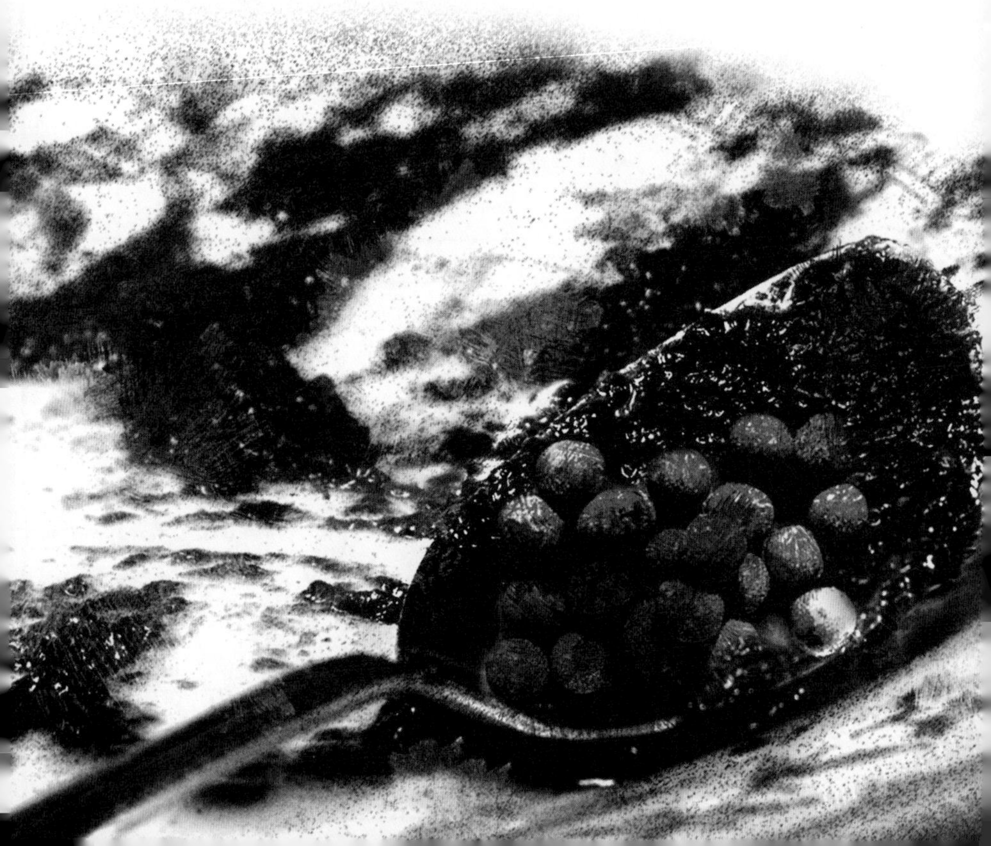

Muzz Elliott turned pale. "I had hoped that it would not be taken that far."

"Inspector, do you think we should warn the driver?" Saskia asked.

Max Taranis coughed. "Before we jump to conclusions, I think it might be prudent to speak to the guard and make sure there has been no sign of Luzio. If the steward is still missing, I will speak to the driver. I advise you to return to your room and stay there until I bring word." He stood up quickly, accidentally bumping the edge of his plate and sending peas rolling across the table. Embarrassed, he bowed and strode off.

Saskia stared at the peas on the table. She was suddenly reminded of the strange manners tutor she had met at Spaniards House, who had been particular about the proper way to eat peas. Madame Raphael had told her about the Companion—that he would always be near when she needed help. She looked up.

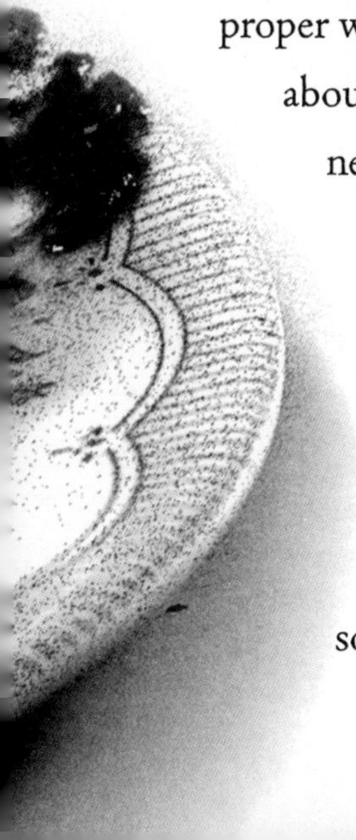

Sadie was staring at her sister curiously. "You're thinking about Madame Raphael," she whispered. "You always get that look on your face when you do."

Saskia nodded once. "I think we should ask for some help."

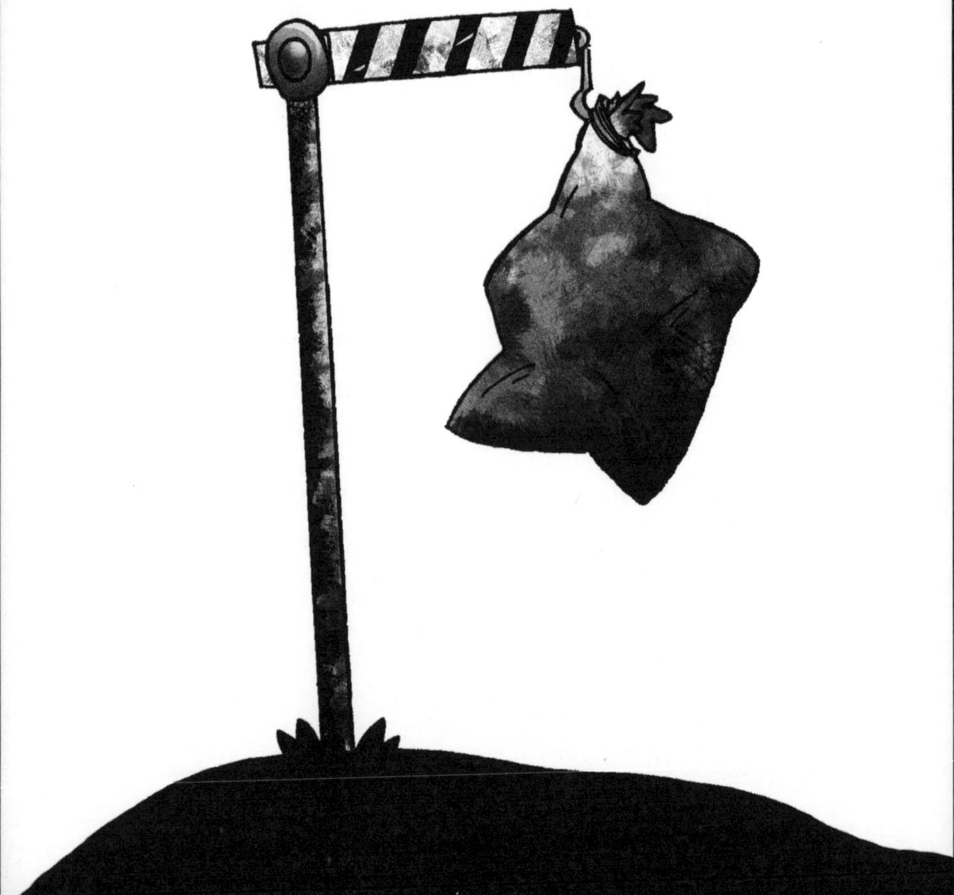

Unbeknownst to Saskia, someone else was calling for help at that same moment. Italian-accented shouts were coming from a large sack dangling from a mail collection point at the junction with the Loire Valley line. A rotund man had been placed in a thick brown sack and thrown from the door of the train, just like a bag of mail. He struggled to free himself from the ties that bound his wrists and feet. His yelling was in vain. Luzio would have to wait until the morning to be collected.

Chapter Eight

At the Château Gates

ERIK COULDN'T TAKE his eyes from Foojack's hands as they gripped the steering wheel of the Bugatti. He had the fists of a giant. Each finger was dirty, with bitten nails. On the back of his left hand was a distinctive tattoo of a swallow, which had faded over the years. He smelled of yesterday's sweat.

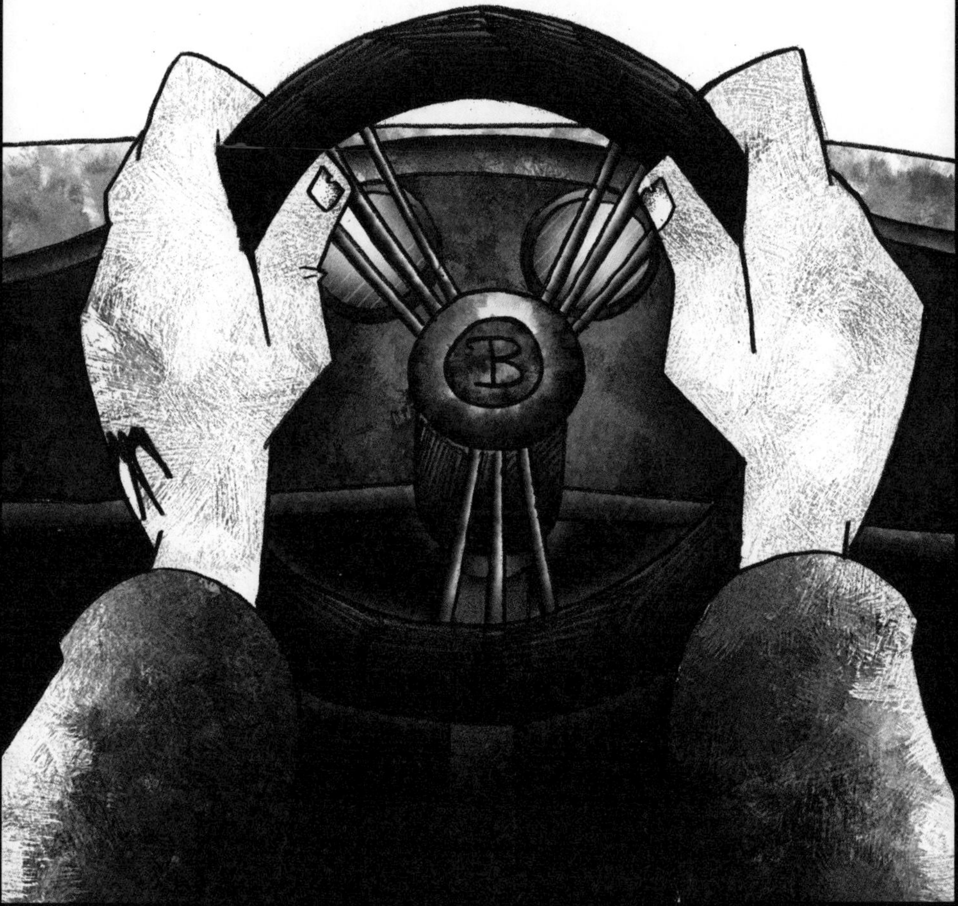

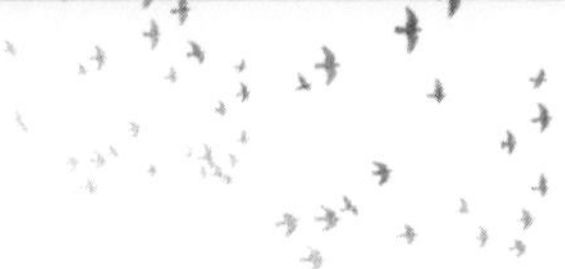

"So . . . you are Erik?" the man asked with a slightly nasal accent as he turned a tight bend and accelerated the Bugatti up the hill.

"What do you want with us?" Erik countered, trying not to breathe for fear of inhaling the odor that billowed from under the man's jacket.

"We get paid to do what other people don't want to. Yours was a name on the list—along with that journalist, Dorcas Potts."

"We're on vacation. Why should we be on a list?" Erik asked. Far above them he glimpsed what looked like a castle.

"Vacation?" Foojack asked suspiciously. "Then why is it so important for Le Sentier Rouge to have you and the woman stopped?"

Erik shrugged. The car following them was about a mile behind. He wondered what Dorcas Potts would do—if she would try to escape or wait until they were at the château.

As the Bugatti turned the next corner, Erik saw a sprawling
castle ahead of them. It looked like a fortified town, with
high walls surrounding a building within. A small bridge
spanned a deep ditch. The road ran straight to the main
gate, which was held in place by thick iron chains. Over the
entrance, carved in stone, were the words Château Autruche.

"Why are you bringing us here?" Erik asked.

Foojack looked at him. He seemed to be trying to work
something out in his head.

"Have you lived well?" he asked.

"Quite," Erik replied.

"And your father—what is his business?"

"He's a robber and a villain," Erik replied. "Reminds me
of you."

"A robber . . . a villain?" Foojack laughed.

"There is no justice."

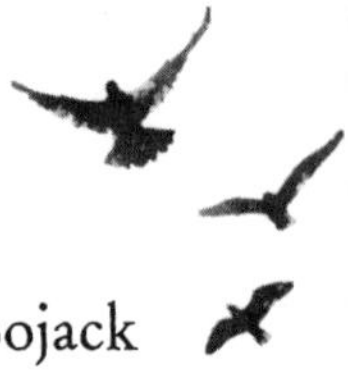

"When will we be set free?"

"It will be like the birds flying from the château." Foojack pointed to three white doves that flew high above. "That is the only way you will ever escape."

Foojack drove quickly toward the gates over stones that stuck out from the bridge like crooked teeth.

"It is a shame. Removing one with such promise is not what we like to do. Le Sentier Rouge—the Red Way—is a brotherhood. Perhaps in another time things could have been different, Erik."

Foojack leaned on the car horn, and the gates to the château opened. Erik felt a rush of cool air as the Bugatti sped through the arch and into a large courtyard of terracotta tiles that led to the steps of the house. The car swerved around a dip in the ground.

"Been meaning to have that pothole filled," Foojack grunted.

The high walls pressed in on them from every direction.

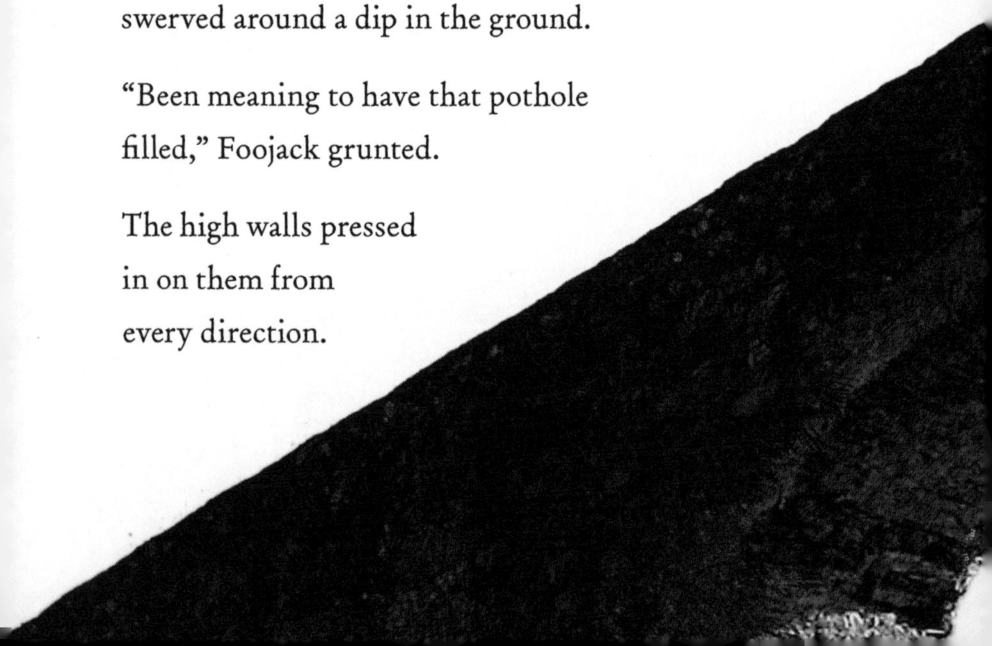

On a balcony overlooking the gate, Erik spotted two armed men staring down at them.

Foojack stopped the car and got out. Erik wondered for a moment whether he would be able to escape the fortress if he made a run for it now, but before he could open the door, Foojack yanked it open and pulled Erik out of the car.

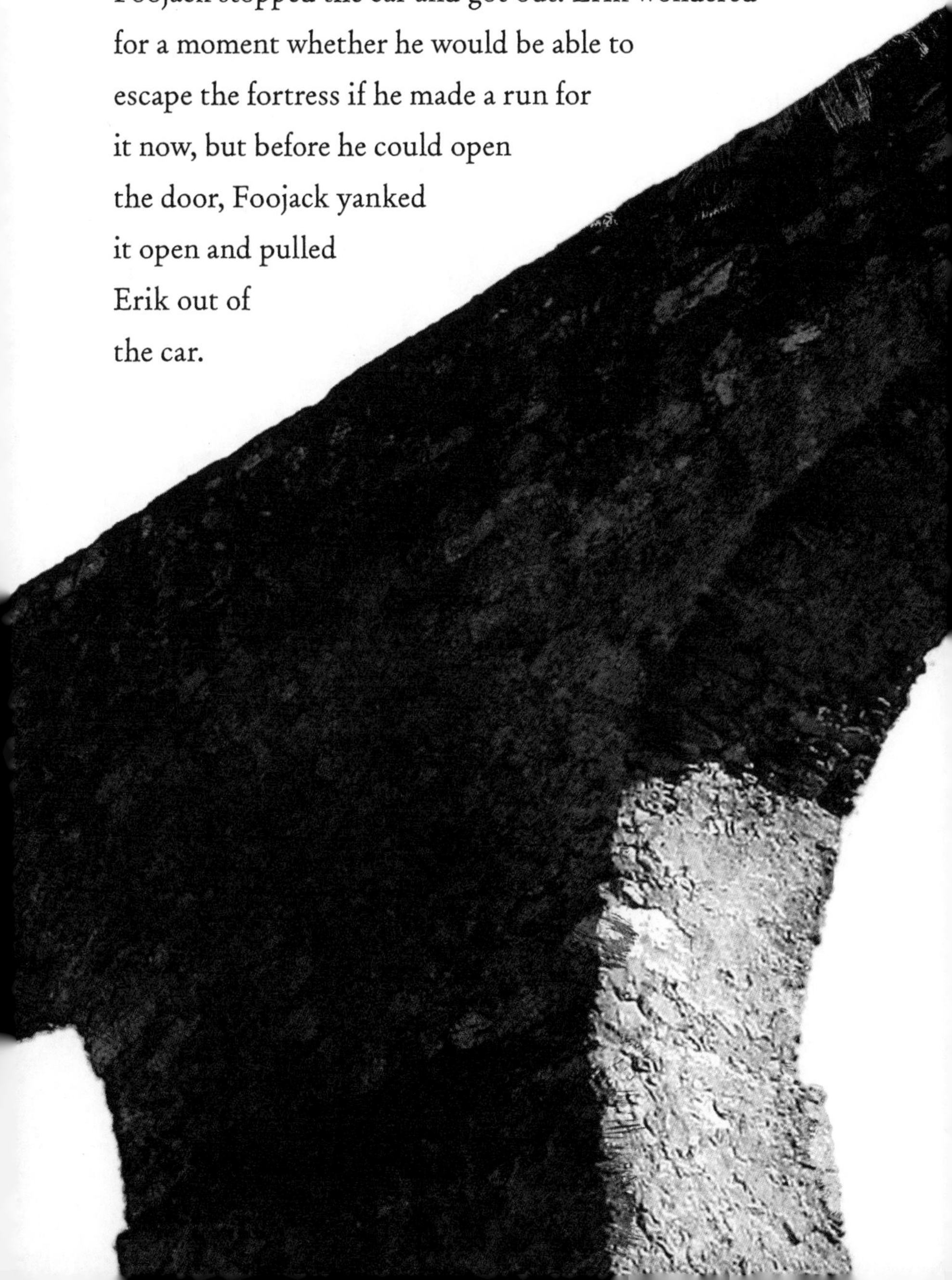

His massive hand gripped Erik's shoulder and propelled him forward.

"Where's Dorcas Potts?" Erik asked, looking around the empty courtyard.

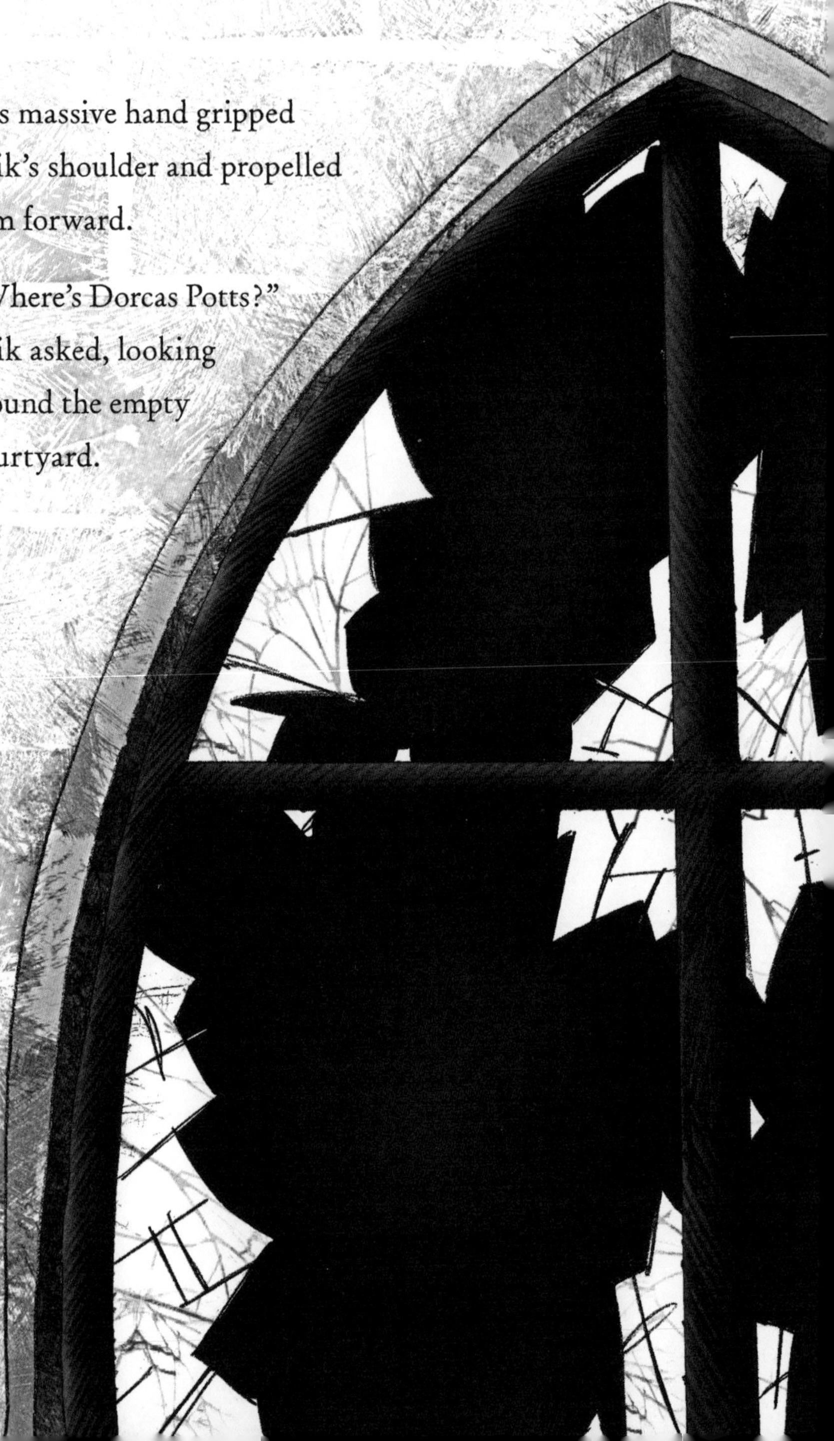

"She is coming soon. La Sauvage will see to that." Foojack grinned. "This way."

Erik was pushed toward the doors of what looked like an old chapel. There was a bell rope hanging down the weathered brick wall. Of all the parts of the château, this place looked the least cared for. Plaster cracked from the walls, the door hung on rusted hinges, and small blackbirds flew in and out of the large broken window.

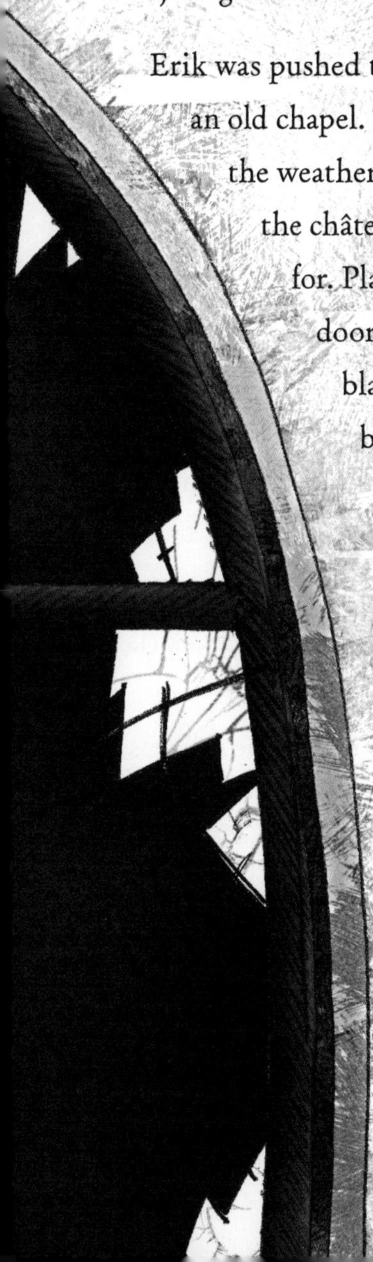

"The prison?" Erik asked as Foojack opened the door.

"The church," Foojack replied proudly. "Château Autruche was once a monastery—a place of importance for pilgrims trying to find God. Then, like everything else, the world took it over."

"And it has become a den of thieves?" Erik asked.

"Very good." Foojack laughed, his deep voice echoing through the dark shadows. "I hope you like this place. It is quite fitting that you should spend your last night here."

Foojack pushed Erik inside the church. It was cold and dark. The door slammed behind him and sent a spiral of birds squawking to the rafters. Erik looked into the shadows. At the far end he could see the remains of a table pushed against the wall. It was draped in old rags, and a broken cross lay awkwardly upon it next to an empty glass bottle. There were no chairs or any other furniture—just a small rail that ran in front of the table. Below the rail was a padded velvet mat, which was old and seemed to have been torn up by rats.

Outside, Erik heard another car come into the courtyard. He caught the sound of harsh voices, yelling, scuffling feet. The château gates slammed. Erik heard Dorcas Potts shouting, and then there was nothing.

Erik wondered what they would do to her. He felt alone, frightened . . . like the night he had been abandoned by his father—the old tramp who had dumped him at the door of Isambard Dunstan's School for Wayward Children. Erik remembered the way the fog had swirled about the long drive and in and out of the trees. He had thought they had come to break into yet another house, for that was how they spent most nights. Erik would be forced through a tiny window or drain while his father kept watch. Then, once Erik had opened the front door, he would have to stand guard while his old man ransacked the house, filling pillowcases with anything that shone brightly, regardless of its value.

He remembered clearly his father's last words before he had disappeared down the long drive of the school.

"Stay here until I get back," he had said as he pulled his tattered coat about himself, tugged his cap, and then coughed and spluttered for several minutes until he could draw his breath again. "I'll be back, my lad—just popping to the shops for some cigarettes, and then we'll be off."

Erik had thought for several days that it must be a long, long way to the shops. Miss Rimmer, who would become headmistress of the school, had been warmer back then. She had opened the door and ushered him inside with a kind smile.

Erik had been given a custodian's job at the school and a room in the tower, well away from the noisy dormitories of cackling girls who spent the nights brushing their hair, shivering in the cold drafts, and telling each other ghost stories. The girls would shriek and scream and insist on the light being left illuminated throughout the night. Miss Rimmer would silence their ramblings and plunge them into a fearful darkness. During the day, Erik would be allowed to attend the lessons and sit at the back of the class in a world of his own.

Now, Erik made his way closer to the table. As he got nearer, he realized it was an altar that had not been used for many years. Looking up, he saw that the walls and ceiling were covered in paintings of angels. Their faces shone in the half-light as they gazed down at him.

In three paces he was at the altar rail. He sat on the dusty velvet and worried about Dorcas Potts. He felt uncomfortable—out of place—as if he shouldn't be there. The last time he had been in a church was when his father had robbed it of its silver.

he said loudly.

"Fine mess I'm in now . . ."

Whoever he was expecting to reply didn't. He was alone in the cold darkness of a secluded French château. The only thing he could hear were the muffled wing beats of the roosting birds high above him. Erik slumped against the rail and, without thinking, turned and faced the altar.

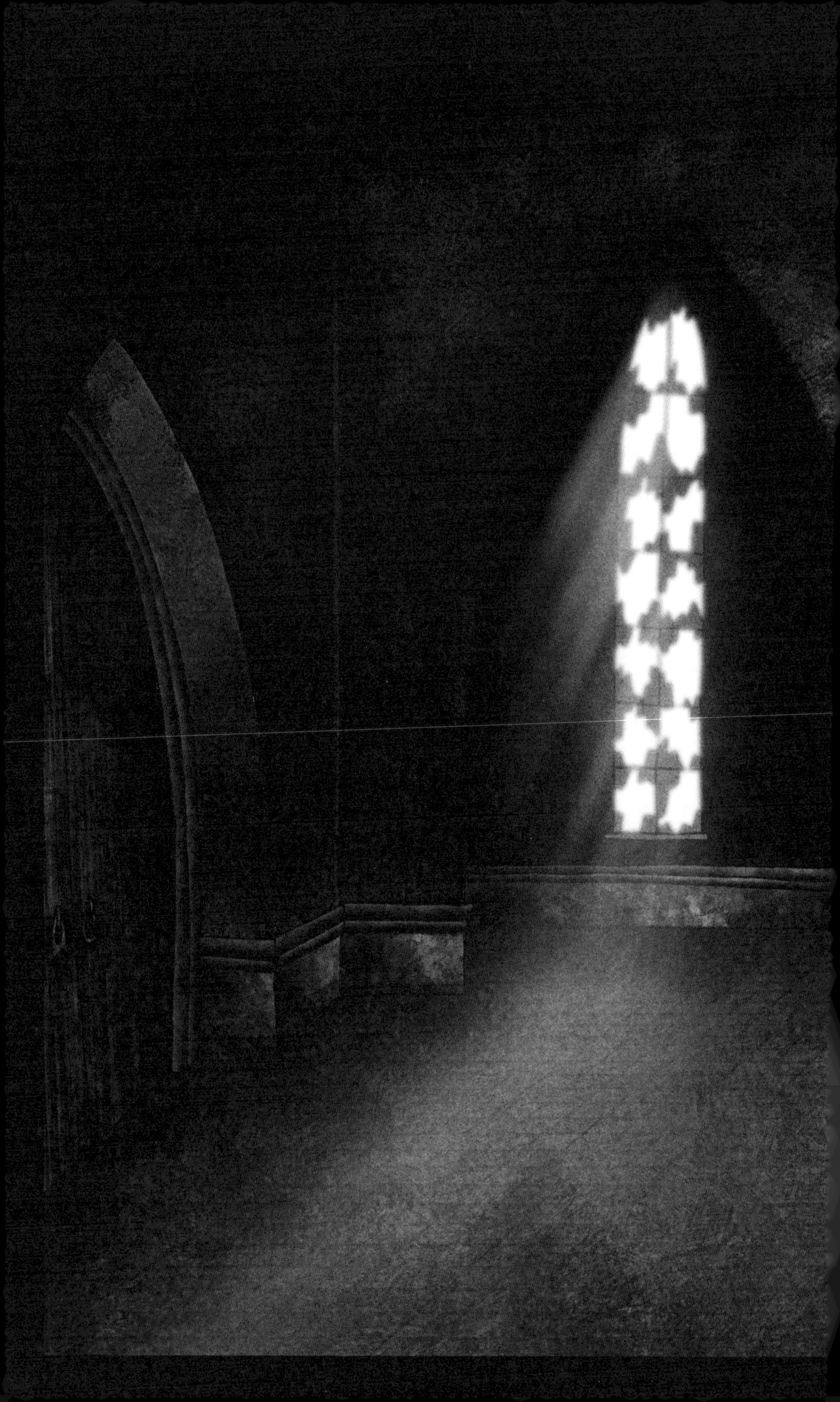

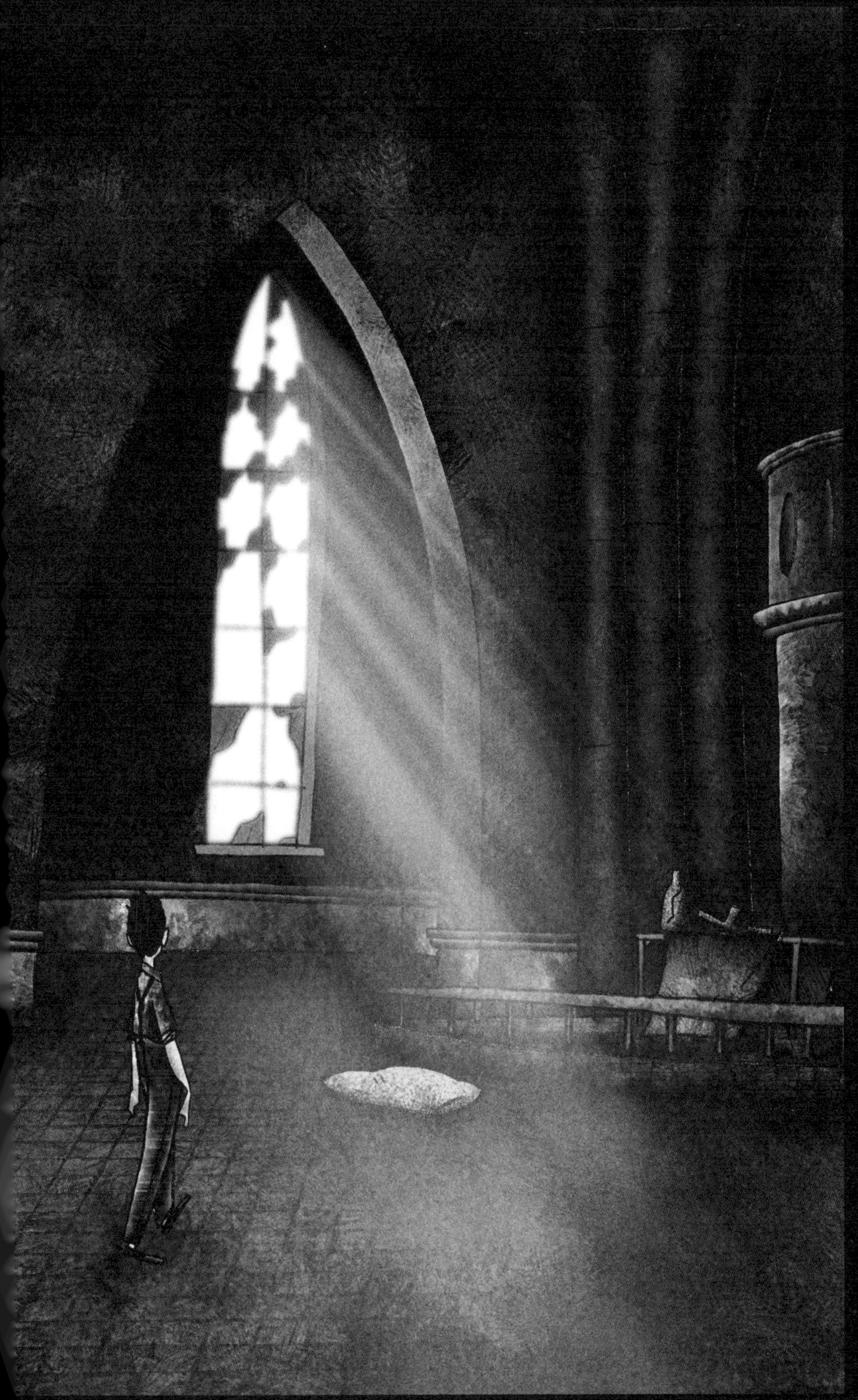

Staring back at him through years of dust and grime was the painted face of a man etched onto the wall. The only thing he could really distinguish were the eyes. They were soft and warm and seemed to be full of life.

"I don't know what you're looking at," Erik said boldly to the painting.

"You, Erik," said a woman's voice from somewhere close by.

Erik didn't dare move. For a moment he thought the voice had been inside his own head. He kept staring at the wall, fearful of turning around to see who might be there.

"Who. . .?" was all he managed to say in reply. He felt someone standing near him, watching him.

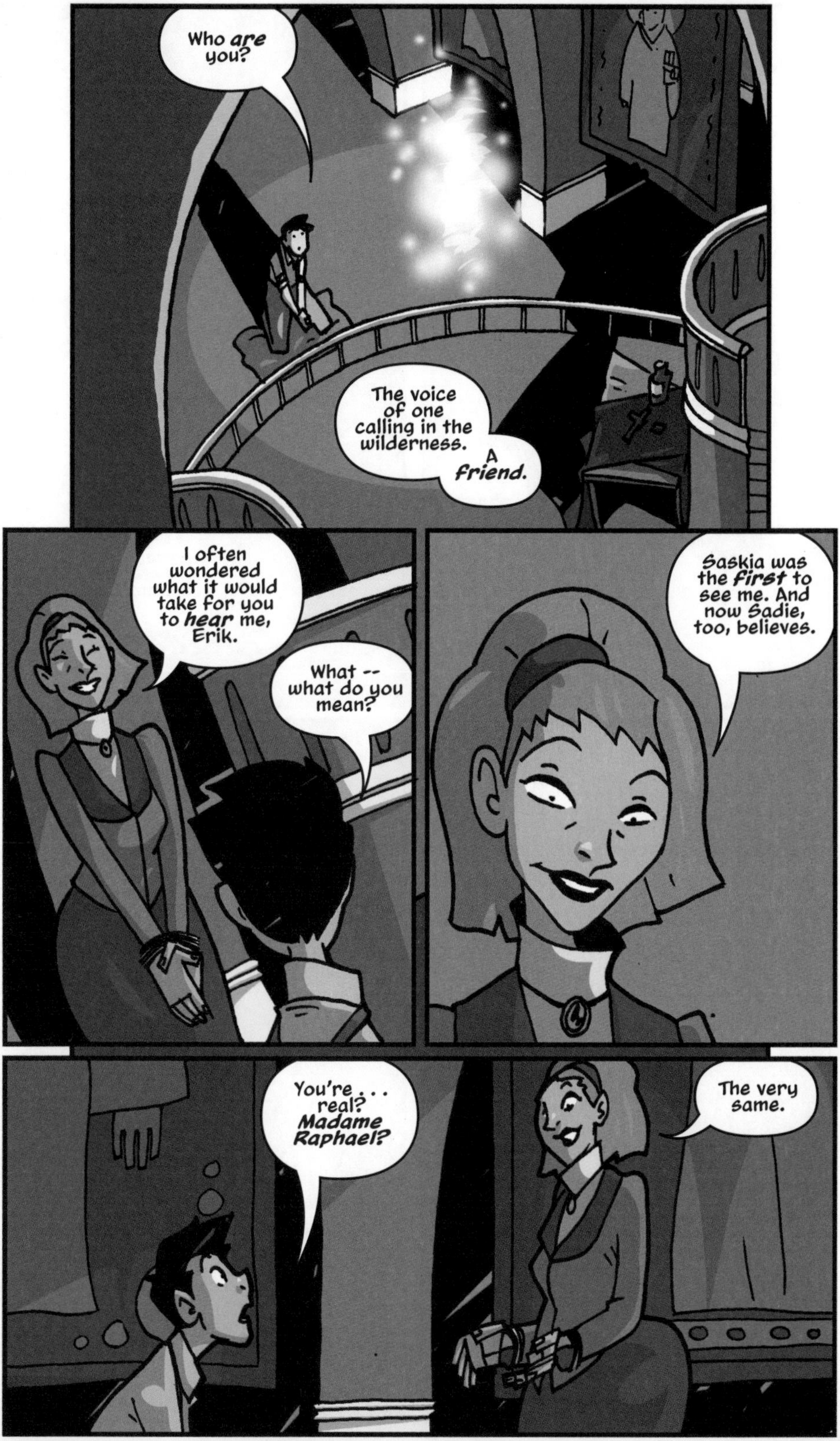

Who are you?
The voice of one calling in the wilderness.
A friend.
I often wondered what it would take for you to hear me, Erik.
What -- what do you mean?
Saskia was the first to see me. And now Sadie, too, believes.
You're . . . real? Madame Raphael?
The very same.

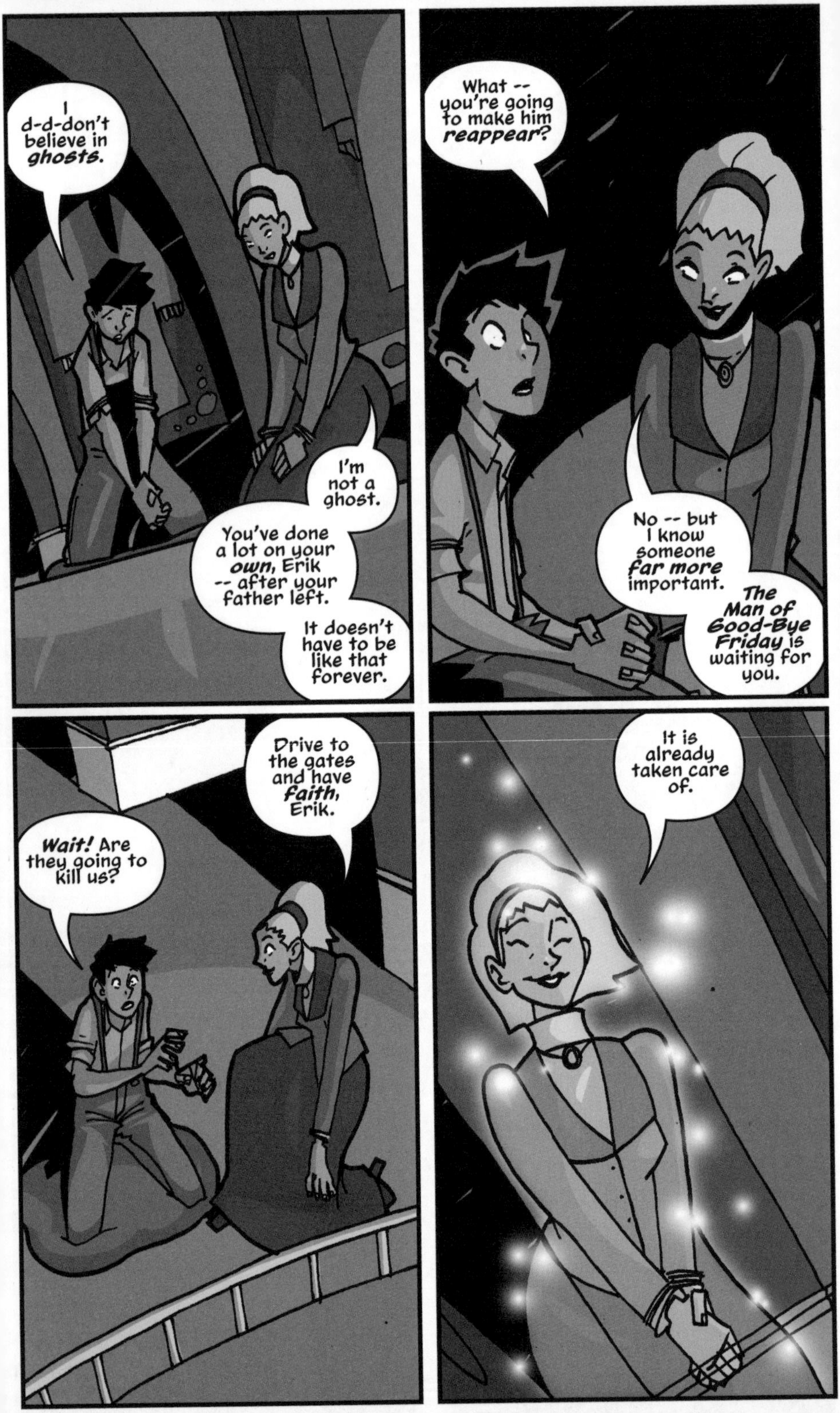
I d-d-don't believe in *ghosts.*
I'm not a ghost.
You've done a lot on your *own,* Erik -- after your father left.
It doesn't have to be like that forever.
What -- you're going to make him *reappear?*
No -- but I know someone *far more* important.
The Man of Good-Bye Friday is waiting for you.
Wait! Are they going to kill us?
Drive to the gates and have *faith,* Erik.
It is already taken care of.

Erik stared into the darkness, willing the woman to stay. But he knew he was alone once again. Erik had never believed Saskia when she spoke of the mysterious woman who had appeared to her at Spaniards House and in the alley at Hampstead. He had thought she was just a figment of Saskia's imagination, a ruse to pass the time, an imaginary friend. Even when Sadie claimed to have seen the woman, he had thought she was just playing along to amuse Saskia.

"Drive to the gates and have faith,"

Erik said again and again as he stared at the wall.

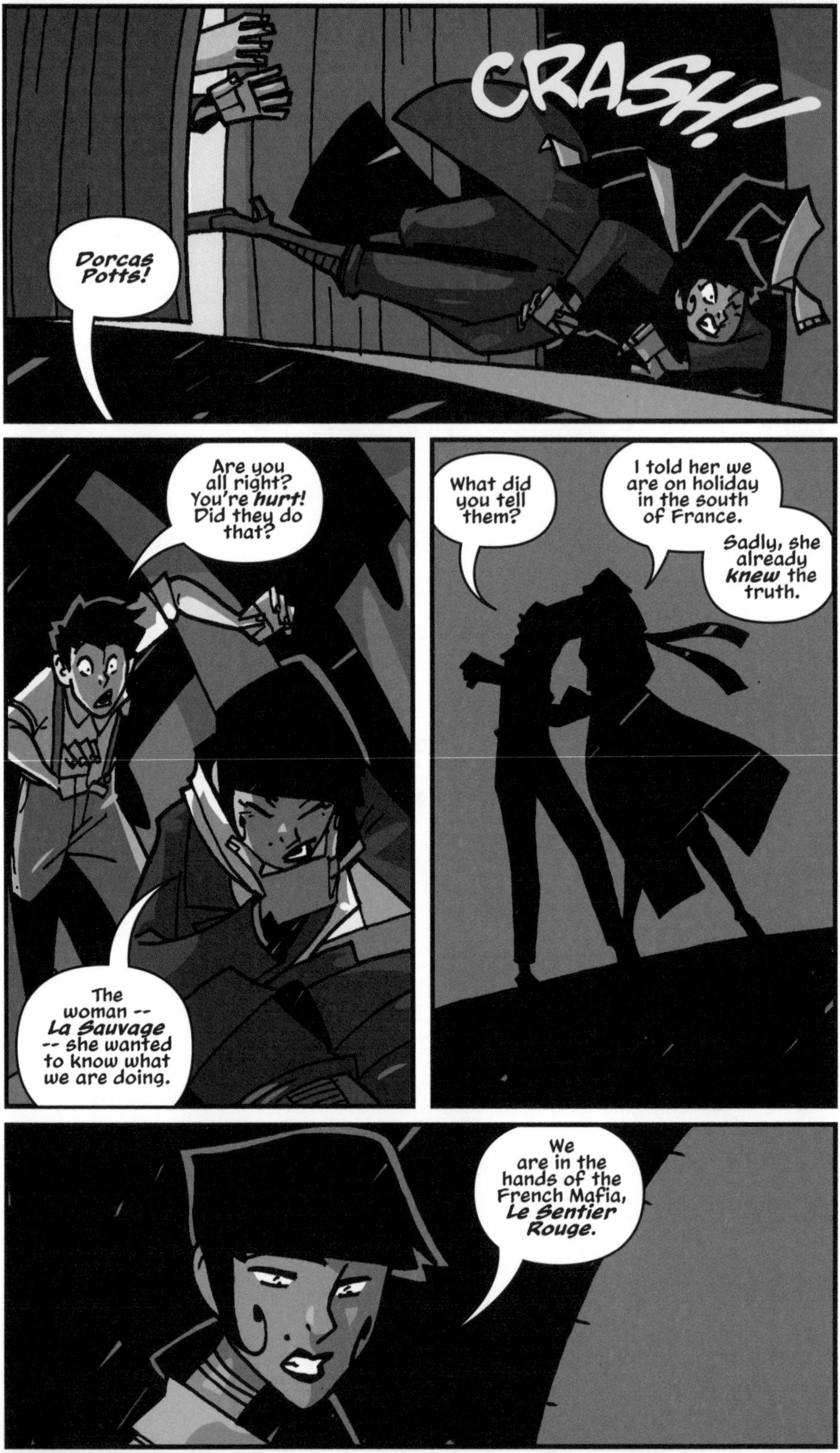
CRASH!!
Dorcas Potts!
Are you all right? You're *hurt!* Did they do that?
The woman -- *La Sauvage* -- she wanted to know what we are doing.
What did you tell them?
I told her we are on holiday in the south of France.
Sadly, she already *knew* the truth.
We are in the hands of the French Mafia, *Le Sentier Rouge.*

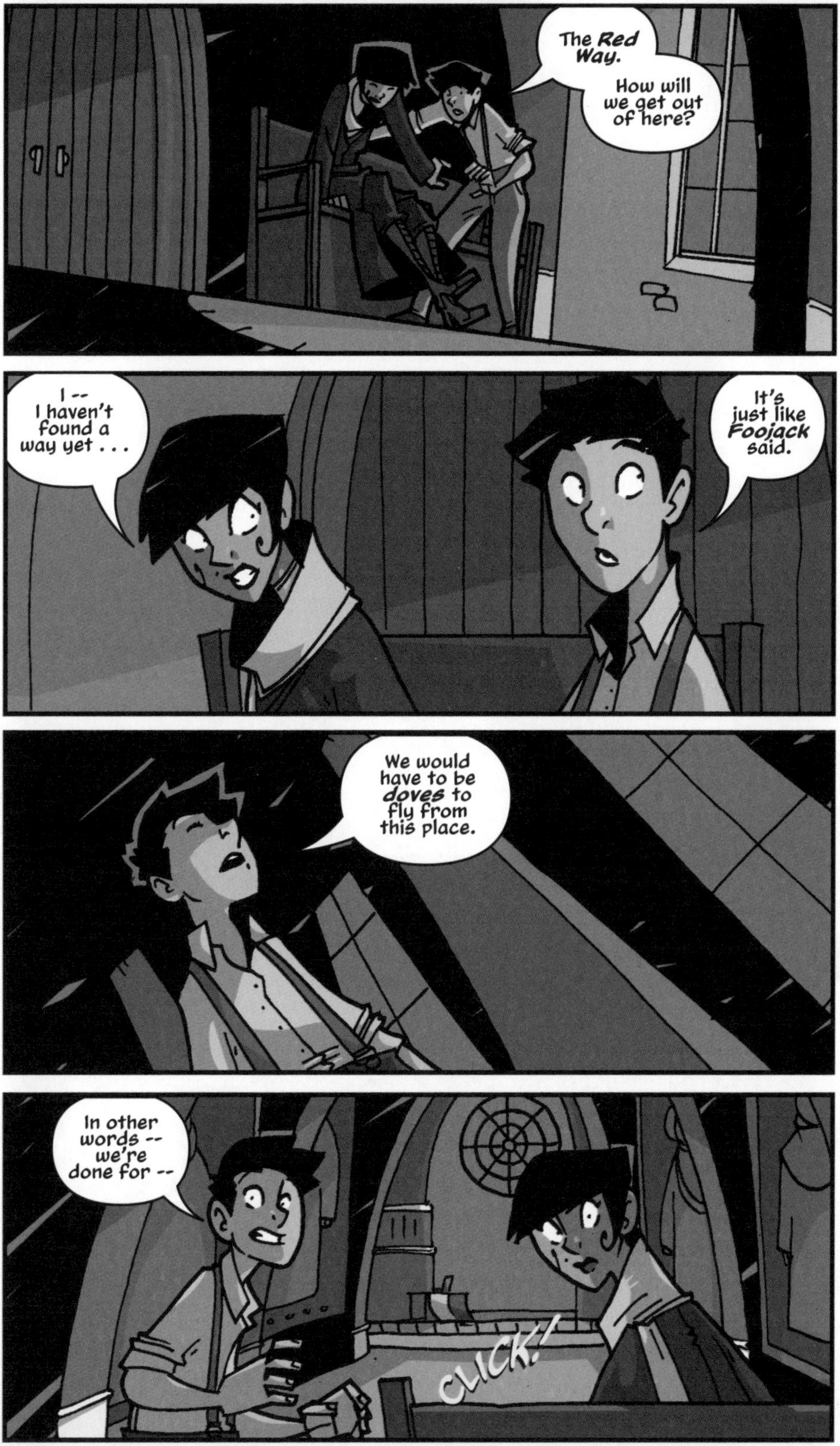
The *Red* *Way.*
How will we get out of here?
I -- I haven't found a way yet . . .
It's just like *Foojack* said.
We would have to be *doves* to fly from this place.
In other words -- we're done for --
CLICK!

At that moment the door to the church opened again. Foojack stood in the opening. He was a giant of a man and blocked out most of the light. In one hand he held a gun. Hanging from his other hand were the keys to the Bugatti. Foojack was alone.

Stepping inside, he kicked the door shut with his heel. At first he didn't speak. He just cast his glare from Erik to Dorcas Potts and back again.

"This is a bad thing," he said gruffly, looking at the gun. "I never thought I would do such as this. It is not the way of Le Sentier Rouge."

Erik's heart began to beat faster as he stepped in front of Dorcas Potts to shield her from the gangster.

Foojack laughed. "You could be my son. Same age, same hair . . . same kind of father."

Foojack walked closer.

"What are you going to do to us?" Erik snapped. His feet were planted firmly on the ground, and his arms were folded.

"Time to use your head, Erik," Foojack said as he let the keys slip from his fingers to the floor. "If I was to look away for a moment, and if someone was to grab that bottle from the table and smash me over the head as I fired my gun, and then grab the keys to the automobile . . ."

The man grinned. Erik looked at Dorcas Potts.

"You would do that?" Erik asked.

"It is not your time," Foojack whispered to Erik. "Madame Raphael and the Companion would not like it."

Foojack suddenly aimed the gun at the roof and pulled the trigger just as Dorcas Potts grabbed the bottle and smashed it on the altar rail. There was a loud crash, and broken glass sprayed across the floor. Foojack fell to the floor in a mock faint.

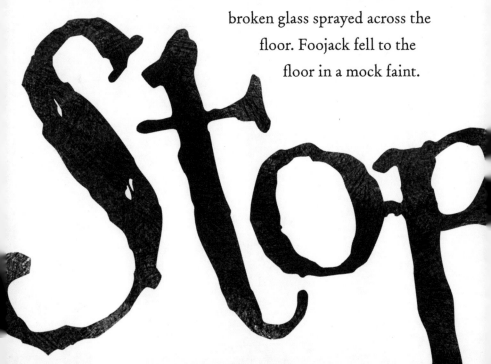

"Follow me," Dorcas Potts shouted as she grabbed the keys to the Bugatti from the floor.

Erik raced to the door behind Dorcas Potts. In a flash, they were both outside. The Bugatti was by the steps of the château.

As they leaped into the car, La Sauvage ran out the front door.

"Stop them!" she shouted.

Dorcas Potts pressed the accelerator, and they charged toward the closed gates.

"The gates!" yelled Dorcas Potts as one of the men on the balcony saw them and raised his gun.

In his mind,
Erik heard
Madame Raphael's
words: "Drive to the
gates and have faith."

"Just drive," he said. The sound of shouts and
gunfire filled the courtyard.

"We're going to crash!" Dorcas Potts screamed as the
gates came closer.

From the corner of his eye, Erik saw two men running
across the courtyard toward them. He kept his eyes
focused straight ahead.

They were only feet away from the gate now. It was held
shut by a thick chain.

A spray of bullets hit the side of the car. Erik ducked. The
Bugatti swerved wildly.

"Hang on!" yelled Dorcas Potts.

The car spun around, then suddenly jerked to a halt.

"What happened?" cried Erik.

"Wheel—stuck in a pothole." Dorcas Potts jammed her foot harder on the accelerator. The engine shrieked, but the wheel spun uselessly in the hole.

There was another gunshot, and a bullet hole appeared in the seat next to Erik's shoulder.

"Try reversing!" called Erik. Dorcas Potts shifted gears, and the car moved a fraction of an inch.

"Still stuck." She shifted back to drive.

"Don't worry—just keep trying," said Erik. He thought to himself, "Have faith."

One of the men
was almost at the
car. He reached
out his hand
to grab Erik.

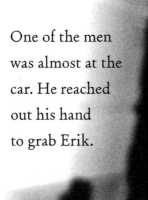

Erik flung himself away from the
man. The shift in weight was just
enough. The car jolted and shot forward,
sending a spray of gravel from the hole.

As the car hurtled toward the solid iron gates, a stone
dislodged from the pothole and flew through the air,
blasting the lone rusted link in the chain. The iron rings
fell to the ground. Instantly the gates swung open, and
the car flew through the arch and over the bridge.

Erik grinned and whooped in triumph. "Faster!" he
shouted. "This is a Bugatti!"

"How did you know we would make it?" Dorcas Potts
yelled above the engine.

"A friend told me," Erik said. He looked back and saw
Foojack stumbling from the church. "Strange," he
muttered to himself. "Foojack knew her as well."

Chapter Nine
French Cocoa

MUZZ ELLIOTT, SADIE, AND SASKIA spent the rest of the day in their luxurious cabin on the ROTHSCHILD EXPRESS. Muzz Elliott, on the advice of Inspector Max Taranis of Scotland Yard, had locked the door and wedged it shut with a stiff-backed chair. He told her that until they reached Cannes in the morning, no one was to leave the room.

The twins were engrossed in the final chapter of MURDER TRAIN while they all awaited news from Max Taranis.

At last Saskia closed the book and sighed. "I can't believe it was the countess the whole time!"

Sadie looked anxiously at Muzz Elliott. "Is there a countess on this train?"

"It's possible," Muzz Elliott replied.

"We can ask Max Taranis when he comes back," said Sadie. "What do you think he's doing anyway?"

"Trying to find Luzio, searching the train with the guard, keeping an eye on the driver?" Saskia guessed.

"I should have left you both in Hampstead, where it is safe." Muzz Elliott stared out the window at the sun sinking behind the mountains.

"Erik and Dorcas Potts should be nearly in Cannes," Sadie said brightly. "When we phoned from Victoria Station, he said they would leave right away."

Muzz Elliott smiled. "I suppose I am glad that you both have an interfering nature. Dorcas Potts is just the person we need. In the meantime, I will order some cocoa, and we shall then sleep. If anything happens, Max will come find us."

With that, she pressed the buzzer for the steward. Within the minute there was a knock on the door. Muzz Elliott slid open the narrow slat and peered through.

"We would like cocoa and cake for three people. And I would like my cocoa hot—VERY hot," she said to the man outside. "Any news of Luzio?" she added before he could leave.

"No, madame," came the muffled voice.

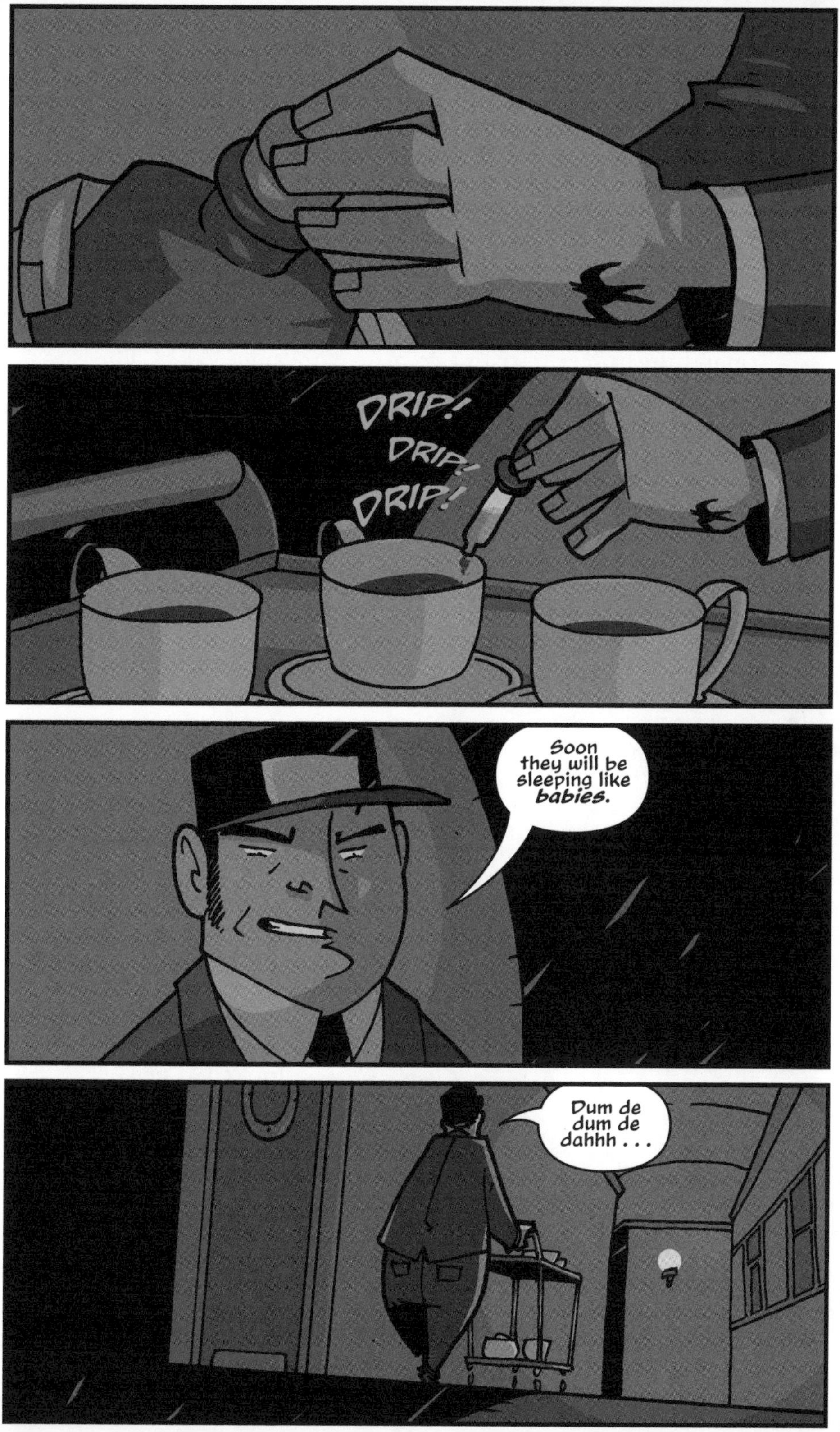
DRIP!
DRIP!
DRIP!
Soon they will be sleeping like *babies*.
Dum de dum de dahhh . . .

The knock on the door came quickly. Muzz Elliott looked through the slat before taking away the chair and slipping the bolt. The steward backed into the room, head down and muttering to himself. He pulled a tray of drinks on a trolley with tiny wheels. Each china mug stood on a matching saucer next to two miniature spice cakes. The cocoa steamed, each cup hot and frothy and sprinkled with grated chocolate.

"French cocoa," the man warbled in a voice more suited to an aging aunt than a small, rotund Parisian. "You have never tasted anything like it."

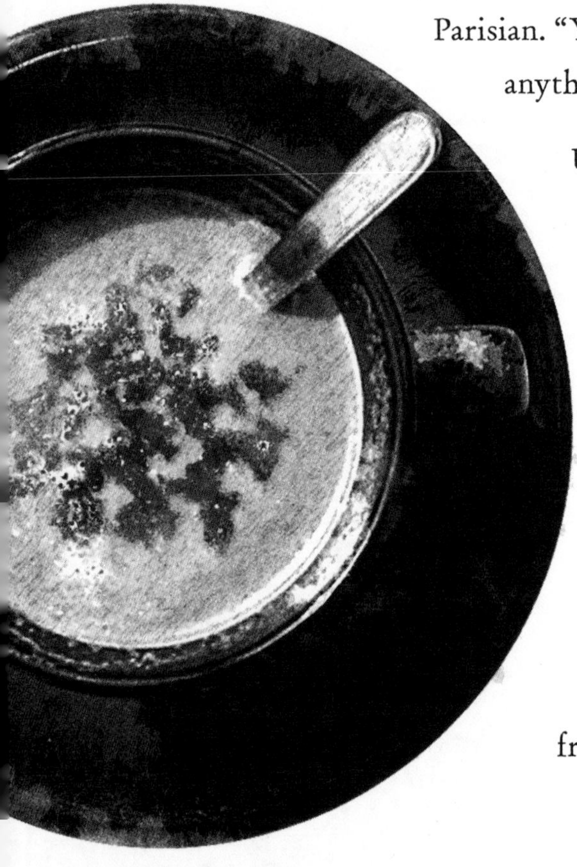

Unlike most stewards, he didn't wait for the tip. His left hand stayed firmly in his pocket as if he didn't care for the gratuity. He looked at neither Muzz Elliott nor the twins before scurrying ratlike from the room.

"It tastes different from British cocoa," Muzz Elliott commented as she sniffed the cup and wondered aloud what the sweet odor was that seemed to spill over the brim of the cup.

Sadie took a sip. "Peppermint?"

"Lemon?" her sister guessed.

"Sleepy," replied Muzz Elliott. She lay back on the soft pillows of the sofa and closed her eyes.

Saskia watched as Muzz Elliott fell instantly asleep. Then she turned to Sadie, who was sitting on her bunk holding the cup in her hand. She reached out as if to find an imaginary table floating beside the top bunk. Then without warning, she let go of the cup, and it crashed to the floor. Hot cocoa splattered across the carpet. Saskia could do nothing. Her arms drained of life and fell to her sides like lead weights. The face of her sister merged with the wall so she appeared as a headless ghost floating in the air. When Saskia attempted to speak, her lips clung numbly to her face.

"Drugged . . . ," she finally managed to mumble, half asleep.

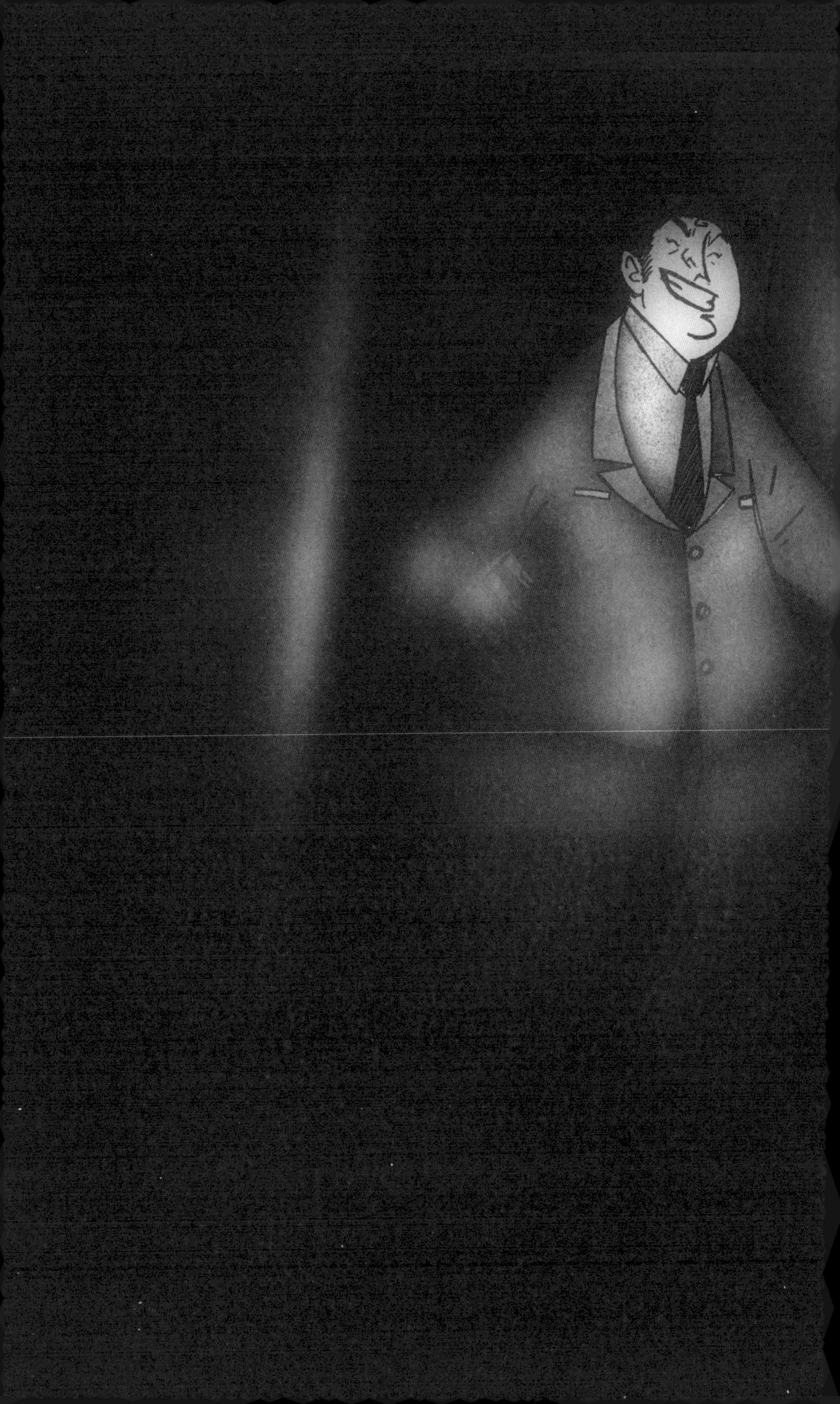

The door to the compartment
opened. Saskia heard the
sound like it was traveling
underwater. Forcing open
her heavy eyelids, she could
make out the round shape of
the steward. He seemed to be
laughing, though Saskia could
not understand at what.

As she fought sleep, Saskia
saw the steward lift her sister
from the bunk and place her
in some sort of large trunk
on wheels.

"Leave the note. Make sure they can see it," a voice commanded from the corridor.

The steward giggled. "This is so beautiful," he said with a flamboyant wave of his hand. "I just love the smell of French cocoa."

Saskia lay helpless. She tried to shout out, but a dark wave of sleep washed over her. With every ounce of strength, she attempted to lift herself from the floor. Invisible hands seemed to smother her face and force her down. With her last moment of consciousness, she thought three desperate words:

"Companion, help us."

Then came sleep—deep, deathly, and complete. She heard no more. The rattling of the train became the rushing of the tide against a beach. In her mind she walked through the waves barefoot as the sun set.

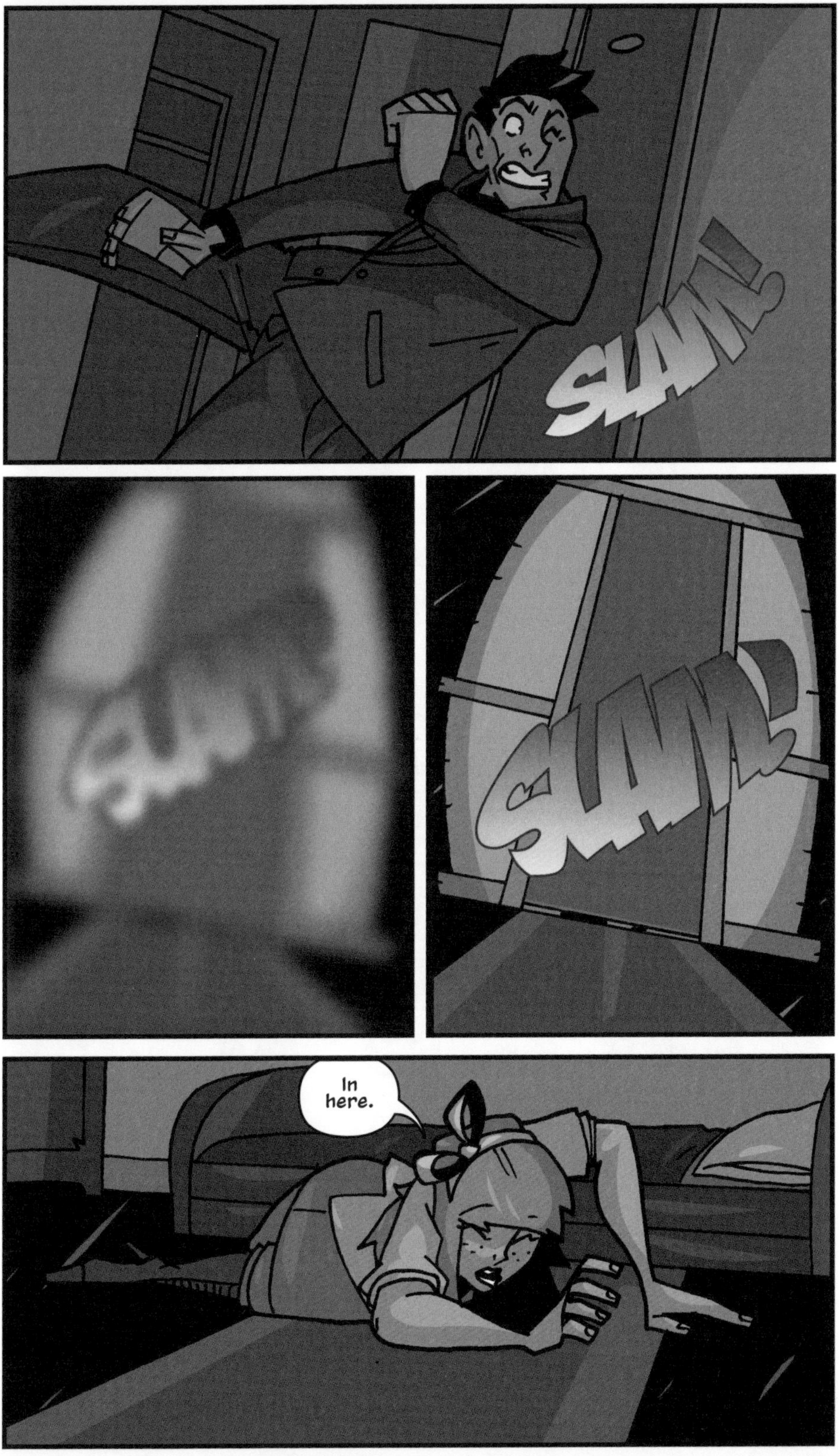
SLAM!
SLAM!
SLAM!
In here.

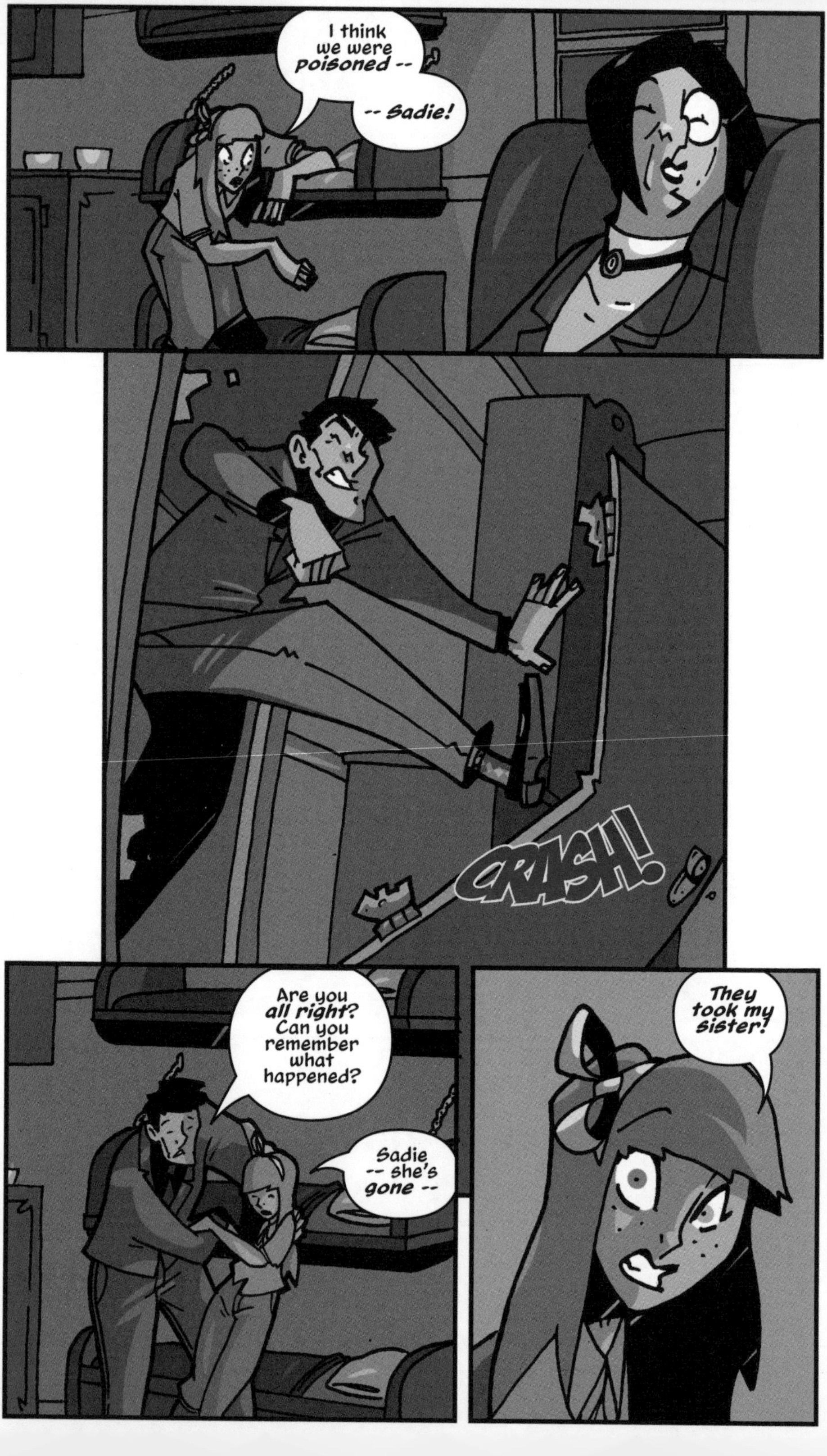
I think we were poisoned --
-- Sadie!
CRASH!
Are you all right? Can you remember what happened?
Sadie -- she's gone --
They took my sister!

"Who did this?" he asked.

Saskia's eyes slowly cleared, and the buzzing in her head gave way to the steady rumble of the train. "We had cocoa.... It smelled sweet.... They took her away.... We must catch them," she babbled.

"Did you see them?"

"I think so," she replied, unsure if what she had seen was only a dream.

Max Taranis sighed. "I think they are gone. The train stopped in the middle of the night—a car was on the track. They must have sneaked off the train then, taking Sadie with them. Who did you see?"

Saskia tried to think. It was as if her brain had been turned to a glob of marmalade. "It was the steward—the one who came last night. He was a Frenchman—small and round. And someone was waiting for him in the corridor."

"It must have been a disguise. There are no stewards who fit that description." Max Taranis picked up a broken piece of Sadie's cup from the floor and lifted it to his lips. He sniffed the dry cocoa smeared on the shattered rim.

"You were drugged by a powerful narcotic," he said solemnly.

"They took her away . . . my sister . . . Sadie," Saskia sobbed.

Inspector Taranis looked at Sadie's empty bed. There, placed neatly on the pillow, was a crisp vellum envelope. On it was Muzz Elliott's name, written in bold black letters. Muzz Elliott slowly roused from her sleep. She looked up at the inspector, then down at herself, apparently confused about why she was still dressed and on the sofa. She saw Max Taranis holding the letter.

"A postman?" Muzz Elliott asked, holding her head and wincing in pain.

"Another blackmail note, Muzz Elliott," he replied.

Muzz Elliott sat up. "Max Taranis. I take it I have been drugged?" she said benignly, as though it were an everyday occurrence.

Max Taranis nodded. "And," he said as he opened the letter,

"Sadie has been kidnapped."

The inspector's eyes scanned back and forth across the crisp, expensive paper.

"Instructions?" Muzz Elliott asked as she tried to stand.

"Precise and very clear. They even mention me by name," he said, folding the note and slipping it into his pocket. "Whoever kidnapped Sadie knew who I am and why I am here. Sadly, my presence has complicated things for us all."

"What does it say?" implored Muzz Elliott. She held her head as if to stop it from throbbing.

"You are to go to the Hotel Carlton and check into Suite Otero and await instructions," Max Taranis said without looking at the letter. "If you do not, then . . ."

"Typical cowards," Muzz Elliott replied. "They would never have dared to take me."

"So are we just going to wait till we get there?" Saskia asked, frustrated that they were doing nothing to find her sister.

"In times like these it is pointless to go after the criminals," the inspector said. He looked in the mirror and straightened his tie. "We shall set a trap and draw them in."

"But what if they . . . ?" Saskia could not finish the sentence.

"Whoever has taken Sadie will have a plan. Your sister will be safe for the time being. Muzz Elliott is being manipulated, and it is my job to find out who the manipulator is."

Not a mile away from the speeding train, on a high mountain pass, the Bugatti drove erratically along the open road. Dorcas Potts gripped the wheel of the sleek car and stared ahead of her, while Erik looked behind to see if they were being followed. In the distance, a single automobile gave sluggish chase.

"Are they any nearer?" asked Dorcas Potts. She slipped the car into a lower gear to take the incline.

"Just the same as before—it's like they don't want to catch us," Erik replied.

"We're only twenty miles from Cannes. They're probably

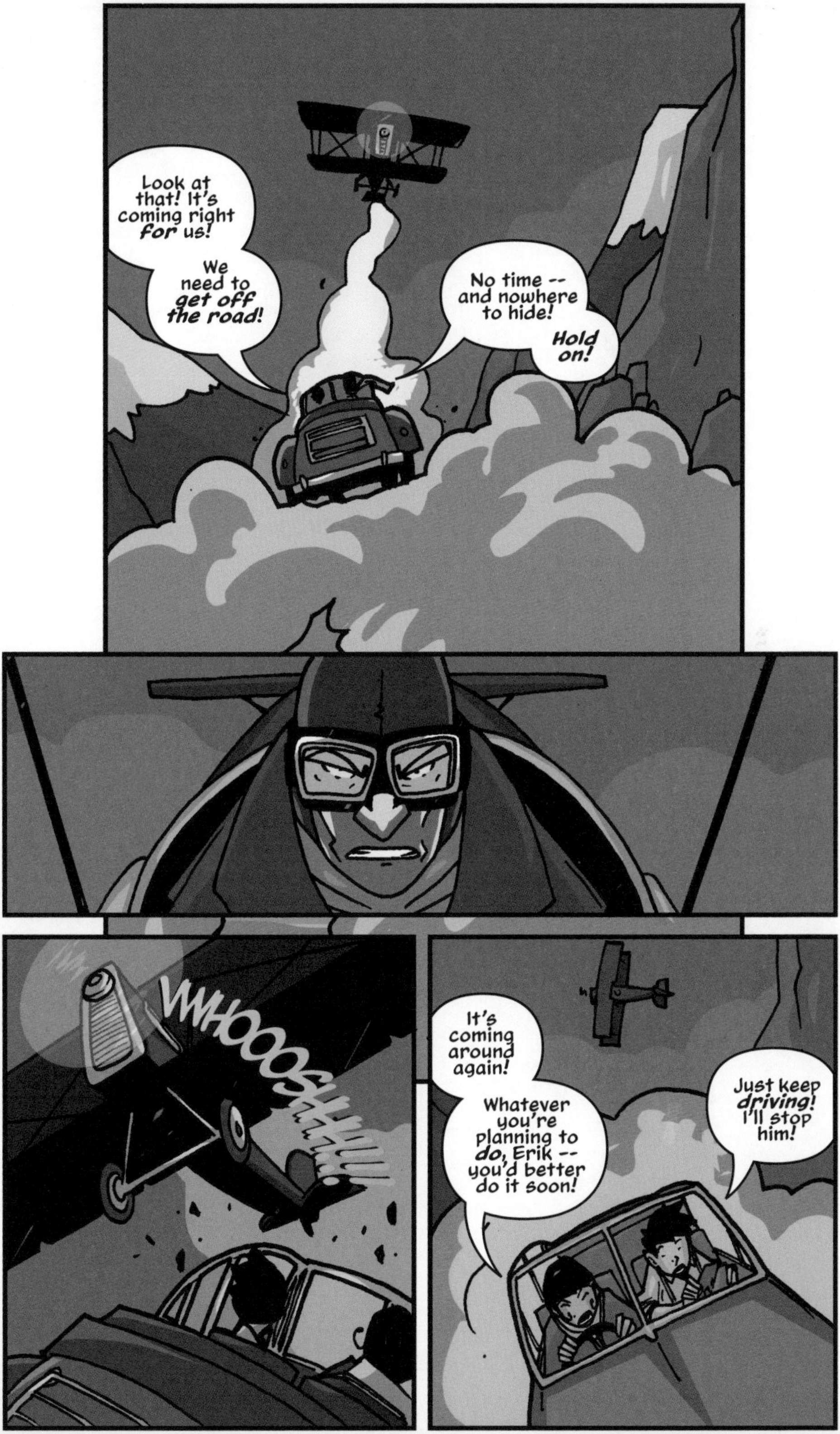

Look at that! It's coming right *for* us!
We need to *get off the road!*
No time -- and nowhere to hide!
Hold on!
VWHOOOSHHH!!
It's coming around again!
Whatever you're planning to *do*, Erik -- you'd better do it soon!
Just keep *driving*! I'll stop him!

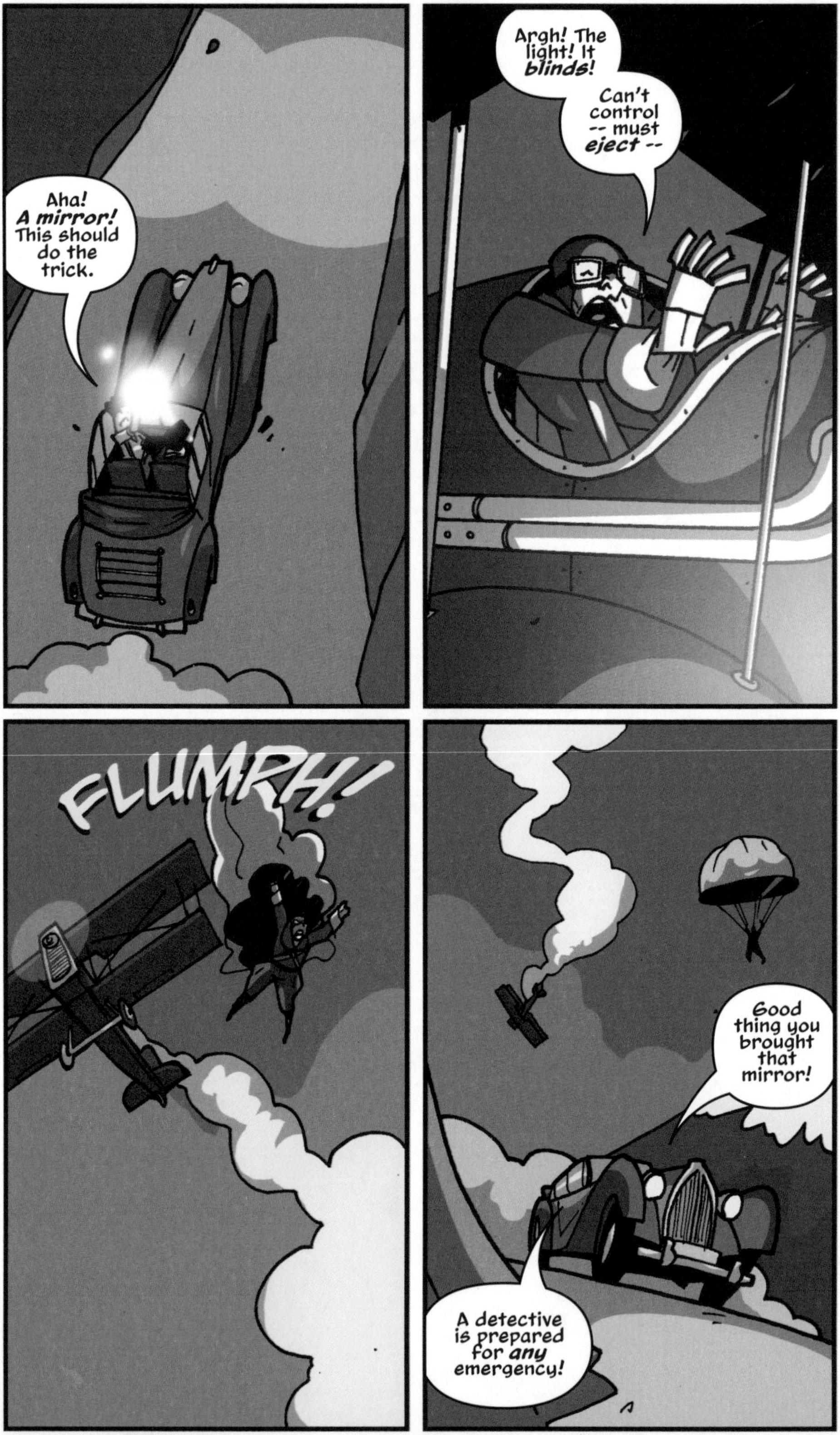
Aha! *A mirror!* This should do the trick.
Argh! The light! It *blinds!*
Can't control -- must *eject* --
FLUMPH!
Good thing you brought that mirror!
A detective is prepared for *any* emergency!

Erik looked to the sky and watched the plane fall. There was a billowing of white canvas high above it. A man dangled like a Christmas ornament from the strings of a parachute.

Dorcas Potts laughed. "You're a quick thinker, Erik Morrissey Ganger."

Erik smiled. He didn't really know what he had done. All he could think about was seeing Madame Raphael for the first time. Saskia had said he would see her when he really needed to—but he had never believed her. Angels didn't speak to people like him. They were for special people—good people. He knew he had done so much wrong in his life, and he never dreamed that someday an angel would visit him.

"Do you believe in angels?" he asked Dorcas Potts. The car reached the top of the winding road, and for the first time they could see the vast blue of the Mediterranean far below.

"I believe in what my eyes can see and my mind can understand. I gave up on the tooth fairy in sixth grade," Dorcas Potts scoffed in her American accent.

"I think I met one in the chapel at the château," Erik said, not caring what she thought.

"Well, if it helps you, then fine."

"**It's Complicated**," Erik said quietly as he tried to puzzle it all out. "Saskia has an invisible friend she often talks to. She's called Madame Raphael. Sadie and I didn't believe her at first, but Sadie started to change her mind several months ago, and when I was alone in the chapel, Madame Rapahel—the angel—came to me."

"Does Muzz Elliott know about all this?" Dorcas Potts asked.

"I think she does," Erik answered. Then he added, "Strange thing. Foojack mentioned Madame Raphael's name when he came to set us free."

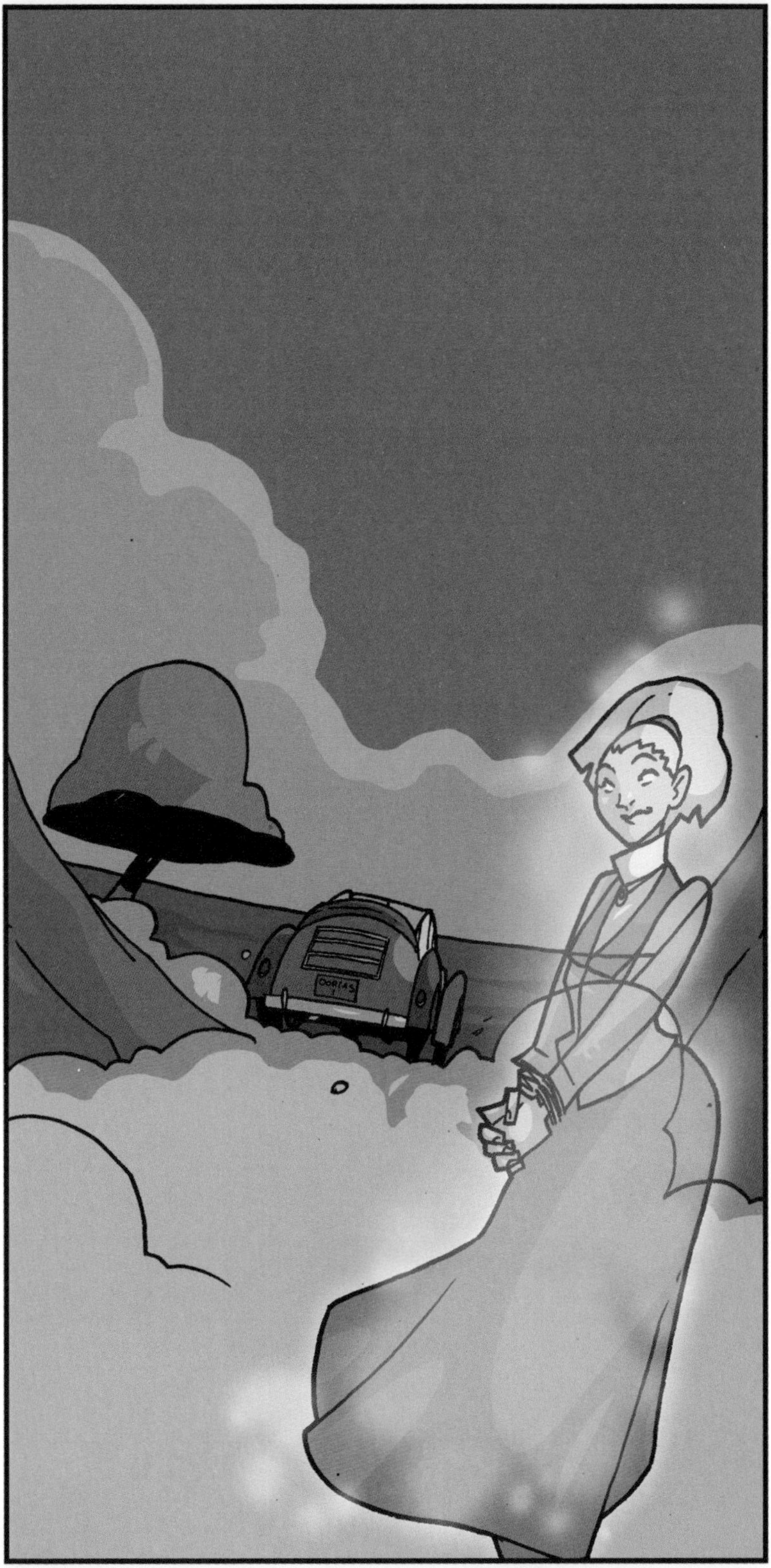

Erik glanced behind him. "Look out! They're not far behind," he cried.

Skirting the bends in the road behind them was the black Citroën. It was crawling up the hill, but it was closer now than it had been before.

"We can beat them to Cannes and hide the car," said Dorcas Potts. "Then we can find Muzz Elliott."

She pressed the gas and the car sped forward, spitting a hail of stones from the wheels.

Chapter Ten

The Great Mogul Diamond

THE CLOCK ABOVE THE ENTRANCE to the Hotel Carlton struck the tenth hour. The chimes mingled with the hum of traffic that dodged in and out of the palm trees on the Boulevard de la Croisette. Beside the ornate brass doorway stood the uniformed concierge in his flat military cap and jacket with gold braid. With the final strike of the hour, a long, burgundy Rolls-Royce slowly came to a halt on the road in front of the hotel. A flurry of doorkeepers swarmed like bees and welcomed the occupants of the car.

A patent leather boot stepped onto the freshly swept sidewalk. Another soon followed. A tall, elegant man in a London morning suit appeared from the car. His salt-and-pepper hair looked like it had just been combed, and his thin mustache turned up at the corners. He shaded his eyes from the bright sun with a hand that bore a small swallow tattoo. Close behind came a rotund Frenchman with an identical swallow tattoo on his left hand. He carried a small bag and muttered to himself. A top hat balanced on his head.

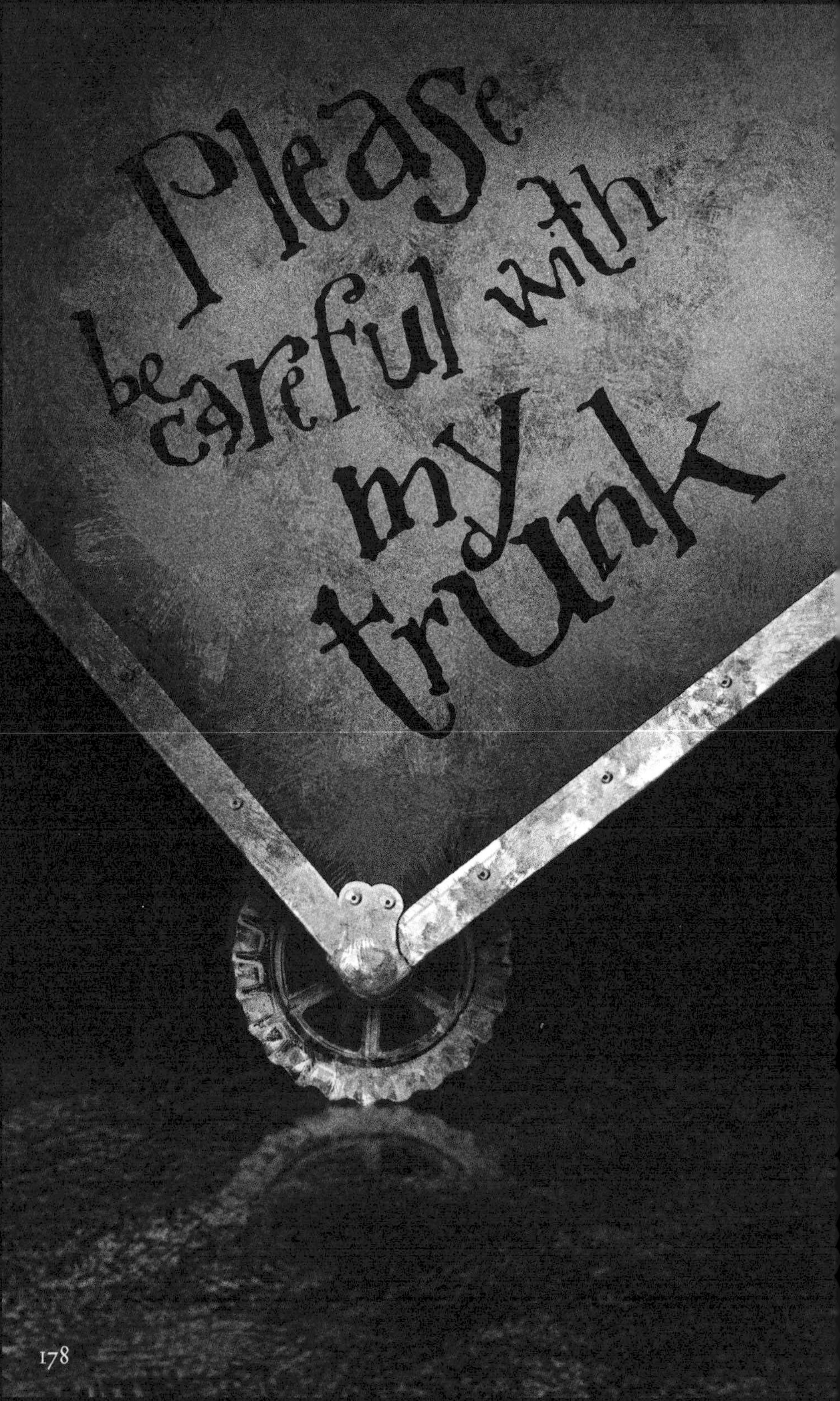
Please
be careful with
my
trunk

"Please be careful with my trunk. It has traveled all the way from London," the tall man said with dignity, waving several doormen in fine silk jackets out of his way. "Take it straight to my room."

The small man said nothing. He followed along, stopping every now and then to sniff the roses along the sidewalk. The door to the hotel was held open. All the other hotel guests gathered around and stared.

"That's Monsieur Largo," whispered a woman to her child, pointing to the tall man. "Saw him when I was your age. He put on the best fireworks display I've ever seen."

From out of the Rolls-Royce came a large trunk. Two iron wheels flipped out of the side as soon as it was tipped on its end. Handles appeared as if by magic, and the doorman pulled as hard as he could.

"It feels like there is a body inside," he joked as he followed the small man to the door.

"There is," the man replied with a short, sharp laugh. He walked through the door and into the grand lobby. "Monsieur Largo, please would you wait for me," he wheezed.

"Claude." The tall man turned to him. "Not in front of my audience."

"But—" Claude would have gone on, but Monsieur Largo's raised (and neatly trimmed) eyebrow bid him to stop.

"Is my suite ready?" Largo bellowed. He stood several feet from the front desk that seemed too small for the vast, marble-columned hotel lobby. "I am Largo, pyrotechnic extraordinaire—ready to perform at your auction."

A man with a long mustache scuttled over to him and bowed. He looked nervously at the trunk that was now rolling toward him.

"Your keys, Monsieur Largo," he managed to say just as Largo snatched them from his hand and took off after his trunk with the smaller man in tow. "The usual: Suite Bonaparte," the manager called out.

Largo nodded without looking back and then stopped after just six paces.

His eyes were drawn to the window of the jewelry store in the corner of the hotel lobby. There, in a glass case, was the largest diamond he had ever seen. It shone in the reflected light of the chandeliers and looked as though it cast its own reflection across the marble floors.

He smiled at the guards who stood at each side of the case and noted their piercing expressions.

Claude scurried closer to his master.

"**The Great Mogul Diamond . . . is it really true?**" whispered Claude.

"Before our very eyes," Largo said greedily and then thought for a moment. With a click of his heels he turned and faced the valet eye-to-eye. "Do you have a reservation for a Muzz Kitty Elliott?" he asked. The man scanned the list in his hand and then nodded. "Good," said Largo with a smile. "Claude, Bonaparte cannot be kept waiting."

• • •

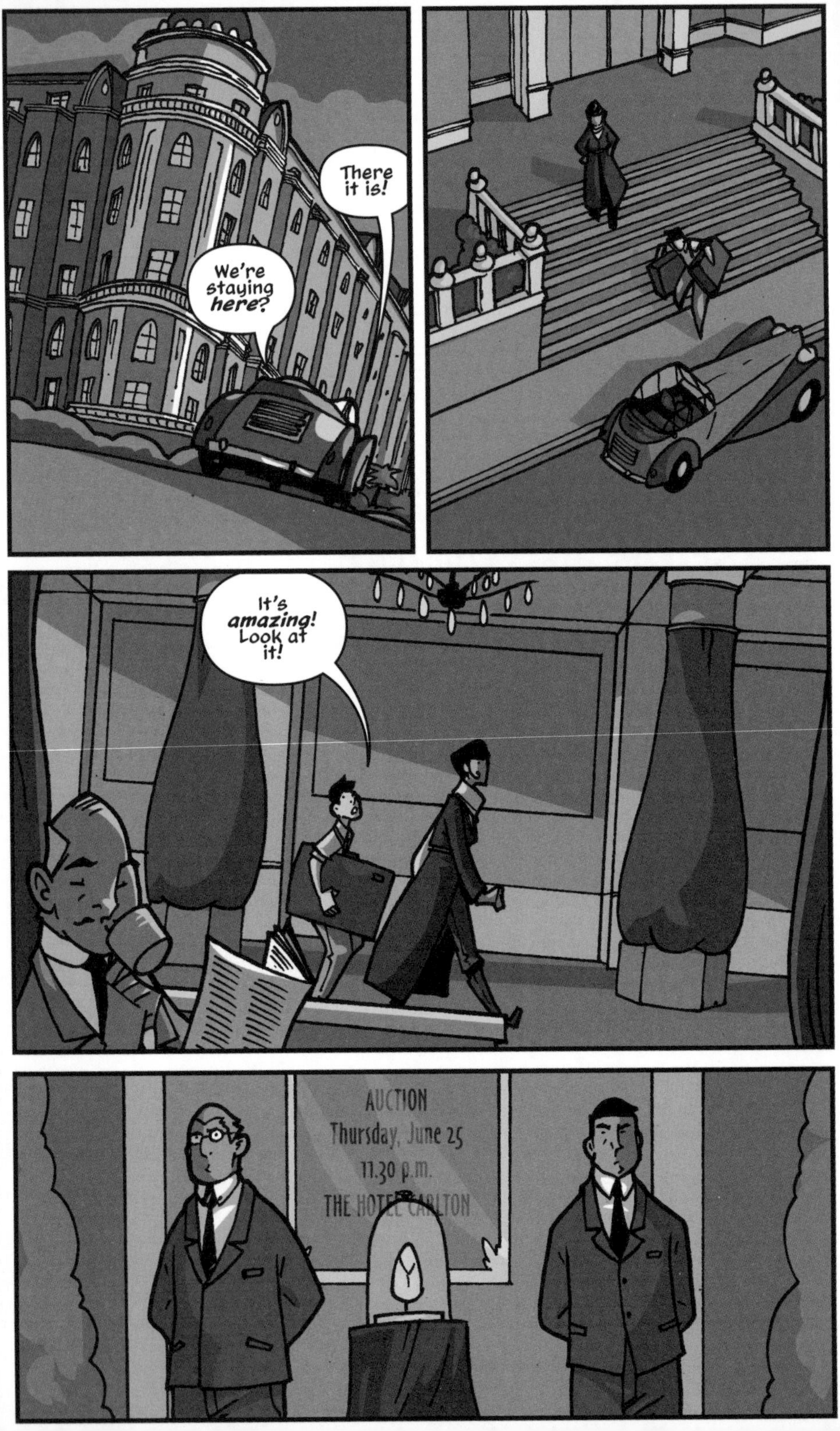
There it is!
We're staying here?
It's amazing! Look at it!
AUCTION
Thursday, June 25
11.30 p.m.
THE HOTEL CARLTON

"The auction is tomorrow. Do you think someone will buy it?" Erik asked, looking on with wide eyes.

"I'm sure someone will. The hotel is full—no doubt with guests who will attend the auction. We only just got rooms. I wired ahead before we left London," Dorcas Potts replied.

The valet approached them. "Can I help you?" he asked, looking like he had stepped in something toxic.

"Dorcas Potts—Potts and Co.—the TIMES," Dorcas Potts said loudly.

"The madame journalist?" he asked. Dorcas Potts nodded. "Here to cover the sale of the Great Mogul Diamond?"

"The same," Dorcas Potts replied. "And this is Erik; he's my assistant." Erik nodded. "Our rooms?"

The man fumbled in his pockets, searching for the keys. "I am afraid that due to the auction, these might not be the rooms you expected. They have a spectacular view, and I am told the air is very good."

The valet smiled and stepped away before she could ask any questions. Dorcas Potts looked at the fob that was tied to one of the keys with a piece of string.

"Room 739 — floor 7,"

she read aloud. Then, calling
after the valet, she asked, "Has
Muzz Kitty Elliott checked in yet?"

He fluttered back toward her and smiled. "Muzz Elliott
has not yet arrived. The train is late. You are the second
person to ask about her today. Is she . . . famous?"
he asked.

"Extremely—a writer of distinction," Dorcas Potts said, pushing Erik toward the elevator. She tossed the car key to the manager. "Here—take my Bugatti and clean it for me. That's a good chap."

The hotel manager shuddered with disdain.

• • •

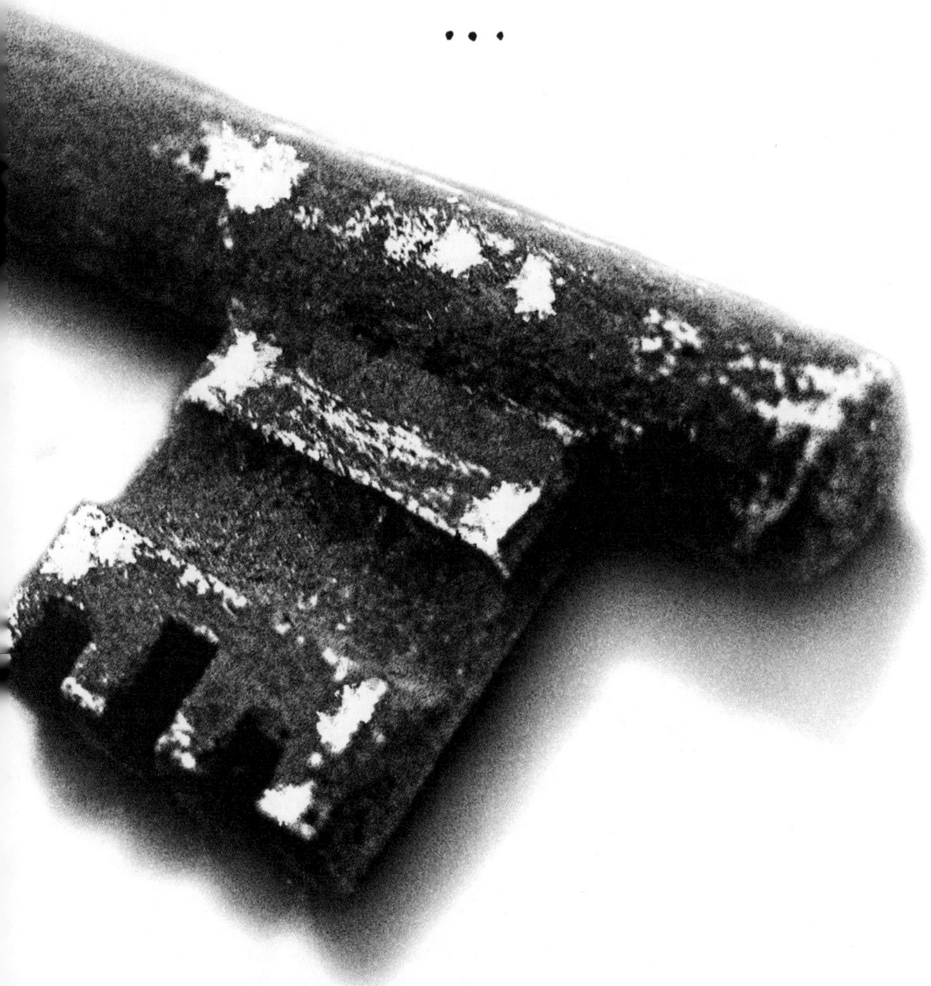

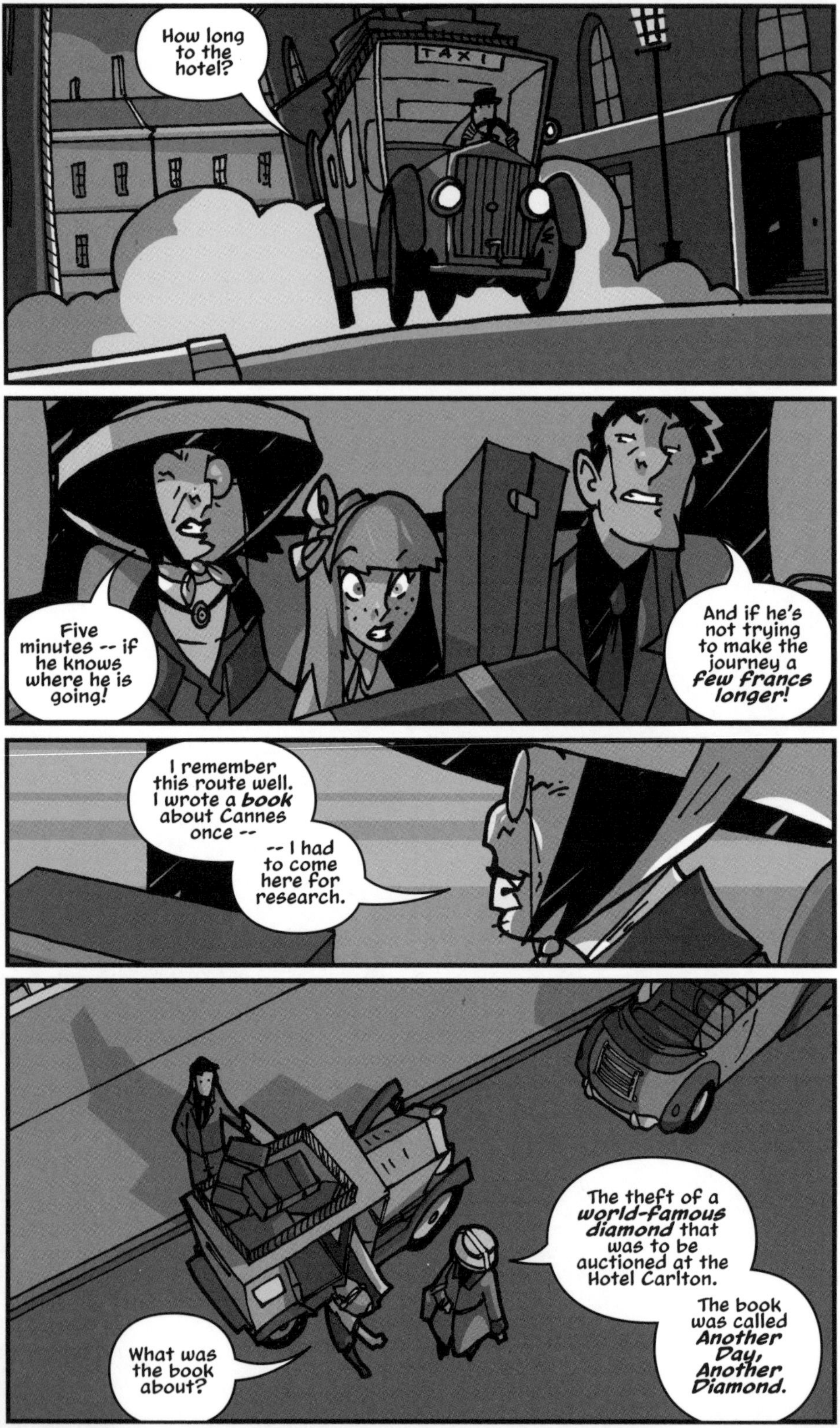
How long to the hotel?
Five minutes -- if he knows where he is going!
And if he's not trying to make the journey a *few francs longer*!
I remember this route well. I wrote a *book* about Cannes once --
-- I had to come here for research.
What was the book about?
The theft of a *world-famous diamond* that was to be auctioned at the Hotel Carlton.
The book was called *Another Day, Another Diamond*.

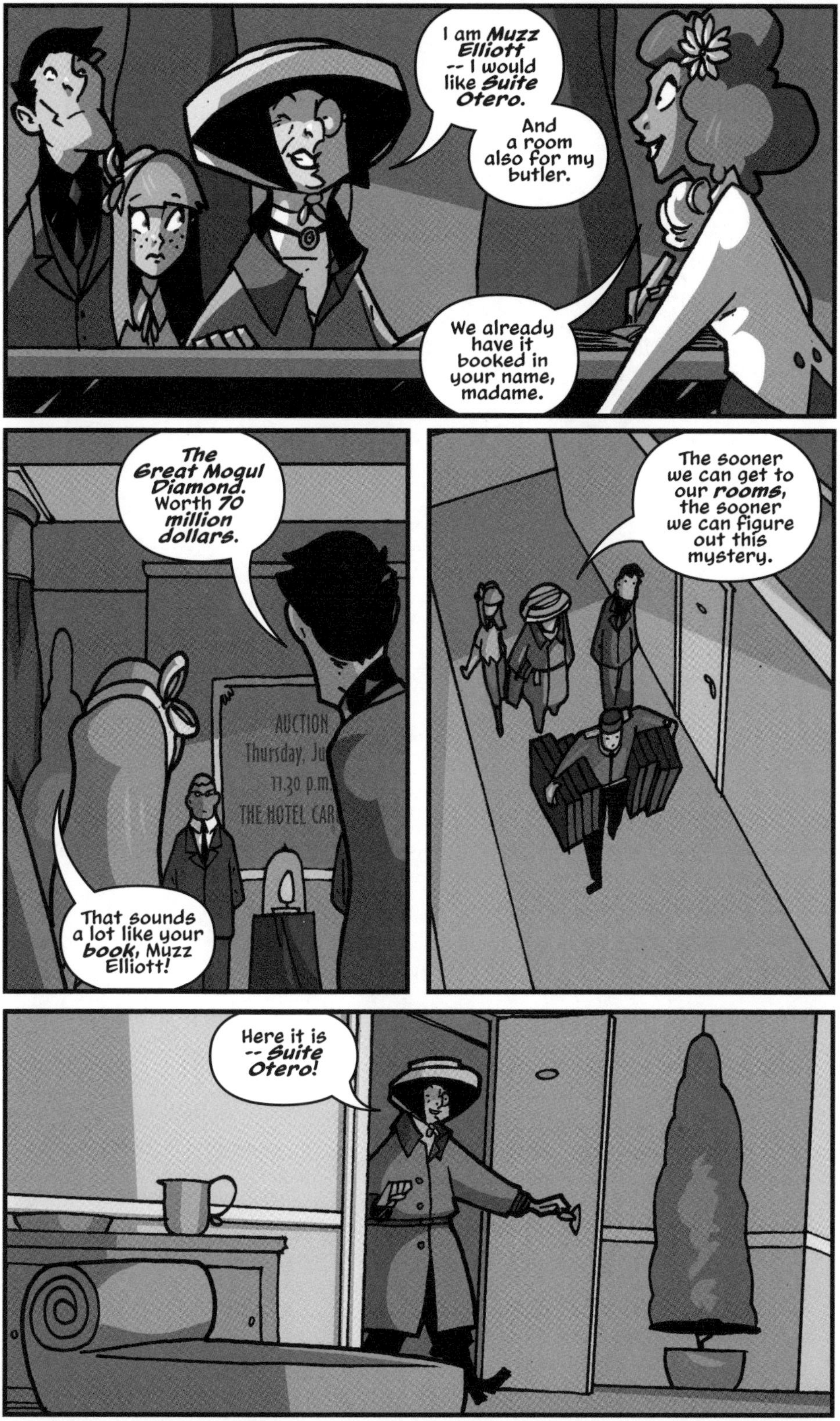

I am Muzz Elliott -- I would like Suite Otero.
And a room also for my butler.
We already have it booked in your name, madame.
The Great Mogul Diamond. Worth 70 million dollars.
AUCTION Thursday, Ju
11.30 p.m.
THE HOTEL CAR
That sounds a lot like your book, Muzz Elliott!
The sooner we can get to our rooms, the sooner we can figure out this mystery.
Here it is -- Suite Otero!

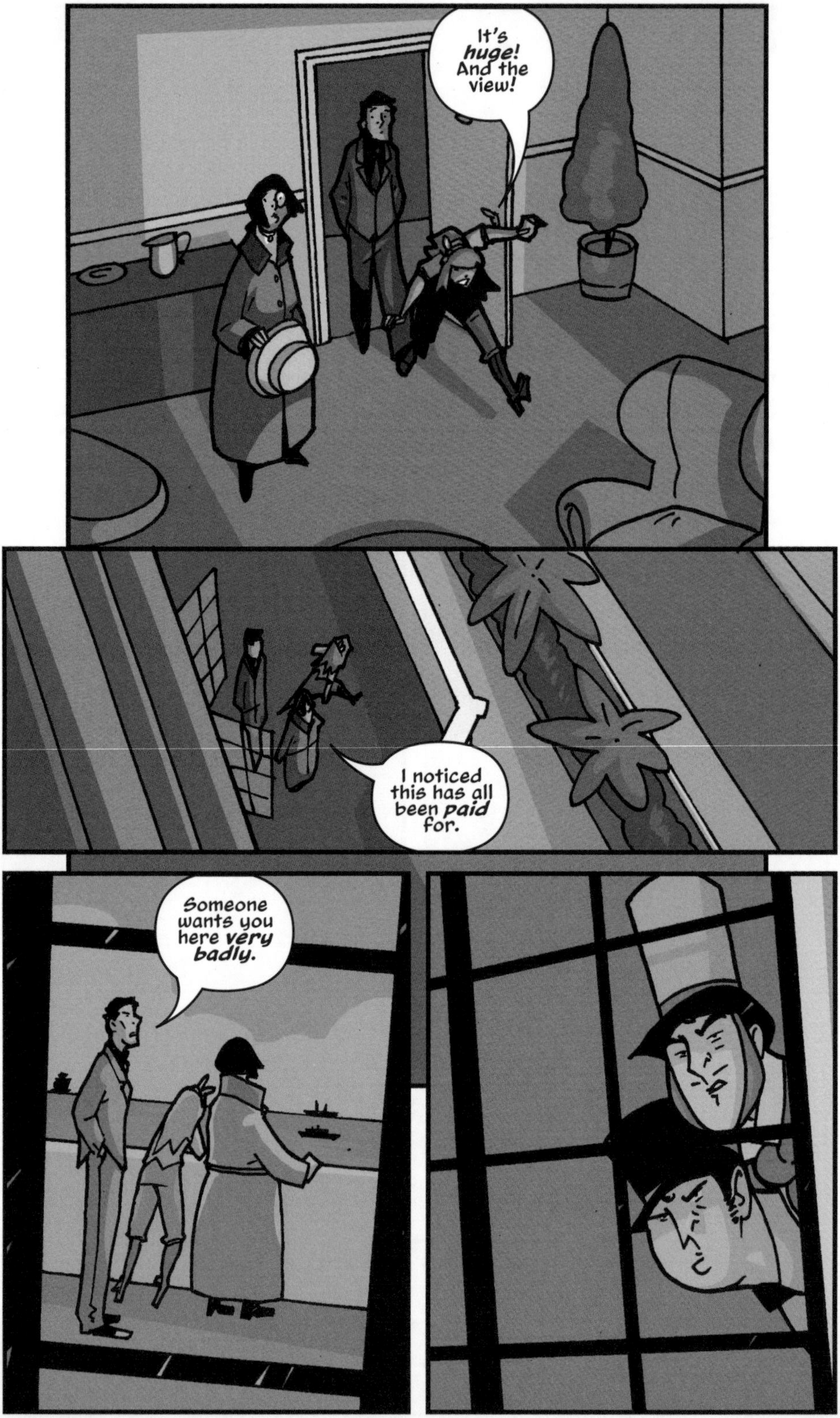
It's *huge!* And the view!
I noticed this has all been *paid* for.
Someone wants you here *very badly.*

In Suite Bonaparte, the trunk began to move.

"Don't you think it is dangerous having Muzz Elliott so near?" Claude asked, wringing his hands.

"Under our noses is better; this way we can watch her," Largo replied. He kicked the trunk with the heel of his boot. "It has taken much thought to get us here, my dear Claude."

"And the ransom note—how shall it be delivered?" asked Claude.

Largo opened the two large doors that led to the balcony. He stepped outside for a moment, then came back into the room.

"Adjoining balconies," he explained. "When they are at dinner, you will break into Muzz Elliott's room and leave the note for her to see."

"Do you think she will do what we want?"

"We have kidnapped one of the girls she chose as her own daughter—of course she will." Largo kicked the trunk again.

Inside the trunk, Sadie was now fully awake. The effects of the drugged cocoa had worn off slowly, and it had taken her a long time to figure out where she was. Now she listened hard to the muffled conversation outside the trunk.

"But what if she doesn't—what will you do?" Claude asked.

"Quite simple. As part of my performance tomorrow night, I will explode the trunk at the end of the Carlton Pier. Muzz Elliott will not be the only one who goes to pieces," he said with a laugh.

Sadie swallowed hard. She had to escape. Suddenly she saw in her mind the image of her sister trapped in a sarcophagus, dangling from the ceiling of the tunnel below Lord Gervez's house. She remembered how frightened she had been as she watched the tunnel fill with water, thanks to the trap set by the villains Potemkin and Straker.

Saskia, too, had been frightened, but Sadie remembered how her sister had grown suddenly calm and discovered the way to free them all from the trap. Saskia said that she asked Madame Raphael and the Companion what to do, and then she had discovered the way out. And on the train, Saskia had prayed to the Companion, and the train didn't crash. Sadie had been kidnapped, but at least she was still alive. And while she was alive, there was still hope of escape.

Sadie took a deep breath and prayed, "Um, hello? Madame Raphael? It's Sadie Dopple—remember, I saw you once at Spaniards House?" She stopped, thinking this was all very foolish, but something urged her to go on. "If you can ask the Companion to show me how to get out of here, I'd really appreciate it. Thanks . . ."

There was silence. No one answered. But strangely, Sadie felt a sense of calm creep over her.

• • •

Outside Suite Otero, Erik rapped on the door and called out. "Sadie! Saskia! Are you in there?"

He heard the lock slide back, and Saskia opened the door and pulled him inside. Dorcas Potts followed. Muzz Elliott and Max Taranis were standing by the window.

"You made it! I'm so glad you're both here!" Saskia blurted, hugging Erik.

"The French Mafia tried to kill us. Kept us in a castle. Madame R—" Erik stopped himself and gulped. "Tell you later," he mumbled to Saskia. Then he looked around the room. "Where's Sadie?"

"She's been kidnapped," Saskia said forlornly. "They took her from the train."

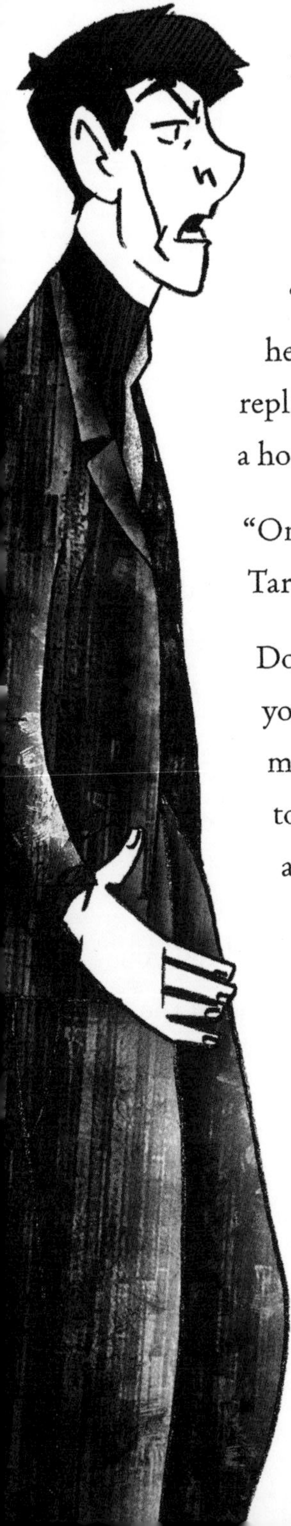

Max Taranis made his way to Dorcas Potts and stuck out his hand. "Dorcas Potts, journalist and detective," he said. "I have heard so much about you."

"Max Taranis, cop and buffoon . . . I have heard so much about you," Dorcas Potts replied, eyeing the man warily. "I take it this isn't a holiday visit?"

"On the case, Miss Potts, on the case," Inspector Taranis answered her.

Dorcas Potts turned to Muzz Elliott. "When you told me about your problem and asked me to make inquiries, I thought you might be planning to come down here on your own, Muzz Elliott, and I wasn't going to let you do it. But I didn't suspect you'd be leaving that evening. It's a good thing the girls phoned Erik."

"I have been alone for a long time and have grown used to settling matters on my own. But I am glad you came."

Dorcas Potts looked sideways at the inspector and said, "Do you still need me now that you have the famous Max Taranis?"

"It is always a pleasure to have a friend nearby," Muzz Elliott said, nodding toward Dorcas Potts. "Mr. Taranis thought I was the offender until mysterious circumstances on the train confirmed all the conversations he had been listening to on my telephone."

"Still snooping?" Dorcas Potts asked Max Taranis with a cold stare.

"Only doing my job, Miss Potts. Just like you." His left eye twitched. "And if you will excuse me, I have a few inquiries to make. I take it you won't interfere in what I am doing?"

"I never dabble in incompetence, Inspector," Dorcas Potts parried.

Max Taranis seemed at a loss for a comeback; his mouth fell open. He gulped the air like a fish, smiled at Muzz Elliott, and left the room.

"So it's blackmail and now kidnapping?" Dorcas Potts asked. Muzz Elliott nodded. "Did the kidnappers leave a note?"

"Max Taranis took it—we never read it," Saskia answered.

"It said we had to check into this room," said Muzz Elliott. "When we arrived, it was already in my name and everything had been paid for—in cash—far in excess of what we would ever spend."

Erik studied the room. Everything seemed to be in its place. Two bedrooms went off from the parlor. The bathroom was down the corridor, and French windows led to the balcony. The scent of gardenia flowers hung in the air. It was the perfume Muzz Elliott always wore.

"Why here? why now?"

Dorcas Potts wondered out loud.

"It is the best hotel in France," Muzz Elliott replied.

"There's something more than that."

"Much more," Muzz Elliott said. "The mysterious events on the train that I spoke of—they were just as I wrote in my book MURDER TRAIN. It is like they are trying to re-create the plot to every book I have written. Even this hotel and the Great Mogul Diamond. I wrote about them all. It is a clever trick—to use my own mind and inventions against me."

As Muzz Elliott explained to Dorcas Potts all that had happened, Erik beckoned to Saskia. He was itching to speak to her alone. The two quietly maneuvered to the doors of the balcony. They were soon outside, looking down on the palm trees of the Boulevard de la Croisette and the merry-go-rounds and market stalls under their canopy.

"I saw her—Madame Raphael, I mean," Erik said sheepishly.

"Did you?" Saskia looked at him in surprise.

Erik nodded, still looking down. "I think she saved my life. I didn't think we would get away from the Mafia, but somehow we escaped—it was just as she said."

Saskia nodded. "I know what you mean. It was that way for me, too, back in the tunnels. . . ." Both of them were quiet for a while, thinking of how their lives had been spared.

"She said something else strange," continued Erik after a while. "She said the Man of Good-Bye Friday was waiting for me."

Saskia gasped. "She said that to Sadie and me too—the night we saved Lord Gervez and discovered what had happened to all his treasure!"

"She did?" said Erik, brightening. "I was hoping you would know what she meant."

Saskia looked glum. "I can't work it out either. It's her way to talk in riddles. But I have a feeling we'll know what she meant when the time comes."

A warm sea breeze blew around them. "What happened to Sadie?" Erik asked.

"We were drugged, and then two men snatched her from the compartment of the train. But I have a feeling she is nearby."

Erik turned to Saskia.

"We have to find her".

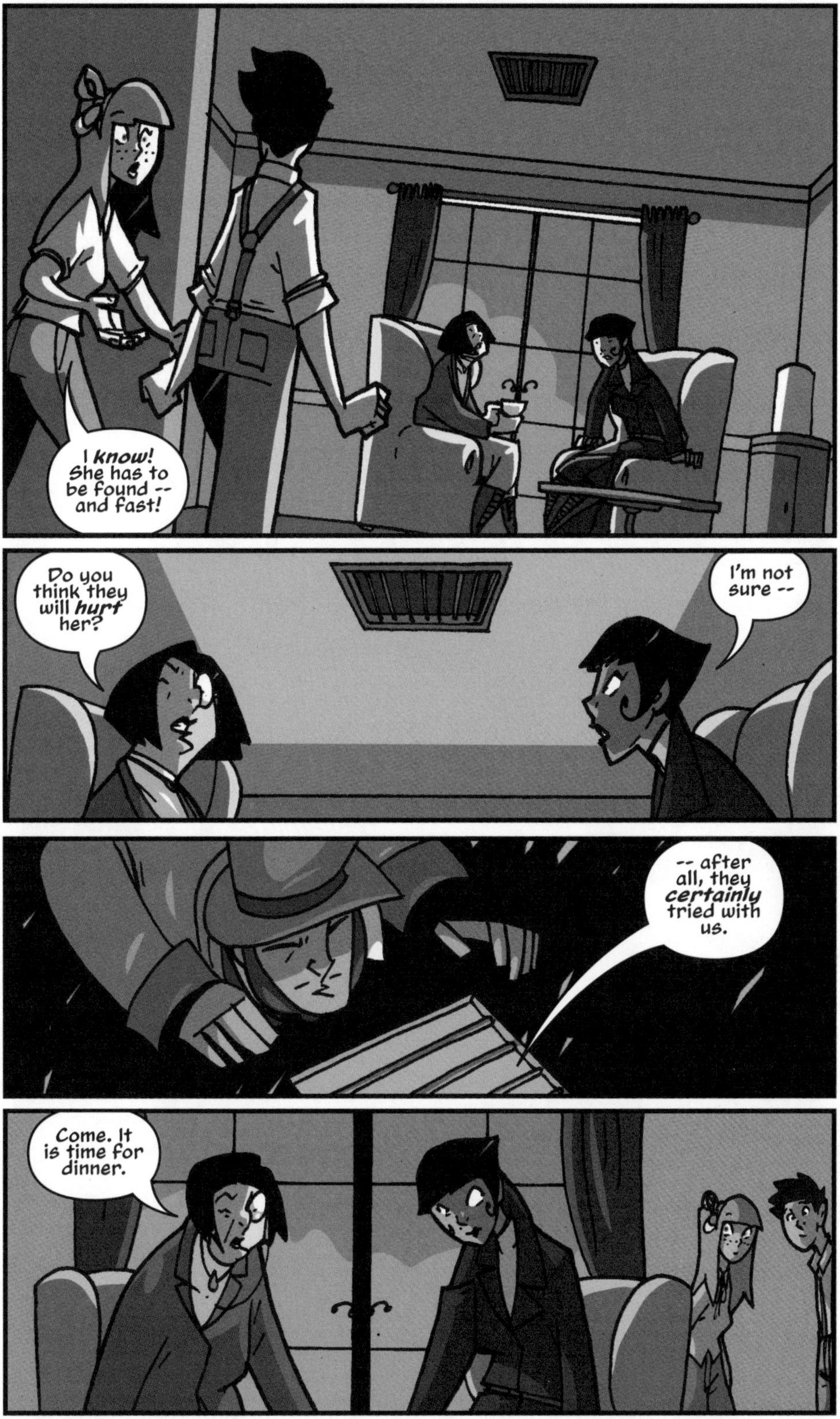
I *know*! She has to be found -- and fast!
Do you think they will *hurt* her?
I'm not sure --
-- after all, they *certainly* tried with us.
Come. It is time for dinner.

. . .

Claude inched along the balcony connecting Suite Bonaparte
with Suite Otero. As soon as he heard the door to Suite
Otero click shut, he stepped over to the French windows
and pulled out a small tool, which he jiggled in the lock.
In a few moments, the door swung open, and he slipped
into the room. Glancing quickly from side to side, he hurried
to a nearby table and placed a single sheet of paper on it.

Steal the Great Mogul Diamond. Bring it to the tower of the Château de la Castre by midnight tomorrow, or you'll never see Sadie Dopple again.

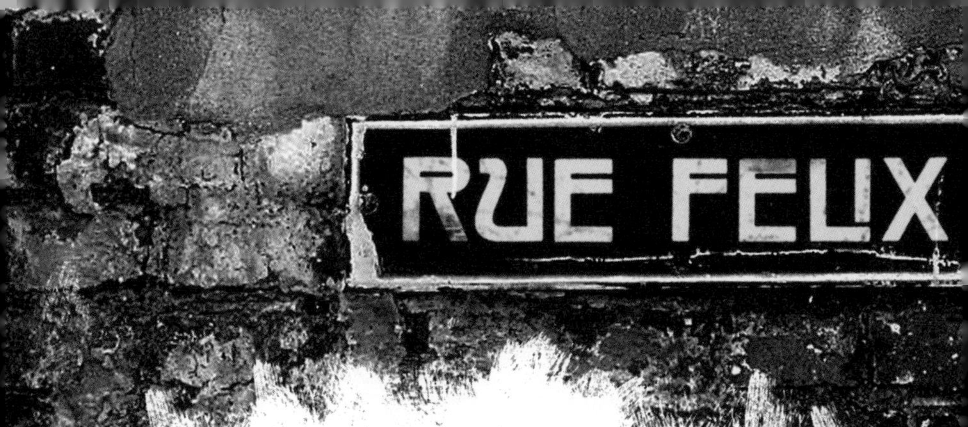
RUE FELIX

Chapter Eleven

A Chance Encounter

IT HAD BEEN a long, fitful night in Suite Otero, and Saskia was glad it was finally morning. Muzz Elliott had not said a word apart from moaning in her sleep. She had dressed, paced the balcony, and sat at her desk looking into the mirror on the wall as if searching for an answer. Finally, after an hour, she had telephoned Dorcas Potts and asked her and Erik to meet them at Café Poet on Rue Felix at nine thirty.

Saskia followed her along the Boulevard de la Croisette. Muzz Elliott walked briskly, dodging the cracks in the pavement. She seemed distracted, and Saskia noticed that she kept looking behind her with every other step.

“Is it far?” Saskia asked as they turned off the boulevard and onto the busy Rue Felix, dodging taxis and impromptu tables of local card players that hugged the shadows beneath the trees.

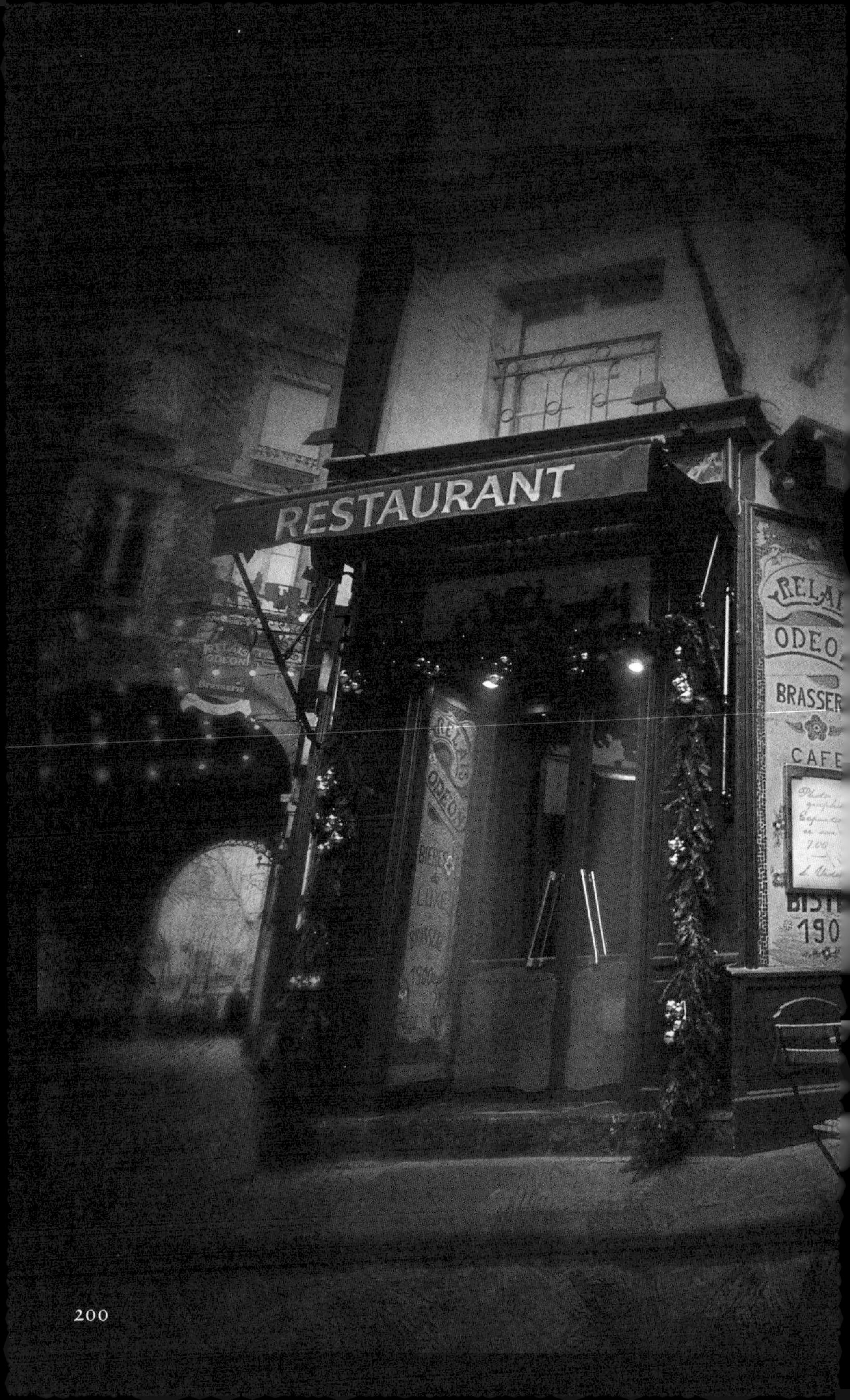
RESTAURANT
CAFE

Muzz Elliott either did not hear or chose not to reply. Her gaze was now fixed on the castle that towered over the painted houses and terra-cotta roofs of the old town.

"Did you say something?" she asked as they drew near a small café with a low awning that shaded four tables. "Café Poet—at last." She slumped into a chair at a table for two and looked around her. "You and Erik could sit inside if you wanted—I'm sure you two have a lot to catch up on?"

It was not a question that needed to be answered. Saskia knew Muzz Elliott wanted to talk privately with Dorcas Potts.

"Through there?" She pointed to the other side of the café in a dark, narrow street shaded permanently from the sun.

"It would be nice," Muzz Elliott said with a half smile. "There are shops if you want to explore, but be careful. We don't know who is watching us."

Saskia smiled in return.

Erik and Dorcas Potts arrived a few minutes later.

Saskia beckoned Erik over to her. "Muzz Elliott wants to talk with Dorcas Potts alone," she explained in a whisper. "I think she got another letter. I heard her talking in her sleep."

"A ransom?" asked Erik.

Saskia said nothing. She was staring at a small, rotund man walking along the narrow alleyway toward them. He was neatly dressed in a small top hat and pin-striped trousers. He wove in and out of the people who crowded the street.

"It's him," she said in a whisper, glancing at Muzz Elliott, who was deep in conversation with Dorcas Potts.

"Who?" Erik asked. He looked around at the sea of people that pushed back and forth like a human tide as they hurried to the marketplace.

"The steward from the ROTHSCHILD EXPRESS— the man who drugged us."

Saskia dived into the throng of people that crowded the narrow street. Erik checked the café tables.

Muzz Elliott and Dorcas Potts were talking closely. He hesitated and then gave chase. Saskia was somewhere ahead in the crowd. He barged his way through artists and street vendors selling fish and warm bread, trying to find her.

The alley turned. A shaft of bright sunlight burst across the cobbled street, and Erik caught a glimpse of Saskia as the crowd parted for a moment.

 "Saskia!" he shouted.

Far ahead, the man in the top hat stopped and looked around. Then he carried on walking, glancing sideways at his reflection in the glistening shop windows. Saskia stepped from a doorway and waved Erik toward her.

"That's him," Saskia said as Erik got nearer. "The man from the train."

Erik watched the small top hat bob up and down.

"We should follow him—he might lead us to Sadie," Erik said. He gripped her hand and dragged her through the street.

They kept up a brisk pace, scouring every inch of the street, until they were both panting for breath. "We've lost him," said Saskia sadly.

The bla of a car horn

ring

behind them

made Erik turn around.

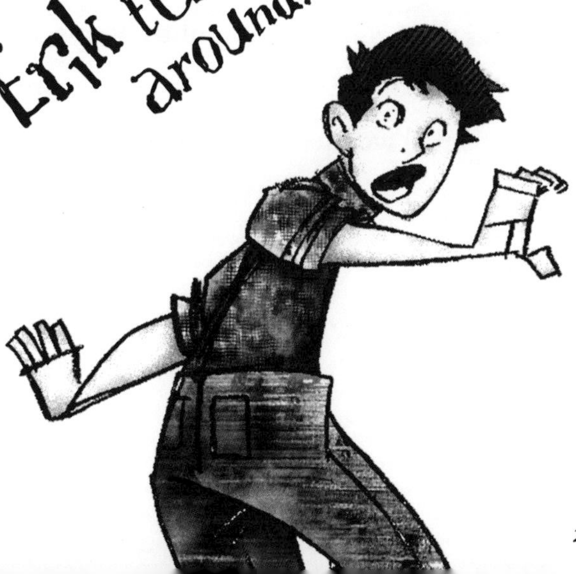

It was then that he saw the man. He was walking the way they had just run.

"It's him—he's turned back!" Erik said. "He must be going for the harbor."

"Sadie could be there," Saskia said. They both began to run.

The short Frenchman was crossing the boulevard. He minced across the cobbles. Cars screeched to a halt to avoid hitting him. Then he disappeared down a flight of steps by a large brass telescope on the harborside.

"Did you see where he went?" Saskia asked.

"It's the boat dock—we went there this morning before we came to the café," Erik said.

Just as they got to the top of the steps, they heard the sound of a boat engine. Looking over the harbor wall, they saw a small wooden steamboat put out from the wharf. On the steamboat was the man. He looked out to sea, not realizing he was being watched.

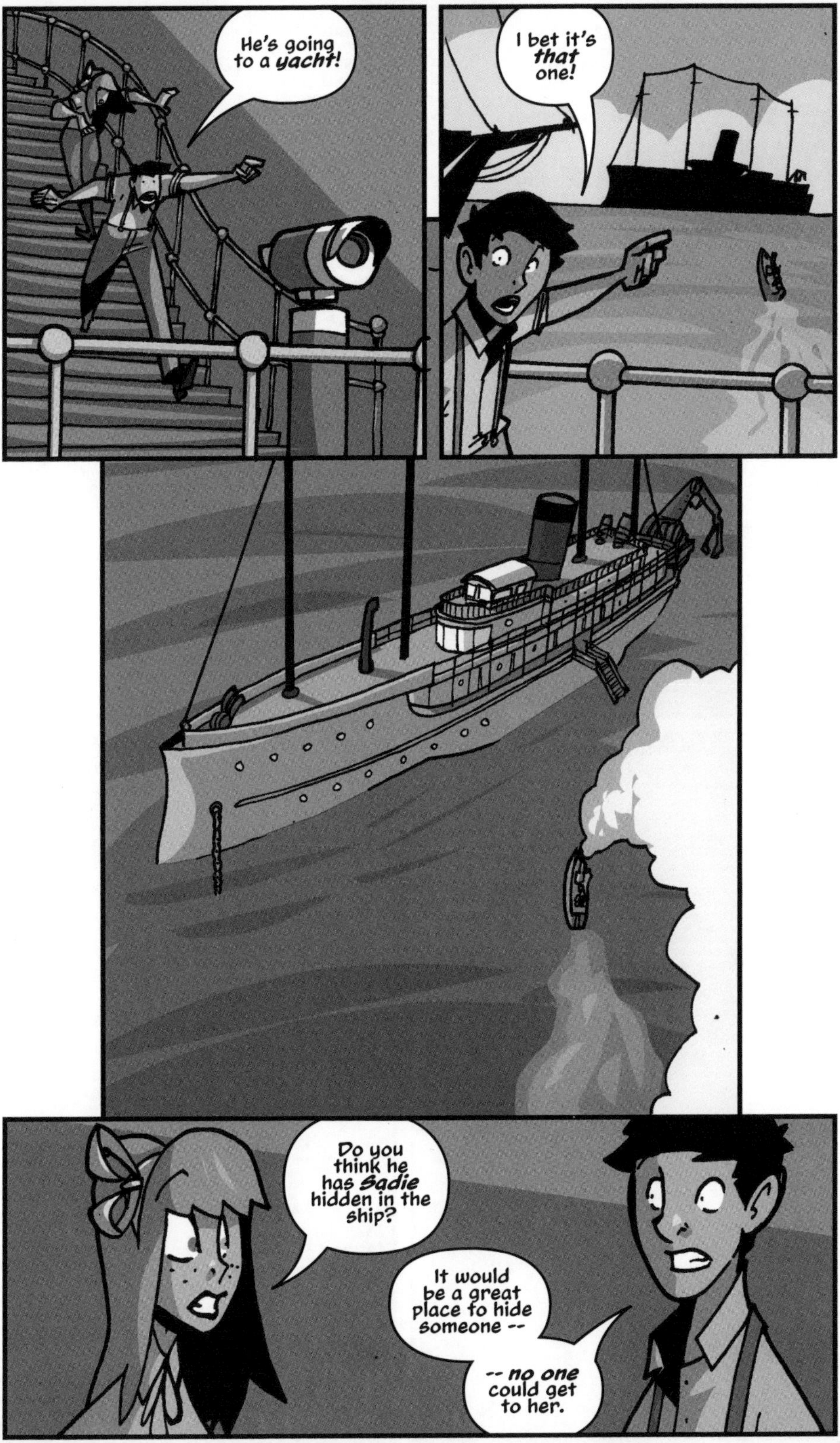
He's going to a *yacht*!
I bet it's *that* one!
Do you think he has *Sadie* hidden in the ship?
It would be a great place to hide someone --
-- *no one* could get to her.

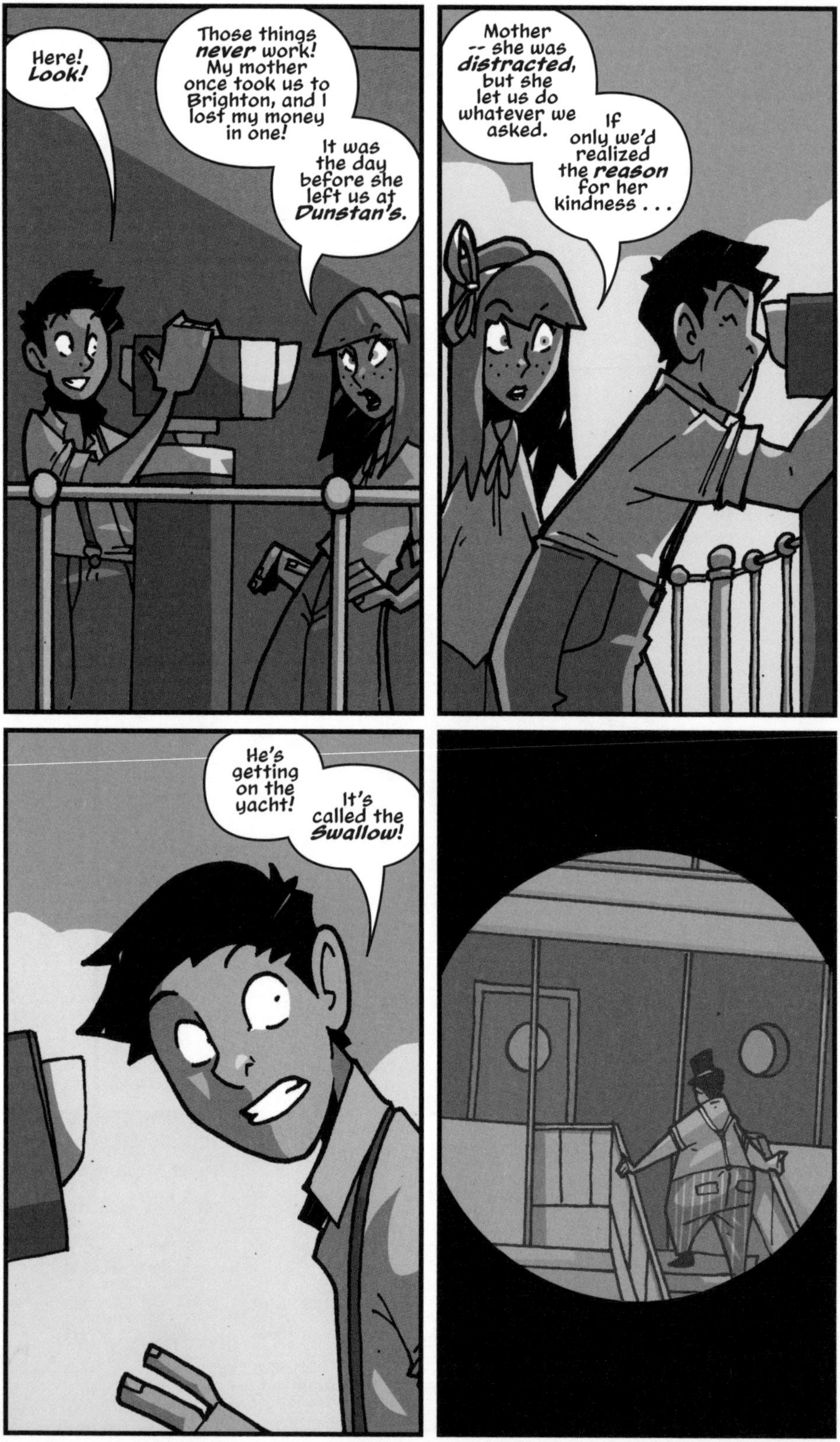
Here! Look!
Those things never work! My mother once took us to Brighton, and I lost my money in one!
It was the day before she left us at Dunstan's.
Mother -- she was distracted, but she let us do whatever we asked.
If only we'd realized the reason for her kindness . . .
He's getting on the yacht!
It's called the Swallow!

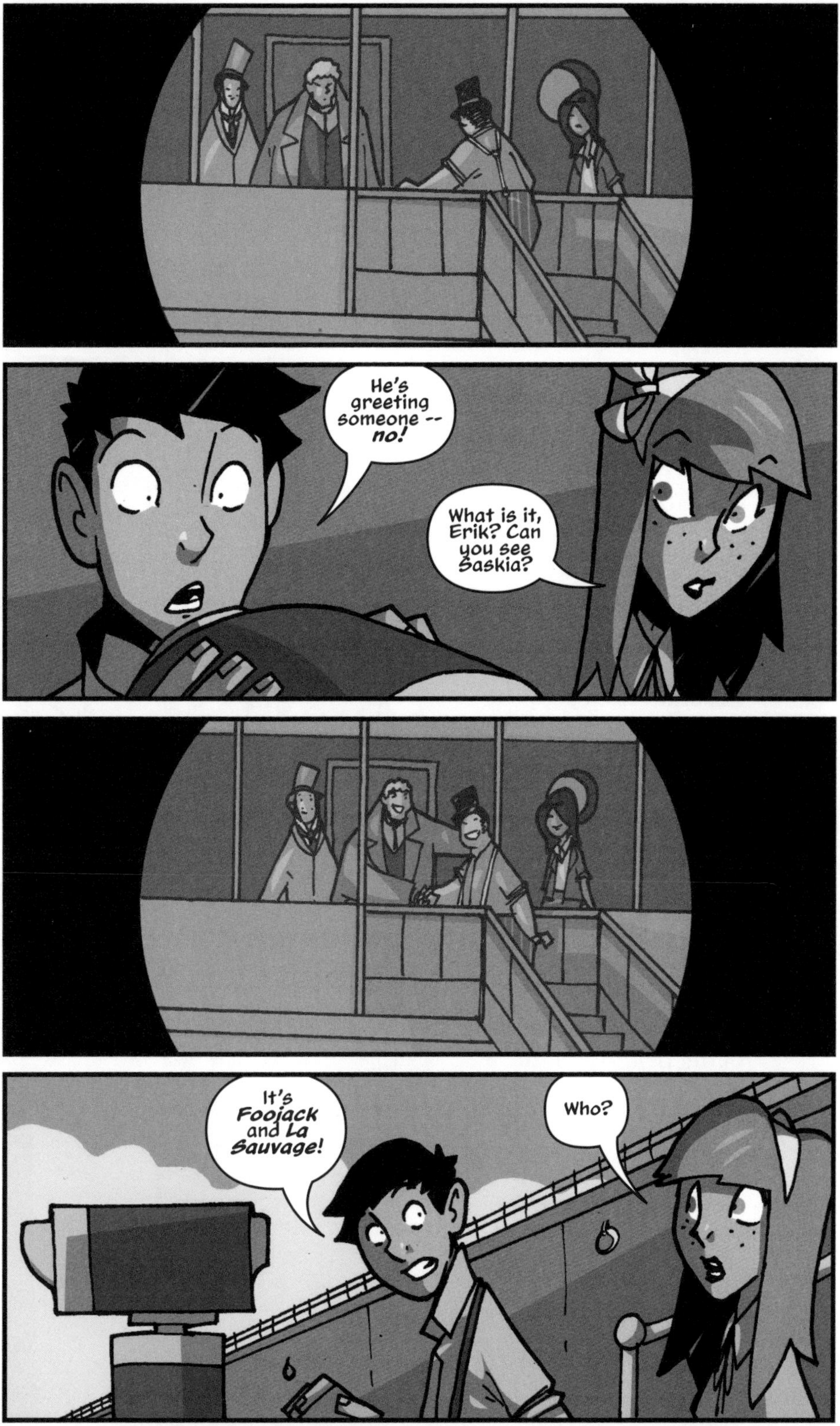
He's greeting someone -- no!
What is it, Erik? Can you see Saskia?
It's Foojack and La Sauvage!
Who?

"It's the man and the woman from the château."

It was unmistakably them. The sight twisted Erik's stomach as he looked through the long lens of the telescope. Then there was a sudden darkness as the shutter closed, the time allotted by the quarter franc over.

"So they are the ones who have Sadie," Saskia said. The thought of her sister being held by Mafia members sent her into a panic. "We have to tell Muzz Elliott— NOW!" she screamed as she ran off.

They're part of Le Sentier Rouge— the Red Way. The Mafia."

• • •

Dorcas Potts stared at Muzz Elliott across the empty coffee cups that littered the table. "So they want you to steal the Great Mogul Diamond?"

"Yes," Muzz Elliott replied gravely, "and I'm sure they want me to do it just as in my book ANOTHER DAY, ANOTHER DIAMOND."

"How can you know?" asked Dorcas Potts.

"Why else would someone take such pains to copy my books? Life imitating art. It's the perfect setup. The police will connect the crimes with me, even if I am not caught in the act."

Dorcas Potts looked at Muzz Elliott's lined face. She seemed a lot older than she had just a few days earlier, and Dorcas Potts could see that concern for her sister, Cicely Windylove, and her adopted daughter was weighing heavily on Muzz Elliott.

"We'll get Sadie back," Dorcas Potts resolved. "I'll steal the diamond and give them what they want."

"Too much of a risk, Dorcas Potts. You could go to prison," Muzz Elliott protested.

"So could you. Anyway, with respect to you, I am younger and far more likely to get away with it."

"But I wrote the book—I know what to do," Muzz Elliott replied with a fatigued sigh.

"Then tell me. It has to be done by midnight tomorrow, and the auction takes place tomorrow night."

"If you follow the plot of the book, they won't even know that it is gone," said Muzz Elliott smugly.

"How?" The hairs stood up on the back of Dorcas Potts's neck.

"Plotting a way of getting Sadie back without me?" Max Taranis asked from the next table.

"Inspector," Muzz Elliott faltered. "We didn't think you would be awake at this time."

Just then Saskia ran up to their table. "I've found the man from the train—the steward who poisoned us!"

"What do you mean? Who?" Dorcas Potts asked. Erik came careening behind Saskia and screeched to a halt next to the table.

"We saw the steward," Saskia said. "He is on a yacht called the SWALLOW. It is docked in the bay by the islands. Erik watched him board."

"Are you sure?" Max Taranis muttered.

"It's true, Inspector. It is him—I'm sure of it."

"And you saw all this?" he asked Erik.

"Everything," Erik replied. Then he looked at Dorcas Potts. "And Foojack and La Sauvage—they were on the ship too."

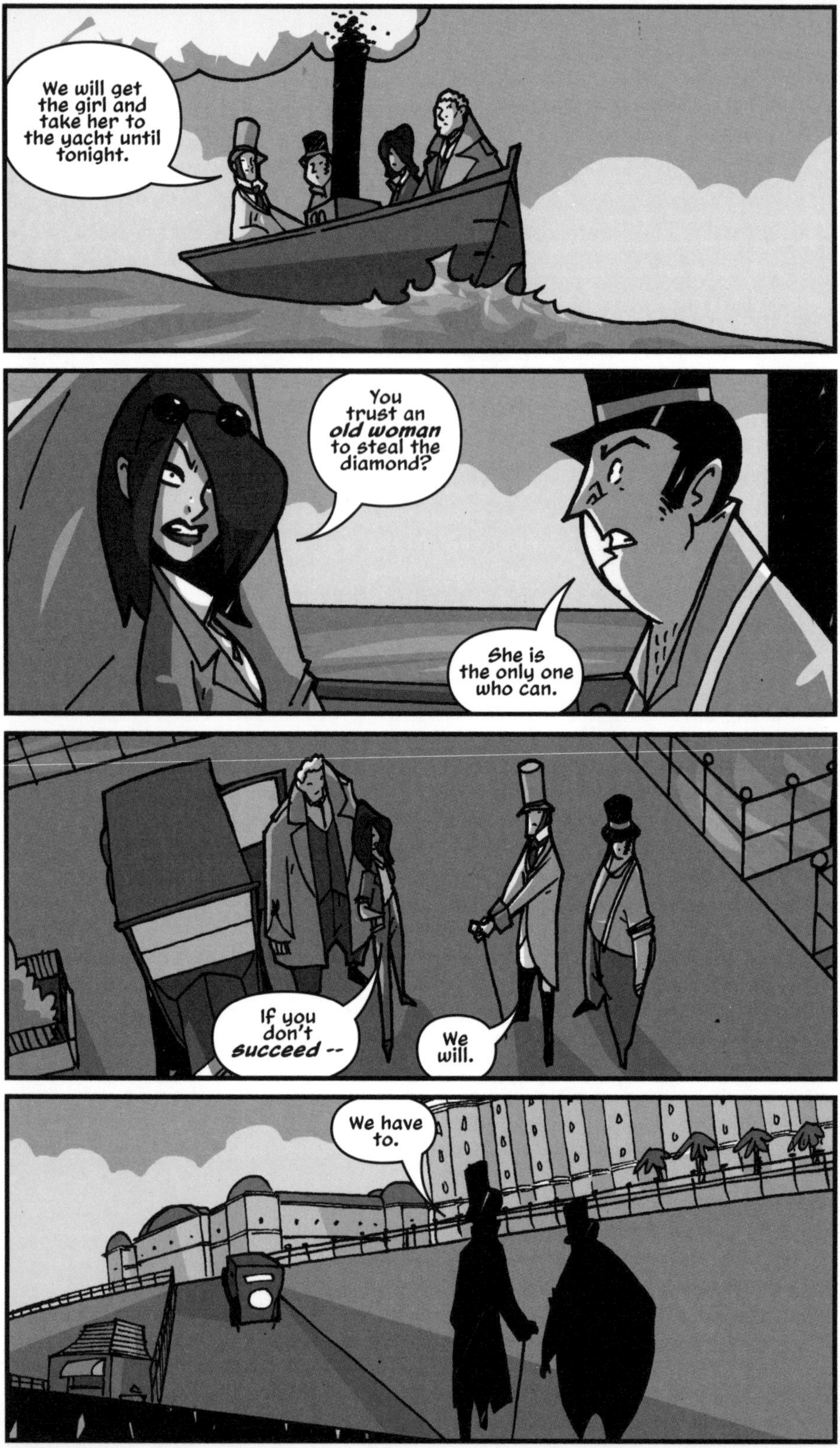
We will get the girl and take her to the yacht until tonight.
You trust an old woman to steal the diamond?
She is the only one who can.
If you don't succeed --
We will.
We have to.

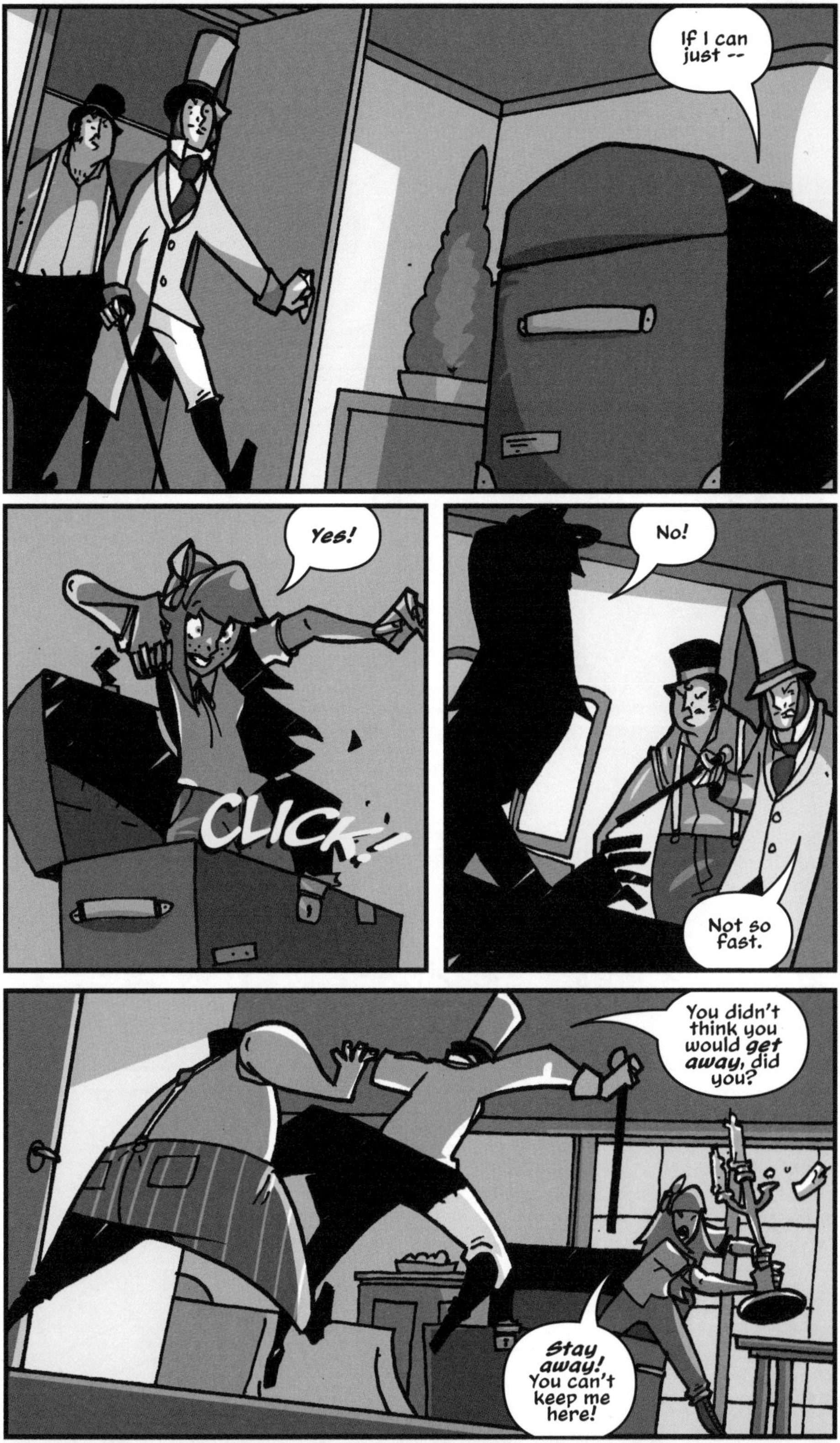
If I can just --
Yes!
CLICK!!
No!
Not so fast.
You didn't think you would get away, did you?
Stay away! You can't keep me here!

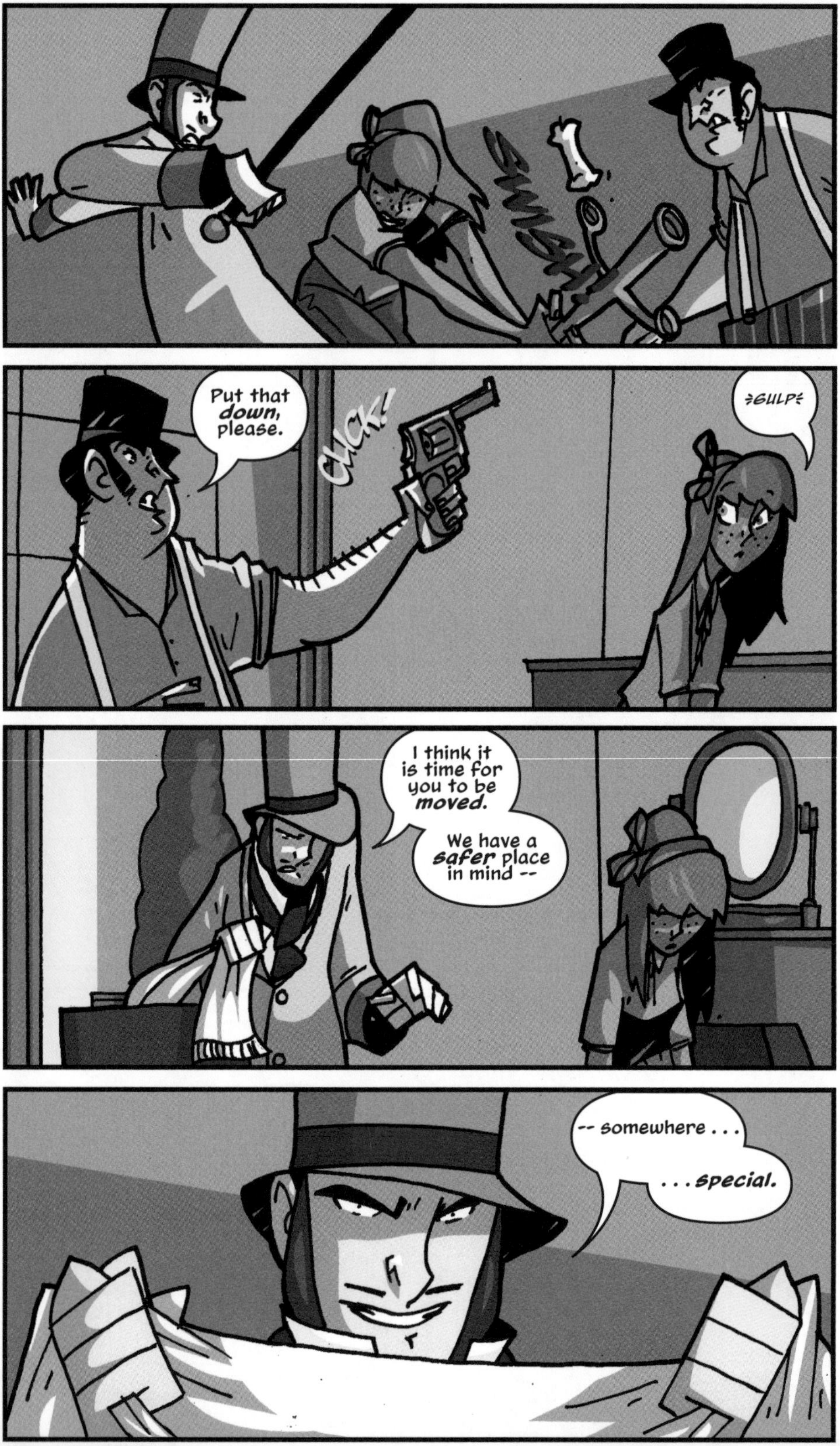
SWISH!!
Put that *down,* please.
CLICK!
GULP
I think it is time for you to be *moved.*
We have a *safer* place in mind --
-- somewhere . . .
. . . *special.*

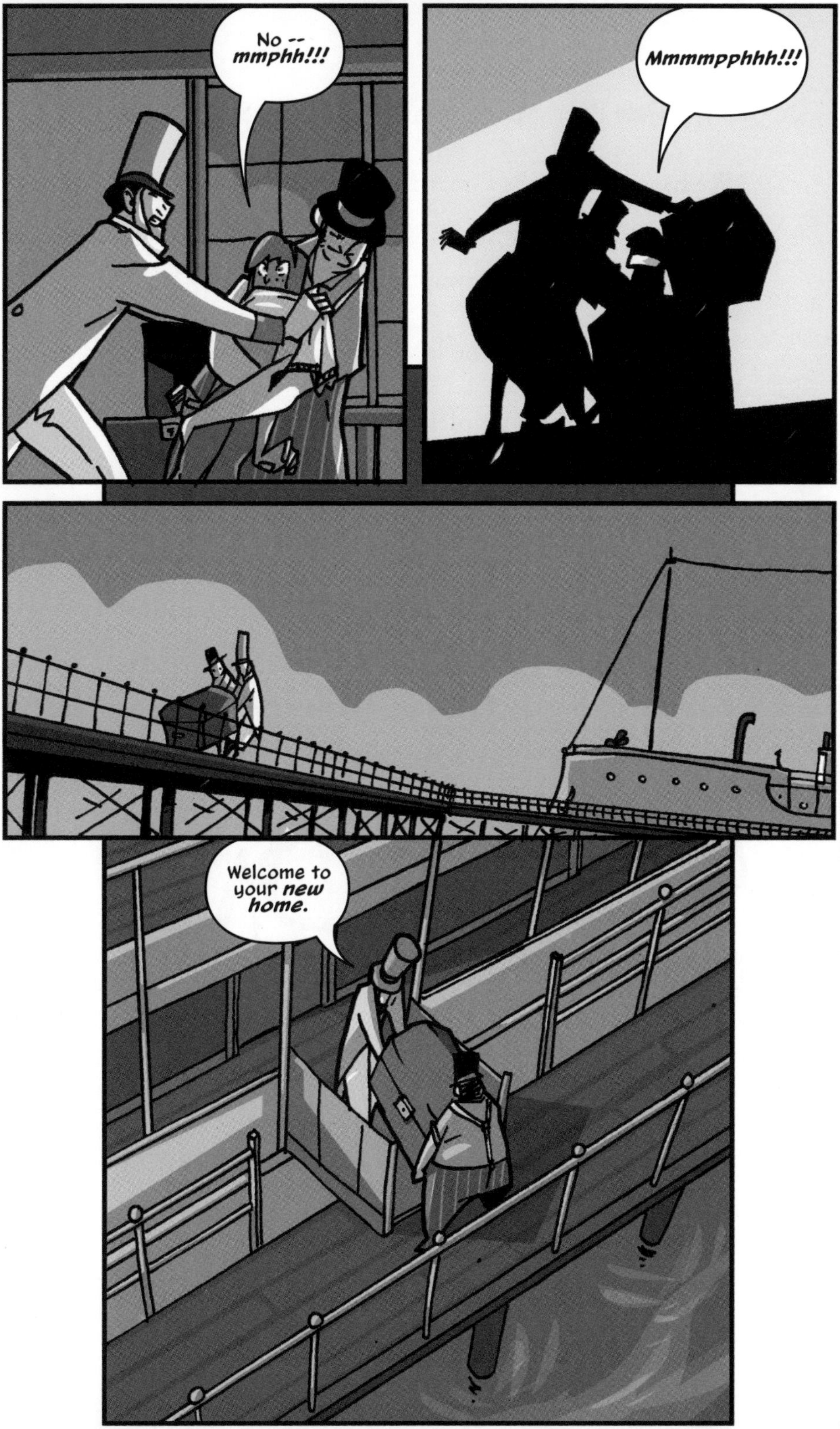
No -- *mmphh!!!*
Mmmmpphhh!!!
Welcome to your *new* *home.*

At the Café Poet, Max Taranis was eyeing Saskia sternly.

"We have to steal the Great Mogul Diamond—it's the only way to get Sadie back," Saskia said. An older couple at the next table edged away.

"But I'm an officer of the law," Max Taranis insisted.

"You won't be the first officer of the law to get involved in a crime," said Dorcas Potts.

"We're only borrowing it," added Saskia.

"We need you, Inspector," Muzz Elliott said calmly. She smiled at the man at the next table who had tipped chocolate down his white suit, then lowered her voice. "It will only work if we have someone on the inside."

 "ANOTHER DAY, ANOTHER DIAMOND?" he asked with a wink.

Muzz Elliott took a final gulp of cold coffee. "See, Saskia—he does read my books."

Chapter Twelve

Meetings and Partings

"DO YOU THINK we should do it?" Erik asked Dorcas Potts as they walked away from the Café Poet with Saskia and Muzz Elliott trailing behind.

"We are only borrowing the diamond to get Sadie back," Dorcas Potts snapped, only half listening. "We'll just snatch it from the safe and have it returned before the end of the auction."

She didn't sound convincing. Erik could tell she was thinking of other things and didn't want him to speak. He ignored the hints of her tone and carried on. "But what if we get caught?"

"Then we shall all rot in a French prison." Dorcas Potts turned and looked back down the road. There was no sign of Muzz Elliott or Saskia. "I want to check the route to the tower—you coming?" she asked.

Erik hurried to match her quick pace as she turned the corner by the Hotel Splendid and disappeared into the narrow cluster of alleyways that led to the marketplace.

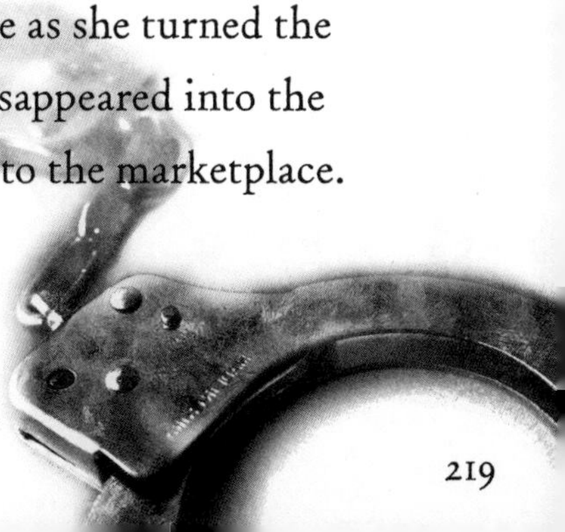

They began to climb up a steep hill that took them into an older part of town. "Is it far?" he asked.

"There," she said, pointing to the top of a tower that poked high above the surrounding terra-cotta roofs. "I need to keep time. If we have to be here by midnight, then timing is crucial."

Erik looked back through the crowded street. It was crammed with people looking into the rows of shops and sitting at tables outside small cafés. It was so unlike Hampstead.

What they were planning to do didn't feel right. Erik couldn't understand why they didn't just tell the police and storm the ship. Sadie had to be on the SWALLOW. Saskia had seen the man from the train, and La Sauvage and Foojack were there—it had to be the place.

"Why don't we just tell the police?" he finally asked.

"We are the police," Dorcas Potts huffed in reply. "It's bad enough having Max Taranis of Scotland Yard breathing down our necks without involving anyone else."

Her reply only confirmed Erik's suspicion that there was more to Dorcas Potts's professional history with Max Taranis than she was letting on.

"Good thing Max Taranis is with us," Erik noted. "He can vouch for us if things go wrong. My father had a cop on his side—he used to pay him off from every job he did."

"Your father never came across Max Taranis," Dorcas Potts countered. They turned onto another narrow street that led even higher. "I wouldn't be surprised if he turned us in just as we started the heist. Then he would get the glory—just like he wants."

Erik didn't reply. As they had turned the corner, he saw someone dart back into the cover of a doorway several paces behind them. Even in the crowded street, this didn't seem right. He pressed himself against the wall as Dorcas Potts walked on, and he waited, looking back at the road behind them. Sure enough, a head slowly appeared. Eyes peered around the corner, searching back and forth. Erik looked away and turned up the hill. It was all he needed to see. They were being followed by the short man he had seen on the ship. He ran to catch up with Dorcas Potts.

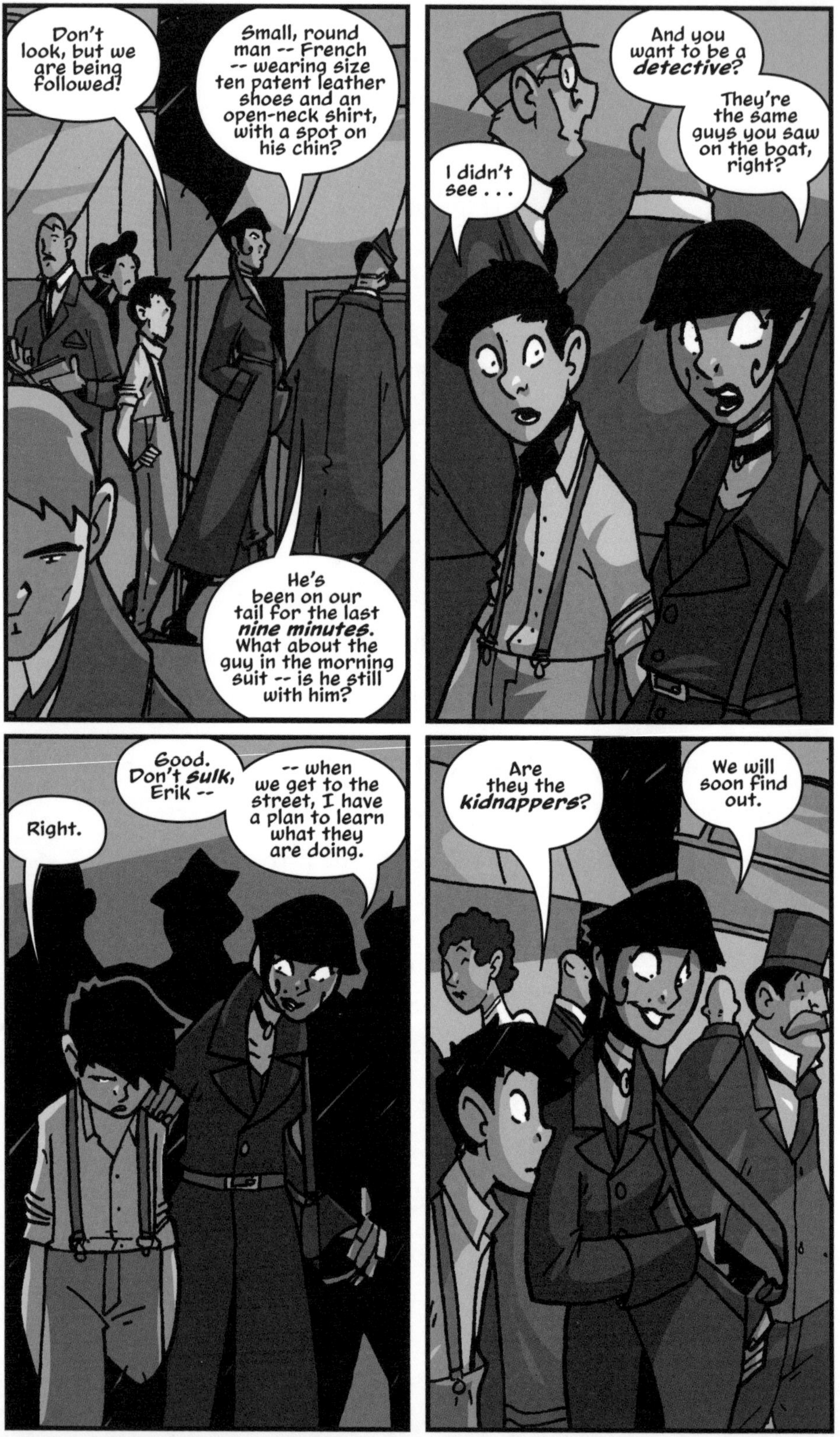
Don't look, but we are being followed!
Small, round man -- French -- wearing size ten patent leather shoes and an open-neck shirt, with a spot on his chin?
He's been on our tail for the last *nine minutes.* What about the guy in the morning suit -- is he still with him?
And you want to be a *detective?*
They're the same guys you saw on the boat, right?
I didn't see . . .
Right.
Good. Don't *sulk,* Erik --
-- when we get to the street, I have a plan to learn what they are doing.
Are they the *kidnappers?*
We will soon find out.

Up ahead, the tower
rose from the red-
tiled buildings that
surrounded it. A fresh
breeze swirled about them
like a fine dust as it blew through
the alleyways.

"What are you going to do?" Erik asked.
Dorcas Potts looked ahead. There, leaning
against the wall of a bread shop was Foojack,
his hand gripping the inside of his coat.

"Take this," she said as she thrust the
purse into his hands. "Run! Now!"
she shouted and set off up the
crowded street.

Erik started sprinting, gripping
the purse under one arm. Dorcas
Potts sped ahead, diving this way
and that as she ran through
the crowd.

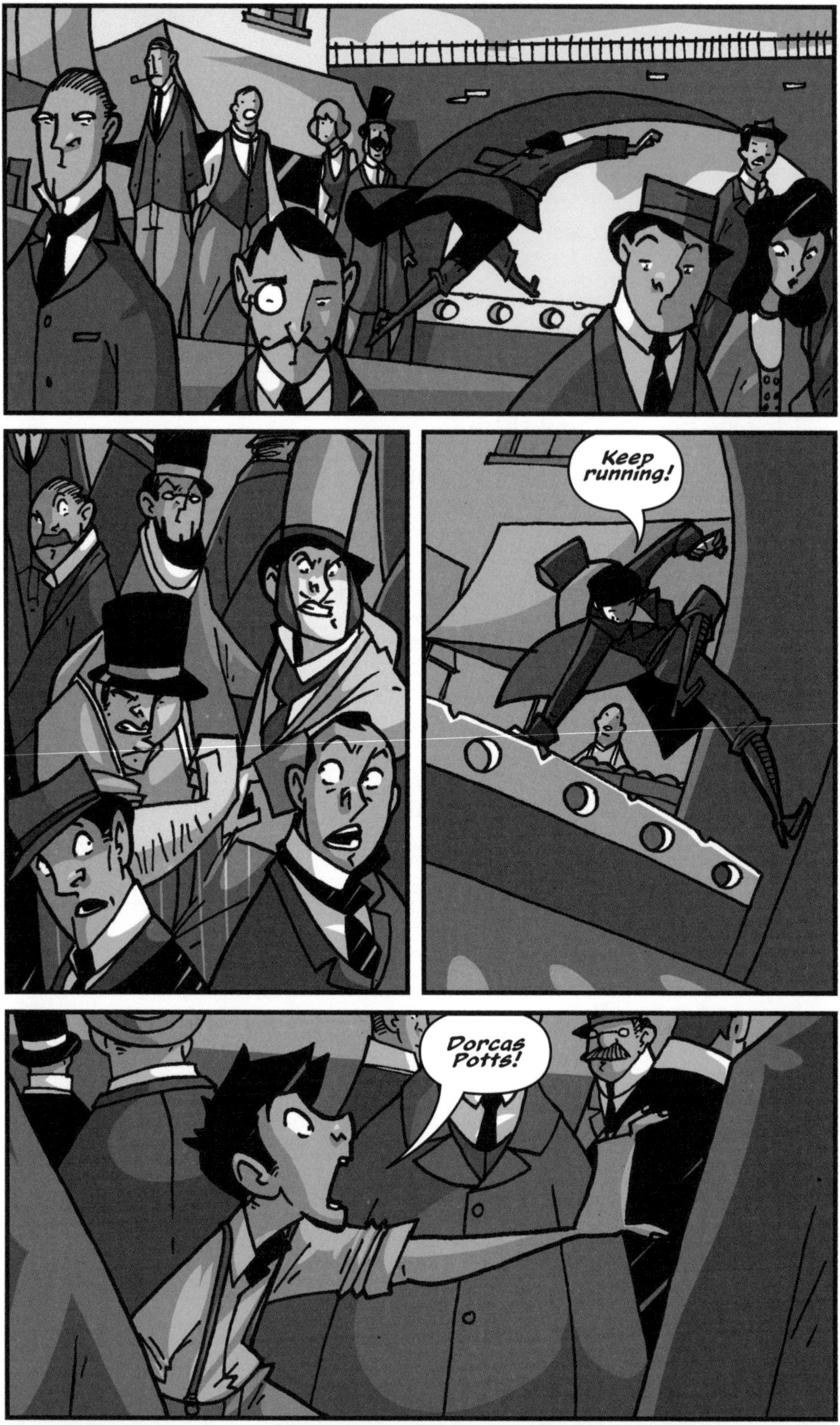
Keep running!
Dorcas Potts!

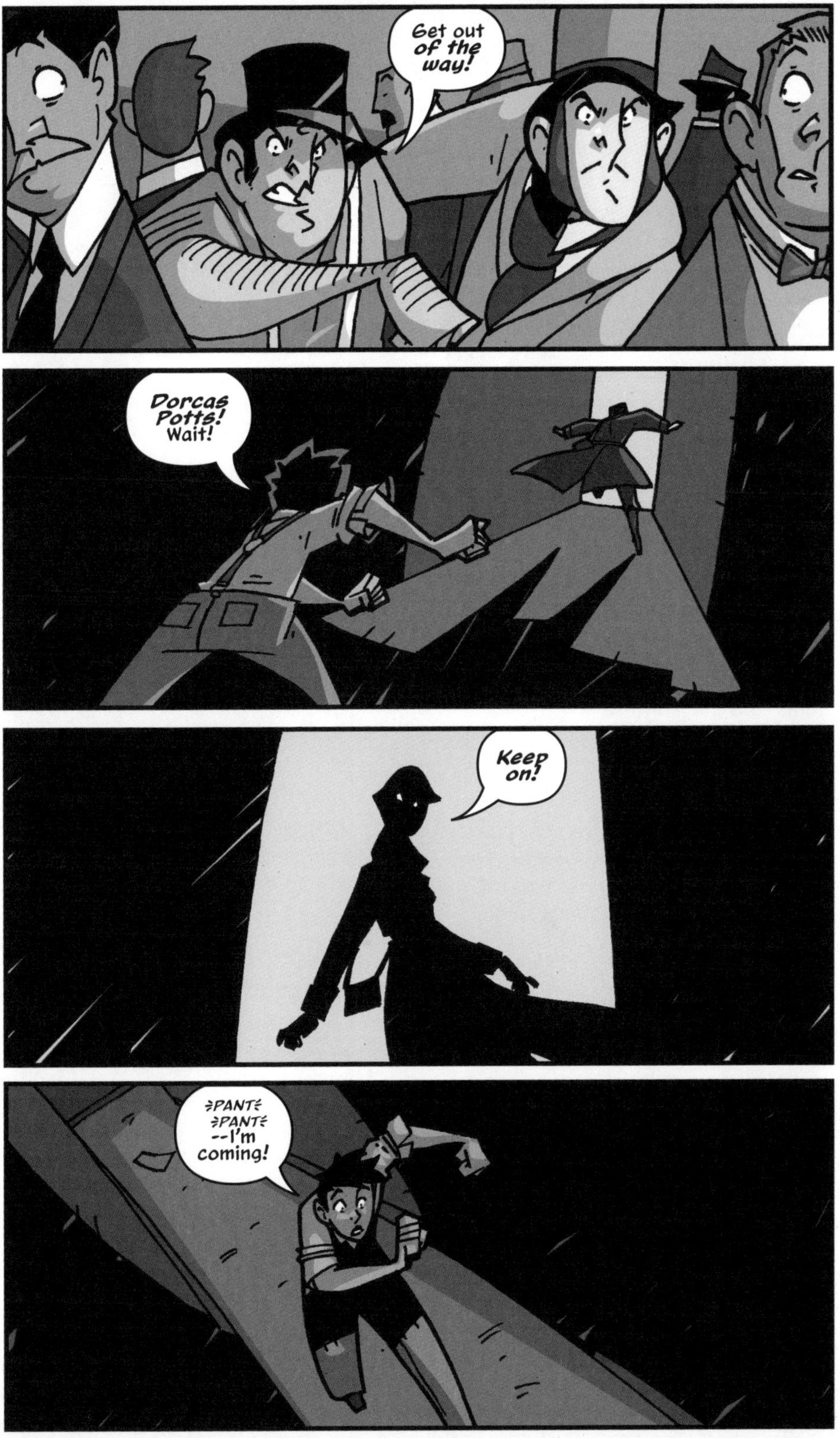
Get out of the way!
Dorcas Potts! Wait!
Keep on!
≠PANT≠ ≠PANT≠ --I'm coming!

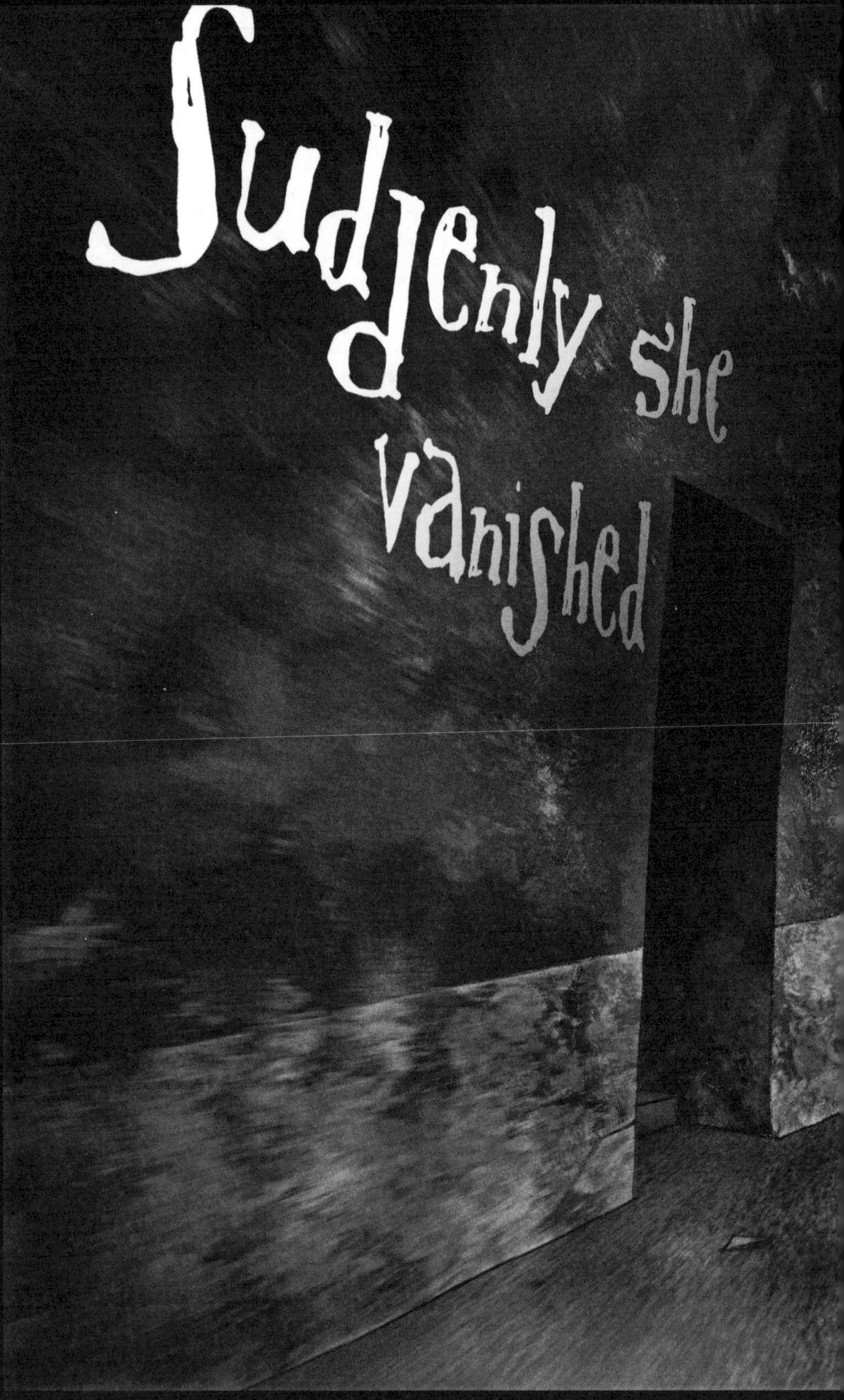
Suddenly she vanished

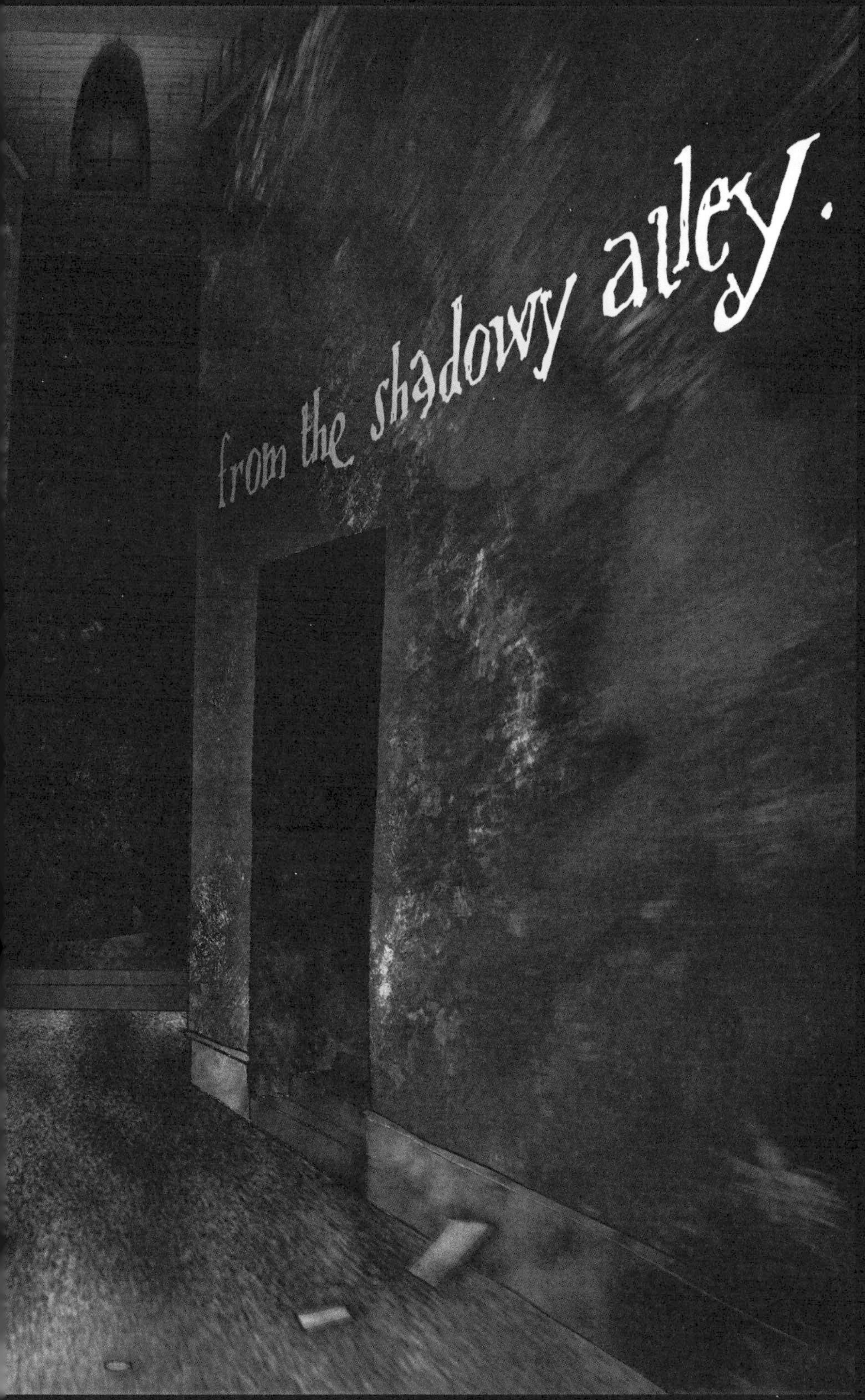
from the shadowy alley.

One instant she was there, and the next she had disappeared. Erik saw no one. All he heard was the slam of a car door and a squeal of tires. Then she was gone. He broke from the covered alleyway, blinking hard to adjust his eyes to the light. There was no sign of anyone, but in the distance he could hear the revving of an engine echoing through the narrow streets. The footsteps behind him sounded closer. Erik jumped to one side and hid in a small clump of bushes that had grown up out of the old stones by the nearest building. He pressed himself against the wall and waited.

Through the small branches, he saw two men run into the narrow street. They stopped in the road and looked around. The taller man rubbed his hands together and smiled.

"It worked—they ran like chickens straight into the net."

"We haven't gotten to do any of the real work since we got off the train," grumbled the shorter man sulkily.

"There is always time. Even if they get the diamond, I have no intention of returning the girl. If we give her back, they will be onto us, and I want to spend the money." The taller man snorted a laugh and set off down the hill with the short man puffing behind.

"That's why she ran ahead," Erik said to himself. "She knew it was a trap, and she didn't want me to get caught. . . ."

• • •

In the backseat of the long black car, Dorcas Potts sat quietly.

"Where is the boy?" asked La Sauvage from the front seat.

"You don't need him," Dorcas Potts replied, looking out the window.

"But we need YOU, Dorcas Potts. You have interfered too much in all of this, and Foojack has a rather large bruise he would like to discuss with you."

Dorcas Potts smiled to herself and pondered how La Sauvage would react if she knew what had really happened back in the chapel.

"So why kidnap me? You already have Sadie," Dorcas Potts said as the car wound its way toward the harbor.

"Insurance," La Sauvage replied. She brushed her auburn hair from her face. "And to stop you from finding out any more than you already have. I heard you were a better detective than Max Taranis."

"Max Taranis couldn't find his own foot in the dark." Dorcas Potts looked at the door handle, trying to calculate if she could leap from the car.

"The doors are locked," La Sauvage said, looking back at Potts. "I knew you would think of escaping."

"So will you let us go when you have the diamond?"

"We are Le Sentier Rouge; we have a code of honor. You will be released."

"But I know what you look like," Dorcas Potts countered.

"Today, yes . . . tomorrow, perhaps not. People can change and never be recognized again," the woman replied. "Once we have the diamond, you will be set free—as long as you promise to go back to London and never look for us again."

"Would you ask a cat never to chase a mouse?"

"Depends who you think is the cat."

The car stopped at the quayside, and Dorcas Potts was pulled from the back by a burly man with a mouth full of gold teeth. He gestured toward the yacht with his gun.

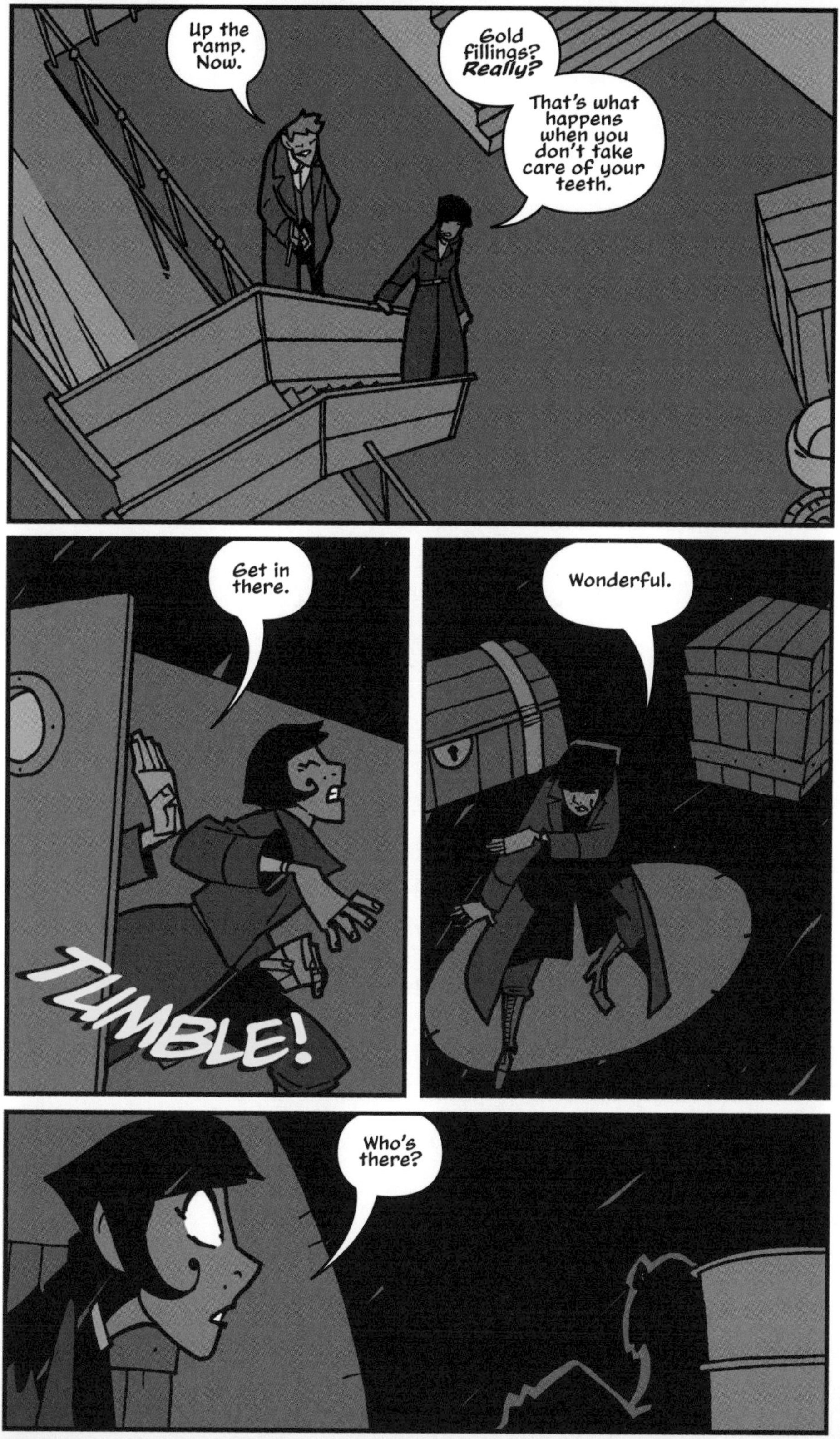
Up the ramp. Now.
Gold fillings? *Really?*
That's what happens when you don't take care of your teeth.
Get in there.
TUMBLE!
Wonderful.
Who's there?

. . .

As soon as the two men had gone, Erik walked down a
narrow, sloping street, still clutching Dorcas Potts's purse.
As he passed an open door, he heard a deep voice coming
from inside. "Narrow is the path, Erik . . ." He couldn't
decide if the voice terrified him or compelled him, but it
seemed to be calling to him, drawing him inside.

He peered into the arched doorway. Inside he saw what
looked like a museum. It was empty of people but full of
strange objects: dusty suits of armor, stuffed horses, and
a large, ornate chair. The far end of the room was dimly
lit with candles, and a shaft of light shone through a dirty
leaded window.

"Who are you?" he asked,

entering the room and walking slowly forward. His heart
pounded in his chest, but it wasn't fear, exactly. Somehow
he sensed that he was meant to be here.

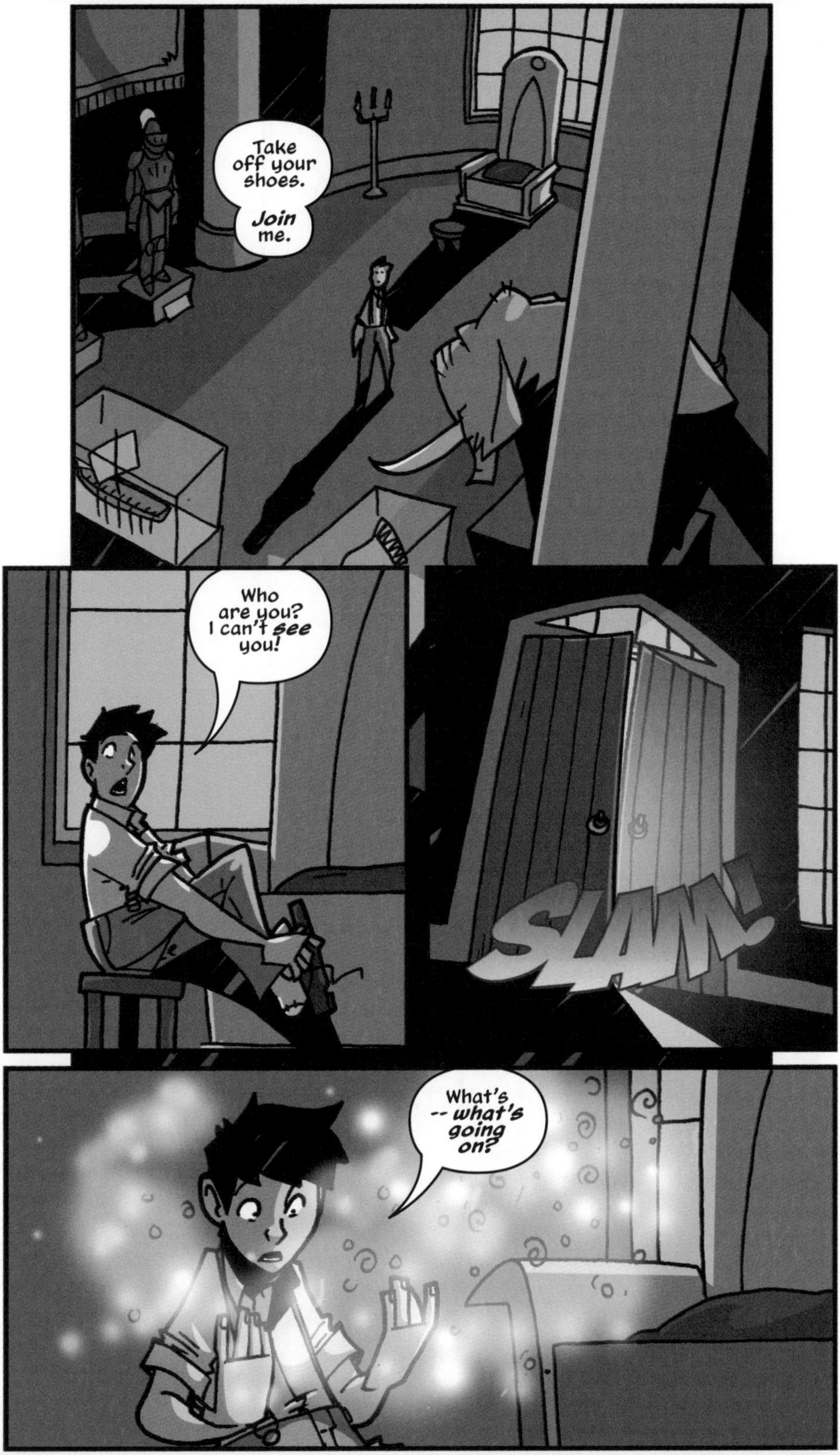
Take off your shoes.
Join me.
Who are you? I can't *see* you!
SLAM!
What's -- *what's going on?*

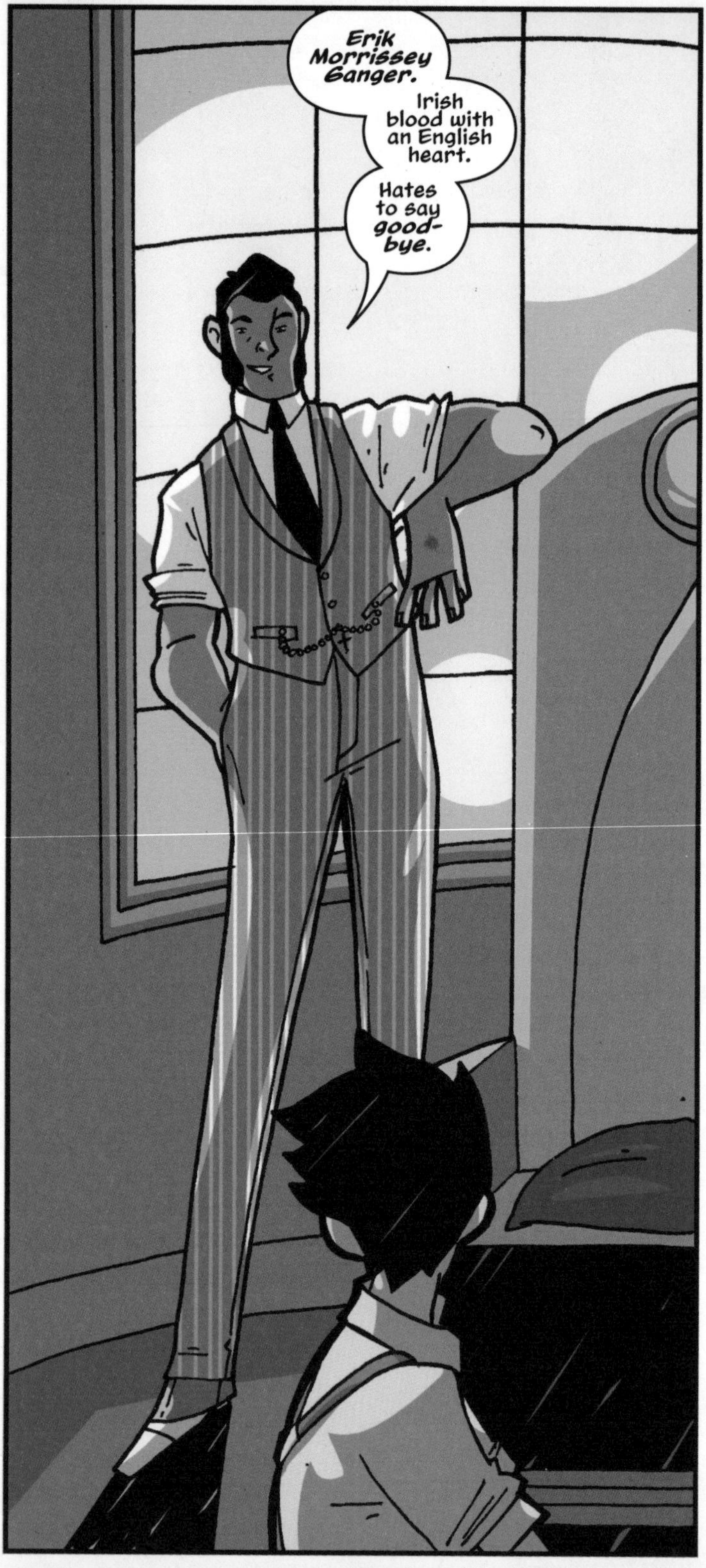
Erik Morrissey Ganger.
Irish blood with an English heart.
Hates to say good-bye.

Erik looked up. The man had appeared in the blink of an eye. He stared at Erik with warm, brown eyes. His skin was olive colored, and he had an incredibly large smile, with dazzling perfect white teeth.

"How . . . ?" Erik asked, unable to finish his sentence.

"How do I know your name?" the man replied, finishing Erik's thought for him. "Known you a long time. From the streets of Shoreditch to the time when your father left you at that school. Do you still wonder if he is coming back?"

"You've been following me all that time?" Erik asked, not knowing what else to say.

"For even longer than that." The man held out his hand for Erik to shake. "And you thought you were alone—with no one in the world."

"Who are—?" Erik began as he took hold of the man's hand, but he stopped speaking at once.

Erik stared openmouthed as he looked at the hand that gripped his own. A deep scar covered the back of his hand. Erik could feel on the man's palm that the wound went all the way through. It was circular with jagged edges.

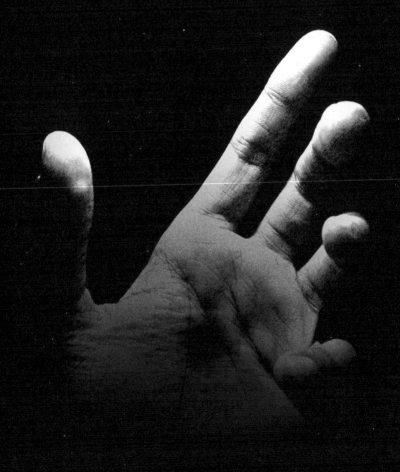

"Everyone does that," the man said. "They take my hand and see the scar and don't know what to say. I have one here, too." He held out the palm of his other hand.

"Will they heal?" Erik asked as he traced the hole with his finger.

"Not for a while," the man said slowly.

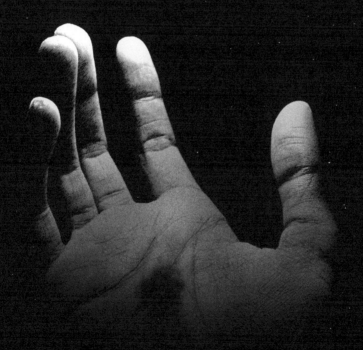

"Now . . . you are supposed to ask me who I am. That's what usually happens—people either scream, fall on the floor, or ask me my name."

Erik wasn't frightened or uncomfortable. There was something about the man that made Erik feel he didn't even need to know his name.

"I know who you are. My father told me stories about you. He talked about your hands—hands that created the world surrendered to cruel nails," Erik whispered. He looked at the floor, not wanting to meet the man's eyes.

"But you didn't believe your father," the man replied, his voice graver than before.

"He left me—left me alone . . . with no one!" Erik shouted and rose to his feet.

"Yes, I know how that feels," the man said somberly. "On a dark Friday long ago, I, too, felt totally alone."

Something in the man's voice made Erik look up at last. The man stared at him with deep eyes. "The Man of Good-Bye Friday," Erik whispered. "Madame Raphael told me you were waiting for me."

"Your father left you for your own good," the man explained. "That's what he thought. He didn't want you to grow up as a thief. He knew that way of life was wrong, so he took you to the school."

The man gripped Erik on the shoulders. Erik felt warmth radiating through him. It was like standing in front of a campfire on a cold evening.

"Then why didn't he tell me that instead of saying he was going for some cigarettes?" Erik asked.

"Just like you never like to say good-bye, neither did he. And in your heart, you know it."

Erik knew it was the truth. He had hidden from that reality for all these years. The coughing he had heard as his father had walked off into the night had been to cover the tears of leaving his son behind.

"Where is he?" Erik asked.

"With me," the man replied. "And he has been since the day after he left you."

"So he . . . he died?"

The Man of Good-Bye Friday looked at Erik kindly for a long moment. And then, almost imperceptibly, he nodded.

"Did he know he was going to die?" Erik asked.

"Of course," the man said. "He had been sick for some time—I think you guessed that."

Erik put a hand over his mouth to stop the quivering. He breathed hard and looked at the floor.

The man folded his arms around Erik and held him close. Erik could feel the warmth of his skin and smell the strong scent of lemongrass. Tears rolled across his cheeks and dripped onto the floor, and for once he didn't even care. It was as if Erik were in the arms of his father once again, and he didn't want it to end. He was wrapped from head to foot in something he wasn't sure he'd ever touch again. One by one old, painful memories flashed through his mind, but with each one, he felt something deep inside him begin to soften and heal. He savored the moment, hoping that it could go on and on.

Then it was over.

Looking up, Erik suddenly realized he was alone. The man was gone, like he had never been there at all. Erik looked behind him and saw that the door to the street was open. His shoes were back on his feet. The bustle of the crowd outside filled the room with unwelcome noise. All was as it had been before.

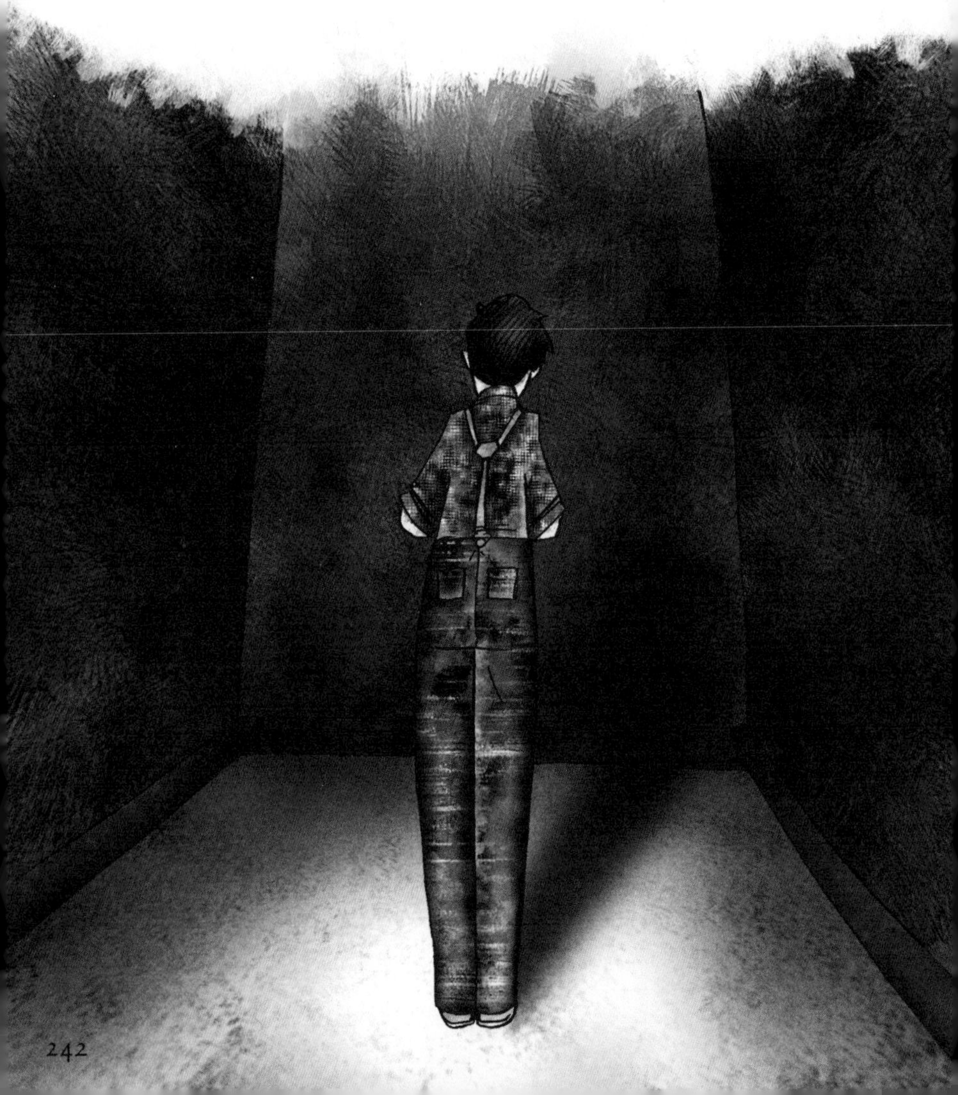

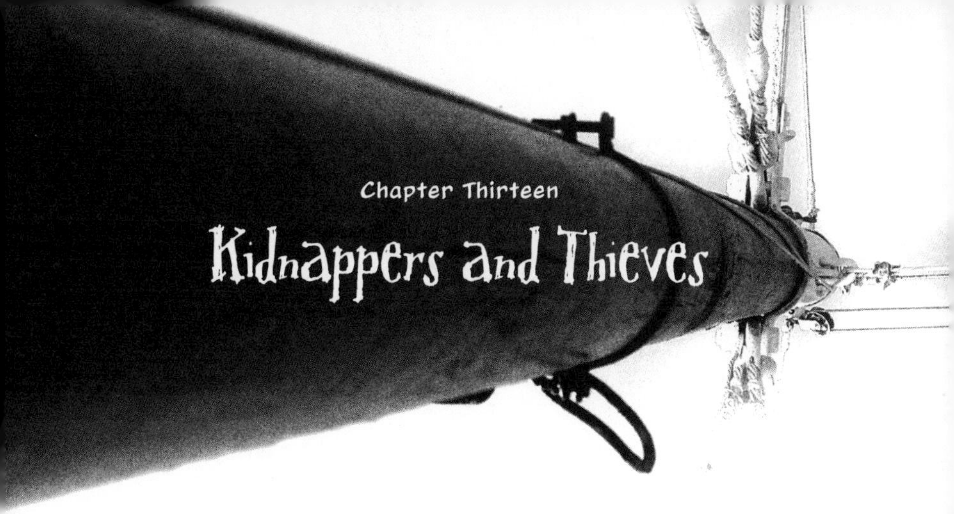

Chapter Thirteen

Kidnappers and Thieves

IN THE DEEP WATER just beyond the islands, the SWALLOW rocked gently back and forth in the changing tide. The rigging of the tall masts glinted in the last rays of the sun setting behind the hills. In the windowless room, Dorcas Potts could hear muffled voices overhead. She stared at the figure in the corner.

"Who's there?" she asked.

"Dorcas Potts?" came an anxious voice.

"Sadie!" said Dorcas Potts, rushing toward the corner. "Are you all right?"

"Yes, I'm fine. Is Erik here too?"

"No," replied Dorcas Potts. "They caught me alone."

Footsteps grew louder from the deck above. "I think they're coming," Dorcas Potts said in a whisper.

"What do they want from us?" Sadie asked.

"They will exchange us for the Great Mogul Diamond. It's being auctioned tonight, and they want Muzz Elliott to steal it. Apparently she wrote a book about a diamond theft at the Hotel Carlton."

"Another one of her books coming true!" gasped Sadie.

"Yes," said Dorcas Potts. "It looks like the events on the train were all to frighten Muzz Elliott into following the plot of ANOTHER DAY, ANOTHER DIAMOND." The footsteps grew louder.

"Why do they need Muzz Elliott to steal the diamond?"

"That, Sadie, is a question I cannot answer. But . . . I do feel there is more to this than we think." The footsteps stomped along the corridor toward the cabin. "They could have easily stolen the diamond themselves. They are the most powerful criminals in France. Why would they pick an old woman to do it for them?"

"Why, indeed?" said a voice. The door opened, and a figure stood in the twilight outside. "You have to be careful what you say on board a ship such as this. Walls have ears."

"Muzz Elliott?" Dorcas Potts screeched in amazement.

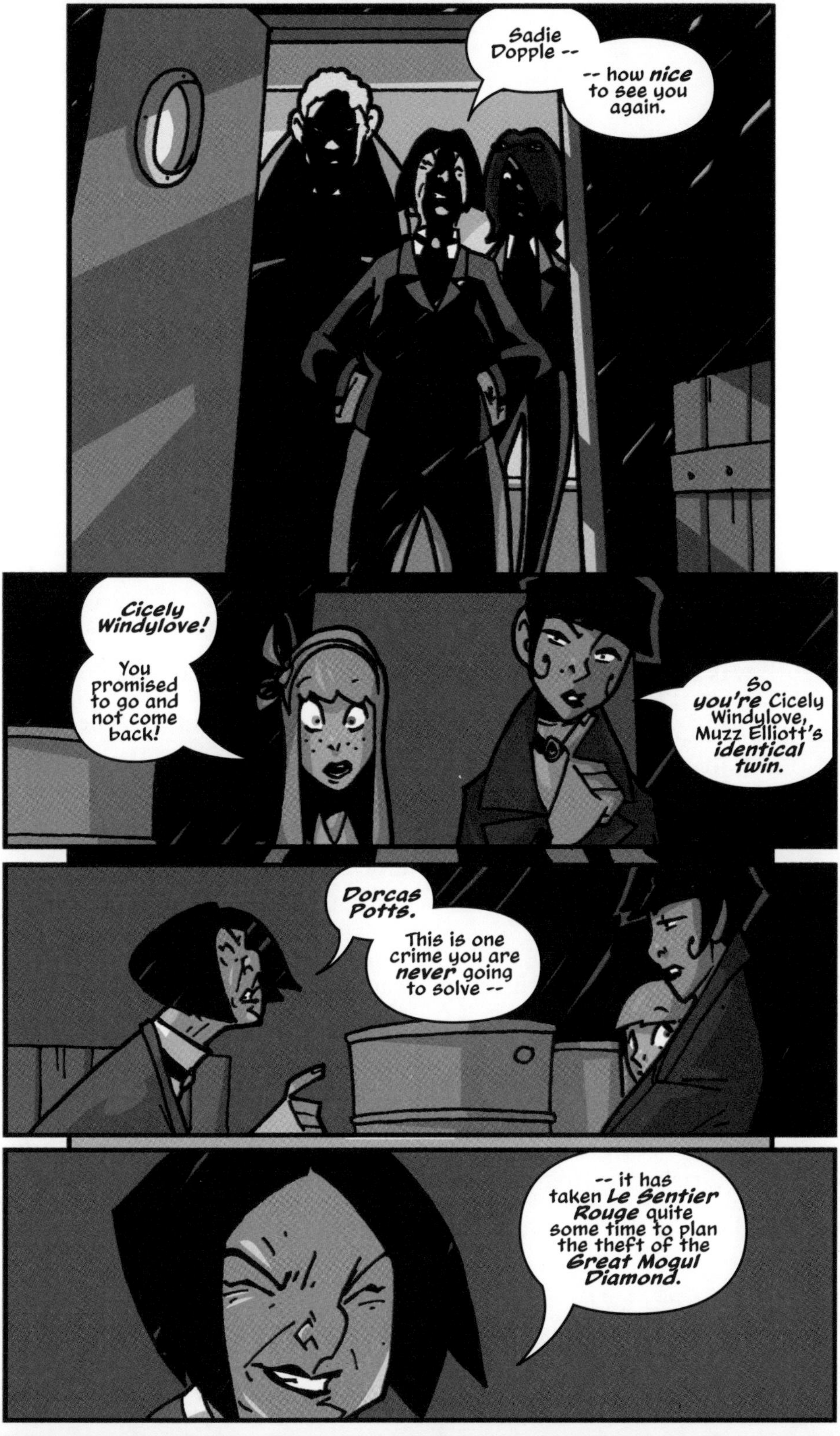
Sadie Dopple --
-- how nice to see you again.
Cicely Windylove!
You promised to go and not come back!
So you're Cicely Windylove, Muzz Elliott's identical twin.
Dorcas Potts.
This is one crime you are never going to solve --
-- it has taken Le Sentier Rouge quite some time to plan the theft of the Great Mogul Diamond.

"You would do this to your own sister, after she let you go free when you tried to kill her?" Sadie asked.

"She did not treat me like a sister,"

spat Cicely Windylove. "All I wanted was a share of what was rightfully mine. But she disowned me. There was no other option but to try and take her place. And then when I discovered where the treasure was hidden, she wasted it all on that wretched school and on you and your miserable sister. No, she has not treated me like family. Why should I do the same to her?"

"But she came all this way because she thought you were in trouble," countered Sadie. "She received a note that someone had recognized her at the scene of a crime and assumed it must have been you. But she came here anyway and risked taking the blame instead of turning you in. Blood is thicker than water."

Cicely Windylove laughed cruelly. "I was the one who sent that note! I wanted to see if Kitty was naive enough to fall for the oldest trick in the book—the bond of twinship—so I had a member of Le Sentier Rouge call and threaten her. She took the bait, and now I will be rid of Kitty Elliott once and for all. She can never make up for a lifetime of being the favored sister, but I will have her do one last thing for me. She will steal the diamond, and my friends and I will get paid. But the police will be waiting for her. Foojack has told them that I, Cicely Windylove, intend to commit the crime. Kitty Elliott will be committed to the Îles du Salut. In turn, I will live out the life I deserve at Spaniards House."

"You would send her to the Devil's Island prison?" said Dorcas Potts.

"The same," replied Cicely Windylove with a wink.

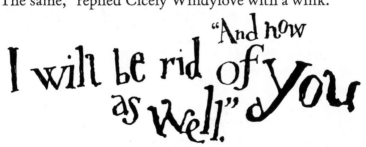

"And now I will be rid of you as well."

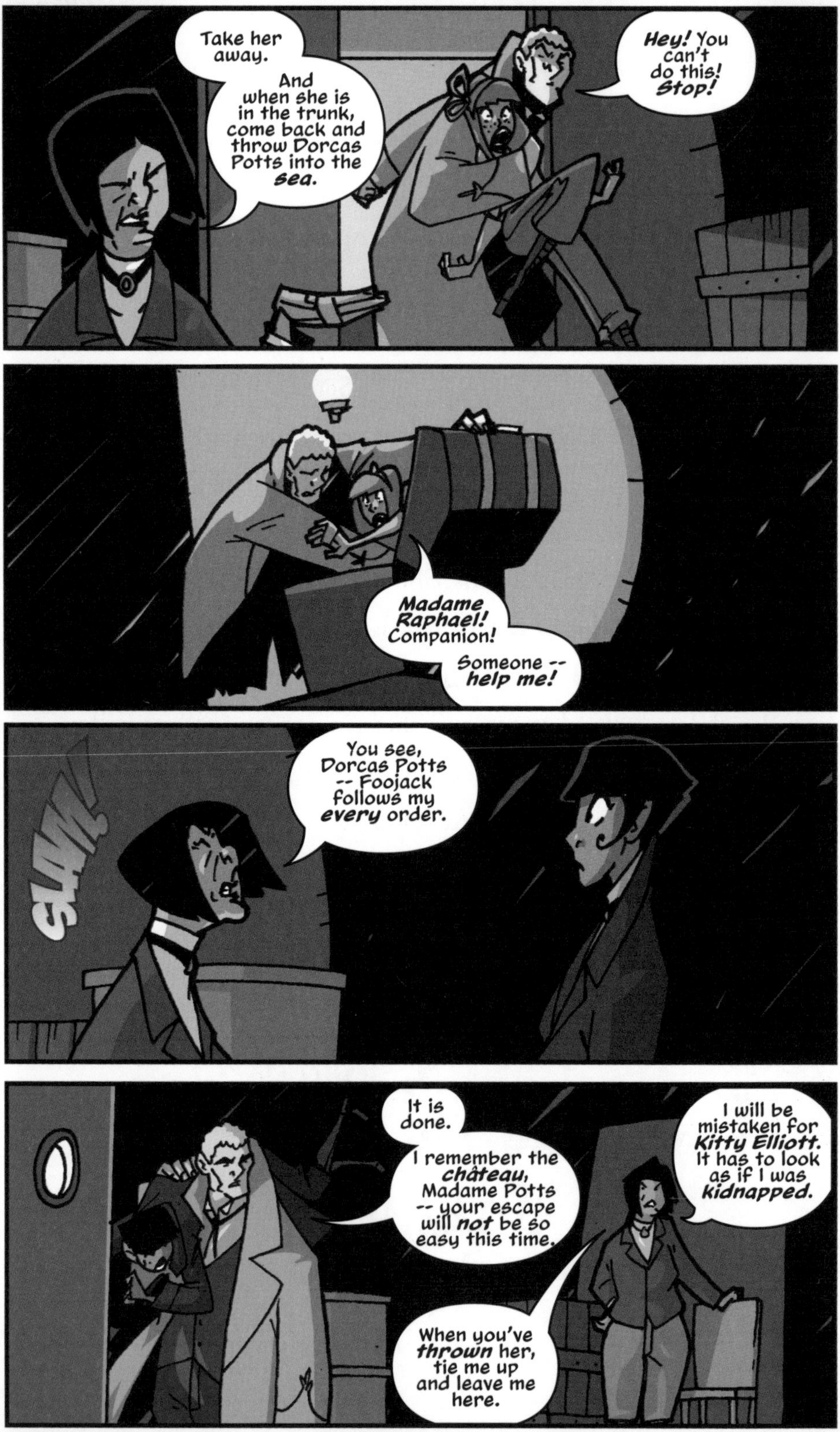
Take her away.
And when she is in the trunk, come back and throw Dorcas Potts into the sea.
Hey! You can't do this! Stop!
Madame Raphael! Companion!
Someone -- help me!
SLAM!
You see, Dorcas Potts -- Foojack follows my every order.
It is done.
I remember the château, Madame Potts -- your escape will not be so easy this time.
I will be mistaken for Kitty Elliott. It has to look as if I was kidnapped.
When you've thrown her, tie me up and leave me here.

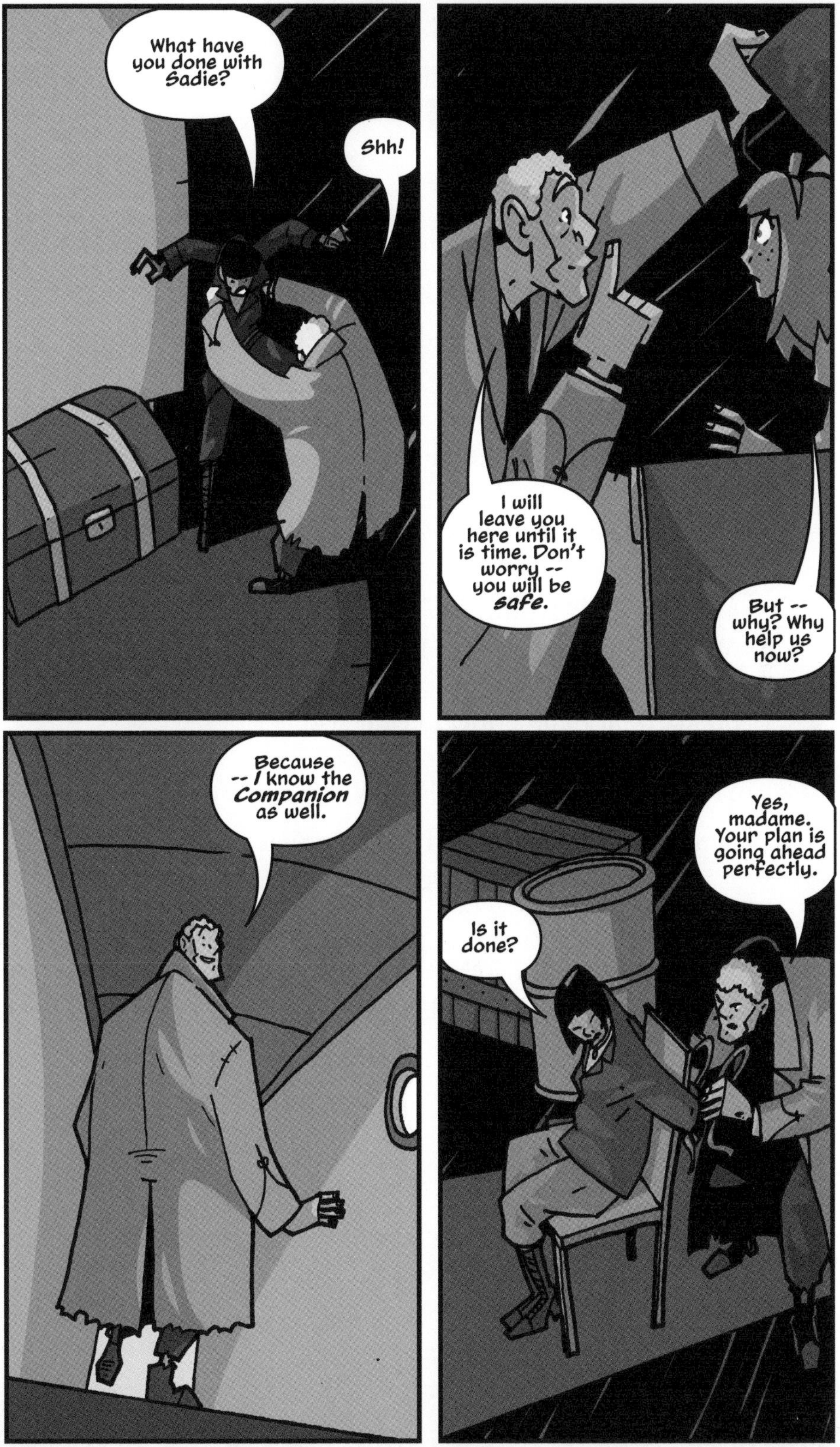
What have you done with Sadie?
Shh!
I will leave you here until it is time. Don't worry -- you will be *safe*.
But -- why? Why help us now?
Because -- *I* know the *Companion* as well.
Is it done?
Yes, madame. Your plan is going ahead perfectly.

In the lobby of the Hotel Carlton, Muzz Elliott clung to the straps of her purse and looked around as she paced the white marble floor. Erik and Saskia waited in the shadows of a large pagoda palm.

"Erik—it's time. You know what to do," directed Saskia.

"I don't feel right about this, Saskia," said Erik.

"There's no other way!" hissed Saskia. "Not if we want to save Sadie and Dorcas Potts. I'm not going to lose my sister!"

"I don't want to be a thief like my dad."

"You're not like your dad, Erik. We're only borrowing the diamond temporarily. We'll tell the police as soon as we get Sadie and Dorcas Potts back."

More and more people streamed through the hotel doors and into the lobby. They filed neatly into rows of velvet

seats and waited for the auction to begin. The Great Mogul Diamond stood proudly on a steel pedestal in the center of the room surrounded by the covetous eyes of Spanish princes, elderly Russian counts, and the like. Max Taranis stood by the main door watching everyone who entered the hotel.

Muzz Elliott looked at Erik and Saskia and nodded.

"We've got to do it, Erik!" whispered Saskia. "NOW!"

With a heaviness in his heart, Erik stepped out from under the shadows of the palm tree. Saskia followed close behind.

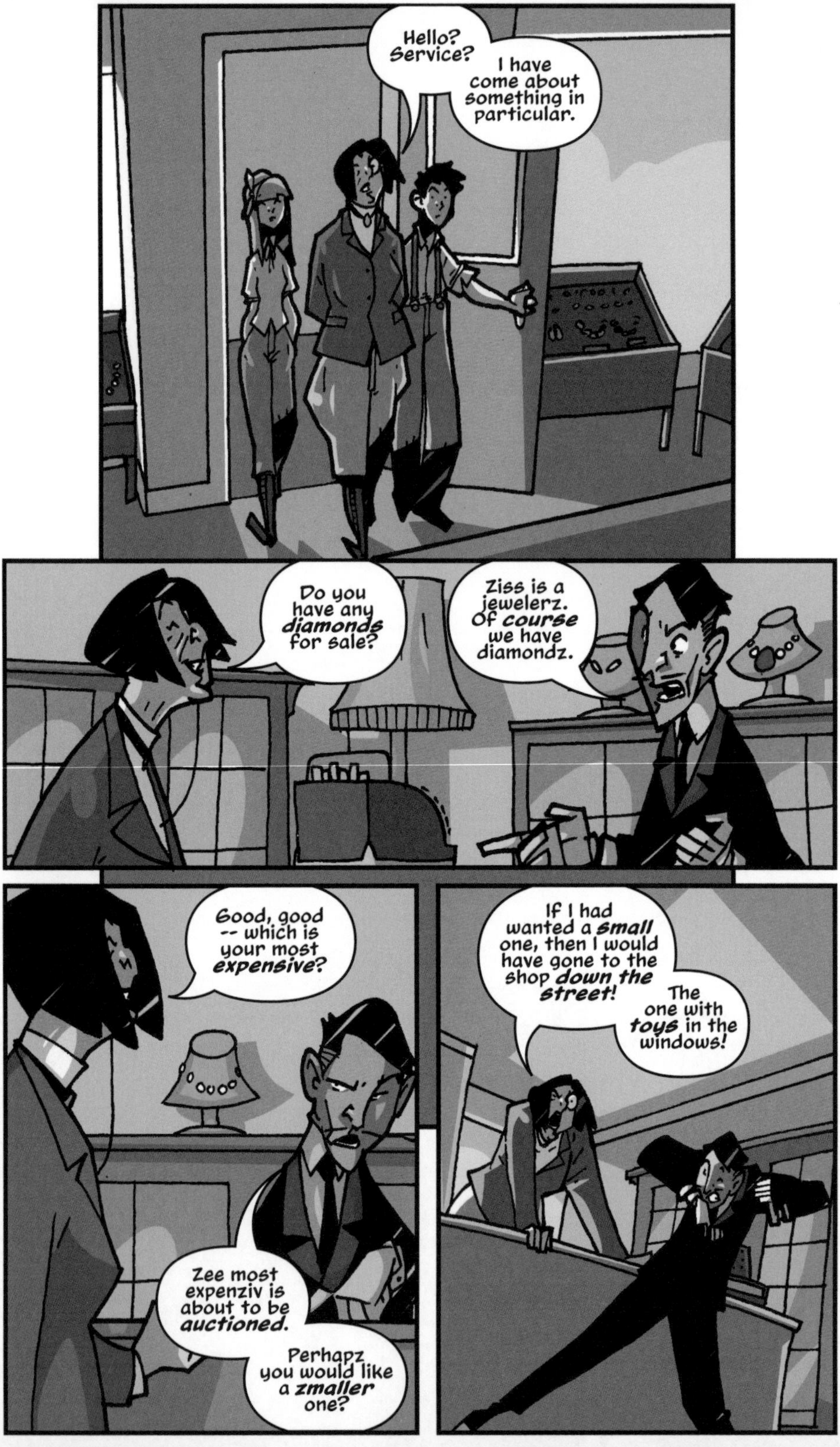

Hello? Service?
I have come about something in particular.
Do you have any *diamonds* for sale?
Ziss is a jewelerz. Of *course* we have diamondz.
Good, good -- which is your most *expensive*?
Zee most expenziv is about to be *auctioned*.
Perhapz you would like a *zmaller* one?
If I had wanted a *small* one, then I would have gone to the shop *down the street*!
The one with *toys* in the windows!

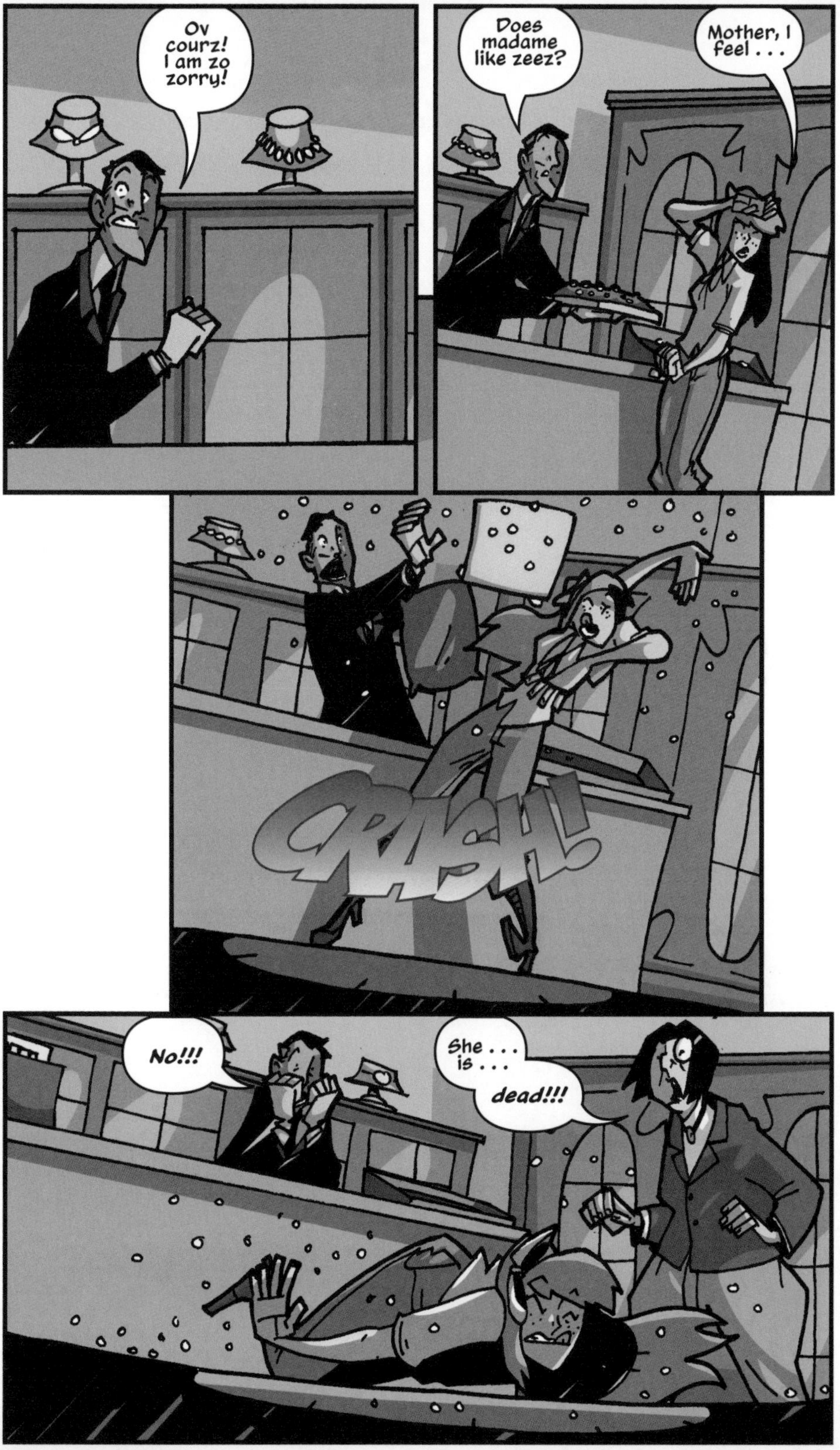
Ov courz! I am zo zorry!
Does madame like zeez?
Mother, I feel . . .
CRASH!
No!!!
She . . . is . . . dead!!!

The man threw his hands in the air and moaned. He gabbled in such a chaotic mixture of English and French that his words were indistinguishable.

While the man continued to rant about the scattered diamonds and Muzz Elliott fussed noisily over Saskia, Erik sneaked into a side room and through two open doors. His heart beating fast, he pulled on a pair of gloves, crossed the floor, and lifted the gilt-framed portrait of Napoleon from the wall. Just as Muzz Elliott had said, the safe was there. It was just as she had written in ANOTHER DAY, ANOTHER DIAMOND. She had done her research well.

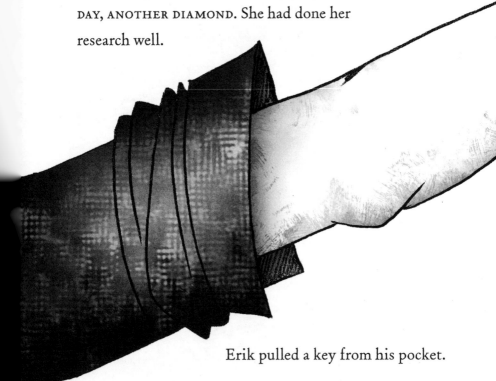

Erik pulled a key from his pocket.

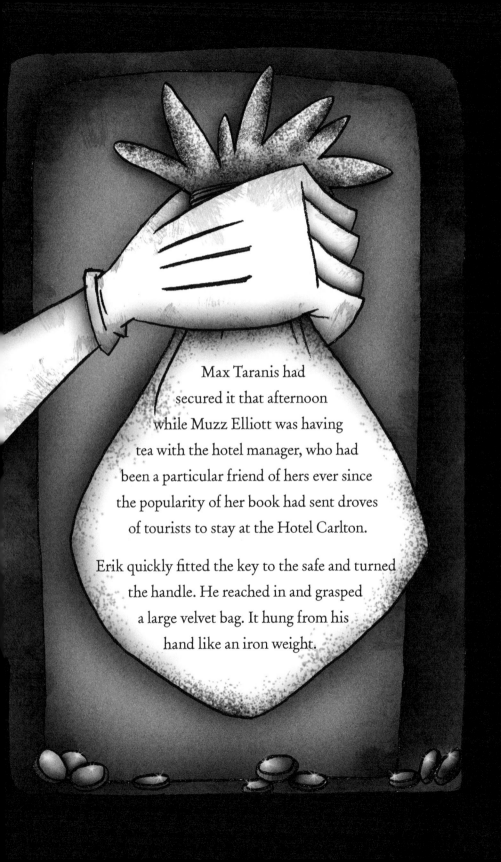

Max Taranis had
secured it that afternoon
while Muzz Elliott was having
tea with the hotel manager, who had
been a particular friend of hers ever since
the popularity of her book had sent droves
of tourists to stay at the Hotel Carlton.

Erik quickly fitted the key to the safe and turned
the handle. He reached in and grasped
a large velvet bag. It hung from his
hand like an iron weight.

His hand lingered inside the safe for a moment. He heard a faint voice in his head, almost like a whisper. "The old order has passed away. All is new." Erik stopped, surprised. His dad had said that to him, a few days before he had left Erik at Isambard Dunstan's. Erik knew now that his dad had wanted to remove him from a life of crime, but here he was, his hand in a safe, about to steal the largest diamond in the world. Yet this seemed different somehow. He thought of Dorcas Potts being shoved into the car and driven off and of Sadie, trapped on the yacht. How could he return without the diamond, knowing this could be the only chance to save them?

Still holding the velvet bag, he withdrew his hand and closed the safe door. He put the picture back on the wall and returned everything to how it had been.

Soon he was back in the shop. The assistant hadn't noticed his absence. Muzz Elliott had seen to that by glowering over the man as he rendered what first aid he knew.

"Shall I give her zee kizz of liveliness?" he was asking.

"I don't think that will be necessary," Saskia blurted out, unable to play dead any longer with the Frenchman's lips hovering inches from her face.

"You have saved my daughter—what a brave man!" Muzz Elliott cried.

Erik edged to the door as the assistant helped Saskia to her feet.

"Ziss is zo irregular," he whispered to Muzz Elliott as she ushered Erik and Saskia from the shop. "I have not counted zee diamondz—what if one is missing?"

"Then I shall mail it to you. They really were too small. I was after something far grander."

As they left the shop, they did not notice the tall, elegant man in the long coat. He stood by the pagoda palm with a smile on his face and his long arms neatly folded. The round, gold clock above his head chimed the half hour.

"Eleven thirty—time to get the diamond to the castle and rescue Sadie and Dorcas Potts," said Saskia.

"Do you have the jewel?" asked Muzz Elliott.

Erik nodded. "It was just as you said: a false diamond is on display for the auction, and the real Mogul is in the—"

His words were cut short by the bellowing of the auctioneer.

"Lords, ladies, and gentlemen, the auction is about to begin and will be celebrated at midnight by Monsieur Largo—pyrotechnic extraordinaire."

"Quickly," Muzz Elliott whispered. She put her head down and made for the exit.

The man by the pagoda palm stepped forward. "I presume you are Cicely Windylove?" he asked in crisp English.

Muzz Elliott stopped, looked him in the face, and smiled.

"The police?" she asked. "Looking for Cicely Windylove in connection with the theft of a jewel?"

"Chief Inspector Balzac of the gendarmerie, madame. Will this matter be handled quietly?" he replied and held out his hand.

"Life is nothing but temptation and heartbreak served out in equal measures," Muzz Elliott replied.

"She's not Windylove," Saskia insisted. "That's her sister."

"It is just what our informant told us she would say. Muzz Elliott is being held captive at this very moment. This woman has taken her place and used you to steal the Great Mogul Diamond."

Saskia looked at Muzz Elliott, confused.

"Inspector," said Erik, seizing his chance. "I have the jewel here. I never intended to keep it. Take it now." He shoved the velvet bag forward. "I won't be a thief any longer."

"That's not a diamond," said Saskia, snatching the bag and hiding it behind her back. "Are you crazy, Erik?" she said under her breath. "We need that to get Sadie back."

"Careful, Erik," whispered Muzz Elliott. "You don't want to blow our cover if there are any spies at the auction."

"Hand over the bag, girl," said Chief Inspector Balzac. "We wouldn't want to make a scene in front of all these people."

Muzz Elliott looked hard at Saskia. "Find Sadie—that's what matters," she whispered as she pulled a silver pen from her purse. Suddenly she lunged forward at Balzac's arm.

"Go!" she shouted.

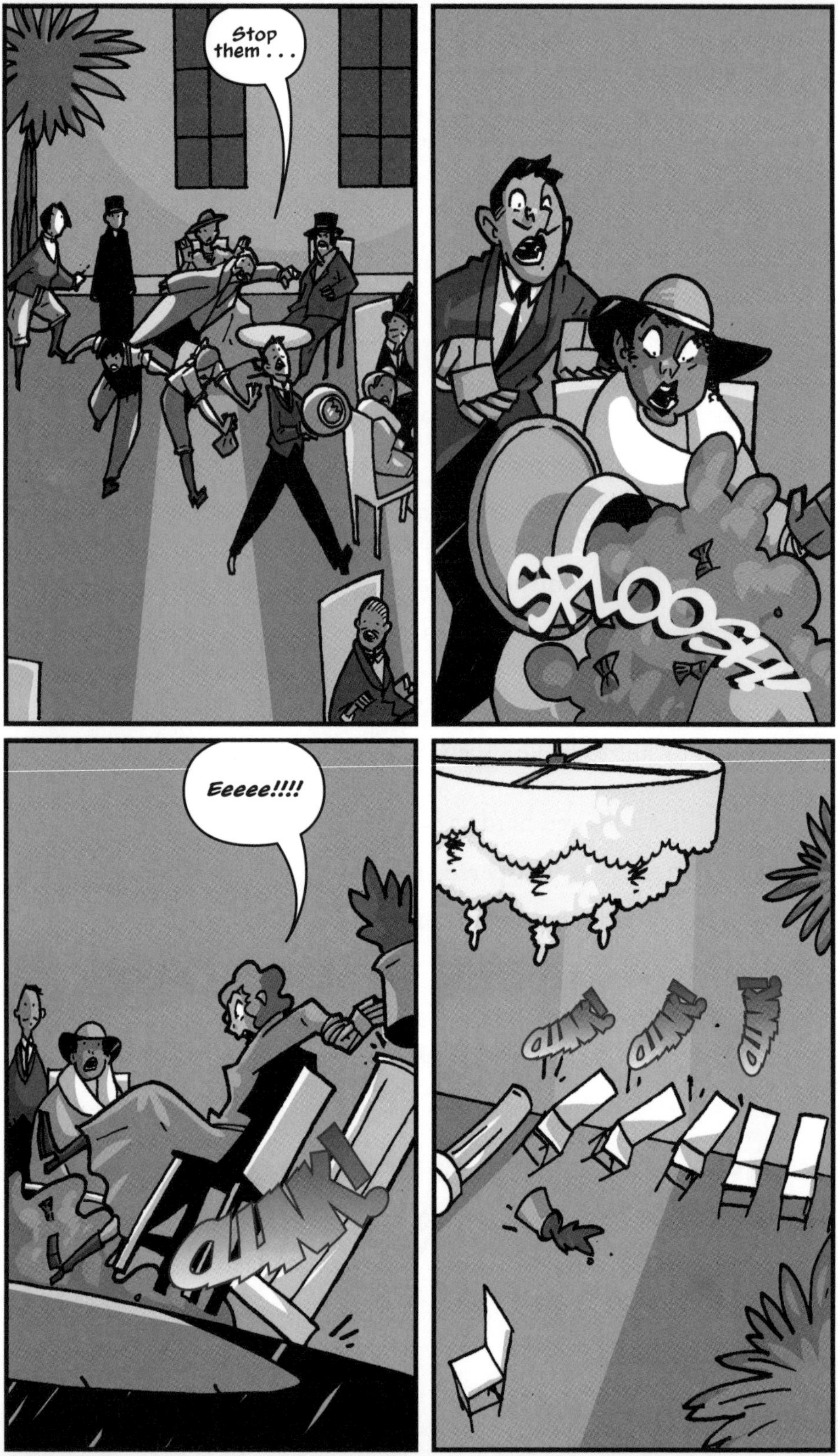
Stop them . . .
SPLOOSH!
Eeeee!!!!

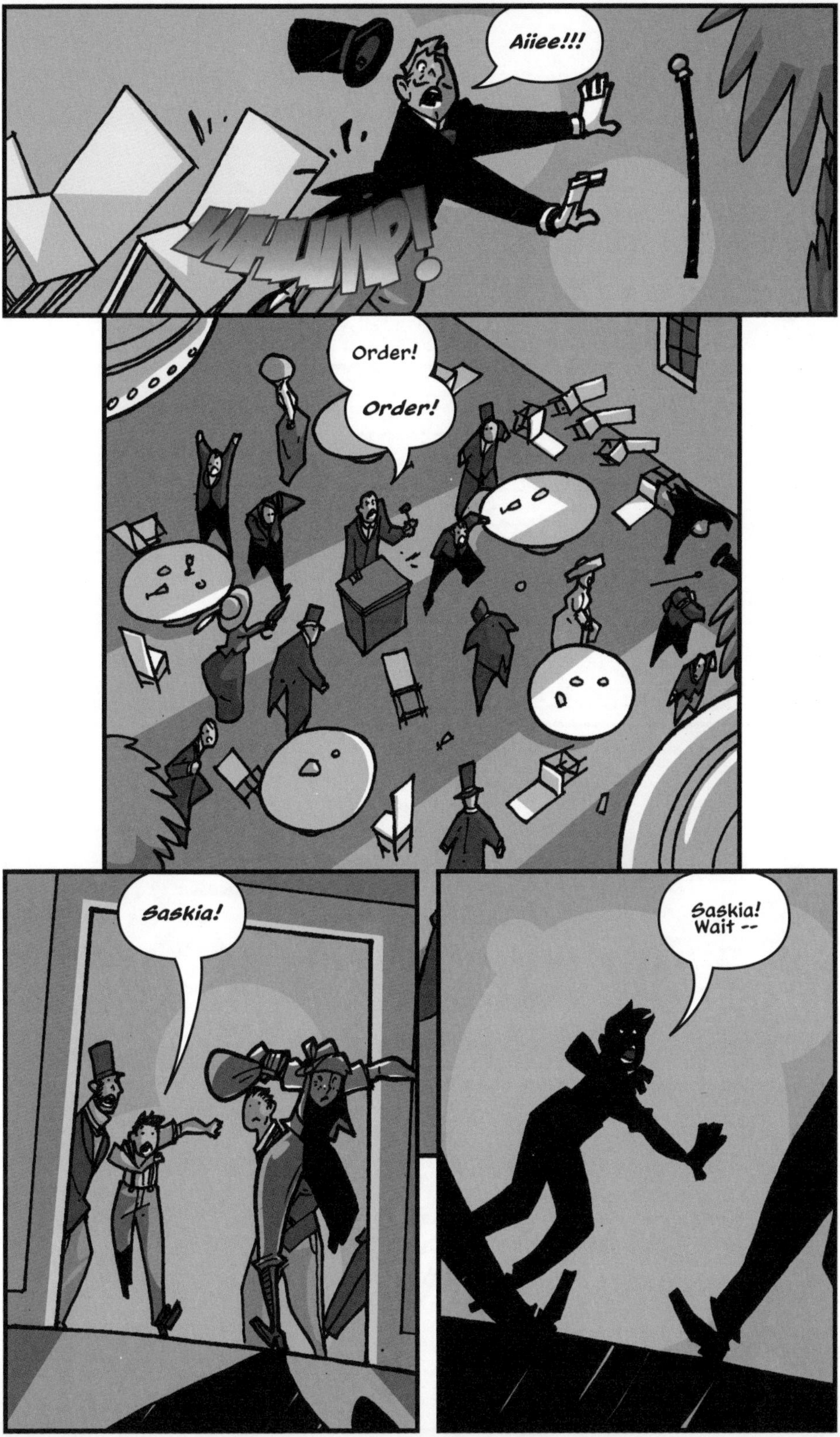
Aiiee!!!
WHUMP!
Order!
Order!
Saskia!
Saskia!
Wait --

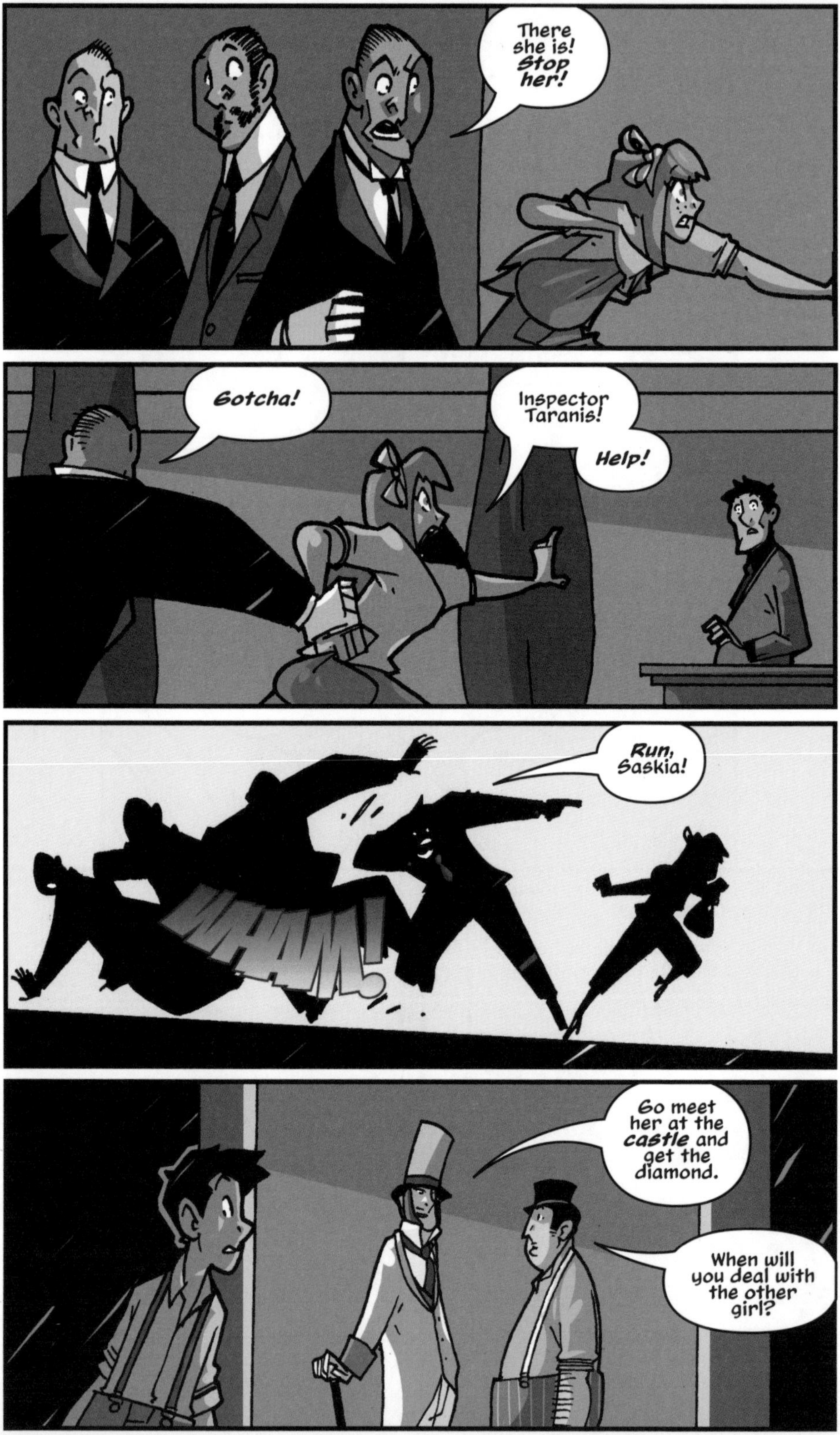

There she is! *Stop her!*
Gotcha!
Inspector Taranis!
Help!
WHAM!
Run, Saskia!
Go meet her at the *castle* and get the diamond.
When will you deal with the other girl?

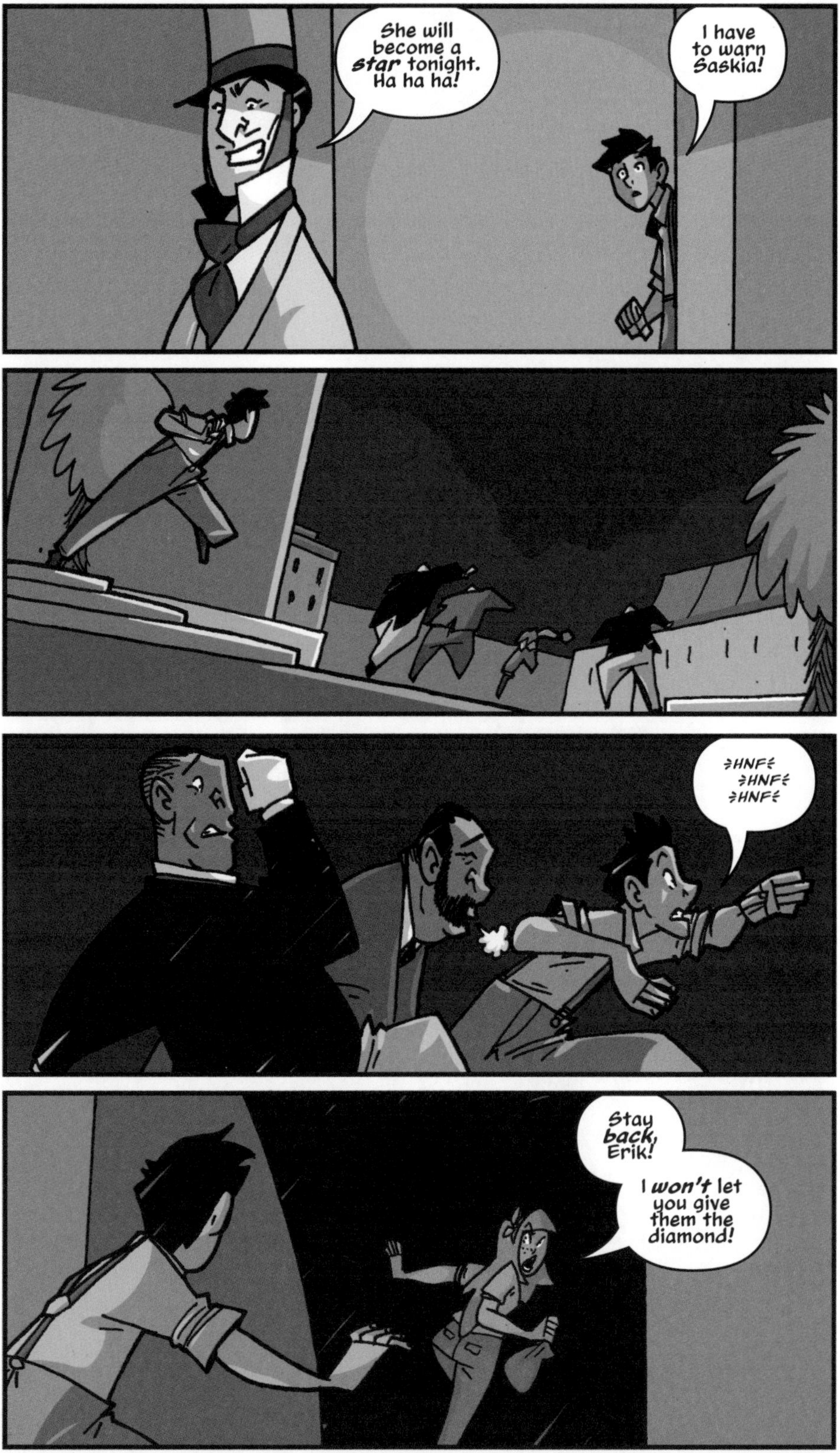
She will become a star tonight. Ha ha ha!
I have to warn Saskia!
HNF HNF HNF
Stay back, Erik!
I won't let you give them the diamond!

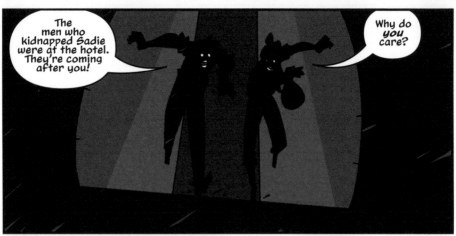

The men who kidnapped Sadie were at the hotel. They're coming after you!

Why do *you* care?

Because I want to *help!* Surely you --

Stop right there! The *diamond.* Now.

Wait! What about my *sister?*

Ah -- your sister --

-- she will be part of the *main event!*

It's *explosive!*

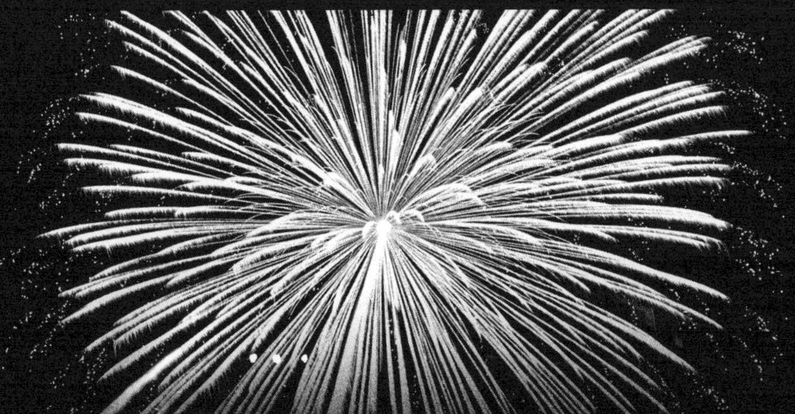

• • •

The pier of the Hotel Carlton was packed with spectators in ball gowns and dinner suits. Largo stood at the end of the pier and surveyed his audience.

"With a click of my fingers, the sky shall explode, and the trunk will be transformed," he announced. He paused for dramatic effect and raised his left hand in the air. The swallow tattoo twitched as though it were about to fly from his hand as he snapped his fingers. At the same instant, his other hand pressed the detonator in his pocket.

• • •

Erik and Saskia looked out from the castle ramparts at the pier in the distance. They watched as the sky erupted in a brilliant display of fireworks. Colors exploded and fell like sparkling raindrops. At the climax of the performance, a trunk flew into the air like a rocket and shattered with a bang. Something large fell from it into the sea.

Saskia watched in disbelief. "That was the trunk they took Sadie away in."

She stood in shock, trying to picture her sister in her mind.

There was nothing but darkness.

Chapter Fourteen

A Case of Mistaken Identity

THE FINAL FIREWORKS faded in the night sky. A chorus
of voices shouted in praise from the distant harborside,
and a brass band accompanied a woman in a silver dress
who crooned to the crowd. Erik stood in silence looking
out to sea. Saskia slumped against the outer wall of the
castle, crying.

"Back at the hotel, after I opened the safe, I heard a voice
in my head," Erik thought out loud. "It said, 'The old
order has passed away. All is new.' I didn't want to go on
with the theft. I kept thinking that it wasn't right. But I
wanted to help Sadie, so I did it anyway. Now it looks like
I stole the diamond for nothing," he finished bitterly.

"It doesn't matter now. Nothing matters now that Sadie's gone."

"My father is dead," Erik said after a pause. "I met a man—
well . . . I think he was a man. He was the one Madame
Raphael told me about—the Man of Good-Bye Friday. He
knew all about me—everything. He said my father was with
him. Dead, I mean. Do you think it will be the same for
Sadie? And what about us? Can we be with him someday?"

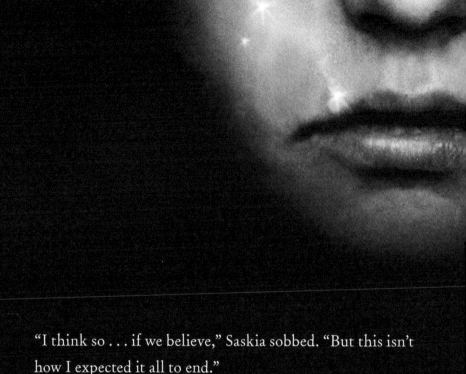

"I think so . . . if we believe," Saskia sobbed. "But this isn't how I expected it all to end."

"We have to put it right," said Erik. "Muzz Elliott is most probably under arrest because they think she's Cicely Windylove. We can still help her. We have to find the Frenchman and return the diamond."

"I don't care what happens next—not without Sadie."

"And there's Dorcas Potts," Erik continued. "We can find her and stop Le Sentier Rouge. We'll get the diamond and tell everything to the police." Erik paced back and forth as the plan formed in his mind. "We could get a boat at the harbor and go to the SWALLOW. We have to do it, Saskia. For Sadie—we have to go."

Erik was crying now too. He held his breath as tears trickled down each cheek.

Erik rubbed his eyes with his sleeve. He coughed and pulled Saskia to her feet. "We have to get Dorcas Potts and stop them."

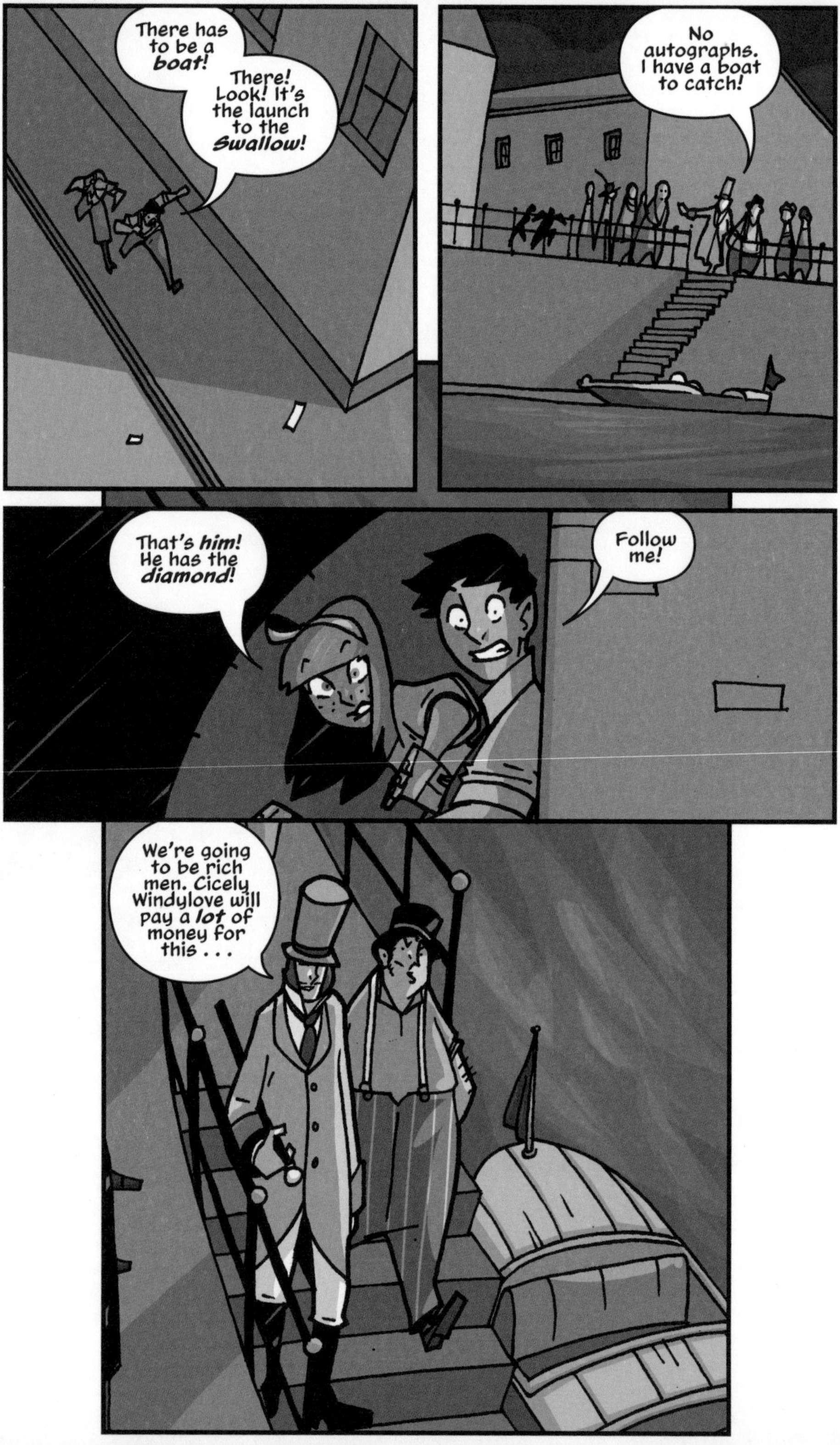

There has to be a *boat*!
There! Look! It's the launch to the *Swallow*!
No autographs. I have a boat to catch!
That's *him*! He has the *diamond*!
Follow me!
We're going to be rich men. Cicely Windylove will pay a *lot* of money for this . . .

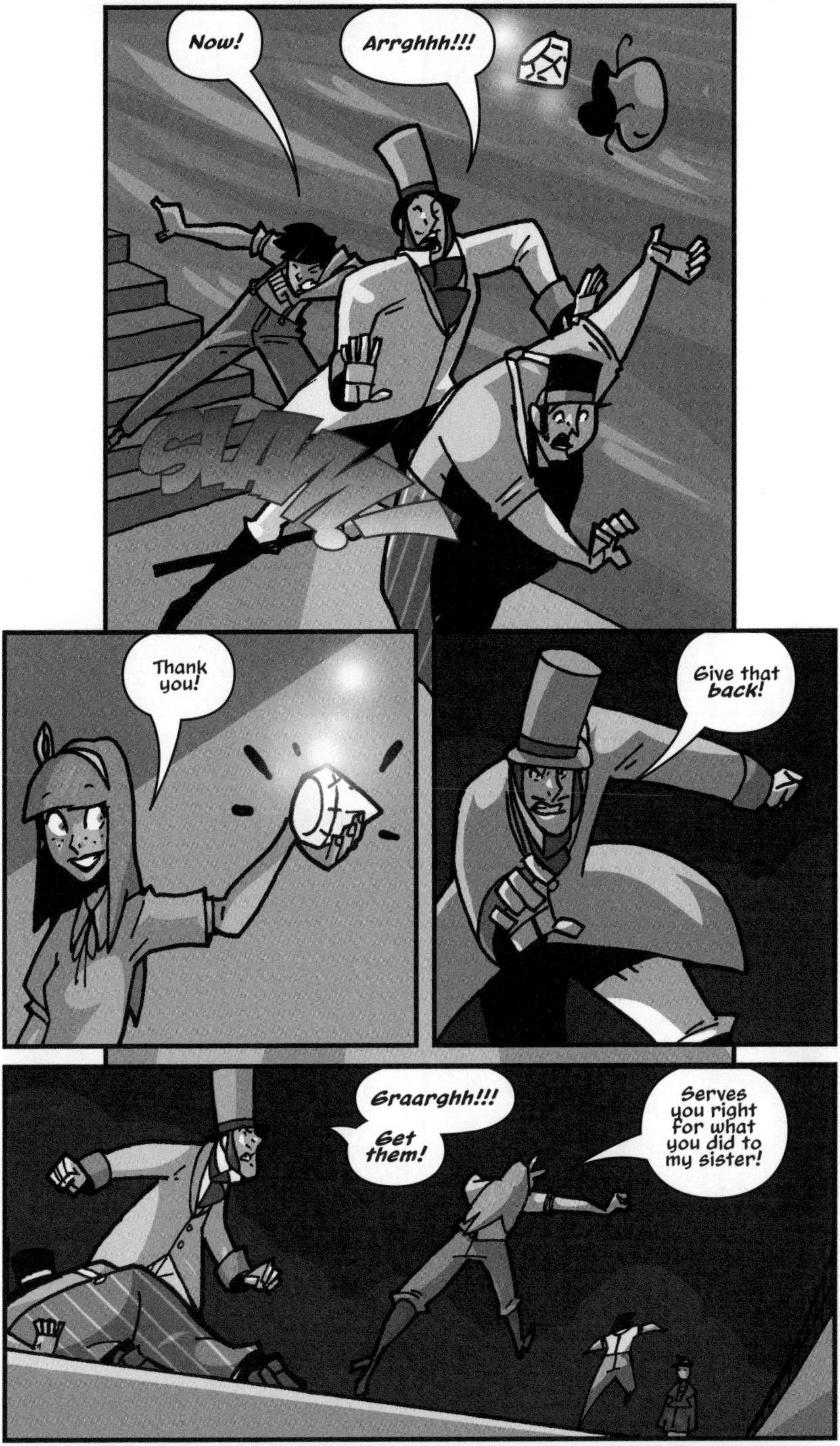
Now!
Arrghhh!!!
SLAM
Thank you!
Give that back!
Graarghh!!!
Get them!
Serves you right for what you did to my sister!

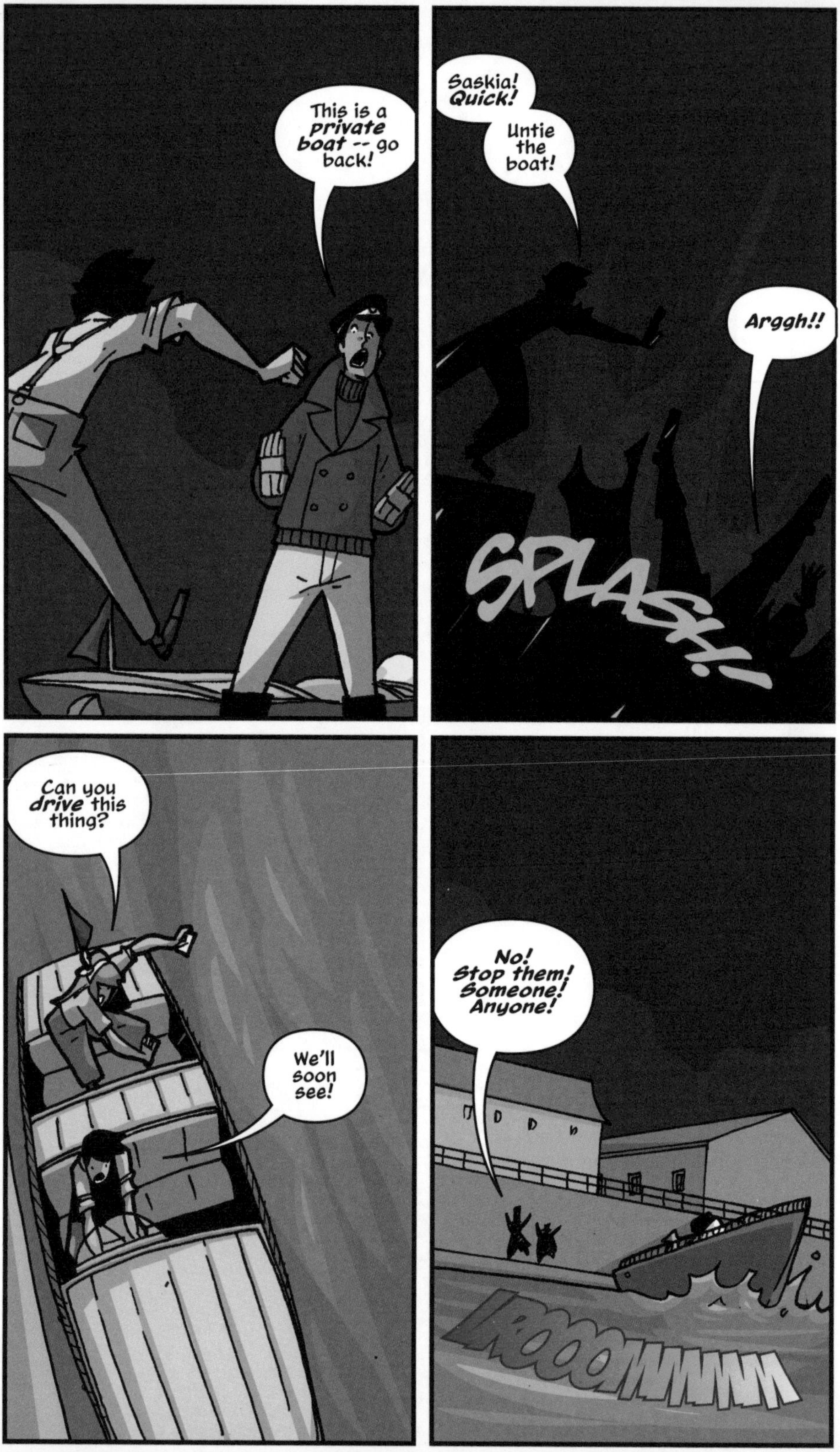

This is a private boat -- go back!
Saskia! Quick!
Untie the boat!
Arggh!!
SPLASH!!
Can you drive this thing?
We'll soon see!
No! Stop them! Someone! Anyone!
VROOOMMMMM

The engine roared, and the twin propellers whirred like a funnel cloud, spewing a jet of water from under the boat and across the jetty. Largo and Claude were momentarily submerged by the wave.

"Quick! Get my other boat," Largo demanded. "We have to catch them."

Erik pointed the speedboat toward the dim shadows of the islands that lay off the coast. He knew the SWALLOW would be there, moored in the darkness. All he could think of was finding Dorcas Potts and putting a stop to Le Sentier Rouge.

Gripping the wheel tightly, Erik aimed the boat out to sea and pressed the throttle down further. Like an aquatic racehorse, the boat lifted from the water.

"They won't catch us now," Erik shouted into the wind and spray that blew in his face.

Saskia turned back just as a beam of light touched her shoulder. She stared into the brightness that seemed to be closing on them.

"They have a boat!" she screamed.

Erik slammed the wheel to one side, sending spray high into the air as the speedboat made a sharp turn.

"If we get to the SWALLOW, we can find Dorcas Potts. She will know what to do," Erik said.

"They're gaining on us—go faster!" Saskia urged.
The beam of bright white light drew closer.

"Okay, here goes!"

Erik tugged the
throttle until it was
fully open. The boat
lifted even higher as it sped across
the still, black water. In the distance they could see the
SWALLOW sitting majestically in the calm of night. A single
red light marked its position. Four tall masts and a funnel
stood out in the moonlight.

Erik turned the boat and raced toward it.

A shot cracked the air behind them. The bullet snapped
through the wood on the side of the boat and hit the
engine. There was a sudden lurch and the smell of fuel,
quickly followed by acrid smoke and luminous flames that
leaped from the hatch.

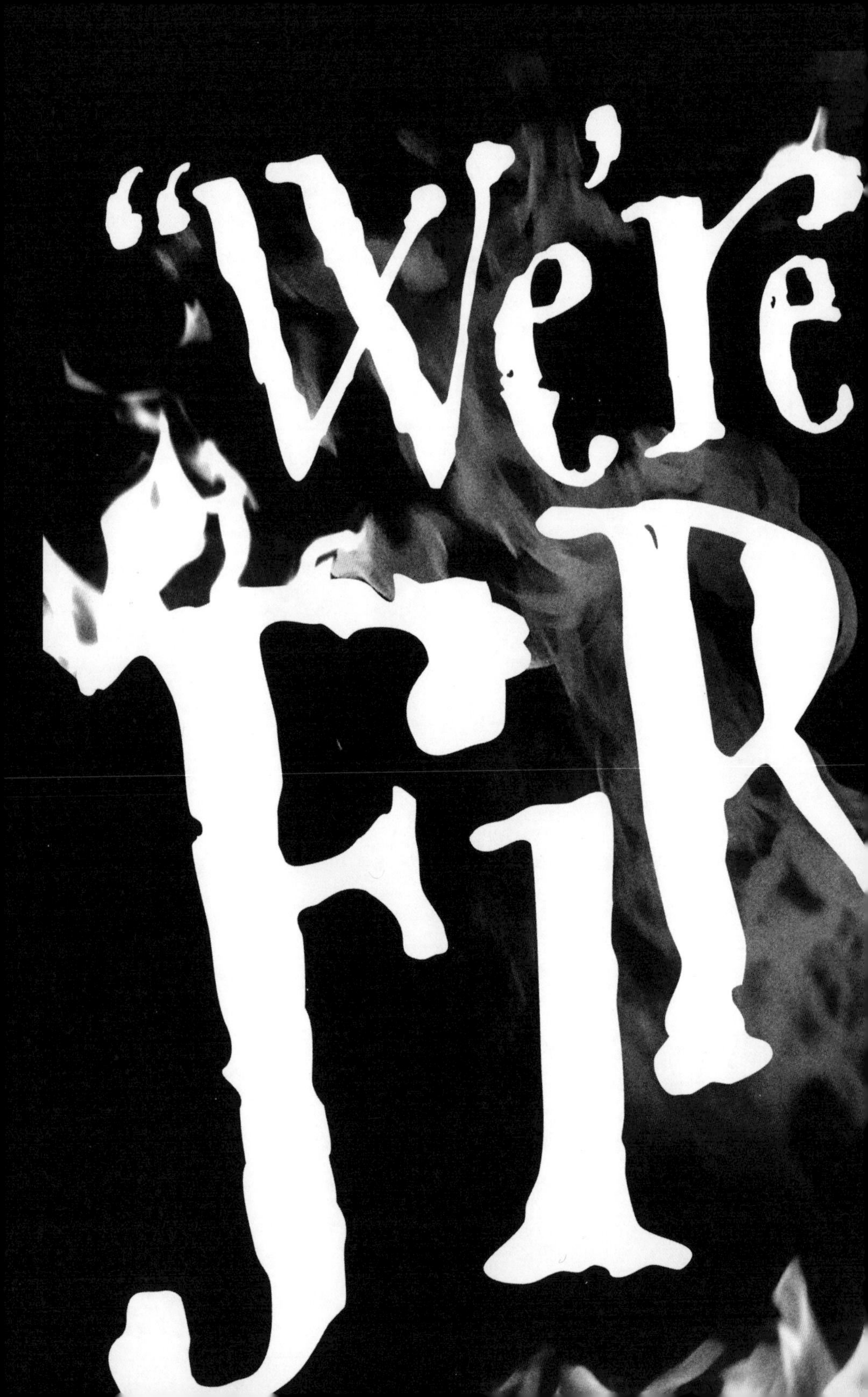
"We're
FIR

on Ell!"

Saskia
screamed.

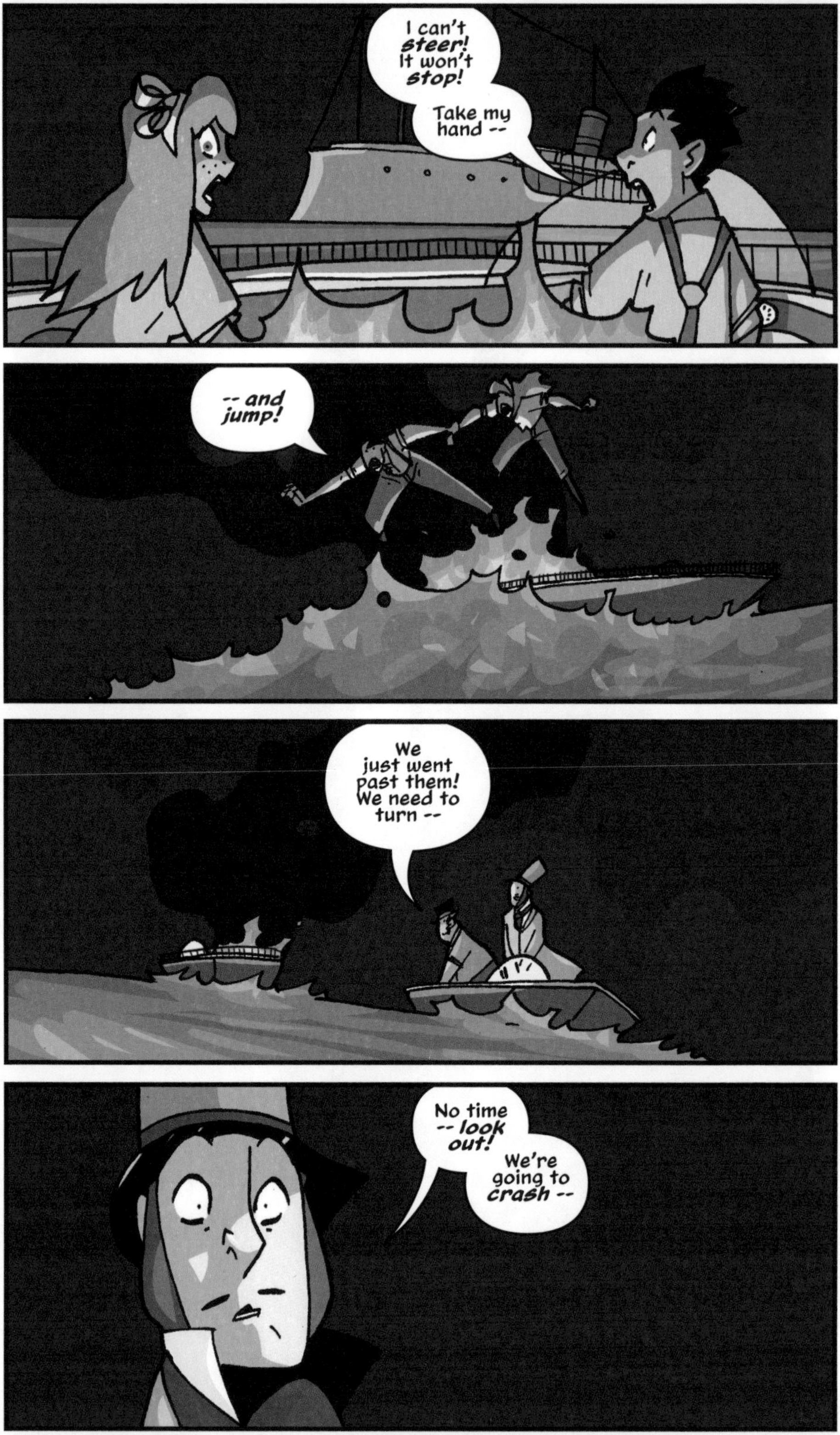

I can't steer! It won't stop!
Take my hand --
-- and jump!
We just went past them! We need to turn --
No time -- look out!
We're going to crash --

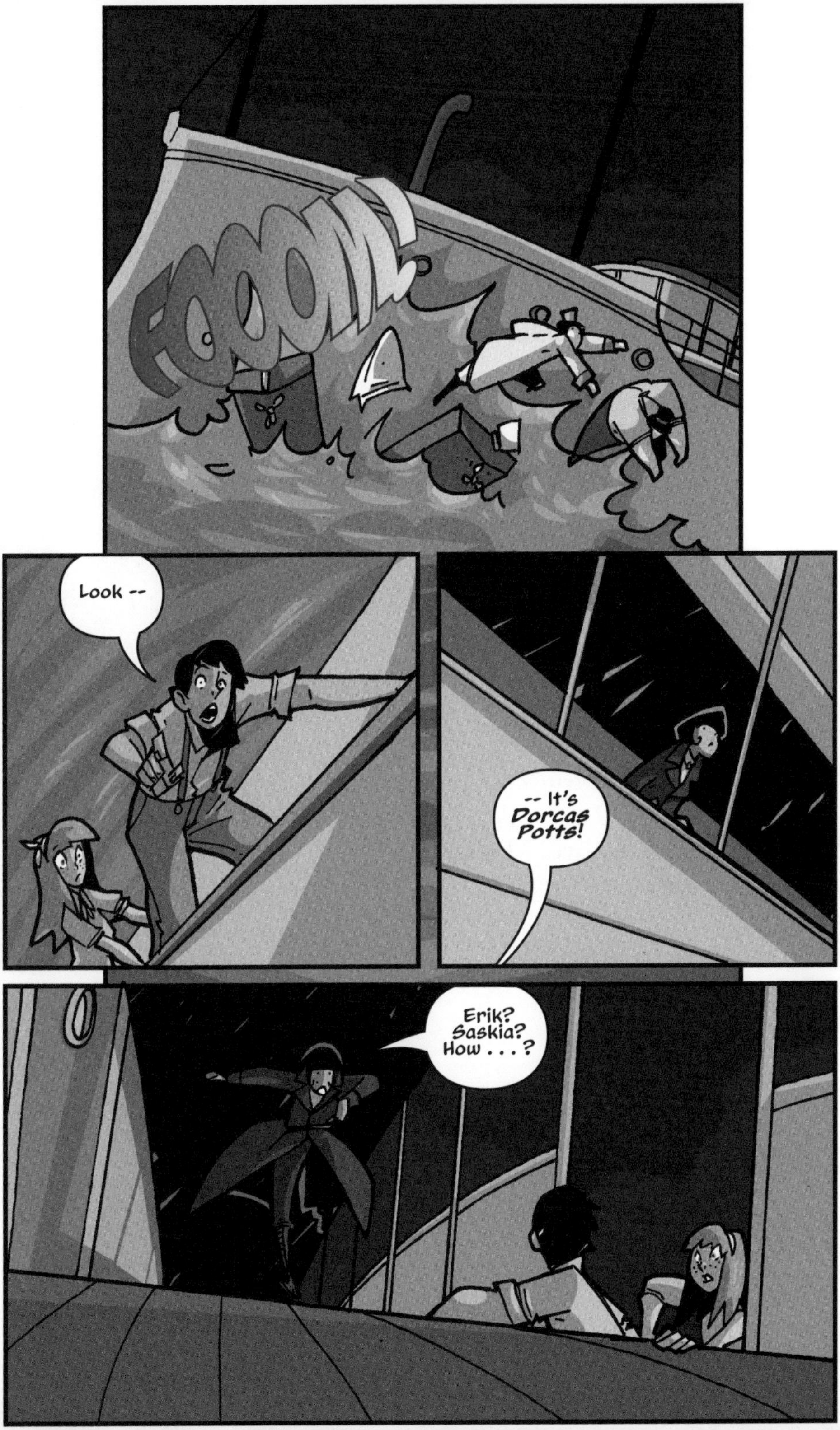
FOOOM!
Look --
-- It's Dorcas Potts!
Erik? Saskia? How . . . ?

“We came to find you,” Saskia said, bending over with exhaustion. “Sadie is dead. Largo killed her. He blew her up even though we got him the diamond.”

“Dead? Don’t be ridiculous. She’s still here on the boat,” Dorcas Potts said.

“But . . . we saw the trunk explode in the sky,” Saskia replied, confused.

“Foojack took her out of the trunk before he left with La Sauvage,” explained Dorcas Potts. “There was nothing in the trunk but heavy rope.”

“Then she’s alive?” Erik said.

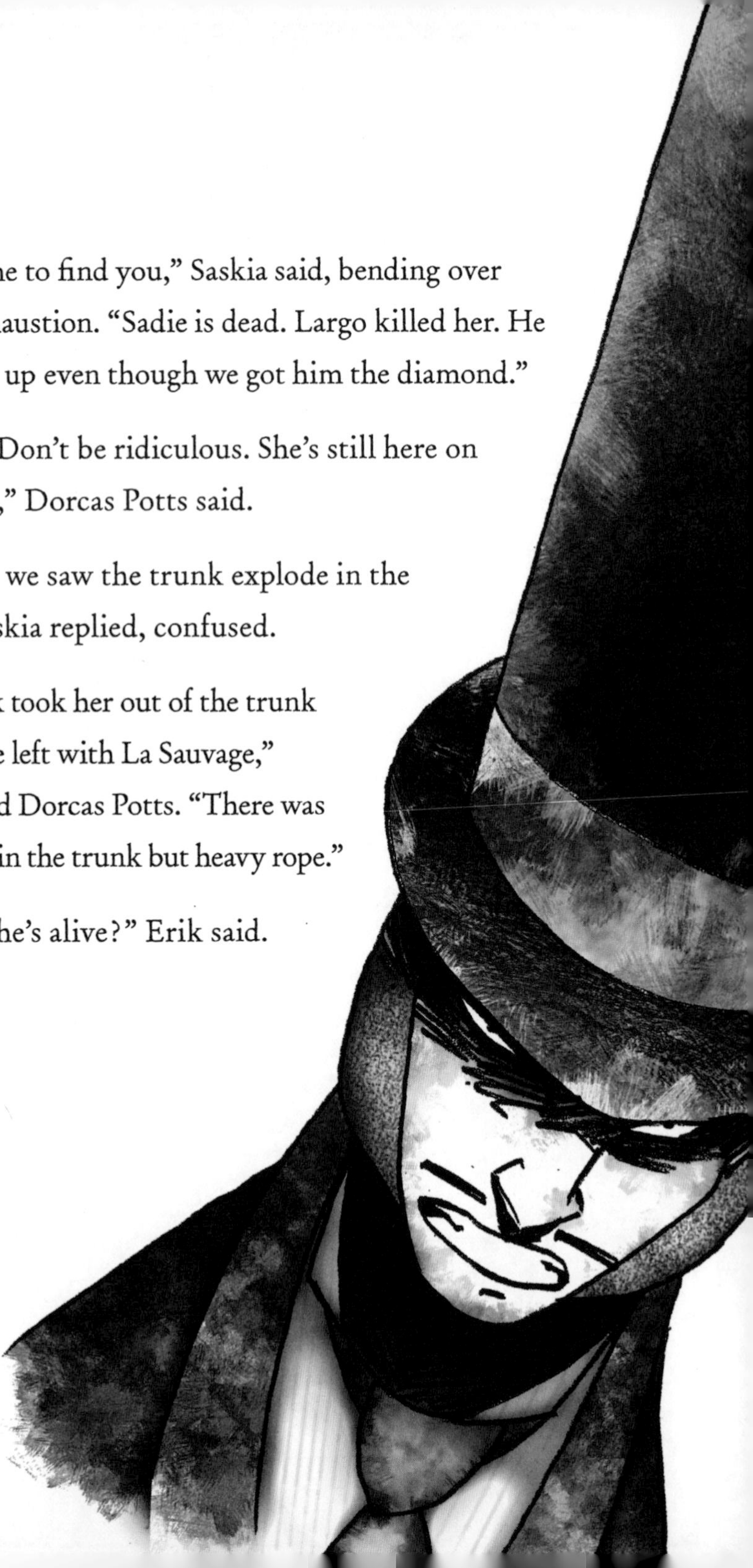

"Not so fast," Largo
said from the far side
of the boat.

Claude appeared by his elbow,
looking drenched and just a little singed.
"You have ruined my plans and wrecked my
boat. If you were not here, this would have all
gone so well. Now . . . the diamond?"

"Did you kill my sister?" Saskia asked, unable to
believe Sadie was still alive.

"She was just the icing on the cake, a contrivance
of elegance," Largo replied with great delight. He
stepped toward them.

"NO I wasn't!"

shouted Sadie from the darkness.

Largo turned. Sadie stepped into the light holding the end of a long rope.

"It can't be! You're—dead," he gasped.

"Not me, mate," Sadie laughed and let go of the rope.

There was the whoosh of sail unraveling. A long beam of wood crashed to the deck just next to where Largo was standing. He and Claude disappeared under a thick pile of white canvas. Erik ran across the deck toward them. A ghostly, canvas-clad figure got to its feet as another scrabbled around on the deck, trying to escape.

Erik leaped on top of them. There was a dull thud.

"Serves you right for trying to make Sadie part of your fireworks display!" called Saskia.

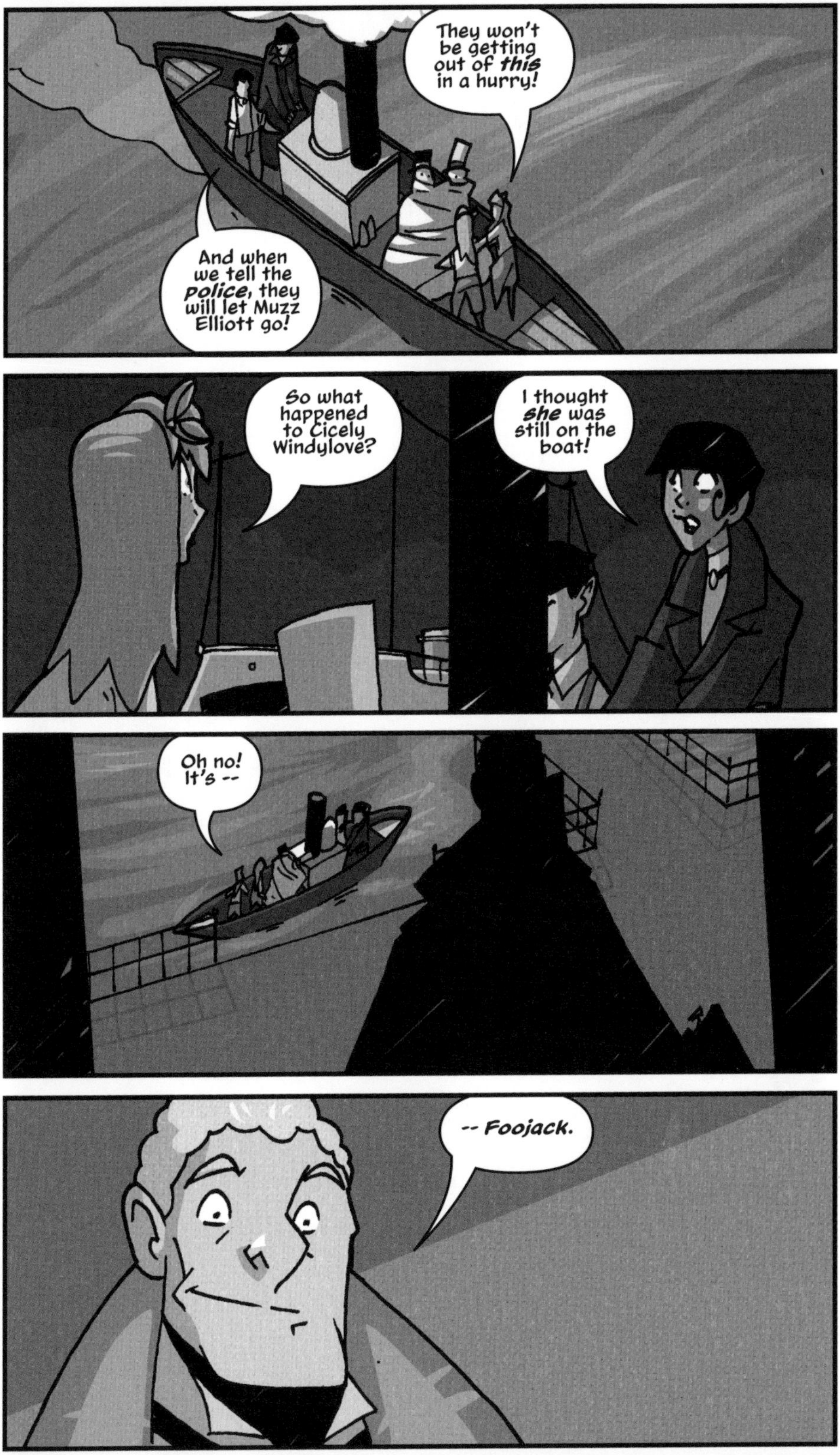
They won't be getting out of *this* in a hurry!
And when we tell the *police*, they will let Muzz Elliott go!
So what happened to Cicely Windylove?
I thought *she* was still on the boat!
Oh no! It's --
-- Foojack.

There was no point in trying to escape. Foojack held the gun in his hands and looked menacingly at them. As they climbed the steps, he pointed to two long, black cars waiting at the dockside.

"Dorcas Potts, Erik, and the girls in that one. Largo and Claude in this one."

"I don't take orders from you," Largo retorted.

"You do now," Foojack said. "Things have changed around here." He waved Largo and Claude toward one of the cars with the barrel of his gun.

"Where are you taking us?" asked Saskia.

"I'll explain everything when we get there," said Foojack with an unexpected smile. He lowered his voice. "Don't worry. You're safe now."

• • •

Erik and the twins sat in the backseat of the car with Dorcas Potts up front. It smelled of fresh leather and beeswax. A police officer was in the driver's seat.

They saw Foojack slide into the car in front of theirs and pull out onto the road. The policeman followed.

"Where are we going?" Saskia asked again. The policeman looked back at her and smiled kindly but shook his head.

"Must not speak English," Sadie guessed.

The car raced on; soon they had left the city and were in the dark of the wooded countryside. They could see nothing but the other car ahead of them. The road twisted and turned as it went higher into the mountains. Then suddenly the driver slammed on the brakes.

They were in a large, empty field. A metal building stood several yards away.

"We're at the airfield," Dorcas Potts observed.

The policeman stepped out of the vehicle and motioned for the passengers to do the same.

As they emerged from the car, Erik, Sadie, and Saskia saw another car driving across the runway toward them. It stopped, the doors opened, and Muzz Elliott and Max Taranis got out, followed quickly by Chief Inspector Balzac. Foojack got out of the first car.

"Do you have them all?" Balzac asked Foojack.

"Largo, Claude, and La Sauvage are handcuffed in the car, and you'll find Cicely Windylove tied up in the hangar."

Muzz Elliott turned to Balzac.

"So you get the Mafia to do your dirty work?" she asked angrily.

"Mafia?" Balzac asked. "This is not the Mafia."

Max Taranis laughed. "Mad Jack, is it really you?" he asked the man with the gun.

"Long time, Max Taranis," Foojack replied.

"You know him?" asked Dorcas Potts.

"An old friend I didn't recognize," said Max Taranis.

"I am a captain in the secret service," Foojack explained. "Undercover . . . making sure you stayed alive. Le Sentier Rouge has been our target, and we were waiting for just the right opportunity to put them away."

"Foojack tipped us off about the diamond theft," said Balzac. "We knew what you were planning all along, so

we put the real diamond on display at the auction and a fake in the safe."

"You mean this isn't the real diamond?" said Erik, holding out the jewel in amazement.

"No, Erik," said Balzac, "but we had to let you think it was so Le Sentier Rouge wouldn't know we were onto them."

Erik stared at the fake diamond in his hand. Balzac placed a hand on his shoulder. "You did the right thing by trying to give it to us, son. If you had been caught with the real diamond, the consequences could have been grave."

"Without all your help, the case would never have been solved," Foojack said. "I think your father would have been proud of you, Erik." He looked at the boy and smiled.

The sound of a plane engine made them all turn and look up. A large plane was coming in to land.

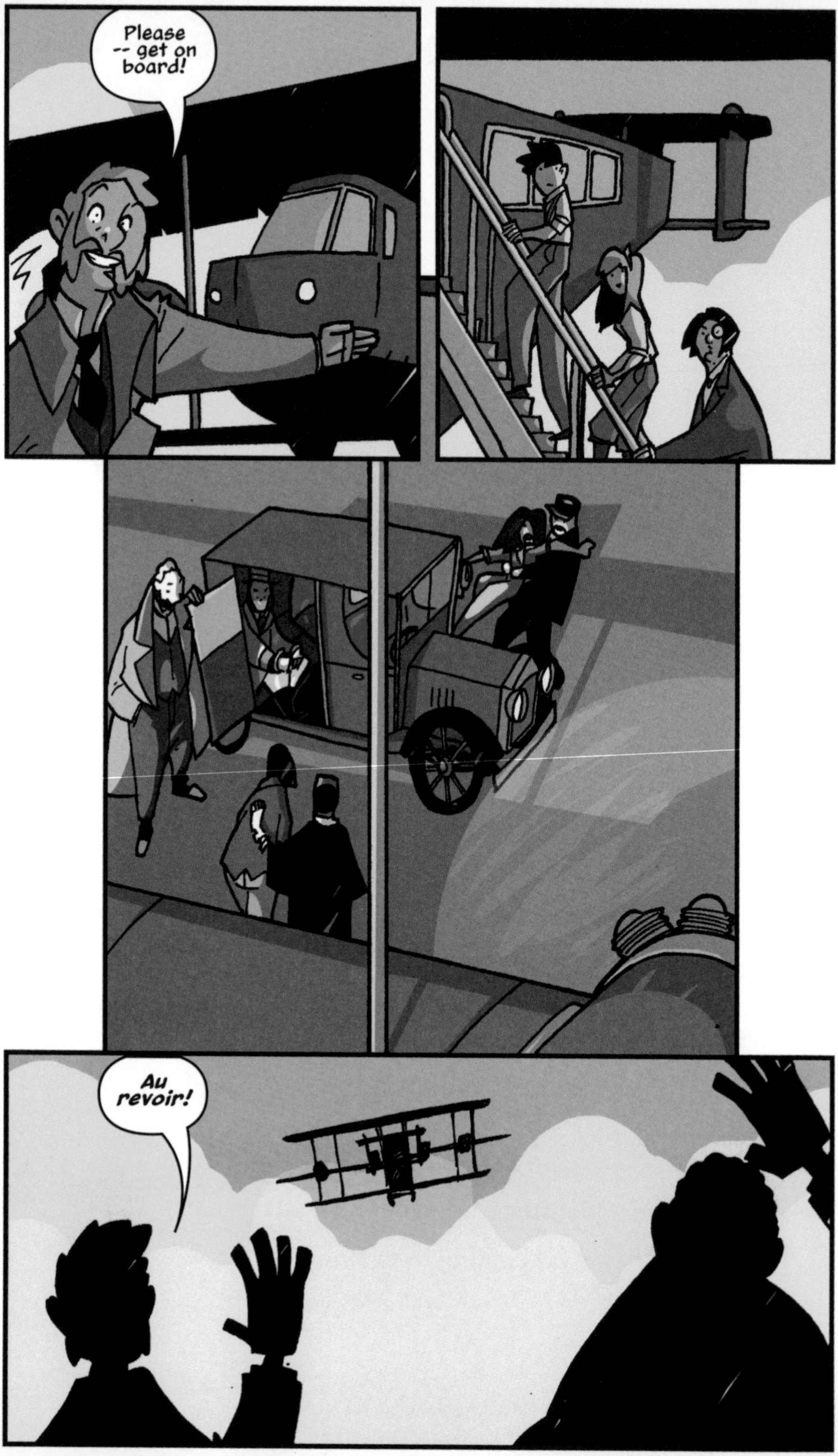
Please -- get on board!
Au revoir!

"So were you in on the plan to infiltrate Le Sentier Rouge, Inspector?" Muzz Elliott asked Max Taranis as the plane flew over Paris.

"I was as much in the dark as you were, Muzz Elliott," replied Max Taranis. "I followed you on the train to investigate the blackmailing. I had no idea Le Sentier Rouge was involved until we got to Cannes."

"Typical. No clue as to what was really going on," muttered Dorcas Potts under her breath.

Max Taranis laughed. "It was a pleasure working with you," he said, winking at Dorcas Potts.

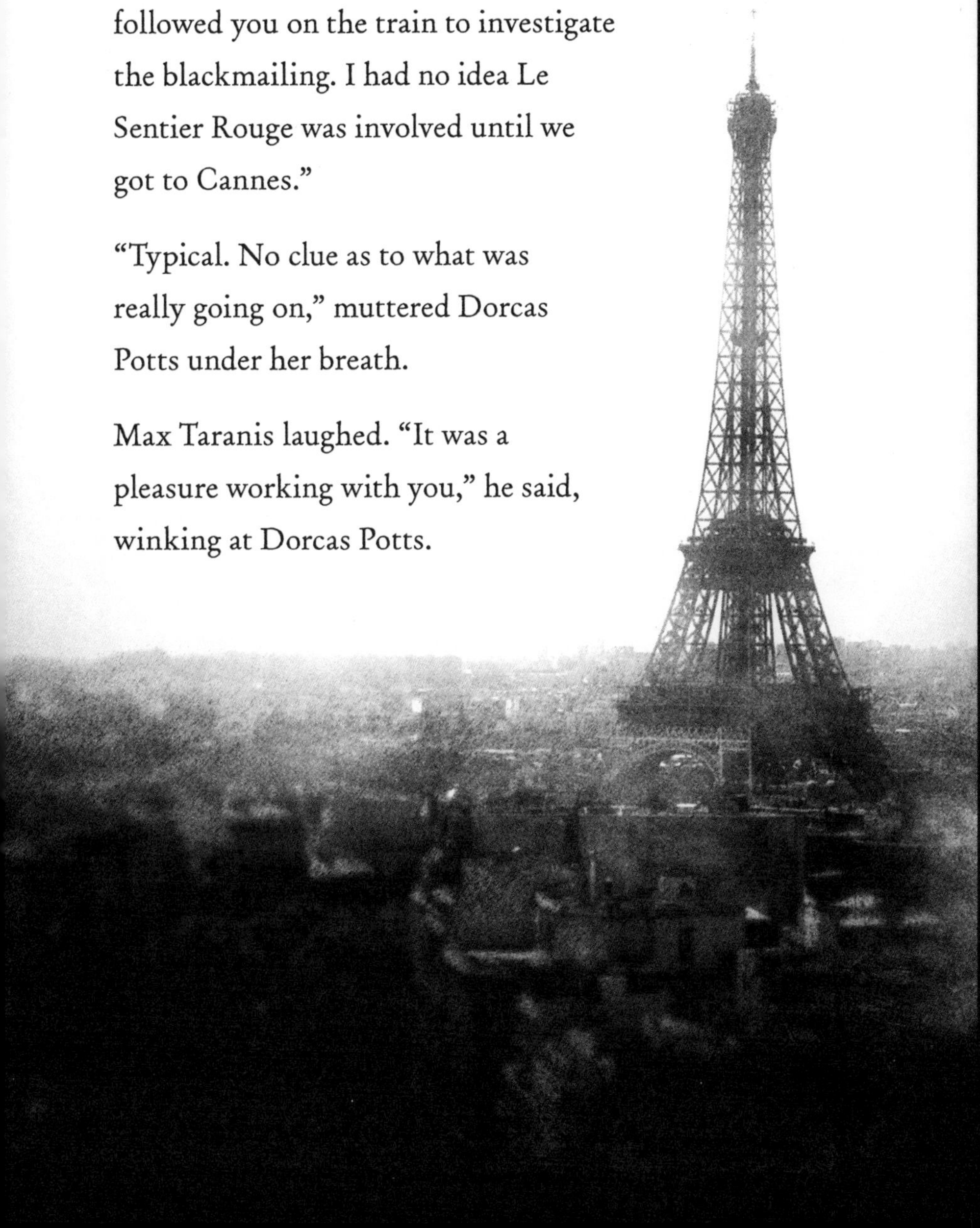

Dorcas Potts turned to Muzz Elliott. "So you are rid of your sister at last."

"Yes," said Muzz Elliott. "I had hoped she would reform. It is not easy to be treated so harshly by your own kin." She sat in silence for some moments, then looked up and smiled at the twins. "But I have new family members now. And more loyal family you could never ask for."

Sadie and Saskia clasped hands and smiled at her.

Erik looked down on the lights of the city. He was thinking of his own father, who he had assumed for so long had abandoned him. But Erik remembered the Man of Good-Bye Friday and his scarred hands. He supposed in a way he had new family now too.

He looked at the gem in his lap. Inspector Balzac had told him to keep the false diamond as a reminder to stay away from a life of crime. It had been a very full three days. "It's good to be going home," he said. He sat back and something crinkled in his pocket; he reached inside, puzzled.

"It will be nice to take a break," agreed Dorcas Potts. "But Balzac had better get my Bugatti back in one piece like he promised."

Saskia chuckled, but Sadie's attention was caught by Erik, who stared at the piece of parchment he'd just unfolded.

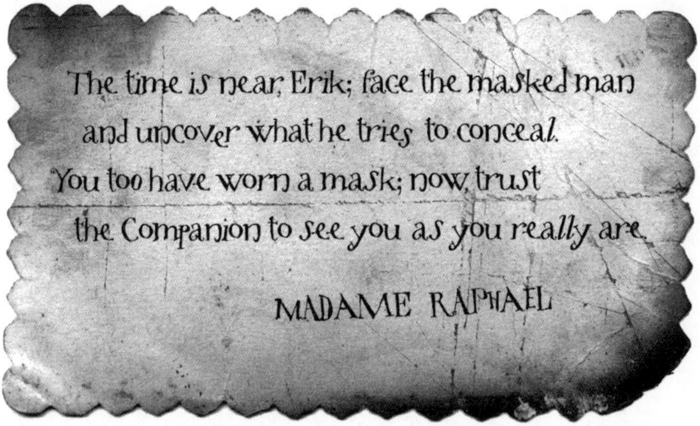
The time is near, Erik; face the masked man
and uncover what he tries to conceal.
You too have worn a mask; now, trust
the Companion to see you as you really are.

MADAME RAPHAEL

Erik wordlessly passed the note to the twins. As they bent their heads over it, he gazed out the window. Whatever lay ahead, he felt ready to face it now; it was time for a new beginning.

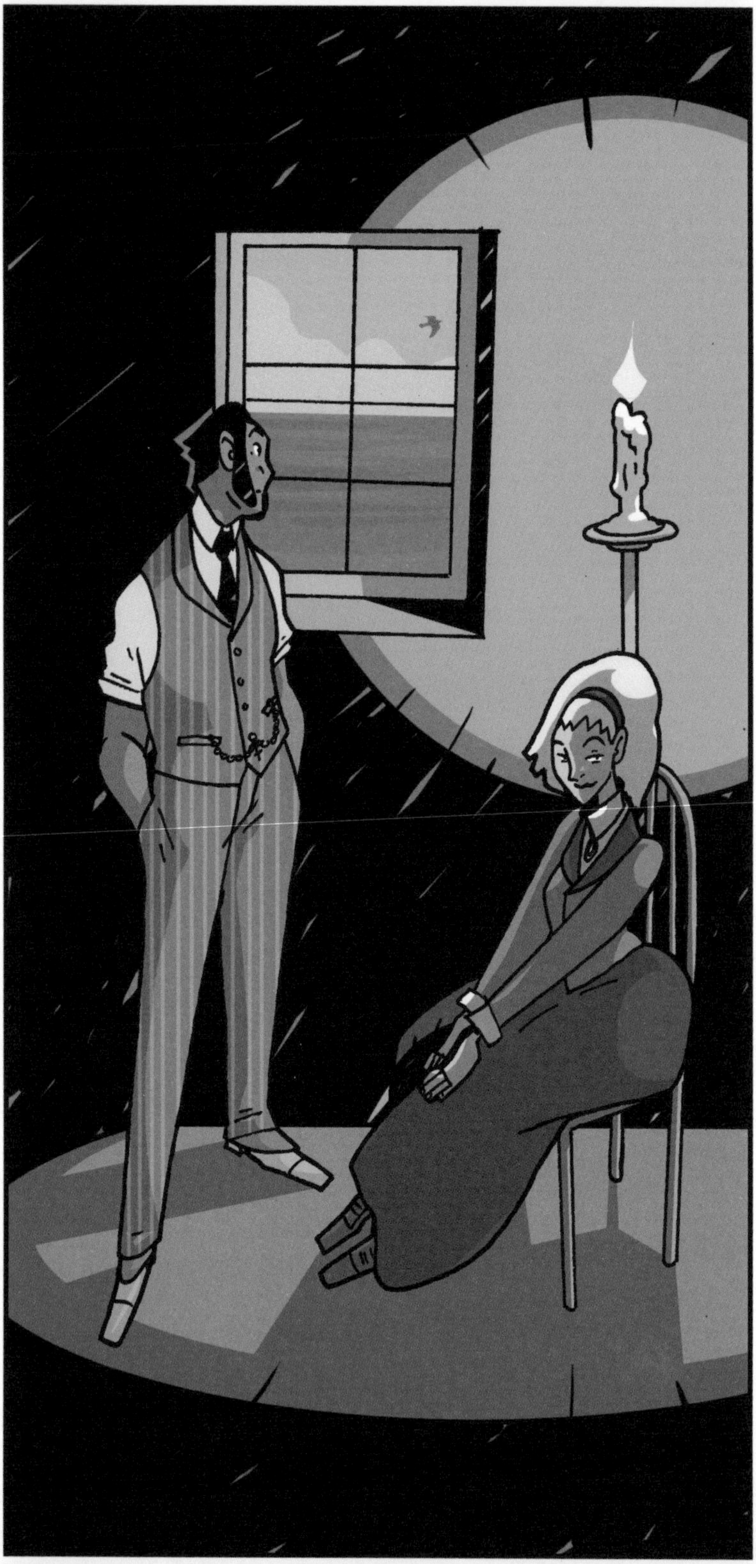

In a dark room of a high tower
that overlooked the sea, a lone
candle burned.

"Do you think they listen to what
we say?" Madame Raphael asked a
tall man in a pinstripe suit with holes
in the palms of his hands.

"Sometimes," he replied, watching the birds
that flew out to sea.

"And when they get it wrong, do we try again?"

"Always," he said simply.

"But doesn't it make you angry?" Madame Raphael dared
to ask.

"If you had ever been one of them, you would understand."

"Look what they did to you," she said as she lifted one of
his scarred hands.

"It was worth it," he said, and he smiled as he looked out
across the sea.

About the Artists

DANIEL BOULTWOOD was born in London. He studied illustration at Richmond College and went on to work in computer game concept design. From there he moved into flash animation, creating games for DreamWorks and Warner Bros., where he refined his style to the animation-inspired work it is today. He lives in London in a shed with two cats.

TONY LEE (adapter) began his career in games journalism and magazine features, moving into radio in the early nineties. He spent over ten years working for television, radio, and magazines as a feature and script writer, winning several awards. In 2005 he adapted G. P. Taylor's SHADOWMANCER into a graphic novel for Markosia.

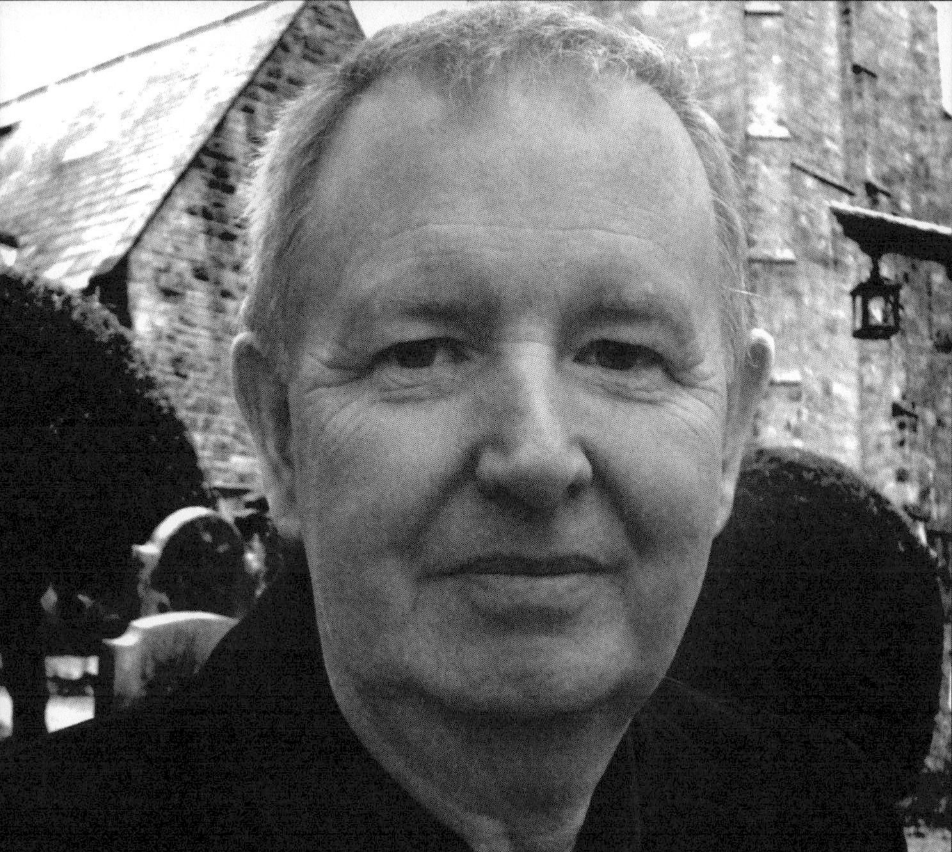

About the Author

A motorcyclist and former rock band roadie turned Anglican minister, G. P. Taylor has been hailed as "hotter than Potter" and "the new C. S. Lewis" in the United Kingdom. His first novel, SHADOWMANCER, was a #1 NEW YORK TIMES bestseller in 2004 and has been translated into forty-eight languages. His other novels include WORMWOOD (another NEW YORK TIMES bestseller, which was nominated for a Quill book award), THE SHADOWMANCER RETURNS: THE CURSE OF SALAMANDER STREET, TERSIAS THE ORACLE, MARIAH MUNDI: THE MIDAS BOX, MARIAH MUNDI AND THE GHOST DIAMONDS, MARIAH MUNDI AND THE SHIP OF FOOLS, THE FIRST ESCAPE, and THE SECRET OF INDIGO MOON. Worldwide sales for Taylor's books now total more than 3 million copies.

G. P. Taylor currently resides in North Yorkshire with his wife and three children.